LONG THE IMPERIAL WAY

LONG THE IMPERIAL WAY

HANAMA TASAKI

GREENWOOD PRESS, PUBLISHERS
WESTPORT, CONNECTICUT

To my Mother

PUBLISHER'S NOTE

This book is based on the author's experiences in the Japanese Imperial Army during the three years he served in China as a private. It is not a translation, and is published just as he wrote it.

CHAPTER HEADINGS

The translations of the Japanese chapter headings are as follows:

LONG THE IMPERIAL WAY

CHAPTER 1

THE VASTNESS of the countryside was terrifyingly depressing. There were simply no distinctive features to it like hills, or rivers, or woods. There was just the plain, and it extended and extended until it was lost in the hazy mist of the horizon. To be sure, there were the villages here and there partly hidden under scraggly clumps of trees, and the waving fields of *kaoliang* and wheat, and the roads winding among them, but they were sprawled indiscriminately, as if some giant had angrily tossed them out of a bag and let them fall whichever way they wanted. To one born and raised on an island they were not distinguishable landmarks but incongruous parts of the endlessness and monotony of the plain.

Private Takeo Yamamoto of the Hamamoto infantry company of the Japanese Army gazed with awe and a depressing feeling of futility at this expansive panorama of the North China continent. He was squatted, well hidden among the tall, thick grass on a low hill overlooking the plain. The hill was the only distinct break in the geography of this district for as far as one could see. The soldier held a rifle propped against his shoulder, for he was on sentinel duty and certainly not on the hill to enjoy the scenery.

Takeo was used to the wide spaces and incongruity of the continent by now (for he had been serving in China for over half a year), but he had never seen anything in such a scale as

1

this and had to take hold of himself from time to time to keep his deeply ingrained sense of duty from becoming lost in an aimless contemplation of the surrounding. But his mind kept going astray, and his eyes kept wandering off into space. . . . Now, the scenes at home were comforting. One had any number of different, interesting things to hold one's attention or even to keep one entertained. There were hills everywhere with neat rows of verdant trees on them or symmetrical patches of cultivated land on their slopes. Valleys always had sparkling streams and rivers running through them over interesting formations of rock. Then there were the minutely squared-off rice paddies. Towns and roads were where everyone would expect them to be and not scattered haphazardly.

It is hot, Takeo thought, his mind wandering off into space again. There was a hot midday sun shining down from a clear autumn sky, and there was nothing over Takeo's head but some grass he had tied to his cap to camouflage himself.

This time, however, his mind did not wander far, for a train's whistle sounded in the distance and jarred him back to his sense of duty. He swept his eyes hurriedly along the railway which ran across the plain and past the hill directly below him. There was a thin slanting column of black smoke against the skyline far to the left, and it was approaching swiftly. Takeo could hear the faint chug-chugging of the locomotive, growing stronger with each beat.

The tracks themselves were mostly hidden by the tall stalks of *kaoliang* which grew thickly on both sides of them, and Takeo peered intently at the tasseled tops of the crowded grain for any signs of movement underneath. The main duty of the guard Takeo was standing was to keep a careful watch for guerrilla bands out to harm the railway, and they had been told that it was a valuable line connecting the capital with Suchow, a vital North China base they had captured only a month ago. The *kaoliang* fields offered ideal cover for the guerrillas, who had already overturned a train and cut the line at several places. All of their raids had been conducted at night, but the soldiers on sentinel duty were warned that the enemy might attempt similar attacks in broad daylight anytime now, for they must have been most certainly emboldened by their successes at night.

Satisfied by the normal movement of the *kaoliang* fields under a light breeze which was blowing across the plain, Takeo next looked at the narrow dirt paths leading toward the tracks. Only the usual desultory movement of farmers was to be discerned, and he saw no groups of appreciable size which could merit even his slightest suspicion. Completely at ease, he gazed fondly on the train which came thundering out of the fields under a trailing canopy of black, belching smoke to rush noisily across the tracks below him and to disappear again into the fields. But the black banner of smoke from the locomotive was visible for some time over the even top of the grainfields, and as it lurched jerkily but resolutely across the endless plain it looked futile and weak, and even comical, until it disappeared in the mist over the horizon.

After the smoke was completely lost to sight, the train whistled again, and the long plaintive wail of the whistle, wafted ever so faintly across the clear autumn air, awoke a sudden feeling of forlornness and homesickness in Takeo. It came so suddenly, it gripped his heart and almost choked him. As he looked longingly at the spot over the horizon where the train's smoke had disappeared, he asked himself, Who will be helping the harvest at my home this year?

His mother had written him in her last letter, "Please put yourself at ease, because the Young People's Corps has promised to help the harvest."

His parents were quite old, and it would be hard on them to bring the harvest in all by themselves, even if theirs was a small farm of only six *tan* (an acre and a half). Takeo was their only son, and he had been doing all the heavy work on the farm for some time until he had been called into the army. Like most farms in Japan, their farm, too, was dispersed in strips over a wide area, covering hills and valleys.

For the hundredth time he told himself, If they only had an ox, it would do the work in my place.

Not very long after he had entered the army, Takeo had made up his mind that he would save enough money from his army pay to buy an ox for his parents. Fortunately, he did not smoke or drink, and he had been able to save nearly all of the five-yen-fifty he had received monthly during his four months of basic training in the barracks at home and the eight-yen-eighty he had begun to receive after coming to the front as a full-fledged private nearly six months ago. He had now over fifty yen in the bank, and when he had left home, a good two-year ox had cost from a hundred fifty yen to two hundred yen. . . . He was not going to learn to smoke and drink, now that he was in the army, as so many of his comrades were doing, and if he had to stay at the front even after the necessary sum was saved, he would send it home and give his parents the pleasure of buying the ox.

"Is there nothing amiss?" The low, gruff voice of Private First Class Tanaka immediately behind Takeo almost made him jump.

"No, sir!" Takeo answered quickly. "A little while ago, a train passed. Otherwise, there has been no change."

Takeo had been so lost in his favorite contemplation on the purchase of an ox that he had not heard the Private First Class creeping softly up through the grass behind him. Private First Class Tanaka was the head of the Sentinel Post on the hill and was usually in the well-camouflaged dugout shelter about fifty yards to the rear, which was the rest station, with the four other soldiers who made up the post. But the Private First Class was a strict sentinel-post leader and supervised every sentinel change and kept prowling about all the time to keep the sentinels on their toes.

"At what hour did the train pass?" the Private First Class asked.

"Yes, sir," Takeo answered and found himself at a loss to answer further, for they had had strict orders to check the exact time any train passed under the hill and Takeo had forgotten to do so.

"I have asked, What hour did the train pass?" Private First Class Tanaka repeated angrily.

"Yes, sir," Takeo stammered and confessed, "I did not look at my watch." His eyes were kept constantly to the front, for he was not supposed to relax his vigil while answering a superior, but Takeo could feel the angry eyes of his superior glaring disgustedly at him from behind.

Private First Class Tanaka was a Second-Year-Soldier, or a soldier in his second year of service. Takeo and his other comrades, who had entered the service at the same time as he, were First-Year-Soldiers, or soldiers in their first year of service. The first year of service in the army was supposed to be a sort of period of apprenticeship, and the First-Year-Soldiers were held in complete servility by their superiors, who included the Second-Year-Soldiers, the Third-Year-Soldiers, and the Reserves. The Second- and Third-Year-Soldiers were regulars who had been serving their compulsory two-year term in the conscription army when the war on the continent had started, and they had been dispatched immediately to the front. The Reserves were men who had already completed their service in the conscription army and been discharged once, but who had been called back to the colors with the outbreak of war.

"You are a good-for-nothing soldier." Private First Class Tanaka's voice sounded derisively behind Takeo.

"Yes, sir," Takeo answered stiffly.

"Repeat the Rules of the Sentinel Post," the Private First Class demanded.

"Yes, sir," Takeo answered, and he now felt a little relieved, for he had memorized well the Rules which had been handed them the previous day when they had first learned that they were coming to this post. Takeo recited in a confident voice:

"First, this Sentinel Post shall be called the Helmet-Mountain-Sentinel-Post.

"Second, since there are remnants and guerrilla bands in the neighborhood, one must constantly watch the surrounding and be especially careful of the railway.

"Third, if one recognizes anything amiss, one should immediately report it to the Sentinel-Post Leader and be especially careful that he is not seen by the enemy."

It was a beautiful recitation, accomplished without a single flaw, and even the Private First Class seemed to be satisfied as he grunted, "All right. Be careful," and turned and went away. Like most of his comrades, Takeo had only gone to elementary school, but he had a good head for memorizing, which stood him in valuable stead in the army, for a great part of the soldier's task in the army was memorizing.

Even after the Private First Class had gone, Takeo felt for some time the alertness and tension the sudden visit of his superior had instilled into him. His eyes roaming over the countryside now had purpose back of them. He looked at the village about a kilometer on the other side of the railroad tracks, where his platoon was quartered, and although he could not see its streets, he examined its surrounding carefully for any suspicious-looking groups among the natives leaving and entering it. Next, he looked carefully at the roads leading to the station house beside the railway below him where the rest of his squad under Corporal Jiro Sakamoto was quartered. There were some natives leading a short train of loaded donkeys approaching the tracks, and he watched them carefully while the sentinel standing in front of the station stopped them and examined the loads on the donkeys. After some time the natives were allowed to pass, and they crossed the tracks and disappeared among the waving *kaoliang*.

The hypnotism of the plain, however, was not to be resisted long, and soon Takeo's eyes were gazing blankly once more at the wide, entrancing spaciousness of the plain. He let go of his rifle and let it rest by itself against his shoulder. The alertness of his mind was once again replaced by the fatalistic depression of a moment ago.

What is death? Takeo asked himself all of a sudden, or, rather, his mood suggested the question to his mind. It was not like a philosopher or student deliberately pondering on this mightiest of questions since the beginning of time, but the question simply suggested itself out of his mood at that moment, and Takeo thought nothing more of it than if he had asked himself, What are we going to have for dinner? On the other hand, too, it was as if the great space before him had asked him the question. In any case, it was the space which had created the mood that called the question to mind.

If we die, we are going to the Yasukuni Shrine. We are going to become gods, Takeo told himself, merely repeating a popular sentiment in the country at that time. But, somehow, Takeo was not satisfied. The Yasukuni Shrine was only a locality in the country, and he was sure death was something bigger.

Takeo had come to think a great deal about death since his arrival at the front. He had already participated in a big campaign, the Suchow campaign, and he had seen many deaths as well as himself narrowly escaping death many times. Death had seemed at home nothing much more than the burning of incense and the reading of *Sutras* by Buddhist priests, but at the front this comforting conception had been jolted badly by the sight of many mangled and disfigured corpses.

I wonder if there is a heaven and a hell? Takeo next asked himself. The Buddhist priests usually said there was, but, How did they know? and Takeo did not trust them. Or were they reincarnated or reborn into something else after death, as his grandmother used to say? Therefore, she had never eaten the flesh of any living thing nor killed even the tiniest insects, for she had claimed every living thing on earth possessed the soul of a former human being. But this too was hard to believe, however much Takeo had loved his grandmother and trusted her.

Maybe death was just what it seemed — the end of everything! On the battlefields he had seen corpses which had been flattened by tanks, and, again, he had helped burn the corpses of comrades killed in combat, in order to get the ashes to send home to their families, for in the Japanese Army all the dead were cremated and their ashes sent home in little wooden boxes wrapped in white cloth. Death had seemed simple enough there — just the ceasing of the bodies to function. What remained had seemed no different from the ashes of the firewood on which the bodies had been cremated.

Takeo closed his eyes and held his breath. Maybe this would give him an idea what death was like, but he simply felt uncomfortable and was soon gasping for breath. No, death could not be as helpless as all that! For just a fleeting moment, Takeo felt alarmed, and he even forgot the great space before him.

A sense of rebellion and defiance, however, soon took hold of him " . . . *Courageous is the heart which vows, I will not return until we have won the war. . . .* " This phrase of a popular ballad repeated itself in his mind. Takeo had a habit of singing snatches of songs whenever he was preoccupied in thought, but this time the songs themselves became his thought. Other tunes and phrases of popular martial songs he knew turned over and over in his mind: " . . . *If you were born a son of Japan, then die on the battlefield . . . ,* " and " . . . *Dedicated to the Emperor, our lives are glorious as the morning sun. . . .* "

A feeling of keen exultation took over in him. Certainly, there was no question about it! He would die for the Emperor! There was nothing as beautiful and noble in all the world. He and his comrades were willing to lay down their lives at any time for the Emperor. Surely, there must be a reward for such an unselfish, sacrificing deed as that . . . *To die was to live in the great soul of the Emperor. . . .* Takeo did not realize it, but he was repeating a phrase he had read in a magazine not so long ago.

His eyes now had a new light in them. The trance which had covered them was no longer there. His were the eyes of a conqueror and victor, proud and exalted. For he had assayed to challenge that fear of death, which had been gnawing at his heart ever since he had heard the first fear-provoking whistling of the bullets over his head in combat, and he had won. He was more than satisfied. He was certain he had won brilliantly and decisively, and he would no longer be troubled by that fear again. Now his spirit was one with the proud, exalted spirit of the victorious Imperial Japanese Army.

This was the first time since entering the army that Takeo had been able to give such free rein to his power of thinking. Like so many people, even in ordinary society, whose thoughts are usually dominated by the necessity to obey or to be servile to others, Takeo felt a sharp exhilaration when he found himself thinking out a problem under his own free will. The value or accuracy of the conclusion attained was, of necessity, limited by the narrow range of his thinking power, but the joy of thinking freely easily made of the conclusion a cherished and valuable belonging: as a child, whose toys are usually strictly selected by his parents, keeps and cherishes dearly some pebbles he has found on the beach. Thus Takeo found himself giving greater value to the conclusion he had reached under his own free volition than to anything he had been taught forcefully, and he did not stop to compare it with others or to weigh it objectively.

From now on, I will really do it! Takeo vowed in his heart. His hand went back to his rifle and grasped it firmly. His eyes now had grim, cold purpose behind them.

This time, he heard the footsteps in the rear as Private First Class Tanaka approached with Private Kan, another First-Year-Soldier, who was to succeed his watch. When the two stopped just behind him, Takeo called in a low voice, "Nothing amiss!"

Private First Class Tanaka answered, "All right!" and the two crept through the grass to Takeo's side.

"Rules!" Takeo said and began reciting the Regulations of the Sentinel Post. He again recited them perfectly and ended his recitation smartly with the usual, "I have ended!"

"Repetition!" Kan, the new sentinel, called and he began to recite the rules, but this soldier was something of a dandy and had not studied the rules seriously, and he had to be corrected and reminded at several points.

"Memorize them better!" the Private First Class scolded.

"Yes, sir!" Kan answered.

"I beg of you," Takeo said politely and gave place to the new soldier.

"I am obliged," Kan answered and took his station.

"Do your best!" Private First Class Tanaka exhorted, and he led Takeo back to the rest station.

Before the dugout, the Private First Class ordered, "Halt! Fall out!" Takeo answered, "I am obliged." He bowed politely and entered the dugout and put his rifle and that of his superior on the improvised rifle rack.

An old Reserve, Private Hosaka, was awake and squatting near the entrance, smoking a cigarette contentedly. "Hard work!" he called when the two entered the dugout. Two more soldiers were asleep in the back.

"I have been obliged!" Takeo said as he squatted down beside the Reserve Private. They all said, "I have been obliged," whenever they came back from standing guard. It, of course, meant that the soldier returning from an hour's watch felt obliged to his comrades in the rest station for having stayed in readiness to give him support in an emergency.

The exact meaning of this greeting, as well as numerous others used in the soldier's daily life, had long lost their significance, and the soldiers used them without caring so much for what they meant as for when to use them. Even more than at home, life in the army had been a series more or less of formal greetings. The soldier was early initiated into the fundamental principle that his life as an individual ended when he took off his civilian clothes and put on his uniform. From that moment on, his body and soul belonged to the Emperor, he was told, and strict rules of behavior and living were set down for him to follow faithfully, and often those rules were more important than life itself.

"It must be hot outside," the Reserve said, dropping his cigarette butt and grinding it under his heel.

"Yes, it is hot," Takeo answered politely.

"They should build a roof," the Reserve said loudly, throwing a meaningful glance at the Private First Class, who already had his Infantryman's Manual out and was studying its pages intently. Reserve Private Hosaka was lower in rank than the Sentinel-Post Leader but a senior in service, and army etiquette allowed him a great deal of leniency.

"Honorable Senior Soldier, why don't you take a rest?" Takeo suggested, in order to save an embarrassing situation. A soldier of the same rank but senior in service was to be addressed, "Honorable Senior Soldier."

"No, I am not sleepy. I shall stay up a little longer," the Reserve answered, lighting another cigarette. After a little pause, Takeo asked somewhat timidly, "Has the Honorable Senior Soldier ever thought about death?"

"Everybody has," the older soldier said half laughingly and looked patronizingly at Takeo, for he could almost have been the latter's father in age.

"No, I mean really deeply," Takeo insisted.

"When everybody first comes to the front, he thinks about it."

"What does the Honorable Senior Soldier think about it?" Takeo asked, for he liked this older comrade, who was also a farmer, and trusted his friendship for him.

The Reserve blew the smoke from his mouth and looked smilingly at it as it rose to the ceiling. After a while, he said, "If you die, you lose."

"It isn't as simple as all that," Takeo protested.

"We have been at the front almost a year longer than you

have, and I have seen many die in that time, and none have gained by it," the Reserve said.

"Such a thing, we do not know," Takeo persisted.

"Whether it is a loss or a gain, you mean? If you die, your parents, or your wife, or your children will cry a great deal. They will suffer. I have a wife and three children, and so I cannot die."

"Not that kind of gain or loss," Takeo said. "We are giving our lives to our country without any selfishness, and so there must be some reward."

"That is so. We will receive a bonus and a medal, but one's life cannot be exchanged for such things."

"By reward, I do not mean such things." Takeo blushed a little as he added hesitatingly, "I mean about the life after death."

"Such a matter, we do not know," the Reserve laughed but, becoming serious, said, "Anyway, let us not die, and let us go home alive."

After a while, the Reserve ground the butt of his cigarette under his heel and said, "Well, shall I go and sleep? . . . Say, when you wake me up, start waking me fifteen minutes ahead of time. If you wake me up at once, I am frightened." The instruction he addressed to the Private First Class, who merely grunted without taking his eyes from his book.

After his older comrade had gone, Takeo sat for some time staring blankly ahead of him and thinking. He was troubled. All his former doubts seemed to be returning. The faith he had achieved a moment ago appeared frail against the practical arguments of Private Hosaka. Takeo felt a vague discontent. He had forgotten something. Surely, it was not like this when he had felt that glorious exultation a moment ago!

"Don't be just dumb! Study something!" Private First Class Tanaka scolded.

"Yes, sir," Takeo answered with a start. This was the second time the Private First Class had caught him unawares. The

Private First Class must think him a sluggard, Takeo thought.

Taking out the little notebook containing the Imperial Rescript Promulgated To The Armed Forces, which every soldier carried in his breast pocket, Takeo said good-naturedly in a shrewd attempt to hide his embarrassment, "Honorable Private First Class studies very hard."

"You study, too," the Private First Class looked up from his book this time and glared at his subordinate.

"Yes, sir," Takeo said and quickly looked down at his opened book.

He could not concentrate for some time and merely made believe he was reading the Rescript. But his eyes soon began to make out the words. He had memorized the Five Articles of the Rescript fairly well already, but he still had the Introduction and Conclusion to memorize. Every soldier had to memorize the Imperial Rescript if he wanted to become a Private First Class, and sometimes a soldier was beaten for not knowing the Rescript. Takeo now tried to forget everything and began to concentrate on the Rescript.

" . . . *Be resolved that honor is heavier than the mountains and death lighter than a feather.* . . . " As Takeo's eyes came to this passage, a keen, almost painful sensation struck him. The same exultation he had felt on the hillside overlooking the plain swept over him. It was like a flash of inspiration.

This is it! This is the feeling! I must not forget it from now on! Takeo thought, and began avidly reading ahead. As he read, he thought to himself, If this was a war to defend our country, they might understand this feeling of mine better. However, Takeo felt that his faith in a meaningful death was something uniquely his own, and he felt as strong a jealousy for it as he did for his most cherished memories.

In the meantime, Private Kan out on the open, grassy hillside was succumbing to the same trance that had held Takeo, as he gazed long at the vast monotonous plain under the broad sky. His eyes resting vacantly on the endless, waving tops of the grainfields, he began repeating to himself one of his favorite mottoes, or rather two of them. *The peace of East Asia . . . The peace of the world*, he kept repeating to himself over and over again.

Those were the aims for which they were fighting, they had been told at home, though in the army they merely mentioned one's patriotism to the Emperor. Kan had never had much time or opportunity to think much about those aims and they wouldn't have made much sense anyway, but he liked the sound of them and their friendly tone.

The sweet smell of the grass was strong in his nostrils, and the sun was making him sweat, and he began to feel sticky all over. There was a light breeze blowing, however, so that it was a pleasant kind of stickiness. Kan became strongly conscious of his body and of the pleasant feeling of the blood coursing through his veins. He began to feel a strong sexual urge. He thought of some special girls he had known at home and of the prostitutes he had met in the cities. He had been a lathe mechanic in a munitions factory and had been initiated early into the baser secrets of life. A soldier very seldom had any time by himself to enjoy his own thoughts, and Kan was certainly enjoying his one hour alone on the hill. All sorts of lewd thoughts began to pass through his mind, and the urge was so great that he closed his eyes and groaned.

One night in the training barracks at home, after Kan had been beaten by a Senior Soldier, he had gone into the latrine and, closing the door, had wept long and bitterly. This was the first time, since then, that he had felt really alone.

CHAPTER 2

IT WAS a bright, sunny morning. As was always the case on the morning following the day ending a stretch of guard duty, Takeo felt gratifyingly rested. Soon the bustle of roll-call, breakfast, and the eternal after-meal sweeping up was ended, and Takeo and his comrades were seated in the shade of the tree in front of the native store in which their Squad Three was temporarily quartered in the village.

As he threw away the butt of the second cigarette he had chain-smoked since breakfast, Private Shunzo Miki said, "Really, what they call the army is a hateful place!" Miki was a bulky farmer's lad, outspoken and honest.

The words were spat out with much venom, some bravado, and a little defiance. Private Miki and his friends under the tree, including Takeo, were all First-Year-Soldiers. Miki did not have the self-assurance yet to give the stock soldiers' complaint that inflection of tragedy and loneliness, sometimes mingled with a sigh, which the older soldiers managed to put into it.

"Really, that is so!" agreed Private Kan with mock pugnacity.

The savagely domineering Second- and Third-Year-Soldiers and the proud Reserves were inside, still lying on their matted beds, recovering from the fatigue of eating a breakfast cooked and served them by the First-Year-Soldiers.

"I am going to unload myself," Private Miki said, and got up to go to the backyard where they had their latrine.

15

"Don't fall in," laughed Private Kan, and everyone laughed.

"You'll hear me if I do," retorted Miki good-naturedly and disappeared inside the house.

"He has been going regularly to the toilet since yesterday," said Kan, the son of a factory foreman, and a very talkative fellow.

"He has diarrhea," said Private Yamamoto.

"He eats too much," said Kan.

"Really, he eats too much," two or three others agreed.

"Hey, somebody get me some water!" a voice shouted imperiously from inside the house.

"Yes, sir!" smartly answered Kan but quickly added in an undertone for the benefit of his Same-Year-Comrades, "He should get it himself."

But he rose and went inside and to the rear where they kept the water in a large earthen vase.

Takeo said, "He shouldn't go if he wants to complain."

"He is always complaining," someone else said.

"But he moves around all right," replied Takeo.

There was a tinge of jealousy in the tone of their voices, and right at that moment there was a mutual invisible bond of jealousy among them for a comrade who was doing a little more than they. Kan, who was a diplomat, had known the danger of what he was doing and so had uttered his little complaint to his comrades before going to undertake his task. But he had fooled no one, for they all knew how servile he was before the older soldiers.

To be jealous from time to time, however, was part of a soldier's daily life, and nobody made much of it. On this occasion, too, it was quickly forgotten, and Kan, still complaining, soon came back to be accepted into the group. It was only when such occasions piled up that one had to watch out, and a fellow very seldom let it come to such a pass.

A squad in the Japanese Army was a very complicated organization, as was the whole army, enmeshed in a maze of intricate feudalistic concepts. From the very first day that a youth entered the army, he was taught the absolute necessity of respect. True, to be sure, as in every army! But how uniquely, how very, very uniquely so, in the Japanese Imperial Army. First came worship for the Emperor, then respect for the superiors all the way down the line to anybody who had been in service longer, irrespective of rank.

Thus, when Kan and his comrades had entered their regiment's barracks at home, they had been taught to get the meals for the older soldiers from the kitchen, serve them, wash the dishes after meals, sweep and scrub the floors, make the beds, oil the shoes, do the washing, and, in fact, to do all the menial tasks for the older soldiers, while the latter sat around to watch with critically prying eyes. All these the new soldiers had to do besides undergoing an intensive combat training. All these, they still had to do at the front here in China besides undertaking real combat, marches, and duties . . . even though Kan and his Same-Year-Comrades had been promoted to full privates from the sub-privates they had been during training. This made them equals in rank with most of the older soldiers, but the latter were still senior in service.

The primary requisite for promotion, they had been told, was "one's attitude in the squad." In other words, Kan and his comrades soon learned that to be promoted, one had to be in good with as many of the older soldiers as possible. Of course, it was different in the case of the few brilliant ones, as in the case of Jimbo who had been to college. He was now in Officers' Training School. The ordinary First-Year-Soldiers, however, had to vie constantly with each other to curry the favor of the older soldiers, and there was always a keen sort of rivalry among them.

"You know that Private-First-Class Tanaka didn't even say 'Thank you,'" grumbled Kan when he returned to his place among his comrades. "The water was for him."

"That one is a bad one," said Miki who had returned from his excursion to the backyard in the meantime.

"That one is only a Second-Year-Man. There are many more

Third-Year and Reserve men. He shouldn't be so haughty," continued Kan.

"It is good to be an old soldier. You can sleep all day long and let the First-Year-Soldier do all your work. It is better than having a wife," observed Miki.

Suddenly loud voices were heard around the corner farther down the street, and a large group of jostling, laughing soldiers appeared, pulling and coaxing along a lively, recalcitrant donkey. They were all old soldiers and seemed to be having a very good time. As they approached, the First-Year-Soldiers of Squad Three politely got to their feet.

"Hey! You got a she-donkey at your place! Bring her along. We're going to give this he-donkey a good time!" shouted the soldier who was pulling the donkey. Most of the old soldiers were dressed merely in their undershirts, though they had their trousers on by special order of the Platoon Leader, who had constantly to worry about surprise enemy attacks. Many of them had towels twisted around their heads to keep them cool and only a few wore shoes, the rest wearing clogs made from wooden blocks.

The old soldiers of Squad Three, who had been resting inside, came out to see what the commotion was about in front of their quarters. Some of them were already putting their trousers on, while others were still in their *fundoshi* or loincloth. Everybody rested and slept in his underwear, for it was too hot, and only the First-Year-Soldiers, who had to work, wore uniforms all day long. But even the old soldiers had to wear trousers to go out in the street.

"Hey, you can't do that to our girl," shouted Private First Class Tanaka with mock belligerence.

"What are you saying! Let your girl have a good time once in a while!" somebody shouted back, and everybody laughed.

"Shall I go and get the donkey, Honorable Private First Class?" asked Kan of Private First Class Tanaka, who was busily putting on his trousers in the doorway.

"Yes, go and get it," was the answer.

All the First-Year-Soldiers, who welcomed this break in the monotony, ran into the house and to the backyard where the donkey shed was located next to the kitchen. The old native couple and their son, the original occupants of the house, who had been forced to move into the storeroom beside the shed when the squad of Japanese soldiers had moved in, came out to see what was happening. When the Japanese troops had come, the womenfolk had fled, but these three had stayed to look after their property the best they could.

The old woman worriedly followed Kan when he entered the shed where the donkey was tied. "What? What?" she hesitatingly asked, using one of the few native words which she knew the soldiers understood.

When she pulled the sleeve of Kan's coat to attract his attention, the latter roughly brushed her aside and scolded, "Don't bother me, old lady!" Takeo, whom the old woman reminded strongly of his own mother at home, gently guided her aside and tried to allay her fears with words from his scant native vocabulary. "Don't worry," he said. "By and by, the horse comes back."

The old man and his son remained discreetly at a distance, but the old woman could not be comforted. She followed the happy crowd as they surged out of the house, pulling the excited donkey behind them. Soon, the soldiers were dashing down the street toward the village square with their reluctant animals. This was not the first time the soldiers had turned to the donkeys to furnish them much needed entertainment, and they went about their task surely, like people observing a ceremony of an oft-repeated festival. Donkeys were plentiful in North China, and the soldiers were always able to turn to them to while away their time when the monotony of the occupation became unbearable, for these animals, with their insatiable capacity to mate, never failed the expectant soldiers.

When the old woman saw the he-donkey being dragged by

the crowd ahead, she realized what was in store for her own she-donkey. She let out a loud shriek, followed by a cataract of mournful wails. She dashed toward Kan, who began to have difficulty with the donkey which started backing away at the sound of her master's voice, and, holding on to his arm, began pulling and pleading vehemently as only an old woman who has flung the proprieties to the winds could. Just then the he-donkey, too, turned around to see what was going on and, noticing the she-donkey, began braying excitedly. Many natives, attracted by the commotion, came out of their homes and the side streets to watch, and other soldiers came on the run to join the happy, milling crowd. The he-donkey began to kick when its braying went unheeded, so that those near it had to move fast to keep away from his vindictive hoofs.

Soon, the narrow cobblestone street was nearly filled from end to end with the noisy crowd. It so happened that all this commotion reached its height in front of the medicine store which the Platoon Commander was temporarily using as his headquarters. Lieutenant Yaichi Kondo appeared at the door of his quarters, hurriedly buttoning the flap of his trousers, for he too seemed to have been resting in his underwear inside the house. His young interpreter was with him.

Everybody seemed to stop long enough to salute the Lieutenant; even the donkeys seemed to hold themselves for a moment, but soon the animals were at it again, and the crowd surged wildly around them, while the old woman resumed her shrieking. The interpreter went beside the old woman, but he was soon a very harassed man, as Kan begged him to get the old woman off his arm and the old woman turned the full vehemence of her tirade on him. The interpreter had to scold the woman soundly to calm her down, and for a while the two looked as if they would get nowhere, shouting the way they did at each other. The interpreter finally seemed to have made sense, and went to the Lieutenant to report his findings. The Lieutenant smiled patronizingly as he always did when listening to his interpreter and, nodding importantly, stepped toward the old woman with his interpreter beside him.

"Old woman, you do not have to worry," said the Lieutenant. The interpreter translated in the local vernacular. The old woman seemed to have been deeply impressed by the authority in the officer's tone, for she let go her frantic hold on Kan's arm to turn around and face the Lieutenant. The latter, though, did not seem very dignified in his undershirt and trousers and without his long sword.

The old woman, nevertheless, concentrated all her fervor now on the officer. "She says her donkey is still a virgin and too young. She says it was born only last winter," the interpreter explained.

The old woman continued pleading docilely now and almost childishly, but Lieutenant Kondo had already learned enough. He had to consider the prestige of his and his subordinates' position before the many natives who had gathered. It would be a complete loss of prestige to halt the proceedings now, and, besides, he was not averse to a little fun himself.

"Tell her, the soldiers will not hurt her donkey and that they will pay her for using it," replied Lieutenant Kondo and, turning to the soldiers, said, "You must all pay ten sen each to this old lady."

There was a very audible undertone of disappointment among the soldiers. Some even began suggesting returning the donkeys. For nothing seemed more noxious to the soldiers than to have to pay for some fun they had themselves improvised, even if it was at the expense of the natives. Lieutenant Kondo, fearing the loss of a pleasant morning's entertainment, took two crumpled yen notes out of his wallet and, handing them to his interpreter, instructed him to give them to the old woman. The old woman continued her wailing but accepted the money and did not try to interfere any more.

Somebody mimicked, "Forward march!" Others echoed "Forward! Forward!" And the happy parade once again moved forward down the street. When they arrived at the square, the she-donkey was tied to the large oak tree in the center. The old woman followed at a distance and stood anxiously watching with the groups of other natives who had gathered in the outer fringe of the crowd.

It seemed now as if the whole platoon had assembled in the square to watch the show. Somebody brought a chair for the Lieutenant, who sat in the very front where he could get the best view. In the meantime, his orderly had brought him his long sword and coat, and he wore them and looked important enough to preside at a court-martial.

"Get back, so that everybody can get a chance to see," ordered Lieutenant Kondo with a flourish of his arms. The young, fair officer made quite a handsome figure, seated stiffly in the clearing in the center, and he had an easy time impressing his subordinates. The pushing, cheering soldiers fell back a little, but still many had to stand on their toes and peer over the shoulders of their comrades to get a view of the center of the square. Some in the rear brought boxes and stood on them.

"Let the he-donkey loose!" the soldiers began to shout.

The soldier who was holding the stallion was having a hard time keeping his protégé back, for it was kicking and pulling as if possessed by the devil. The soldier shouted, "Here it goes," and let the wild beast loose. A ringing cheer of anticipation arose from the jostling crowd of soldiers, but the natives merely craned their necks and remained silent and expressionless. The glum silence of the natives was in strong contrast to the noisy exuberance of the soldiers.

The donkey slid on its haunches when it was suddenly released but, scrambling to its feet, wheeled about and made straight for its mate-to-be. It reared majestically on its hind legs and came down solidly on the back of the she-donkey, which stood still and seemed stoically resigned.

However, the misgivings of the old woman were soon borne out, and the he-donkey began to have difficulties. The mare, feeling the pain, kicked back and, throwing her assailant off, bit its neck. The he-donkey retreated to a safe distance and began to bray mournfully. The soldiers laughed and shouted encouragement, and some even went to slap the hesitating animal's flanks. The old woman, who owned the mare, however, began to wail pitifully again.

After two or three more painful tries, the stallion again succeeded in gaining its precarious hold on the mare's back. This time Kan was ready with a bucketful of warm water, which he hurled at the flanks of the animals. Kan, his comrades noticed, was in his element, showing off his "ability to be of service" with that intent seriousness which only he could manage so well. He even lent his hand at one painfully critical stage, and the stallion was at last able to consummate his long struggle. The young mare, by this time, seemed to be in a daze at all the excitement about her, and, except for an impatient twitch now and then, remained resignedly still.

There was little jubilant cheering now, as most of the soldiers watched in raptured silence. Exclamations of wonder were to be heard from time to time. Some were snickering like girls from a Middle School. Even the Lieutenant lost his usual composure and leaned far forward to get a closer view, but nobody was watching him, so he lost little face.

After a fairly long time, the he-donkey seemed to have consummated his exertion, and his wild convulsions ceased completely. But he still held tenaciously to his awkward position on the mare's back and seemed in no hurry to get back on the solid ground.

"Watch him, watch him now!" somebody shouted, and they all seemed already to anticipate what he was pointing at, and they continued to hold their silence. The stallion let go of the mare's mane which it had been clutching savagely between its jaws throughout its late struggle and, raising its nose, bared its lips widely to show the rows of even white teeth, so that it seemed to be laughing heartily though silently. The sudden change of expression was most comical, and the long, raptured silence was broken by an explosion of loud guffaws. This was the climax of the lewd show. The soldiers had seen it often, but each time they maneuvered a show they were not satisfied until they had seen it to its idiotic conclusion.

"Well, that is enough! Private Kan, let the donkey down!" the Lieutenant ordered, now his old imperious self. Any more would compromise the army's dignity in front of the natives. Kan, having been called by name before all his comrades, came to a stiff attention and answered "Yes, sir!" Although he was called simply because he was nearest to the laboring animals Kan felt a happy pride that he, a mere First-Year-Soldier, should be singled out from among all the soldiers gathered there.

He pulled hard at the rope which was still attached to the he-donkey's neck, but the animal seemed determined to enjoy his advantageous position a little longer and would not let go his tenacious hold on the mare's back. The soldiers began to cheer as the struggle started to put on the appearance of becoming a long, drawn-out one. But Kan was desperately determined to obey his commander's order, and he began yanking the rope in earnest, though nobody tried to give him a hand. The mare had to bear the burden of the struggle as she was dragged which-ever way the stallion was pulled, and several times she seemed about to topple over but recovered with that surefootedness which is the principal asset of this type of animal.

"Let him alone. Maybe he wants to do it over again," one of the older soldiers in Kan's squad suggested from the side. Most of the soldiers did not want to see it end yet, and others joined in the suggestion.

Now Private Kan was in a delicate position. If he obeyed this new suggestion of the older soldiers, he would be disobeying his Lieutenant. Some of the First-Year-Soldiers, who were al-ready feeling a little jealous at this one-man show of their energetic comrade, began to gloat at his dilemma. The Lieu-tenant objected, "That is enough. Somebody lend Kan a hand."

Kan, however, was equal to the occasion, and, with a comic gesture and a loud whoop, he gave the rope what he made to appear to be a final halfhearted yank, though, really, all his strength aided by the strength of fighting desperation was in it. It pulled the stallion off, but Kan, by making a clown of himself with his exaggerated motions, had saved the face of the older soldiers.

The old woman who owned the she-donkey quickly came forward, fearing a repetition of the shameful orgy which had just ended, and began to untie her animal from the oak tree. She looked so shamefaced and sad that one would think it was her own daughter who had been soiled in this public square. There were exclamations of sympathy among the natives, though the soldiers remained stoically indifferent.

As if he thought some form of dismissal appropriate, Lieutenant Kondo turned to his interpreter and said, "Tell the old lady to take good care of her donkey."

The interpreter transmitted the officer's words, and tears glistened in the eyes of the old woman. They looked like tears of gratitude at the kind words, and the Lieutenant himself thought so and felt pity for the old woman for the first time. He took out another yen bill from his wallet and handed it to the woman. The woman accepted the money silently, but who would have thought that her tears were tears of anger and chagrin and tears of frustration at her impotence to berate the proud officer, as she wanted to so much just then?

The Lieutenant, happily oblivious to the woman's true feelings, turned to go back to his quarters with his interpreter. The soldiers, too, began to disperse, though a few curious ones still stayed around to look at the donkeys. The First-Year-Soldiers hurried back to their quarters to prepare lunch, for they had been so absorbed by the spectacle on the square that they had almost forgotten how close it was getting toward noon.

Takeo, too, started for his quarters but felt shame and full of pity at the same time when he passed the old woman, tearfully pulling her donkey home. To show his sympathy, he patted her arms and smiled at her. He searched for some words of sympathy in his scant native vocabulary and, failing to find any, said in his own tongue, "Don't worry. She will heal quickly." He used his most assuring tone, and when the woman did not respond, added in the native tongue, "Good. Good." He did not know what he exactly meant by those words, but it was an expression of his sympathy. The words, however, seemed entirely inappropriate, and Takeo felt very sheepish. He left the old woman and hurried to overtake his comrades.

When he reached his quarters, Takeo found Kan and his other comrades already in the kitchen, making ready to start a fire under the rice pot. There were altogether five First-Year-Soldiers in Squad Three, and they were crowded in the narrow kitchen and getting into each other's way, but it was the First-Year-Soldiers' duty to cook the meals for the squad, which numbered sixteen at that time, and no one wanted to volunteer to get out of the way and be called a shirker. Each squad, too, had its First-Year-Soldiers who looked after the squad's cooking, for here at the front there was no central kitchen, so to speak, as in the regiment at home. The orderly cooked the meals for the Lieutenant, and the interpreter ate with the natives.

"Did you wash your hands?" Takeo jokingly chided Kan, who was cutting some vegetable leaves.

"No. What waste it would be! The meal should taste good today."

"Really. Didn't you wash your hands?" Miki now asked accusingly.

"Say, you better wash your hands," the others joined in a little angrily.

Kan grudgingly took a dipperful of water from the water pail and washed his hands. Takeo felt sorry for Kan that his joke should have been taken seriously and went out to get more firewood for the stove. He met the old woman outside gently washing her donkey with some herbs dipped in hot water. The other two men stood by to look on sympathetically and seemed to be giving kindly suggestions but did not offer to help the old woman.

Why are the men so resigned and calm during calamities? thought Takeo as he returned to the kitchen carrying an armful of kindling wood. It was the women who grieved the most and went about to remedy the situation.

"Say, we better give the natives some of our food today in payment for the use of their donkey," Takeo suggested.

"That's right, let us give them some of this beef when it is cooked," said Miki.

"Why shouldn't we give them some rice?" Takeo said.

It was the perennial sympathy of the underdog for the underdog.

CHAPTER 3

THE ATMOSPHERE at Squad Three was weighted by a gloomy tension during roll-call that evening, although evening roll-calls were always trying affairs, especially to the younger soldiers. That hour offered the old soldiers an ideal opportunity to rail the young ones on various pretensions and thus keep them in harness. It was the time, too, when various, usually obnoxious orders were issued from headquarters. Evening roll-calls were always held separately within each squad, and the men of Squad Three were lined up stiffly in single file in the backyard of their quarters.

The count-off was ordered by the Senior Private First Class, Tamotsu Gunji, in the absence of the Corporal, who was away at Platoon Headquarters explaining a very unpleasant incident. The men counted off loudly and smartly, and they looked very much dressed up in their coats, trousers, and shoes, in strong contrast to their general appearance of undress and sloppiness during the day. The few curious natives, who were looking in through the front door, marveled at the strict, disciplined manner in which the men conducted the ritual of the roll-call, and they had a hard time believing that these were the same men who had carried on so disgracefully in the village square that morning, or that these were the same men who lay around lazily in their underwear all day long.

When the count-off was finished, Private First Class Gunji

next ordered, "Turn to the East!" The soldiers made an about-face, for east was behind them.

"Worship the Imperial Palace! The supreme salute!" ordered the Private First Class. The men bowed low and solemnly from their hips, and the silence was impressive while they held the worshipful posture.

"Return to attention! About face!" Once again the line was facing the Private First Class. The faces of the soldiers remained expressionless, and their bodies, rigid and tense.

"Respectful recitation of the Five Imperial Doctrines!" Private First Class Gunji now ordered, and began the recitation himself in a ringing voice. The whole squad joined him and began reciting at the top of their lungs, and the lusty, vigorous voices of fifteen healthy men resounded noisily in the narrow confines of the backyard.

"First, the soldier makes it his destiny to perform patriotism.

"Second, the soldier maintains etiquette.

"Third, the soldier respects martial courage.

"Fourth, the soldier values truthfulness.

"Fifth, the soldier remains austere."

These five doctrines were from an imperial rescript to the armed forces promulgated by the late Emperor Meiji at the end of the last century. They were supposed to constitute the basis of conduct for all the men of the Japanese armed forces, and the Rescript was really a much longer composition, although the Five Doctrines were the main points. Some troops required their men to recite the whole Rescript (a matter of nearly fifteen minutes) during roll-calls, but most were satisfied merely with the recitation of the Five Doctrines. The armed forces of Japan were required to recite the Rescript, all or in part, at both morning and evening roll-calls, and sometimes the men recited it even at the firing lines to raise their morale.

"Face the East! Worship the Imperial Palace! The supreme salute! Return to attention! About face!" . . . The squad went through the same ceremony of worship after their recitation of the Rescript. East was always designated as the direction where the Emperor's Palace was located, though actually it was not always so. East was where the sun rose, and the Emperor was a personification of the sun's glory, and it sufficed one to bow eastward when worshiping the Emperor, wherever one might be.

The other squads in the platoon, too, were conducting the ceremony of worship at the same time, and the loud voices of soldiers reciting the Rescript could be heard from all over the village. For a time, the village sounded like a school at home during class recitation period. This was entirely out of harmony with the grim, realistic atmosphere which pervaded the village during the day.

In place of the Platoon Commander, who was very much occupied at the time, the Senior Sergeant was making the round of the squads this evening to hear the reports of the roll-calls. The jarring clatter of his saber and the hurrying beat of his hobnailed boots heralded his arrival in front of the house where Squad Three was quartered. . . . "Attention!" Private First Class Gunji shouted. . . . When the Sergeant appeared in the backyard where the squad was lined up, accompanied by an orderly with a bayoneted rifle, not even an eyelid flickered among the men standing at rigid attention.

Saluting the Sergeant smartly, the Private First Class recited the evening's report in that smooth singsong manner which was the envied mark of distinction of the self-confident old soldier. . . . "Total number, sixteen; absent, one; present number, fifteen. Count off!" . . . When the count-off substantiated his report, Private First Class Gunji explained, "The one who is absent is the Squad Leader, who is in conference with the Honorable Platoon Commander."

The Sergeant, who had been glaring peevishly up and down the line during the recitation of the report, suddenly pointed at Private Nakamura, a First-Year-Soldier, standing near the end of the line, and said in a voice charged with anger and arrogance,

"The coat's breast-pocket button is loose!"

Private Nakamura was a First-Year-Soldier, but he was a little older than the other First-Year-Soldiers, for he had been sick at the age when he had to take the conscription military examination, and his examination had been postponed. He had married in the meantime, and he was one of the few First-Year-Soldiers with a wife and child. He was also one of the few First-Year-Regulars with a business of his own, having been a tailor in the city when he had been conscripted.

"Yes, sir!" Nakamura answered hastily when he was pointed out. He stiffened perceptibly, and he felt his heart sink inside of him, for he was not of a strong constitution. There was nothing he hated worse in the army than to be singled out for some fault of his own, for while he had absolutely no ambition in the service, he had an exaggerated aversion to being scolded all by himself. They said of him that his "feelings were weak." He blushed deeply as he fumbled with both hands for his breast-pocket flaps. The flap over his right pocket was unbuttoned, and he hastily buttoned it with trembling fingers. He realized with a sudden upsurge of remorse that he had left it unbuttoned when he had removed the picture of his wife and child from the pocket that afternoon to look at it secretly in the latrine, as he did from time to time.

"Be careful the next time!" the Sergeant reprimanded stiffly and he wrote down this flaw in Squad Three's roll-call procedure in his notebook to report to the Platoon Commander together with the other reports of the evening. He left the squad in the same important manner that he had entered it, amidst the noisy rattling of his saber.

When the Sergeant had left, Private First Class Gunji finally ordered the long-awaited "Rest!" Poor Private Nakamura, his face red as a blushing Middle School girl student, felt all the eyes of the older soldiers turned angrily upon him. Private First Class Gunji glared almost murderously at him, for it would also be marked down as the Private First Class's fault that he had not noticed and corrected the disorder of his subordinate before the roll-call.

Several old soldiers in line, especially Private First Class Tanaka, began ranting at the quaking private, "Well, wait," interposed Private First Class Gunji impatiently. "Attention!" he ordered. "Except for the First-Year-Soldiers . . . you are dismissed!"

The dismissed soldiers bowed toward their acting squad leader and consoled, "Thanks for your trouble," as they always did at the end of roll-calls. They always said, "Thanks for your trouble" to anyone who did a little more than the rest even though, at many times, it was no trouble at all. This was one of the many sensitive courtesies of the army.

The First-Year-Soldiers, however, had no one to console them, and they remained stiffly in line and braced themselves for what they had come to expect after many bitter experiences during evening roll-calls. This evening, moreover, they had every reason to expect the full treatment of the older soldiers' stock punishment, for it was a special evening indeed.

First, poor Private Nakamura got it. The open palm of Private First Class Tanaka resounded loudly as it caught the Private squarely on his left cheek. . . . "Fool! Don't you know what roll-call is?" The Private First Class shouted like a madman. Private Nakamura quickly regained his posture after the first shock and mumbled, "Yes, sir." His eyes, which stared straight ahead in the position of a soldier at attention, were filled with stark terror. The other First-Year-Soldiers, standing beside him, too remained motionless and rigid, as if oblivious to what was happening beside them.

"What do you mean by 'Yes,' you fool!" Now it was the turn of Private First Class Gunji, who had lost face the most on account of the erring young soldier. The Private First Class was a left-hander, and Nakamura now got it on his other cheek.

The blow shook him a little, but he took it as stoically as the first.

The other old soldiers stood around angrily, as if any one of them might lend his hand at anytime. They outnumbered the First-Year-Soldiers and they formed an impressive half-circle around the latter. It must have been very special this evening, too, for the more matured Reserves, who usually left the unpleasant task of disciplining the young ones to the Second- and Third-Year-Regulars and remained aloof during such proceedings, were hanging on closely. A few, though, went and sat on benches nearby and lighted their cigarettes.

"Do you call that the posture of attention?" Tanaka began again and swung really hard this time. The blow sent Nakamura reeling to the ground, but he got to his feet in a hurry. "Pull in your chin!" the Private First Class commanded angrily.

These slaps with the open hands were not so painful physically, but the great noise they made was a powerful demoralizer. They ate into one's heart and squeezed it each time. The fisted blows, which were administered on rare occasions, were the painful ones, but they were easier to take, since they were over with quicker — either the assailant hesitated to give more or one blacked out. This practice of disciplining by slapping was not unique to Squad Three but universal in the Japanese Armed Forces, and no subordinate ever thought of resisting, for it would have been insubordination and punishable by death.

"You are all loafing nowadays!" Now it was the turn of Private Oka, the Third-Year-Soldier, who remained a perennial private. As usual, he had drunk a little *chungchiu*, the strong native liquor, before roll-call tonight, and the First-Year-Soldiers could smell his reeking breath, as he went down the line slapping each man, this time soundly on his cheek. The Senior Private was stout and bull-necked, and he had a way of slapping with the base of his palm which made his victims recoil and sometimes topple over. Tonight, however, the First-Year-

Soldiers took it standing, and they were all satisfied that the slapping had come to include all of them at last, as they had been expecting.

"Well, wait!" Private First Class Gunji interposed impatiently when Oka seemed ready to go down the line again.

Turning to the First-Year-Soldiers, he began pompously and in a nasal tone of self-pity, "You know what happened today?" He paused and glared threateningly at his subordinates.

"Yes, sir," Kan answered, for he was always ready with an answer.

"One button loose at roll-call is a trivial matter. This evening we are not scolding you for that!" the Private First Class continued, "Who knows why we are scolding you tonight?"

"Yes, sir," Kan answered. "It is because one rifle of our squad was lost today."

"Why did you let it get lost?" Oka bellowed, and he went slapping each soldier down the line again. This time, Private Nakamura, who had had more than the others, sank to the ground, but he regained his feet shakily.

A rifle in Squad Three had disappeared this day, and no one could account for its disappearance except for the fact that, for over an hour in the morning while everyone had gone to see the rowdy show in the village square, the squad's quarters had been left vacant and unguarded, and anyone could have entered it and walked off unnoticed with the rifle. The loss of the rifle had been discovered only late in the afternoon when the First-Year-Soldiers had begun polishing the rifle rack in preparation for the evening roll-call. The men of the squad had immediately started a search of their quarters and of the neighboring houses, too. Failing to find any sign of the missing rifle, Corporal Sakamoto had finally reported the loss to the Platoon Leader. An intensive search was immediately conducted throughout the village, and numerous natives were interrogated, but no rifle turned up, and it was the consensus that some enemy spy had probably walked off with the weapon. It could have been hidden underneath any of the numerous variegated baggage that had been carried out of the village that day, or it could still be hidden in some remote undiscoverable corner of the crowded village. After a fruitless search before roll-call everyone was certain that the rifle was lost for good.

As usual, the First-Year-Soldiers were being blamed for a fault the whole squad had to assume, for it was an accepted premise that it was another one of the First-Year-Soldiers' duties to guard the prestige of a squad while the older soldiers relaxed or had a good time. The case of Squad Three, furthermore, was a clear-cut one. When the whole squad had turned out with the donkey this morning, it was only natural that the First-Year-Soldiers should have decided among each other who should remain behind to watch the vacated quarters. Officially, it had been the Squad Leader's duty to have assigned somebody to stay behind to watch, as he did when the squad turned out for drills and morning roll-calls, but the argument against the First-Year-Soldiers was that the Squad Leader could not be expected to do everything all the time and the younger soldiers should be alert to uphold him whenever he forgot or was too preoccupied.

"Squad Three is sloppy! The First-Year-Soldiers are good-for-nothing," the other soldiers of the platoon grumbled when they had been called out to search for the lost rifle. They all blamed it on the First-Year-Soldiers, for First-Year-Soldiers had stayed behind in all the other squads this morning.

The First-Year-Soldiers of Squad Three themselves acknowledged their guilt within their respective consciences and felt a deep remorse and alarm at the magnitude of their sin. They could hardly imagine how it could have happened. The suddenness and spontaneity of the excitement when the donkey had been pulled out of its shed in the backyard had lulled their sense of duty momentarily, and when they had followed the mob to the square, they had forgotten completely about their vacated quarters. Then, too, one of their own comrades, Kan, had been the star performer on the square, and that also had helped them forget.

They had suffered a terrible remorse and contrition all day long, and that feeling was at its height now that they all knew their Squad Leader was at Platoon Headquarters probably receiving a hot tongue-lashing from the Platoon Commander. There had been cases, though rare, of soldiers losing parts of their weapons or of others damaging theirs, like twisting a bayonet scabbard, and each time they had heard of the terrible chastisement those soldiers had received. For instance, one of their comrades had lost the brass cover to his rifle's muzzle while out on the field taking combat training one day in the home barracks, and the whole squad had to search the grounds until late in the night; even though it was finally found in the tall grass, the soldier received a terrible beating when he had returned to the squad room. However, this was the first time they had heard of anybody losing a whole rifle.

"Do you know what the rifle is to the infantryman?" shouted Private First Class Gunji.

"Yes, sir," answered Kan promptly. "It is his soul."

"Then why did you let it be stolen?"

The First-Year-Soldiers had no answer to this question — not even Kan who was always ready with an answer. No answer was expected, furthermore, for it was one of those questions which the older soldiers used to silence the young soldiers before beating them. The First-Year-Soldiers remained silent and kept staring rigidly ahead.

"You are too fresh for First-Year-Soldiers!" bellowed Private First Class Gunji.

"Do you understand?" cried Oka and went down the line again — bang, bang, bang.

Private First Class Gunji waited patiently until Oka was finished. Then he continued solemnly:

"You should all know how valuable the rifle is to us. . . . Attention! . . ."

The First-Year-Soldiers stiffened perceptibly, though they were already at attention. Some of the older soldiers standing around, especially the Regulars, came to attention, though most of the Reserves remained slouched the way they were. Private First Class Gunji himself came dramatically to attention and continued in his most solemn voice:

"It fills us with trepidation that there should be the Chrysan-themum Seal of His Majesty the Emperor on each rifle. It means that His Majesty is pleased to own the rifles. . . ."

The superior and subordinates remained respectfully motion-less at attention, as well as the Regulars, and even the Reserves did not move, though they had not taken the trouble to come to attention. It was the absolutely inflexible custom in the army that one should come to attention when the Emperor or any-thing pertaining to him was mentioned, and the Reserves, when they did not come to attention, were only taking undue license in the absence of a higher superior than a Private First Class Regular.

"As the sword was to the samurai, so must the rifle be to the infantryman — it must be his soul. . . . At ease," Gunji ordered, now that the passage about the Emperor was finished.

The First-Year-Soldiers, however, had little time to relax their stiff muscles, for Private First Class Gunji shouted, "It is unpardonable that First-Year-Soldiers should go to see some-thing like what happened today!" and went down the line him-self this time — bang, bang, bang.

Private Okihara, a huge brawny Reserve who, some said, had been a butcher in a slaughterhouse, came ominously forward from where he was leaning clumsily against the mud wall en-closing the backyard. Disgustedly flipping away a still lighted cigarette butt, and baring his teeth in an ugly leer, he too went down the line, this time without saying a word — bang, bang,

bang. He struck with his closed fist, which rocked his victims, and two went down to the ground. Takeo, who was one of the two struck down, quickly regained his feet, though he spat blood from his mouth. Nakamura, the other one, who was a tailor and weakly built and who had received more of his share of beating this evening than the others, remained squatted on the ground with his head between his bent knees.

"Get up, you fool!" shouted Oka and gave him a rough kick.

This did not budge Nakamura, who felt as if he had gone far away to a comfortable distance from all this unpleasant commotion. He heard voices, but they sounded far away, and it was quiet and pleasant where he was.

"Well, wait," interposed Gunji when Oka made as if to kick the soldier on the ground again. "Somebody get a pail of water."

The water came, and they poured it all at once on the head of the fallen soldier. The chilly water woke Nakamura up with a jolt. He opened his eyes and looked dazedly around him and realized for the first time what had happened. He tried to scramble to his feet but was able to do so only after a great effort and had a hard time staying up, for his head seemed to be swinging in a circle. All his comrades, too, were in a very shaky condition. Miki, the big farmer's lad, was bleeding profusely from his nose.

The falling of Nakamura to the ground had taken the vindictiveness temporarily out of the older soldiers. Private First Class Tanaka now demanded in the shrill voice of a fanatic, "If they tell you to do it, will you commit *harakiri* to atone for your mistake?"

"Yes, sir! We will do it," replied the First-Year-Soldiers in unison.

This was not the first time they had been beaten, and this was not the first time they had been asked an impossible question. These First-Year-Soldiers of the Emperor's Army took their beating quietly and answered their superiors meekly. These were men who would have gladly laid down their lives for their Emperor but who asked nothing for themselves in return. They had the courage to charge a thousand enemy but not the determination to stand up for a single individual right. For there were no individuals in the Imperial Army — only absolute servants of the Emperor — and no rights except the right to die gloriously for the Emperor.

Punishers and punished, superiors and subordinates, the soldiers of the Japanese Imperial Army suffered together under a system which tried to make powerful destructive machines of them even beyond the endurable limit of inherently constructive mankind. Shells of the warm, constructive individuals they were born to become, the men lived unhappily within a perversion which tried not to recognize the ethics, constructiveness, and fair play their souls constantly hungered for in their relations with their fellow men. The Emperor's order was to kill and destroy the enemy, and the men had to suffer the consequences for anything which contradicted the order, even for the natural urge to construct.

"Attention. . . . It says in the Imperial Rescript,' 'Understand, that to receive an order from a superior is at once to receive an order from your Emperor.'" Private First Class Gunji declared solemnly. He had memorized well his Imperial Rescript, which was one of the main reasons he held his present superior rank. He continued, "So even if Private First Class Tanaka should order it, you are bound to commit *harakiri*. Are you ready to do so?"

"Yes, sir!" the First-Year-Soldiers replied promptly.

The sincerity of the young soldiers did not have to be put to the test, for just then their Squad Leader, Corporal Jiro Sakamoto, returned from his long conference with the Platoon Commander. He did not look as anxious as when he had left the squad, and the men felt a little relieved. He chased away the group of curious natives who were peering in through the front entrance and closed the door.

"Assemble!" he called to the old soldiers loitering around in the yard. When they fell in line sloppily, he ordered, "Attention!" The Corporal was past master at the art of bringing his subordinates quickly under his control. After a smart "Right dress," which brought the soldiers into perfect line, the Corporal ordered, "At ease." Now fifteen separate individuals, with fifteen separate temperaments, and fifteen different likes and dislikes were one in their attention to their Squad Leader. Corporal Sakamoto did not seem to notice the bleeding, shaking First-Year-Soldiers, though he knew well enough what had been going on. Although he himself did not usually beat the young soldiers and left the sordid task to his senior subordinates, he knew as well as all the other superiors on up to the highest general, who condoned and occasionally practiced it themselves, that the beating was necessary to maintain the unique discipline of the Imperial Army.

"I have been talking with the Honorable Platoon Commander until now, but it seems the rifle cannot be found," Corporal Sakamoto began with dignity. "I asked the Honorable Commander not to report to Company Headquarters, and he said he will not do it. Tomorrow, I plan to go to Company Headquarters. The Sergeant-in-charge-of-arms comes from my village, and so I think something can be done, but until then I wish you will remain silent about it."

The Corporal's cool, matter-of-fact voice was in such strong contrast to the insane tumult of a moment ago that the men listened almost in a daze. The Squad Leader sagaciously made no mention of the terrible scolding they all knew he had received at the hands of the Platoon Commander, and in a short time had his subordinates thinking once again along normal, rational channels. The First-Year-Soldiers were especially relieved, for they no longer needed to keep themselves keyed up almost to the breaking point, and Private Nakamura was the most grateful of all for this rational attitude of the Squad Leader.

"If the one possibility in ten thousand should happen, the Honorable Platoon Commander will report that the rifle was lost in a fire or something," he said. "You must not mention this matter to anybody outside the platoon," the Corporal warned once again. "The Honorable Platoon Commander will make the best of it to the other squads, and you must do the same."

"How about the old man and his son who lived here?" Private First Class Tanaka asked in his hurt, nasal tone. They all knew that several natives, including the occupants of this house, were being investigated at Platoon Headquarters.

"They are stubbornly saying they don't know. The other natives, too, say they don't know. The old man and his son say that they were in their room all the time, and the old woman, as we all know, was in the village square with us."

"The old man and his son should know," Private First Class Gunji protested.

"We tried frightening them, but they would not tell. The Honorable Platoon Commander has told the village master that he will burn the village if the rifle is not found. We may not burn the village right now, but we may, before we leave," Corporal Sakamoto explained patiently, for he was like a father soothing a group of dissatisfied and injured children.

He next turned to the First-Year-Soldiers who were crowded at one end of the line and said in a paternal tone, "I guess you know how wrong you were."

The First-Year-Soldiers answered, "Yes, sir," and some were almost in tears as they heard a kindly tone in a superior's voice for the first time since the beginning of this night's nightmare.

"Attention. . . . It fills us with trepidation that a rifle with the Imperial Chrysanthemum Seal was taken by the enemy. Even if we should commit *harakiri*, we cannot be excused. From now on, we must do our best to recover our prestige. Don't forget — even if we should all commit *harakiri* here in a row, we cannot be excused. But we do not have to do such a thing. We can atone to the Emperor in a much better way. . . . At ease."

Every man in Squad Three was inspired by this short speech of their Squad Leader. All the rantings and beatings of a while ago had been done in such a high level of frenzy that the men had gone through it as if in a dream, but the steady, sincere tone of the Corporal's voice sank into them inexorably with its message of high patriotism. That message easily found an answering chord in the fundamentally sincere will-to-do among the soldiers and proved once again the utter uselessness and imbecility of all the mad show of discipline and obedience which the soldiers had to go through for the greater part of their life in the army; but there was no one to notice the proof of it, for the generals were busy polishing their swords for the parade, and even Corporal Sakamoto, who had proved to himself conclusively what the show of a little sincere leadership could do (for he could feel the inspired response of his subordinates in their expressions and the atmosphere) had himself gone too long through all the stock experiences of a soldier's life to look upon the beating as anything but proper and inevitable.

The Corporal was only glad that he did not have to undertake himself the scolding and beating which were obviously required of the occasion. He was tired, too, from the day's futile search and his long session with the Platoon Commander. Of course, he had no intention of scolding the older soldiers, for most of them were Reserves just like him, and it would have made them lose face before the First-Year-Soldiers.

He turned to the ragged-looking First-Year-Soldiers and said, "Wash your faces and go to sleep. . . . " Then he ordered, "Attention. . . . Dismissed!"

There was the usual responding "Salute!" and the usual "Thank you for your troubles." They all fell out of line, and the First-Year-Soldiers went to the kitchen to wash their badly battered faces with water from the large earthen vases there. They scooped the water from the vases with long-handled dippers and took turns pouring it into their upturned hands. The cold water felt soothingly refreshing on their hot faces, and some even had it poured over their heads. Miki stuck large wads of paper into his bleeding nostrils, which made him look ridiculous, and they all went back to their sleeping room.

Most of the old soldiers were already in bed. Many were smoking their last cigarettes while lying on their backs. Some were still up, however, and since First-Year-Soldiers were not supposed to turn in until all the old soldiers had gone to bed or until, otherwise, they got special permission to do so, Takeo and his comrades remained glumly sitting on the edge of the matted platform which served as their mutual bed.

"Hey, does it hurt?" Oka shouted from the other end of the room where he was lying on his stomach on the single layer of blanket which served as their mattress, smoking a cigarette.

The First-Year-Soldiers were in no mood to answer such a casual question. They remained gravely silent.

"Can't you answer, at least?" Oka angrily demanded and half rose from his blanket.

"Yes, sir. It hurts." Kan again saved the day for his comrades, but he was not as lively as usual.

"The life of the First-Year-Soldiers is hard," now it was Tanaka's voice.

"Yes, sir," they all answered.

"We all went through it, so you have to stand it, too," said Tanaka.

"In our times it was harder," said a Reserve. "The First-Year-Soldiers nowadays have it easier."

"Well, go to sleep," Reserve Private Hosaka called angrily, and he meant it for everyone as well as for the First-Year-Soldiers.

"Yes, sir," the First-Year-Soldiers answered, and they had a hard time keeping the relief they felt from their faces. They all stood up and bowed politely toward the older soldiers as they always did before going to bed, but tonight they bowed more politely than usual.

"The Honorable Squad Leader, the Honorable Privates First

Class, the Honorable Senior Soldiers, we beg to be rested before you," they said in chorus. This was the stock good night of the First-Year-Soldiers when they went to bed before the others, and they said, "The Honorable Squad Leader, the Honorable Privates First Class, the Honorable Senior Soldiers, please rest well," when they turned in after all had gone to bed.

Takeo pulled the blanket way up over his aching head and felt happy relief at the oblivion of darkness. He closed his eyes and tried to sleep but his jangled nerves would not calm down. Nakamura, beside him, was crying silently, and Takeo could feel his shaking shoulders.

Poor Nakamura, Takeo thought. He is older than we but must go through it the same as all of us.

Takeo recalled that first time he was initiated into the army's unique ordeal by slapping. Only a week after they had entered the army post at home, Takeo and his comrades had been ordered to line up after roll-call one evening. There had been about twenty of them in the squad. Five old soldiers went down the line without warning, slapping each soldier soundly on his cheek. Those that could not keep their posture of attention were slapped more than the others.

After a thorough slapping, the Squad Leader, who had been looking at the proceeding without taking part, took over and asked the dazed young soldiers, "Why did we slap you, do you know?" He pointed to each soldier in turn.

"Because we have been loafing."

"Because we do not understand the spirit of the army."

"Because we are worthless."

There was a wide assortment of answers, each as sincere as the one which preceded it. Each time a soldier gave an answer, however, he was slapped without explanation, and those that were too puzzled to answer were slapped until they did, at which they were slapped again.

When it was Takeo's turn, he had answered, "Because we do not polish the shoes of the Honorable Senior Soldiers well enough," and he was slapped for his trouble. Jimbo, the learned one, who had gone to college, tried to quote the Imperial Rescript, and he got it plenty.

When it came to Miki's turn, he had answered honestly, "I do not know."

"That is right!" the Squad Leader had ejaculated, and the slapping had stopped. "When you are slapped, don't give any excuses. You do not trust your superiors enough. . . . Attention. . . . As His Majesty the Emperor has been pleased to admonish in the Imperial Rescript, 'Uninfluenced by the worldly thoughts and unhampered by politics, guard well your single destiny of patriotism.' Our single duty is to be patriotic to the Emperor. You need only to obey what you are told. There is nothing simpler than this. Do you understand?"

They had all answered, "Yes, sir," though it had seemed very complicated at the time. Since that initiation, Takeo could not remember how many times he had been slapped and beaten, although he could not recall having had it as badly as this evening. He had been slapped by officers and non-commissioned officers, as well as the immediate superiors in the squad.

He remembered the standing joke: "The Lieutenant slapped the Sub-Lieutenant; the Sub-Lieutenant slapped the Sergeant; the Sergeant slapped the Corporal; the Corporal slapped the Private First Class; the Private First Class slapped the Private; the Private slapped the Private-Second-Grade; the Private-Second-Grade, who had nobody to slap, went into the stable and kicked the horse."

Takeo's face hurt when he tried to smile, but he felt much calmer. Nakamura seemed to have stopped weeping, for he was not shaking any more, and Takeo soon fell asleep.

CHAPTER 4

IT WAS PLEASANT to be on the march again. Takeo thought so, and every other First-Year-Soldier thought so, too. Except for the few perennial stragglers, most of the young soldiers preferred the march of a light campaign to the occupation of a village in enemy territory. In a light campaign, there was little danger of being killed, and a march offered many interesting deviations from the monotonous routine of life in an occupied village.

The straps of his rucksack felt solid against the shoulders of Takeo, and the hard rifle butt felt substantial in his hand. Each step that he took was a clear impression in his mind. There was nothing hazy or complicated about the march. Everything was real, and there was little danger of breaking a rule of etiquette. All one had to do was walk — one, two; one, two — and the time went by without trouble.

"It is better to be on the march." Takeo turned to Nakamura, who was trudging silently beside him. Private Nakamura was a weak marcher and seldom talked while marching. This time, too, he only smiled.

"That last village was like cow's dung," Takeo said bitterly. Nakamura weakly smiled and nodded.

Takeo, of course, was referring to the village where the squad had lost its rifle and the First-Year-Soldiers had got it so badly because of the incident. The lost rifle never turned up, and the men had to accept the inevitable conclusion that it had fallen into enemy hands. Thanks, however, to the fact that their Squad Leader came from the same village as the Sergeant-in-charge-of-arms at Company Headquarters, the men of Squad Three did not have to assume the grave consequences of having lost a weapon with the Imperial Chrysanthemum Seal on it and were able to get a new rifle through the tacit, considerate manipulation of the Sergeant at Headquarters. The Lieutenant, too, did not carry out his threat to burn the village.

The squad tried to get even before leaving with whoever had stolen the rifle by smashing everything breakable in the native house where they had been quartered and by virtually wrecking the house itself by knocking down posts and pushing over walls. They had also brought along the donkey, which the old woman had prized so highly, to carry their extra provisions. As usual, there had been other squads, too, which had gone on a wrecking spree before departing, for by the time the soldiers were ready to leave a village after any length of occupation, they were a spiteful lot, and they turned their spite on the houses which held no pleasant memories for them. It was almost a general practice for the soldiers to smash the huge earthen water containers found in the kitchen of every native home. Those huge and flimsy vases offered an irresistible temptation to the advanced destructive instincts of the soldiers, and some of them frequently carried their enthusiasm even farther and went through the houses like madmen, knocking down everything in sight. The officers very seldom troubled to see how the soldiers behaved at departure, though they never stooped themselves to carry on like their subordinates.

"Do you think there will be many enemy this campaign?" asked Miki, who was marching on the other side of Takeo. As usual, the troops were marching in a column of four.

"There shouldn't be. This time, our brigade is the only one out on the march," replied Takeo.

"They say some Communist bandits have appeared," continued Miki.

"Then they are Eighth Route Army. They run away fast," said Takeo.

Their platoon was acting as advance patrol today, and Squad Three was scouting the road ahead of the whole battalion. The men were a little more alert than usual, but they expected little resistance, since they were passing through territory from which they had swept the main body of the enemy away but a month ago in the victorious Suchow campaign. Squad Three was the light-machine-gun squad of the platoon, too, and the two machine guns it had were strong assurances to the men.

Oka, who was carrying the machine gun and marching in front of Miki, turned his body slightly and asked, "Give me a match?"

"Yes, sir," Miki answered and lighted a cigarette and handed it to the older soldier.

"Thanks," Oka said and asked, "Are you all right?"

"Sure, I am all right," laughed Miki. "Shall I carry the machine gun?" he offered.

"No, thanks. A little later, maybe."

This was what they all liked about the march. There was a strong feeling of mutual dependence and comradeship, and the soldiers thought little of rank or seniority and the trying rules of behavior. The unending petty clashing of emotions among the soldiers in their close quarters in an occupied village were forgotten temporarily at least in the wide spaces of the roads on a march, and if the enemy ran away, as they usually did in a light campaign, and nobody got hurt, the soldiers could ask for nothing better.

"Little rest!"

The welcome order was relayed from the rear, signaling the regular ten-minute rest taken every hour on a march. Two advance sentinels were dispatched, and the rest of the squad sat down on both sides of the road to lean back contentedly against their rucksacks. Kan took out his cigarette case, damp with sweat, and offered a cigarette to Private First Class Tanaka, sitting beside him. The older soldier took it and offered a lighted match in return.

"Hey, somebody give me some water," a Reserve shouted from the rear.

"Yes, sir," answered Kan and, releasing the shoulder straps of his rucksack, went back and offered his canteen.

"When we pass the next village, some of you First-Year-Soldiers be sure to get some water," said Corporal Sakamoto.

"Yes, sir," the young soldiers answered promptly.

"Squad Leader, how long are we going to march this time?" Oka asked.

"Maybe two weeks. We are marching to the coast," answered the Corporal.

"To the coast? Are we going to board a steamer for home?"

"We're going home. We're going home," the soldiers said here and there.

Nakamura, who had been lying blissfully back on his rucksack, letting the fatigue flow out of his aching body, held up his head in sudden interest.

Home . . . he whispered to himself. He was the only First-Year-Soldier in the platoon with a wife, and he had a little boy who had been born on the day of his departure for the front. He thought of his father's tailor shop where he had been working. It was funny how many thoughts came rushing into one's mind at the mention of the single word "Home." Private Nakamura let his imagination run wild with pictures of his home and his loved ones at home. He closed his eyes and stretched his body comfortably in the dust beside the road.

"Depart!" the order came from the rear, shattering the reverie of Nakamura and many another soldier.

Amid exaggerated grunts and cursing, the soldiers rose to their feet and fell in line. The day was still young, and the men were still fresh. Toward evening, there wouldn't be much grunting and cursing, and a week from now whatever cursing there was would be genuine.

The sun shone hotly, and the air was parched, for it had not rained for weeks now. The tall *kaoliang* had been harvested, and from the bare, rolling fields intermittent breezes raised tiny clouds of dust which raced for short distances and fell down suddenly like so many playful children. The road over which the troops marched was one long continuous column of swirling dust. The dust went into the eyes of the marching soldiers, filled their nostrils and settled between their teeth; it mingled with the salt from the sweat on the men's faces and sank into the pores of their uniforms. If any good was to be attributed to the dust, it was that it made any large movement of troops during the day easily visible and thus offered the enemy little opportunity for their favorite tactics of ambush.

"Do you think we are really going to go home?" asked Nakamura, turning toward Takeo.

Surprised and pleased to find his usually silent comrade talking, Takeo replied half jokingly, "What do you think?"

"They often said that our division was going home, didn't they?" It was too pleasant a thought for Nakamura to keep to himself, and he wanted somebody to fill in the inevitable conclusion of the observation that, therefore, they themselves were going home, but even Takeo chose to remain silent regarding such an impossible observation.

"They say there are almost no enemy in North China now," continued Nakamura insistently.

"None, maybe, in North China, but plenty more elsewhere."

"But our division was sent for the campaign in North China."

After the Suchow campaign, it really had seemed that the main body of the enemy had been driven out of the whole area of North China. The men had never been taught the nature of total warfare, and many believed that if the enemy were routed, the victory was complete. They still considered warfare in the light of the stories of the Russo-Japanese War, in which they had been steeped since childhood.

"But we only came overseas six months ago, and there are many more who have been here a year and two years," Takeo contradicted merely for the sake of continuing conversation.

Nakamura fell silent all of a sudden, for this was the argument which always spoiled his dream of returning, and the old soldiers always mentioned it whenever there was talk of the whole division going home.

Takeo felt a little sorry and said, "Of course, when it comes to the whole division returning, it doesn't matter."

But Nakamura had lost interest in the talk and he no longer felt the happy anticipation of a moment ago. He wiped the sweat from his face with the towel which he kept conveniently hanging from his hip. Most of the Japanese soldiers carried towels suspended from their belts around their hips, with which to wipe their sweat.

"It is a little early for you First-Year-Soldiers to talk about returning. Do you want to go home that much?" asked Private First Class Gunji sarcastically from behind the two young soldiers. A sharp pang of remorse and disappointment gripped Nakamura's heart, and he smiled sheepishly and kept silently plodding ahead.

"Sure, we all want to go home, Honorable Private First Class," laughingly replied Miki in good humor.

"You don't know what it is like to want to go home until you have been at the front one and two years," said Gunji, now seriously.

"You surely must want to go home, Honorable Private First Class," hesitatingly suggested Takeo.

"Two years is a long time. We never thought it would take so long, when we left home."

"We, too, never thought it would be like this when we left home. We thought we would be constantly fighting and that the days would pass before we knew it," said Takeo honestly.

"I guess you didn't know there would be much marching and anything like occupying villages," observed Oka.

"That is so," said Takeo.

"Honorable Private First Class, won't you have a cigarette?" Miki turned around and offered a cigarette to Private First Class Gunji, happy at the opportunity to be friendly with the Senior Private First Class.

"Well, thanks," said Gunji.

"We thought there would be fighting day after day, and that either the enemy would be finished or we be finished. We never thought we would lose, so we thought we would win quickly," Takeo continued.

"But the enemy is smart and keeps running away all the time," said Private First Class Tanaka, marching beside Oka.

"This is a hateful kind of war," reflected Miki aloud.

"Is there any good kind of war?" asked Takeo disgustedly.

"Sure, there is. That is a war where you rape and plunder all you want and don't get killed," laughed Oka loudly, and some laughed with him, though most of his comrades did not accept his vulgar conception of warfare and held little respect for him.

They were now approaching a village, and all eyes were riveted on a crowd of natives standing on the outskirt where the road entered the group of low mud houses. The Corporal peered through his binoculars and reported that the natives were carrying Rising Sun flags of Japan and seemed like friendly villagers waiting to welcome the troops.

"But be careful of ambush," added the Corporal. "You can't tell about these natives."

The squad fanned out and approached the village carefully. The welcome committee, however, turned out to be genuine, and the platoon, led by Squad Three, entered the village in marching formation.

"No enemy in the village," the platoon relayed back to Headquarters.

Soon the order returned, "Advance patrol, pass through the village and halt five hundred meters ahead."

"That puts Battalion Headquarters right in the center of the village where there are the tea and the cakes. Those bastards always take the best places," Oka grumbled.

As the platoon passed through the village, still more natives stood on both sides of the street waving hurriedly improvised Rising Sun flags painted on square strips of white paper pasted on sticks. Some offered hot tea in large jugs and cakes, and they ostensibly tasted the cakes and drank the tea themselves to show they were not poisoned. The soldiers noticed, however, that there were no women among the natives and knew that the latter trusted them little.

"I guess they wave Rising Sun flags when the Japanese troops come and wave Chinese flags when the Chinese troops come," said Miki, looking suspiciously at the smiling, bowing villagers.

The old soldiers knew how true this statement was, for they had often entered the native homes in villages during unguarded moments to find both flags of the warring parties standing incongruously side by side against the walls. When the soldiers had pointed the flags out to the native inhabitants, the latter had only smiled sheepishly and said, "*Mei futze* — it can't be helped."

"The natives don't care who win the war," said Reserve Private Hosaka, who was the oldest in the squad. "They only want the war to end quickly and peace to come."

"You can't blame them. This country has wars all the time," said Reserve Private Aoki.

Coming out on the other side of the village, the platoon advanced the specified distance and halted. Soon the much awaited order arrived, "An hour's big rest. Lunch." A "big" rest was usually for an hour and for eating meals, while a "little" rest was anywhere from five minutes to thirty minutes.

Sentinels were posted, and the soldiers stacked their rifles in neat rows and took off their rucksacks. The older Reserves went ahead to remove their cartridge and bayonet belts and to lift the straps of their canteens and utilities bags off their shoulders, and they piled them all on the ground beside them. Some even removed their shirts. Others, who were less energetic, just leaned back against their rucksacks and closed their eyes, for it had been a hot half-day's march.

"Honorable Squad Leader, may I go back into the village to get you some hot tea?" It was Kan, standing at attention and begging to return half a kilometer into the village to fill the Corporal's canteen with the hot tea the natives had offered the soldiers. Squad Three had been unable to stop to fill their canteens, since they were the advance patrol and had to keep the necessary distance from the main body of the Battalion.

"Well, this is great!" the Corporal gratefully exclaimed and presented Kan his empty canteen. "It would be good to wash my rice down my throat!"

The other First-Year-Soldiers, too, who felt themselves called upon to follow Kan's suit, quickly got to their feet and offered to get tea for the remaining Senior Soldiers of their squad. Soon they were loaded down with large bunches of clattering empty canteens and hurried toward the village. Nakamura, however, was the only First-Year-Soldier who did not offer to go to get tea in the village. He seemed too tired to move and leaned back heavily against his rucksack and kept his eyes closed throughout the commotion.

"Nakamura!" Private First Class Tanaka's angry voice sounded all of a sudden. "Why don't you go with the rest?"

"Yes, sir!" Nakamura answered weakly, and got shakily to his feet. He looked around him and, noticing no available canteens, took his own and chased limpingly after his comrades.

"What a good-for-nothing!" Nakamura could hear Tanaka's disgusted voice behind him, but he did not care and did not hurry his slow, limping pace.

"Say, better not let him do too much. He is weak," Aoki, one of the older Reserves, suggested gruffly between puffs of his cigarette. Private Aoki had been a laborer in a road gang and had a wife and three children waiting for him at home. He cared very little for all the petty doings in the army. As he made everybody know from time to time, so that no one would misunderstand him, he cared little about who got promoted and nothing at all about being promoted himself; all he cared for was to go home alive. He was the kindest among the old soldiers to the First-Year-Soldiers, and he seemed to be specially attached to Nakamura, although his massive, muscular body was the exact antithesis of the frail physique of Nakamura.

Private First Class Tanaka, who had been a store clerk after finishing elementary school, laughed apologetically and said, "But we have to keep them on their toes, you know."

"You are a Regular, too. How about it if you moved around more?" quietly suggested Aoki, but there was no mistaking the steel in his voice. The Reserve had removed his shirt and his huge arms and burly chest were bared for all to see who should doubt the sincerity of what he said.

Tanaka did not feel inclined to belittle Aoki though he was a Private First Class and the Reserve was only a common private. "Sure, we will move when necessary," replied Tanaka in his nasal tone of self-pity. "Isn't that right?" he asked, turning to Private First Class Gunji, who was another Regular and the second-in-command in the squad.

Gunji laughed sheepishly but did not answer. Aoki said no more, and the other Reserves remained silent. But the barb had gone home, and there was no mistaking the sting that it left.

When hostilities had broken out on the Chinese Continent, Aoki and other Reserves like him, who had long finished their services in the Conscription Army, had been hastily mobilized and sent to the front together with the Regulars who had been serving their terms just then in the home post. There had been many among the Regulars, senior in rank to the Reserves, most of whom were ordinary privates, but the latter had made it unmistakably clear from the very beginning that they were going to go by seniority of service and not rank. In the relationship within the squad, which was, after all, the greater part of a soldier's life in the army, the Reserves had insisted that they were going to measure priority by the yardstick of age, and it had seemed very natural, for age was respected by the tradition of the nation. The Reserves easily had their way, moreover, because they were more in number, and, like Aoki, tried and tested in the harsh ways of life. The Reserves sometimes said of the Regulars that they "still had milk around their mouths," and some of the Reserves like Hosaka were almost old enough to be the fathers of the Regulars.

The Reserves had a bone to pick, too, for they had been yanked out while they had been enjoying the most stable years of their lives. Many of them had businesses of their own, and they had been enjoying such prosperity as they had never known or heard of before, for the industrialization of the country had advanced swiftly in their generation, and things which had been luxuries in their fathers' time were already becoming necessities of daily life. They had no ambition in the army and were fighting bravely the way they did only because patriotism to the Emperor had been so inexorably ingrained into them since childhood that it was second nature to obey when commanded in the name of the Emperor.

"If anything else besides fighting has to be done, let the Regulars do it. We don't want to be promoted. They do," the Reserves often said among themselves when at a loss to find an excuse for their extreme laziness.

The older Regulars also tried to excuse themselves for shirking by saying, "It is training. Let the First-Year-Soldiers do it." But sometimes when the work was too heavy, they did lend a hand, for, as the Reserves said of them, they were ambitious to gain the recognition of their superiors after all and were not devoid of ambition like most of the Reserves.

Kan was the first to return from the foray of the First-Year-Soldiers to the village, and in his usual exaggerated manner made the bunch of filled canteens he was carrying by the straps from his shoulders appear heavier than they really were. "Say, that was heavy!" he exclaimed, and went immediately to hand the Squad Leader his canteen, now filled with hot tea. The other

First-Year-Soldiers soon returned. Some had cakes in baskets besides their canteens, and Nakamura had a bowlful of native pickles, which were very popular among the soldiers.

"Hard work! Hard work!" the Second- and Third-Year-Regulars consoled their younger friends and stood up to help them unload their burdens, which was as far as their dignity allowed them to exert themselves, but the important point was that they were exerting themselves. The Reserves lay back to look contentedly at this happy effect on the Regulars wrought by Aoki's little hint of a while ago. We must prod them from time to time, each Reserve said in his mind.

With the arrival of the hot tea, the soldiers quickly removed the metal rice containers which were strapped to their rucksacks and began hastily shoveling the cooked rice into their mouths with their chopsticks. They wanted nothing more during lunch hour than to be over with their eating as quickly as possible and to spend as much of the remaining time as they could in resting for the march ahead.

It was a hot day, however, and the rice, though freshly cooked early that morning by the First-Year-Soldiers, had sweated profusely and tasted flat on the tongue. The beef, barbecued in sweetened soya sauce, was too rich. They would have had a hard time gulping down their food except for the hot tea — and especially the pickles Nakamura had dug up somewhere in the village. The pickles' salty taste gave the necessary zest to the lagging appetites of the men.

"Nakamura, this pickle surely helps. Where did you get it?" Private First Class Tanaka spoke loudly for all to hear, as if he wanted to atone for his previous harsh words which had proved so unpopular with the Reserves.

Nakamura merely answered modestly "It was nothing," and continued to eat. Such indifference did not improve in the least his popularity with the elder Regulars, although they all knew that it only stemmed from his complete lack of ambition in the army. It was what endeared him to the Reserves, however. Kan tried to save the embarrassment of the Private First Class and said, "He took it from the kitchen of the house at the edge of the village. I saw him."

By now, most of the soldiers had shoveled down their last lumps of rice and were washing their containers with the tea that was left over, for the tightly covered metal containers quickly soured in the hot weather if one did not wash them immediately after eating. Others, who could not stomach all the rice their containers held, emptied the white content in piles on the ground beside them. The rice which Nakamura emptied from his container formed a fairly large heap beside him. The fatigue of a march always took away the frail soldier's appetite.

Reserve Private Aoki, who had restrapped his container to his rucksack, noticed the mound beside Nakamura and said, "You had better not fill your container so much if you are not going to eat all. It only adds more weight and weakens you on the march."

Nakamura laughed weakly but did not reply. He thought, I always think this time I will be strong and eat all. Later, while he leaned back to rest through the remainder of the lunch hour, he thought, Aoki is a kind man, but he did not say a word to anyone.

Miki, the First-Year-Soldier from the farm, had eaten all his lunch and leaned over to look at the rice Nakamura had thrown away, when he heard Aoki's comment.

"What a waste!" he exclaimed. "You should have given it to me. I could have eaten more."

"You surely eat plenty!" said Oka.

"No, I am not hungry, but I hate to see all of that go to waste. When you think of the farmers who grew it, it is really wasteful."

"Now, it is not so. You always eat twice as much as the rest," Oka chided, and a few laughed with him.

But Miki's protest had sounded sincere, and since they knew him for the true son of the farm that he was, simple and crude, most of his friends did not join Oka in his laughter. Miki looked appealingly about him, as if he dared not refute Third-Year-Soldier Oka's statement alone.

Reserve Private Hosaka, a true farmer himself, came to the rescue. "It is just as Miki says. When you think how much we toil to raise it, you can't waste rice like that," he said.

"Everybody should try and plant rice once. If they were to bend over one full day and wade in that mud of the paddies, they will know how thankful they should be," Miki said, again taking courage.

"I guess you are right," Oka agreed. He was not one to force an argument when he knew he was in the wrong. He became serious himself and said, "Look at me. I worked at the *Kure* Naval Depot, and when I see the rifles rusting here at the front, I think it is wasteful."

"In fact, if you think so, there is nothing more wasteful than war," observed Private First Class Tanaka, always wanting to have the last say.

Miki rose and went before Corporal Sakamoto. Saluting, Miki asked, "May I go to do the big-service?" ("Big-service" meant to move the bowels. "Small-service" meant to urinate.) The First-Year-Soldiers had to get the permission of their Squad Leader whenever they left the vicinity of the squad on a march.

"Sure, but make it snappy. We are leaving soon," said the Corporal authoritatively. Corporal Sakamoto had been a foreman in a munitions factory and was one of the younger Reserves. He did not speak much before his subordinates and guarded his dignity jealously.

Miki made a dash for a clump of bushes beside the road ahead. Reserve Private Aoki stood up and facing away from the squad began to urinate. He had the cigarette he was smoking still in his mouth, and the smoke from the cigarette seemed to have blinded him temporarily; he turned a little toward Private First Class Tanaka, who was sitting beside him. A few drops must have splashed on the back of Tanaka's neck. "Hey, hey," the latter protested and he began wiping the back of his neck with his palm and tried to move away.

Aoki, the big road laborer, seemed not to hear it and cut the wind loudly. Tanaka had very unfortunately moved behind Aoki and since he had moved on his hands and knees, his face was directly in the path of the wind.

"Hey! Hey! I've got it plenty," laughed Tanaka half-heartedly in protest.

"Say, I beg your pardon," apologized Aoki, as if noticing the discomfiture of the Regular for the first time, but he continued buttoning the flap of his trousers.

Most of the Reserves laughed, though the Regulars remained politely silent. Tanaka, to save his dignity, began hurriedly to put on his shirt and equipment though it was still a little too early to prepare for the march. He had lost much prestige by this incident, and he thought, Aoki is a worthless fellow. But he could not think, I hate Aoki, though that was what he felt, for even in his thinking, Tanaka was careful not to break the rules of etiquette. Tanaka was also scared of Aoki.

"Hey, Miki, are you through? We're starting," shouted Corporal Sakamoto, and he arose to put on his shirt and equipment too. He always did it a little early to get his reluctant subordinates started.

"Honorable Squad Leader, I forgot to bring paper with me," came back the sad answer from behind the bush.

"What a worthless fellow!" Tanaka snorted, and he had merely said out loud what he had been thinking of another.

As the Corporal floundered to find words dignified enough to answer this hopelessly foolish request, Private First Class Gunji, the second-in-command, ordered, "Takeo Yamamoto, take him some paper!"

"Yes, sir, I will take him some paper," Takeo jumped to his feet and repeated in true military fashion, and sped away on his vital mission.

Miki soon came out of the bush and returned hurriedly with

Takeo, pulling up his trousers and grinning sheepishly.

Hosaka, the Reserve who was also a farmer, asked chidingly, "Don't you have any paper?"

"I have, but I left it in my utilities bag," Miki explained seriously.

"Come on, make it snappy. We're leaving in three minutes," Corporal Sakamoto said, looking at his wrist watch and glad of this opportunity to make the observation of the little time left before departure for the benefit of those last-minute Reserves who were still on the ground. He could not directly order about the Reserves on such occasions as this, for it would be hurting their prestige.

Everybody now began getting ready in earnest. When the order, "Depart," came, Squad Three was ready and lined up on the road to the great pride and satisfaction of its Squad Leader.

One, two — one, two — they began to march in the dust. Takeo shook the rucksack on his back by shaking his shoulders to make it rest more comfortably on his back and thought, It is good to be on the march.

CHAPTER 5

"NAKAMURA, put strength in you!" Oka called from behind the First-Year-Soldier, who was showing perceptible signs of weakening. The sun was shining hotly as usual, and the air was clogged with dust. This was the third day of the march since the platoon had left the ill-fated village where Squad Three had lost its rifle, and Nakamura was already beginning to lag. He had not eaten much since starting on this campaign, and he was tiring more than he had done on any other march.

Oka, who was a pillar of strength on the roads, suggested, "Let me empty your canteen for you. That ought to lighten your burden a little." The Third-Year-Soldier's hands were free at that moment, for Miki was taking his turn carrying the squad's machine gun, which Oka had been carrying until a short while ago, and he went behind Nakamura and removed the canteen from the case hanging from a shoulder strap.

"Why, it is full! You drink too much. If you keep water full in the canteen, you get tired quicker," said Oka and began emptying the liquid on the road without asking for permission to do it.

Nakamura kept marching silently and doggedly ahead, and the voice of the elder soldier sounded distant and irrelevant. The weight of the canteen on his shoulder, however, was gone, and it did seem to make a great difference. It was the tried and tested experience of every soldier that, when fatigued on a march, the removal of even the tiniest weight was a help, or vice versa, that the presence of the lightest object was a burden. Thus, often, soldiers discarded such trivial objects as pencils, notebooks, and handkerchiefs from their pockets when they became too tired on a march. Some of the more irresponsible ones even threw away their cartridges and hand grenades, although Nakamura did not have the audacity even to think of it.

I want to drink some water, Nakamura thought to himself, but he did not mention it, for he knew he would be rebuked if he did. He heard the water pouring out of the canteen with such intense longing that he felt as if his own heart was ebbing with it. . . . One, two; one, two . . . he kept plodding, but he thought, I will turn around and wrench the canteen out of Oka's hand and pour the rest of the water down my throat. Of course, he did not carry out this desperate thought, but now the gurgling of the water as it ran out of the canteen's mouth seemed closer to him, and just to listen to it seemed to refresh him as if he had drunk it himself. It was like this whenever he wanted something badly which he knew he could not get. He imagined he got it, and it helped.

"There, that is empty. From now on, you will be comfortable. Next time, don't drink too much. If you want to drink, drink from my canteen," Oka suggested crisply and he returned the empty canteen to the case hanging beside Nakamura's hip. Oka was one of the strongest marchers, and he seldom drank any water on a march except at mealtimes. He was very solicitous of the young soldiers, too, when the troop went on the roads, as if he wanted to make up for his extremely cruel treatment of his subordinates during occupation. "Oka is a different man on the march," the First-Year-Soldiers used to say of him gratefully, which was more than they could say of the other older soldiers.

It was not always the rule, however, that the light drinker was the strongest marcher. There were many who drank freely and sweated profusely until their uniforms were dripping wet, who, nevertheless, kept up with the best of them. Then there was the case of Reserve Private Hikaru Manju, who had been a plasterer at home. He drank liquor on the march. He always kept his canteen full of the powerful native drink made from *kaoliang*, which the soldiers called *chungchiu*, and he drank it as often as the average soldier drank water.

Right then, he must have taken another gulp of the burning "energizer," for his voice could be heard above the clatter of the march, ringing clearly and musically, as it sang a snatch from a popular ballad:

> *Mr. Shosuke Ohara — why did he lose his*
> *fortune?*
> *Because he liked to sleep, drink and bathe in the*
> *morning.*

Everybody laughed. Manju was a good singer, and the whole platoon heard him. It seemed every swig he took made him stronger and more cheerful. Others, like Oka, who liked the stuff, tried to imitate him, but it only took the life out of their legs and made them lightheaded. It was a foregone conclusion that nobody but Manju could drink while marching and thrive on it.

"It is because he has a special body," they all said enviously, though really his body was no different from any of the others — only a little more muscular than the average, maybe.

"It depends on the way you take it," Manju would explain when asked how he did it. "Everybody drinks it to give him strength or to get drunk, but I drink it just like I drink water, without thinking anything about it."

The loud mimicking voice of the happy soldier could be heard again above the beat of the boots on the road: "We're going home! We're going home! Bugles forward!"

This really made his comrades laugh, and some tried to imitate him. For a moment the soldiers forgot their fatigue and wretchedness. The platoon was not on advance patrol today, and the men could relax and be gay if they wanted to, for they were marching with the main body of the battalion.

The gaiety was short-lived, however, for the company was marching in front of Battalion Headquarters today, and the Company Commander, Captain Hamamoto, was not going to have his men appear frivolous and undisciplined to the Battalion Commander. The army was very strict about discipline on the march, and such behavior as the singing of popular tunes and the drinking of liquor was unthinkable in the strictest sense. While in training, they even forbade the soldiers to talk unnecessarily on the march. Captain Hamamoto sent the order back to his troop, "Sing an army song!"

The men at Company Headquarters began the song loudly in chorus. Others to the rear took up the tune, and they sang alternately. They sang:

> *The infantryman's color is the color of the*
> *cHerry blossom.*
> *Look, the cherry blossoms fall on the hills of*
> *Yoshino.*
> *If we are born proud sons of the Yamato race,*
> *Let us die on the fields of battle.*

Like all army songs, the tune was more a chant than a song. The stanzas repeated themselves monotonously. It sounded drab and flat to the soldiers who had been listening to the lyrical popular songs of Manju a moment ago. Before many stanzas were finished, the song frittered away, and the soldiers were again marching glumly and resolutely — one, two; one, two. All the words of an army song sang the praise of some heroic deed or expressed a noble ideal, and it required effort to recall them. Such a song only added to the fatigue of the march. But Captain Hamamoto had gained his end already, for he had silenced the frivolity of his subordinates, and he did not press his men to continue the song.

"Arrival at a fork in the road!" The report was transmitted

back from the advance patrol and relayed to Battalion Headquarters.

"Advance patrol, halt!" the responding order came from Battalion Headquarters. It was followed by another order:

"Honorable Captain Hamamoto, report to Battalion Headquarters!"

The Company Commander quickly buttoned the front of his coat which he usually left open during the march and fastened the heavy sword, which he was shouldering like a rifle, to its proper place on his hip. He had a worried look on his face as he hurried to the rear.

"Maybe they got intelligence of enemy in the neighborhood," Kan said out loud.

That was the thought which had struck everybody simultaneously. As always, it was accompanied by a tired feeling of reluctance and ill omen The men lowered their rifles and leaned heavily against them while they waited patiently in the middle of the road. They had not seen any enemy or heard of any enemy movements since starting on the campaign, and they had been hoping that the march would be finished without a firing engagement. The surroundings, however, looked peaceful enough as the men gazed nervously around them. As usual, the heat waves were rising lazily from the harvested fields for as far as they could see.

When the Company Commander returned, his cheerful and almost jaunty expression dissolved whatever misgivings the men had been feeling. "Close the ranks to the front!" the Captain shouted, standing on his toes at the head of his company. "Can you hear me in the rear?" he asked. He always asked that question when he spoke to an assembly, as if anybody would answer if they could not hear him.

"Yes, sir!" somebody answered in the farthest lines.

The Company Commander began importantly: "Our company has been selected flank patrol. We will take the fork to the left and proceed independent of the battalion until the roads meet farther on. I have been especially instructed that nothing must be taken from the natives. Ours is a march which includes 'propaganda work.' "

The company turned into the assigned road amid audible grunts of disappointment from the soldiers. "What is this? Looks like this isn't a war," grumbled Okihara, the butcher. "They treat the natives too good."

The men had hoped for a little freedom of movement when they had learned of their independent assignment. Company Headquarters was bad enough, but Battalion Headquarters constituted always a strong damper against the wilder impulses of the soldiers. Within the first hour after turning into the new road, the company passed through two villages, and the officers kept such a strict surveillance that not a single one of their subordinates broke the ranks. The Company Commander was the very epitome of a gentleman as he smiled graciously at the natives who came out to wave their flags at the passing column.

This was called "propaganda work." The phrase had become suddenly popular after the Suchow campaign when the great body of the enemy had been allowed to flee into the interior of the continent and the war had taken on the irrefutable appearance of becoming a long, protracted affair. All of a sudden, the orders from higher up had come to include more and more such phrases as "propaganda work" and "propaganda squads," and the soldiers were instructed to "protect the good natives."

The soldiers had been compelled to go through a constant metamorphosis in their attitude toward the natives since coming to the continent. When they had first landed, they had thought little of the native inhabitants. Their sole thought had been of combat — to fight the war as they had been taught in training and to get it over with as fast as possible and to go home. They had expected a swift campaign, for their conception of warfare had been gleaned from accounts of the previous short, decisive wars their nation had fought in its turbulent history, and they had kept themselves relatively aloof from the natives. They had carried their own rations and had been able to subsist by themselves wherever they went. Some officers had even talked about how they were fighting the enemy soldiers and not the natives, and these officers had been strict. There was one officer who had scolded his subordinates for picking apples from trees alongside a road while on a march.

It was the city which had brought about the first sharp change in their attitude toward the natives. There had been street fighting, and snipers in civilian clothes had been everywhere. The soldiers had been forced to advance from house to house in widely dispersed groups, which were easily hidden from the vigilance of the officers. The houses in the city had been full of such tempting luxuries as the men had never seen in such abundance before. They had crammed their rucksacks with sweet-smelling soap, thick towels, watches and silverware, and at one place the engineer soldiers had blown open a safe in a bank, and the huge native silver coins had been piled high on the ground. The soldiers had cast away whatever they had been carrying and had filled their rucksacks with the heavy money. They had crammed the coins into their tent sheets fastened in rolls to their rucksacks, and into their utilities bags hanging from their shoulders, and into their pockets.

The soldiers had not had the least idea what they were going to do with all the native money and all the knickknacks which they had gathered. Some had a hazy idea that they might be able to take them home or at least to send them home. Most, however, had plundered for the mere thrill of possessing all those riches and did not care what they were going to do with them later.

A few had been bold and ruthless enough to rape the women who were found quaking in the houses. These had been mostly the older reserves, for the younger ones had not had the presence of mind to work up the open-faced audacity necessary to carry out the shameful deed. Some of the latter, though, had gone simply wild in the close quarters of the city streets and had started shooting at every native they saw, and some had even fired at the women and children, though their comrades quickly stopped them here, for there was a limit, after all, to the brutality which anyone could bear to witness even in warfare.

These strictly disciplined soldiers of the Japanese Army had given free rein to their impulses the first chance they had got in the city. The unrelenting, oppressive discipline of the past had burst when confronted by the numerous temptations presented by the free fighting in a rich city, and the base acts of license had happened in torrents, as if a dyke had burst, which had been forced to hold more than it was built to withstand. When living under some high ideal, man is easily fooled into believing that his capacity is unlimited, and the leaders of the Imperial Army had tried to teach their subordinates that there was no limit to what they could stand. But there is always a limit, and when men are forced to put that limit to a test, the acts of violence which follow are always remarkable for their abnormality.

The troops had stayed only a single night in the city and had started immediately after the fleeing enemy the following day. Before many hours had passed after resuming the march, the men had been forced to unload themselves of their numerous articles of plunder, which weighted them down more than they could stand. The silver coins and other things which the men had collected in their lust had fairly littered the road over which they passed and the soldiers had kicked them around in the dust like so many pebbles.

Of course, there had been officers who had frowned on this wild conduct of their subordinates, and it seemed the higher the rank, the greater had been their displeasure, although the weaker their ability to keep an eye on the soldiers. The soldiers themselves had had no delusions regarding this displeasure of their superiors, and they had taken care subsequently to indulge in their pranks only when out of sight of the officers. The officers, to be sure, had frowned on this license of their subordinates more because of its debilitating effect upon the troops' discipline than because of a genuine pity for the natives.

The soldiers, however, did not have very long to act like sneak thieves before their officers, for soon the troops were advancing so swiftly inland that the supply trains, consisting mostly of horse wagons, had not been able to keep up with them, and they had been forced to live off the land for almost everything else besides the rice and seasoning articles, like soya sauce and soya-bean paste, which they always carried in their rucksacks with them. In every village the troops stopped to spend the night, the soldiers killed the natives' livestock and poultry for their meals and made free use of anything palatable they found in the natives' usually barren kitchens. Halfhearted attempts had been made by the officers to pay for what the soldiers took, but they had been soon abandoned, since most of the natives fled when the troops came, and it was difficult to find the rightful owners. In the meantime, the officers themselves had become grateful partakers of the booty of the soldiers, and plundering for the sake of filling the larder on a march became an openly accepted practice among the Japanese troops.

Then the days of occupation had followed, when the cooperation of the native noncombatants had become essential to combat the enemy's new guerrilla tactics. It was then the phrase, "propaganda work," had come into use. The strict rule had been laid down that soldiers must pay with their military scrips for everything they took from the natives. Although a few still continued to practice their mischief on the sly, the bulk of the troops had abided by the new rule.

It was only when the soldiers went on the march in pursuit of the troublesome guerrilla bands that they fell back to their old practices. They plundered to replenish their food supply and, whenever they encountered resistance in a village, went through the houses under order of their superiors in search of lurking enemy or hidden weapons and ransacked them for their measly possessions. Although the soldiers had had to abandon all hope of sending any booty home (for the censorship was strict), they had come to prize any articles which could get them a good price in the city, where they hoped to have a good time beyond the range which their scant salaries could get them. Such articles as watches and little pieces of jewelry were popular, for they had to carry whatever they took from the houses in their rucksacks, but such valuables, light in weight and heavy in value, were almost unknown in the poverty-stricken huts of the peasants, and the soldiers who could boast of prize booty were scarce.

The Hamamoto company did not find it overly difficult to obey the order to behave when it had taken the side road to march as a flank patrol, independent of the main body of the battalion. The company passed by two large watermelon patches, almost overflowing with the invitingly ripe melons which littered them at that season of the year, without laying a hand on any of the fruits. The Company Commander had succeeded in infusing into his men some of the pride he had felt when trusted, in preference to all the other companies of the battalion, to go independently on such an important mission as this.

Toward the middle of the hot afternoon, the company again approached a luscious watermelon patch on the outskirt of a village. After commanding the advance patrol to enter the village and to post sentinels at the other end of it, Captain Hamamoto ordered a halt to the march. While the men rested lazily alongside the road bordering the watermelon patch, the Company Commander and his interpreter proceeded toward the usual group of natives who stood at the entrance to the village, waving their flags of welcome.

The officer negotiated with the villagers for the legitimate purchase of the watermelons outside the village on behalf of the men of his company. A bargain was easily reached, since the natives were only too glad to part with their watermelons if that were to mean that the rest of their village was to be left alone, and it was not difficult for the natives to figure out that if the commander of the troops was willing to pay for the watermelons, he would not allow his men to plunder the village. The most courteous exchange of greetings took place following the payment of the bargained sum by the Company Commander, and the latter was able, at the same time, to mention his little piece regarding the "divine destiny of the Imperial Army."

When Captain Hamamoto returned to his company, he announced the agreement reached with the natives regarding the purchase of the watermelons and called for five soldiers from each squad to go and pick two watermelons each for their respective squads. The soldiers who had been waiting, a little puzzled at this strange behavior of their Commander, quickly got into the mood of the occasion and greeted the bizarre announcement with wild cheers, like so many schoolboys on a picnic.

The First-Year-Soldiers in Squad Three immediately jumped to their feet to volunteer before their Squad Leader to go to get the squad's watermelons. Nakamura, too, got shakily to his feet to volunteer with the others.

Private First Class Tanaka, the Second-Year-Regular, however, was on his feet in an instant to motion to the weak First-Year-Soldier, "Nakamura, you do not have to go. I will go in your place." The young Regular was not forgetting the berating he had received the other day at the hands of the Reserves for letting Nakamura overdo himself.

Private Oka, too, the Third-Year-Regular, saw some fun in it and dashed after his comrades into the watermelon field, although it made one more than the specified number for Squad Three. Nobody protested, however, for everybody was in a cheerful mood, and Oka himself was not disappointed, for he had a fine time chopping at the watermelons to see which were the ripe ones. Others did the same, and they left many of the fruits hopelessly gaping with huge cracks in them on the field when they returned happily with their allotted number to their respective squads.

"Honorable Squad Leader, we got the best ones, you know," boasted Oka as they began passing large slices of the fruits around to the squad members.

The soldiers bit hungrily into the cool, juicy slices of the watermelons, and they were greatly refreshed by them. They were the more refreshed by this simple repast because they ate it with the comforting thought that they had come to it by legitimate means. They easily forgot the many watermelons they had wastefully sliced on the field and only felt a warm goodness in their hearts, which was cheering and inspiring.

"I never knew that watermelons could be so delicious!" exclaimed Private First Class Tanaka, now at complete ease with his conscience in more ways than one.

"What a waste!" Miki said aloud to no one in particular when the Company resumed the march and they saw the ground littered with slices showing much of the edible red flesh still left on them. Some natives were already gathering the refuse, probably to feed their hogs.

As the company passed through the village, an elderly gray-haired gentleman came bowing profusely alongside the Company Commander. He looked benevolent and dignified enough to be the village head, and he was thanking the Commander most graciously. The old man had probably never expected such restrained conduct as he had seen from an invading army, and his gratitude seemed genuine and spontaneous.

"Tell him, we who live by the Imperial Way will not injure the good citizens," Captain Hamamoto said to his interpreter, who was walking beside him.

"Thank you. Thank you," the old man replied, continuing to bow respectfully.

"Look at the Company Commander. He looks like he is fighting the war all by himself," said Oka disgustedly to his comrades in Squad Three, which was fortunately marching far to the rear, so that there was no danger of the Commander hearing him.

Captain Hamamoto was the eldest son of a wealthy hotelkeeper at home, and he prided himself as being the heir of the most powerful family in his neighborhood. He felt a close kinship with the old gentleman who walked so respectfully but with such poise beside him. On a sudden impulse, he took out his silver cigarette case and presented it to the old man, saying to his interpreter the while, "Tell him I want him to take it as a souvenir of me."

富堂

CHAPTER 6

THE WATERMELONS had refreshed the men of the Hamamoto company remarkably, and they made good time after leaving the village. Even Nakamura seemed to have regained his strength, and he kept up resolutely with the rest of his comrades. The company arrived at the fork where their road met the main road traveled by the rest of the battalion, far ahead of the designated hour, and the soldiers had over thirty minutes of welcome rest before the battalion's advance patrol came into sight, marching wearily in a thick cloud of dust.

It was nearly sundown when the main body of the battalion came up to where the Hamamoto company was resting. The troops were halted, and each company was assigned a village in the neighborhood to billet for the night after the usual procedure. The villagers, of course, were not consulted, and the battalion's adjutant merely made the assignments on a map, swiftly and efficiently. In no time, the battalion was dispersed, and the companies were hurrying to their respective villages to give their men and horses the rest they deserved as soon as possible.

The Hamamoto company was given the village farthest ahead on the road. It was a good hour's distance away, but the feet of the soldiers were light as they headed for where they knew they would get a good night's rest — barring, of course, a surprise enemy attack, which was unlikely with the whole battalion on the march. It was getting dark when the company reached its village, which was no different than hundreds of others the soldiers had seen in this district — a shabby huddle of mud-walled huts with low-thatched roofs, separated by narrow cobblestone lanes.

As the soldiers marched into the village, however, the huts which lined the street looked warmer and more welcome than the houses of any of the villages they had passed through that day, for home was to the soldiers where they found themselves at the end of a day. The company halted in the middle of the village, and sentinels were immediately dispatched to strategic points on the village fringe. Fortunately, Squad Three was not posted to sentinel duty that night, and the squads that were free were soon assigned the native houses which were to be their respective quarters, after a patrol consisting of representatives from each squad had made a swift survey of the village.

Squad Three got a fairly large soya-sauce store on the main road. The motions the soldiers went through from this point on were a paragon of precision and speed, for the men wanted nothing more than to have everything over with and to be in bed as soon as possible, and this hustling to bed down in a native village was something they had gone through time and time again on countless marches since coming to the continent. There was no seniority or the niceties of etiquette here, and each gave his utmost for the good of the whole.

In a twinkling, the squad's rifles and machine guns were neatly stacked in front of the assigned quarters. Next, the soldiers stacked their rucksacks in double row in front of their rifles and carefully piled their equipment beside them. This done, the Squad Leader divided his squad into two — one to fix the house so that the squad could sleep and cook its big meals there and the other to forage for food.

Nakamura was assigned to the first group, and, as he stood momentarily dazed by the frenzied actions of his more energetic comrades, Takeo, who was also in the same group, pulled him by his arm and said, "If you don't move, you will get scolded!"

They went inside to find the native occupants hurriedly gathering their more valuable belongings to carry out with them. As when the villages were assigned to the separate companies, the natives had not been consulted when their houses were assigned to the squads, and they stood aside in helpless alarm while the soldiers went boldly in and out of their homes.

A few gruff words were enough to cause the natives to flee with their hastily gathered bundles from the house which the men of Squad Three entered.

The men immediately went to work on the interior of the soya-sauce store. They smashed the counters into kindling wood with the clubs which they found handily lying about in the backyard and removed the huge wooden vats containing the store's sole stock-in-trade. They would have smashed the vats, too, only they feared the sticky contents of the vats would mess up the floor and fill the room with their heavy smell. In no time they had the room cleared of all its jumble of disorderly fixtures, and they covered the dirt floor with loose boards they found in the backyard and in the neighboring houses. They also gathered the straw mats which were so abundant in the native homes and laid them on the boards to serve as their beds. The rucksacks and equipment were brought in from outside and placed separately at the head of the mats where each was to sleep that night, and a rifle rack was quickly improvised to support the rifles and machine guns.

"Now, our hostel for the night is finished," said Reserve Private Aoki, the road laborer, and he gazed proudly at the room neatly laid out for the sixteen soldiers of his squad. Well could he be proud of the finished work, for as usual he had taken the lead in the work of demolition and clearing away, and the methodic distribution of his efforts, which only a long life of muscular labor had nurtured in him, had greatly hastened the completion of the neat job.

Nakamura, who was tired enough almost to lie down and go

to sleep at once, felt something ebb away in him when he heard the word "hostel" mentioned, for it recalled to him all the considerate service and comforts of a hostel at home, and he felt limp all over. Aoki took out a cigarette and, lighting it, called, "Let's have a smoke!"

Takeo felt envious and proud, at the same time, of the confident Reserve, and, as he watched the latter smoking while calmly surveying the fruit of their concentrated labor, he was filled with a deep sense of satisfaction at being able to serve his Emperor together with such a capable man as Aoki. He thought to himself that he would at all times gladly and wholeheartedly follow the kind of active leadership shown by the powerful Reserve. He told himself, How happy I would be if I could serve my patriotism to the Emperor by obeying only such a man as he.

When they had finished smoking, Aoki said, "Yamamoto and Nakamura, gather the rice for three meals from each rucksack. We will go to the kitchen to make ready to cook." The soldiers, as usual on a march, had to cook the rice for three meals at the end of a day — for supper, breakfast (for they would depart early the next day), and for lunch, which they would put in their containers to carry, attached to their rucksacks.

Private Takeo Yamamoto answered, "Yes, sir," though Nakamura was too fatigued even to answer the Reserve. Private First Class Gunji gruffly scolded Nakamura, "Answer, at least!" and the latter said weakly, "Yes, sir." This scolding of a weak soldier and of subordinates in general, they called "injecting willpower," in the army.

The soldiers in the other half of the Squad who had been ordered to forage for food dashed down the main road of the village and turned into the side lanes, where they had a better chance of finding the quarries which they sought. Dividing into little groups, they kicked open the bolted doors of the native homes lining the lanes and ran through the front rooms into the backyards where they knew the livestock and poultry were kept. The native inhabitants of the houses thus entered stood discreetly aside while the soldiers searched their homes. In most houses, the natives hid in the inner rooms, and the soldiers found little time or inclination to bother them.

Kan and Reserve Private Okihara, the butcher, who had teamed up in the search, finally discovered a pig in the backyard of the fourth house they had forcefully entered. They were unarmed, for the soldiers were forbidden to use their weapons in killing their quarries, since the sound of rifleshots might be misinterpreted by the officers as an enemy attack, and besides, the firing of rifles in the close quarters of a village would be dangerous. While the two soldiers searched for appropriate clubs in the yard to use as weapons, the animal, sensing its danger, ran squealing out of the house into the lane outside.

The soldiers, now armed with heavy clubs, ran after the fleeing pig, and soon cornered it between themselves farther up the lane. Okihara delivered the first blow which sent the animal reeling backward, crying in the most unearthly fashion. It made a fast about-face and now ran toward where Kan was waiting for it with his club. Kan's blow caught the squealing animal squarely on its forehead, but it did not seem to weaken the swine much and it turned again and charged back toward Okihara with its bristles standing angrily up on its back. It was a huge black animal and would have terrified anyone else but these soldiers hardened by their severe experiences on the battle-fronts as it charged desperately down the lane, grunting and snorting like a wild beast aroused.

Okihara, however, was not one to be easily frightened, especially since the slaughtering of animals had been his occupation before joining the army, and he struck a mighty blow which sent the animal down to its knees. The Reserve, now, struck again and again and soon the swine was lying helplessly on its side, groaning and gasping loudly for breath. Kan ran into a house nearby and came back with a huge butcher knife he had found in the kitchen. With deft and expert motions, the Reserve cut the swine's jugular vein and began skinning its hide.

Kan watched admiringly and gave a helping hand whenever

needed. He said, "If we have this much pork, we won't need anything else." The Reserve was too busy with his work, and he only grunted. Kan thought, How I want to become as nimble with my hands as he.

The job of skinning was over with in a moment, and Okihara now began to slice away the choice flesh of the animal. The soldiers never troubled to take the bones or any parts of a fallen animal too hard to pare with their clumsy knives, and they usually left over half of a carcass to be later reclaimed by the natives or eaten by the dogs. Okihara, however, was doing a cleaner job of it than most of his comrades could manage, and the reed basket which Kan had found in the kitchen where he had got the knife and which he held obligingly for the Reserve was soon filled to brimming.

When the Reserve continued to wield his knife, too preoccupied with his work to notice his already full basket, Kan suggested almost hesitatingly, "Honorable Senior soldier, this is enough. The basket is now full."

The Reserve looked up for the first time and said, "That is so!" With a last swift motion, he cut away the liver and placed it on top of the large pile in the basket. The soldiers all prized the liver, for the liver, according to the usage of their language, was where they believed the courage of a man or beast to dwell. As he laid down his knife and surveyed his half-finished work, Private Okihara grunted, "What a waste!"

"The natives will take the rest," Kan consoled the Reserve.

While they stood there, resting for a moment after their late exertion, the two soldiers could hear the desperate squeals of other pigs, being chased and killed by the foraging soldiers, from all over the village. They even heard the mortal lowing of cattle being slaughtered. The crashing of woodwork as the soldiers cleared away the rooms which were to be their quarters for the night added to the din in the half-darkness of approaching evening and created the atmosphere of bustle before bedding down on a march so pleasantly familiar to the soldiers. Men called to each other in high, excited voices, and in a house nearby some soldiers must have discovered a coop of chickens, which cackled in fearful alarm.

Miki and Reserve Private Hosaka had discovered the chickens when they had forced open the door of a bigger than usual house at the end of the lane. Miki's heart beat wildly when he saw the flock in the backyard, for he was sure there were over twenty. The two soldiers went after the fowls with long poles they found in the yard, and they struck them down with wide, swiping strokes. The chickens scattered all over the yard and flew into the air, and some even flew over the mud walls enclosing the yard. But the soldiers got most of the fowls, and they ran happily back to their squad with their booty hanging tied by their legs to a pole carried on their shoulders between them.

Squad Three was a happy but busy group of soldiers as they chopped the pork brought by Kan and Okihara into little pieces and skinned and cut up the chickens brought by Miki and Hosaka. Others in the squad's foraging party had found some vegetables and eggs, and these they dumped into a pot together with the pork to make into the messy stew which was one of the few dishes they knew how to cook. The pieces of chicken they dipped in soya sauce and barbecued over an open fire, and soon the appetizing aroma of the roasting chickens mingled with the sweet smell of steaming rice to fill the air of the house where the squad was quartered and to flow out into the street.

"Looks like the feasts of the *Bon* Festival and the New Year's Festival have come together," laughed Hosaka gaily.

"We must certainly have a drink tonight," said Manju, who was carrying a jug of native liquor he had dug up somewhere. His red face showed he had already partaken liberally of his favorite booty, and he began singing:

> *Is liquor the fountain of tears*
> *Or the father of sighs . . . ?*

"Let's get it over with quickly and rest ourselves. Tomorrow we start early," said Corporal Sakamoto impatiently.

"Don't take your time. Set the bowls out and line them up," Private First Class Tanaka scolded the First-Year-Soldiers, who were standing idly waiting for the meal to be cooked. They had found enough bowls in the kitchen to go around for all the men in the squad and had washed them in hot boiling water as they had been taught to do with all the native kitchen utensils they used.

When the first batch of chickens was done, Corporal Sakamoto ordered, "Somebody, take some of these to the Honorable Platoon Leader and the Honorable Company Commander."

"Yes, sir," Kan answered, and, before any of the other First-Year-Soldiers could offer their services, put a few pieces of the barbecued chickens in two separate bowls and went out of the house with them.

A non-commissioned officer very seldom joined his subordinates in their wild foraging, and a commissioned officer never even dreamed of engaging in the lowly task. The foraging for the officers was done by their orderlies, who also cooked their meals, and sometimes a Squad Leader like Corporal Sakamoto had the presence of mind and initiative to send his own squad's takings to his commanders. Of course, such action counted greatly when the time came for the officers to decide whom to promote, and the ambitious non-commissioned officer never forgot to take advantage of it.

Kan soon returned, beaming proudly, and said, "The Honorable Company Commander was just beginning to drink *chung-chiu* with his interpreter, and so he was very happy. At the quarters of the Honorable Platoon Commander, the orderly was busy cooking the meal, but it didn't seem like they had anything much." It filled Kan with pride that he was able to impart all these very personal observations of their superiors to his comrades.

The hungry soldiers dispatched their meal with zest and speed, and, after filling their containers with the morrow's two meals they had cooked, unrolled the blankets they carried strapped to their rucksacks. They lay down on the mats which had been spread on the board floor in the room so painstakingly cleared away earlier in the evening and covered themselves with their blankets. The soldiers had taken their shoes off but still had their uniforms on, for that was how they went to sleep on a march.

It was totally dark now, and, except for the occasional barking of. dogs, the village was enveloped in the deep silence of night. Somewhere, a night watch reported, probably to the officer-on-inspection, in a low but clearly audible voice that nothing was "amiss." Hobnailed boots clattered loudly over the road as someone passed hurriedly in front of Squad Three's quarters, but they soon faded into the distance, and silence reigned again.

The First-Year-Soldiers had addressed their customary good nights to their seniors before lying down to sleep. Miki turned in his blanket toward Nakamura, who was sleeping beside him, and whispered, "It was great fun when we caught the chickens today. You should have come." But Nakamura was already fast asleep, and he did not answer. At the other end of the room, Manju, who was filled with the liquor he loved so much, was snoring loudly.

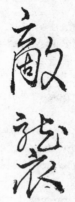

CHAPTER 7

THE SEVENTH DAY found the battalion still on the road and an appreciable distance from its starting point. They had met no enemy resistance thus far and so had not been pressed to turn the march into a running fight or to make up for lost time, as always happened after an engagement. The march had been a stiff one, nevertheless, and the troops had averaged ten *ri* (about twenty-five miles) a day, which meant starting before daybreak and continuing into the evening every day.

The men of Squad Three were bearing up admirably, and Nakamura was the only one who was showing any noticeable signs of weakening. The First-Year-Soldier had dropped out of ranks only once, however, and then had caught up with his comrades in the next rest period. Nobody doubted that he was doing his best, and they all admired his silent doggedness. The thought of this strong light-machine-gun squad, always in readiness to spring into action, was a source of constant assurance to the Platoon Leader, who kept reminding himself that the next time he must cite its leader, Corporal Jiro Sakamoto, for promotion.

"Aren't we going to meet any enemy this time, you think?" asked Kan of Third-Year-Regular Oka, who was marching, as fresh as ever, with the machine gun beside him.

"What is the matter? Do you want to see some enemy?"

asked Oka laughingly, and he shifted the gun to his left shoulder.

"If there were a few, maybe it would be fun," Kan said a little boastfully.

"Better if we reached town soon," interposed Private First Class Tanaka, who was marching in front.

"Why aren't we meeting any enemy this time?" Reserve Private Hosaka turned toward Corporal Sakamoto and asked the question which had been occupying everybody's mind for sometime now.

"It's because we chased all the enemy away from this area during the Suchow campaign."

"Then why do they make us march?" the Reserve next asked.

"Because the railroad to the coast is partly wrecked," the Corporal answered.

"When we reach the coast, are we going home, do you think?" Reserve Private Aoki now asked.

"Going home? We're like baggage, you know. They can send us anywhere," the Squad Leader, who seemed more congenial than usual, replied in a cynical tone.

"We're certainly going home," objected Aoki the road laborer, who had a wife and three children.

"If you want to think so, that's your right," said the Corporal.

"I heard there were many enemy stragglers in this area," Private First Class Gunji, the squad's second-in-command, joined the conversation.

"That's what they say," the Squad Leader agreed.

"The interpreter said they have formed into bands and are raiding the villages," the Private First Class continued.

"They also say there are communist guerrilla bands," the Squad Leader added.

"Then why don't we meet them?" Hosaka repeated his first question.

"Listen, there's a whole brigade on the march besides our battalion. You don't expect the scattered enemy to offer resistance," answered the Corporal loudly, as if he wanted to allay any anxiety their past conversation might have aroused in his men.

"The enemy is smart. He is in civilian clothes. You can't tell him," said Okihara, the butcher.

"Do you think we're going home?" Nakamura surprised Takeo by turning to him and speaking in a spirited voice.

"Will you become a tailor again, when you go home?" asked Takeo in return without answering his question.

"That is so. But I don't want to do anything for one month," said Nakamura.

"I bet you want to see your wife," teased Takeo.

"I don't want to see my wife, but I want to see my child."

"You're strong today," said Takeo.

"I don't feel any different from other days, but the strength comes out when they talk about going home."

"Is that how much you hate the front?"

"I came to die anyway, but I want to go home just this once."

Takeo felt a friendly pity for his older comrade, for they all felt more or less as he did. The only difference was they did not express their feelings so plainly. Takeo tried to imagine how it would be if he had a wife and child waiting for him at home himself.

Just then, the loud voice of their Squad Leader awoke him from his contemplation.

"Message to the rear!" shouted Corporal Sakamoto. "Village in sight ahead!"

Squad Three was again acting as advance patrol today, although it was a much less anxious and alert patrol than the one on the first day. The squad continued to advance, and soon they could make out the shapes of the trees and houses on the village outskirt. From the width of the village fringe which showed itself, the men guessed it to be a fairly large one.

"That's funny. . . . There are no natives out to greet us here," said Oka, who was carrying the machine gun in the lead.

"Probably they don't know we are coming," said Miki, beside him.

"Wait a minute. . . . Looks like natives are moving around inside," said Okihara, the butcher, who was also in the lead, and he stopped in his tracks.

The whole squad came to a hesitating halt about a hundred meters from the village, and the Squad Leader, who was bringing up the rear, proceeded to the front to look through his binoculars.

"What a good target we make, if there are enemy in the village," thought Takeo.

The squad stood in the middle of the road in open view to anyone in the village, but nobody suggested taking shelter, though many felt uneasy where they stood. Anyone would have sounded cowardly and overanxious who made the suggestion. It was like this always in the army; they would think of something good but would hesitate expressing it for fear of seeming too forward, and things would take their inevitable course.

It was then that things began to happen all at once. Before the Corporal could look through his binoculars, Okihara had fired the first shot. It exploded in the ears of his comrades nearby like an artillery shell.

"They are carrying guns!" Okihara shouted, and all the men leaped for the ditches on both sides of the road. The sharp eyes of the Reserve had caught sight of the glint of steel in the hands of the natives he had first seen moving about just inside the village's outer fringe, and the discovery had not been too early.

As they dove for shelter, they could hear the bullets of the answering fire from the village shrieking all around them. Some bullets struck the road just in front of them and spattered dust into their faces.

When the excitement had started, Nakamura had been leaning heavily against his rifle, happy at the respite offered by the pause. As usual, when he rested thus on a march, his head hung limply and his eyes were kept vacantly staring at the dust on the road, his mind blissfully oblivious and irresponsible. At the first explosion he had instinctively turned toward the left, which was the nearer side of the road where he stood. Then, hesitating when he saw a comrade blocking his way, he had turned to the right. But when the bullets began flying, he had fallen flat on the road.

Once in the shelter of the ditches, the men began hastily putting on the steel helmets which they carried tied to their rucksacks, though Okihara and some of the bolder Reserves, who never troubled to wear their helmets in combat, began immediately firing their rifles down the road. These latter never wore their helmets in action, because, they said, the extra weight only hindered the free movement of their heads. They had to carry them around however, since helmets were part of their regular required equipment.

In no time, the squad's two machine guns were in position on both sides of the road and were sending a concentrated volley at the enemy in the village. The machine-gunners, who were Oka and Private First Class Gunji, quickly found their range, and the enemy who seemed to be inside the houses on the village fringe almost stopped firing. Only sporadic shots from widely dispersed points now answered the determined fire of the men of Squad Three.

"The enemy have only rifles. They don't seem to have machine guns," said Corporal Sakamoto and relayed the information back to the platoon, which had halted and was beginning to deploy farther back.

"Squad Leader, let's make for the hill on the left," said Okihara, pointing to the small grass knoll to the left of the village.

Okihara, usually stolid and reserved, seemed always to be sparked into life when the bullets started flying and took upon himself the duty of assistant adviser to the Squad Leader, who was his junior in term of service. He was brave, too, in a coldly savage kind of way and was much respected by all in combat.

Private First Class Gunji, who was second-in-command, however, never liked the intrusion of the Reserve Private, and, right now, too, tried to put the latter in his proper place. "No, let's charge into the village," the Private First Class suggested.

While this argument was going on, Takeo noticed for the first time the still figure of Nakamura in the middle of the road.

"Hey, Nakamura . . ." he started to call, but halted when he noticed the limp position of the arms and the face buried in the dust.

By now, the others also had become aware of the prostrate figure on the road, and before any of them could think of what to do about it, Takeo crept out on the road and began crawling toward it. The enemy seemed to have suddenly come back to life and sent a hail of bullets at the audacious figure moving in the open on the road. The bullets kicked the dust close to Takeo, but none got him, and he was able to grab hold of his friend's feet and drag the limp body of Nakamura back into the ditch.

Nakamura had been shot through his left chest and hip. He was still breathing, though weakly, when Takeo turned him over on his back. Each little breath forced the blood to spurt from the wound in his chest, and he sighed each time, a lonely, hopeless kind of sigh.

Takeo shook Nakamura's shoulders and shouted his name in his ears in the hope of recalling whatever spark of conscious life was left in him. Others who had gathered around the wounded soldier began calling his name.

"Put strength in you!" Oka shouted at the First-Year-Soldier as he had done earlier on the march.

But Nakamura soon stopped breathing, and Takeo, who felt his pulse, announced, "The pulse beat has stopped."

Even as he said it, the color went out of his friend's face, and the grim dust-caked face which stared up at them lost all semblance to the good-natured features of Nakamura they had all known, and it seemed to belong to someone else entirely.

"Come on, let's take the hill to the left," Corporal Sakamoto shouted when he saw that they needed no longer to trouble with the wounded soldier, "We'll come and get it afterward."

The squad deployed and made a dash for the hill, while one machine gun which remained behind in the ditch covered the flank by blazing away full blast at the village. As they had expected, the squad found no enemy on the hill, and they now had an excellent command of the village.

The men could see many figures fleeing along the road at the other end of the village. Oka placed his machine gun on the top of the hill and began firing at these running figures. The riflemen fired a few shots, but the Corporal stopped them.

"Too far . . . you can't hit. . . . Leave it to the machine guns," he said. The other machine gun soon came up to join them and also began firing at the fleeing figures.

"Come on, let's go!" said Okihara impatiently and began recklessly dashing down the hill. The others followed him. By now, the enemy fire had thinned to desultory scattered shots which whined far above the men's heads.

"There aren't many enemy. . . . They seem to have fled," Okihara observed almost disgustedly and he slackened his gait to run alongside the Squad Leader who was following him.

When he had started down the hill, Okihara did not make for the village but, instead, headed for the farthest end of the cluster of houses by going around them. Instinct, nurtured by his long experience at the front and arising out of his inborn disposition to grasp in a flash the essential necessities of combat, had led him to decide the moment he had leaped forward from his cover on the hill that the best course would be to cut the enemy's retreat out of the village. It was an inspired encircling operation which Squad Three was now undertaking on its own free will as the men followed, as if drawn irresistibly toward it, the confident figure of the aroused Reserve. The squad was running over a recently harvested field, and their shoes sank deeply into the loamy soil.

"Let's take it easy," said Okihara, and he slowed down to light a cigarette.

A few others followed suit, but Takeo and the other First-Year-Soldiers, who were still young on the battlefields, kept on running, for they had not yet recovered from the fear instilled in them by the surprise enemy attack, and the bullets were still whistling in the air, though scattered and safely above their heads, as if the enemy were firing from a great distance. Their muscles were tight from fear, however, so that they were quickly fatigued, and the relaxed Reserves, running easily, soon caught up with them and again took the lead.

"Come on," the Squad Leader, who was in the lead, turned around and called to his men, "We've got to get to the road ahead of the platoon."

The platoon had entered the village, and the men of Squad Three could see their comrades deploying through the streets. The Squad Leader wanted to have his men on the road leading out of the village in case the platoon were able to chase out any straggling enemy. After one last spurt, the squad made the road which was on a slight elevation at the end of the village.

Finding nothing on the road, the men advanced, now carefully, toward a rise in the road about a hundred meters outside of the village. They proceeded, scattered on both sides of the road, so that they would not be caught in the open as when they had approached the village.

"Here's one," said Oka kicking a figure sprawled in the road.

Takeo, who was following, looked to see that it was a huge young man. The bullet-pierced face seemed to be smiling happily. A rifle lay beside him, attesting to the fact that he had been one of the enemy attackers, though he was dressed in the typical farmer's garb and was barefooted like most of the farmers hereabouts.

"No wonder we have a hard time finding them," said Aoki

from the other side of the road. "They don't look any different from the rest."

"You surely hit him, Oka," Hosaka praised the Third-Year-Soldier, who was still lugging the machine gun.

"I didn't think I would hit anything at that distance, but I guess it's best to shoot anyway," replied Oka.

"Here's another," said Okihara, but he did not kick the figure this time. There was a woman with a baby still clasped in her arms, lying limp on the road. A bullet had pierced both her and the baby. The woman must have been in the group of fleeing figures at which the squad had fired from the hill, and the soldiers had not been able to distinguish her from the great distance.

"How pitiful!" Takeo exclaimed impulsively. Others grunted low and disgustedly.

"That's war. You can't help it," said Tanaka.

The Reserves who had wives and children of their own remained silent and passed by the pitiful figure without looking much at it.

"Hey!" Okihara exclaimed and raised his rifle to aim. Everybody looked to where he was pointing his rifle and saw a man crouched against the end of a blind ditch. Ghastly fear was written on his face, and he began feverishly to speak, though his words came out only in a mumble and were unintelligible anyway, since they were in the native tongue. Blood was trickling from an ugly leg wound. He must also have been with the group fleeing from the village and was probably hit together with the less fortunate ones who were now lying lifeless on the road.

"He doesn't look like a soldier," observed the Squad Leader. The native was dressed like any other farmer, and he was not carrying any weapon.

"You can't tell," dryly replied Okihara and pulled the trigger. The bullet struck the man squarely on the forehead, and a thin column of blood spurted high into the air as he fell forward on his face.

At the report of the rifle, excited voices suddenly arose on the other side of the road, which made the soldiers almost jump. The voices came from behind a bend in a shallow gully running perpendicular from the road and invisible to the men where they stood. The soldiers soon were able to tell that the voices came from children crying, and they were mingled with the voices of adults trying to silence them. When the children could not be silenced, the adults seemed to have abandoned all hope of keeping their hideout a secret, and a whole chorus of wailing female voices arose from the gully.

"You can't tell these, either," said Okihara and took out his hand-grenade from his utilities bag and made as if to pull out the safety pin. He was going to toss the grenade into the gully.

"Wait a minute," said Corporal Sakamoto, and he and the rest of the squad with rifles held in the ready cautiously approached the hole in the ground from which the voices were rising.

When they looked down into the shallow hole, they saw a large group of women, children, and girls huddled closely together. There were a few men, but most of them were too old to be soldiers. There was no doubt that these were noncombatant villagers who had taken refuge here when the fighting had started. They held nervously to each other, and some hid their heads in their arms. They stopped their wailing and crying all at once when they saw the soldiers with their rifles standing on the ground above them. The silent, cringing figures presented such a sight of helpless fear that the men, who had been acting with the thought solely of a vicious, vindictive enemy, stood dumb and in a daze. For a moment the killers and these totally unprotected victims of warfare remained staring blankly at each other.

Then Manju shouted an obscene word which all the soldiers had learned from the natives, and the men of the squad laughed.

The children began to cry again, and the air of vacant suspense was broken.

"Come on, let's get back to the road. We will have to make contact with the platoon," the Squad Leader ordered peremptorily, and the men turned toward the road. When they reached it a messenger from the Platoon Leader was waiting for them. "The Honorable Platoon Commander says that you must return to the village at once," he said.

The same feeling of relief was felt by all the men of Squad Three when they heard this message to return, for it called an official end to their bold self-appointed mission as a spearhead of the whole battalion's advance. Ever since they had met with the first attack of the enemy, the men of the squad had acted on their own native impulses without waiting for orders from higher headquarters. Though they knew they had done well by encircling the village, thus hastening the flight of the enemy and sparing the platoon and perhaps the whole battalion from the necessity of a heavy frontal attack, still they felt a little scared by the audacity of what they had done and wanted nothing better than to return to the comforting folds of the battalion as soon as possible. These men who had been taught to live almost solely by the orders from their superiors could not stay long on their own free initiative, however much they knew that they were on the right track. The Squad Leader, however, felt a deep satisfaction at what his squad had accomplished and, as he trudged together with his subordinates back toward the village, looked forward to a hearty well-done from his superiors.

But Takeo was thinking, I wonder if somebody found Nakamura's body? And what will they be doing to it?

When the squad approached the village, they saw the main body of the battalion already marching out of it. While the little advance skirmish was under way, the battalion had merely closed the gap between it and the advance company and marked time without breaking its ranks to await the outcome of the battle.

"Hey, line up. The Battalion Commander will soon be coming," said Corporal Sakamoto when his subordinates started back individually in the scattered formation they had become used to in the late skirmish with the enemy.

The squad fell in line to form the official column of four and marched back smartly, with the Corporal in the lead. The Corporal had never felt so proud in all his life as he marched at the head of his battle-tested squad.

They could soon see the Battalion Commander, looking more important than ever on his horse, coming out of the village, preceded and followed by the great bulk of his men on foot. The Battalion Commander and a few others of his headquarters staff, including his adjutant, the surgeon, the intendance officer, and messengers were the only ones on horseback, and they looked majestic in the midst of the great number of troops or foot, marching four-deep in the dust of the road. The really stocky figure of the Commander looked unusually large on horseback, and as he approached the men of Squad Three, his usually dark and roly-poly face seemed to be enshrouded in a magic light of all-comprehending wisdom.

When the squad had come to the specified distance away from the Commander, Corporal Sakamoto called it to halt as he had been taught in training. Presenting arms smartly, he reported in his most military voice, "Advance Patrol Squad is now returning to its platoon!"

He had also wanted to add the information, "No enemy to the front," but the Commander had seemed too important to be bothered by such a triviality, and he had felt that it would make him, a mere Corporal, seem too forward and impetuous.

The Battalion Commander returned the salute with a slight gesture of his hand, which imparted all the more an air of supreme importance, and, smiling paternally, said, "Hard work! Take a little rest and come up with the rear of the column."

"Yes, sir!" the Corporal responded, and he was the very personification of absolute obedience and subjugation.

When the squad resumed its march back to the village, the men could not help feeling a little proud at the distinct recognition they had just received from their Battalion Commander, and it seemed to them as if the other men of the battalion whom they passed on the road were looking at them with envy.

I know now the Battalion Commander saw us dash up the hill under enemy fire, thought Corporal Sakamoto and felt more elated than ever.

Some of the men in the passing column seemed to recognize friends in the squad and shouted, "Hey, were there many enemy?" Some said, "Did any of you get hurt?" while others merely shouted the usual "Hard work!"

To all of these, the men in the squad answered good-naturedly, although the Corporal still retained his dignity of a short time ago and marched along silently with a grave face and without looking to right or left. Reserve Private Okihara, who, among the men, was most responsible for the recognition the squad had received, walked glumly along in his usual fashion and scowled coldly at the soldiers who spoke to them.

When the squad reached the village, they found the other soldiers of their company still going through the houses, outwardly searching for enemy stragglers, but really, as they knew, for the excitement of the plunder. At one place, soldiers were kicking at a locked door. Somebody brought a log, and they soon rammed the door open. The soldiers rushed in with fixed bayonets to see who would get to the lockers and drawers first.

At another place, a group of soldiers came out of a store, each carrying a brand-new towel around his neck and bundles of more new towels and cloth materials under his arms. Soldiers were busily darting in and out of the houses, and they paid little attention to the returning squad. They looked completely martial with the bayonets glistening at the points of their rifles, but right now they were no more menacing than armed vandals robbing empty homes. One, carrying a huge pot, smiled happily as he passed the squad, though nobody could guess what he was going to do with it on a march.

At another place, the squad had to stop when a soldier came dashing out from a yard, chased by a growling, vicious dog. The soldier stopped to turn around and made a pass at the dog with his bayonet when he saw that he was being watched, but the dog merely feinted and kept rushing at the soldier, who was really in a bad way. Okihara picked up a brick and hurled it at the dog. The missile hit the animal squarely, at which it gave a yelp and dashed back into the yard. The soldier did not follow the dog, and without even so much as a smile of gratitude, dashed away down the road, drunk with the excitement of the moment.

"What a hopeless fellow," said Okihara as the squad resumed its march through the village.

When they met a soldier proudly pulling an ox behind him, they asked him where they could find their Platoon Leader. He replied that he had seen the Company Commander questioning some natives on the village square, but he did not remember seeing the Platoon Commander anywhere.

"He is probably going around," the soldier said meaningfully.

The men of Squad Three looked enviously after the soldier as he went away with his ox, for an ox was one of the best prizes of plunder; it could be used as a means of transportation for any surplus provisions and, when needed, could be eaten for food. An ox was even more coveted than a donkey, which was harder to handle and could not be eaten. Squad Three had long ago relinquished the donkey they had taken with them at the start of the march when it had proved too obstinate and eccentric.

The squad found the Company Commander on the village square, as they had been told. The horse-drawn artillery of the battalion which brought up the rear of the battalion's order of march was rumbling by on the main road which passed through the square. Captain Hamamoto, their Company Commander, seemed to be conducting a simple court of investigation in the center of the square. He was surrounded by members of his headquarters staff and was seated on an ornately carved lacquered chair which somebody must have found in one of the wealthier homes. A large desk stood between him and a group of dejected-looking natives, whom he was questioning through his interpreter.

The natives were dressed like any other villagers but were all men who looked young and well built and could be taken for soldiers. They had probably been unfortunate enough to be found in the houses or discovered loitering in the streets by the ransacking soldiers, who had to show something after all for their "search for enemy stragglers." One native had his wrists tied behind him, and a telltale rifle, though rusty and probably unusable, lay by his side. A soldier with a bayoneted rifle held the other end of the rope which bound the native's wrists and stood officiously on guard beside the sad-looking man. The latter had probably had the bad fortune to be in or near a house which had contained the weapon, for no natives would have been caught with a weapon when the Japanese troops entered a village — let alone such a rusty one. Weapons were also what the soldiers were told to search for, and an assortment of old rusty bayonets and rifles were piled up beside the Company Commander. There were even a few muzzle-loaders among the pile. There were always a few soldiers among the plundering mob which ransacked a village, eager to be recognized by their commanders, who found time in their hurried search to pick up these bits of evidence to vouch for their own alertness. The Company Commander, of course, in turn welcomed these materials for a report, later on, to the Battalion Commander, proving his own capability.

Corporal Sakamoto led his squad in front of the Company Commander and, halting it, presented arms as snappily as he had done to the Battalion Commander a while back. The squad's appearance, however, had disrupted the Company Commander's investigation of the natives, and the officer frowned slightly as he returned the Corporal's salute.

"Second Platoon, Squad Three, has returned now from advance patrol," reported the Corporal.

Captain Hamamoto, who was in a hurry to get rid of the squad and to resume his investigation, said brusquely, "Hard work. You'll find your Platoon Commander at the other end of the village. Cremate the corpse right away and make ready to start."

"Yes sir," answered Corporal Sakamoto and, though he had expected a warmer welcome in view of the recognition they had received from the Battalion Commander on the way back to the village, quickly led his squad out of the way of the Company Commander's investigation.

"Really, there must have been a kinder way to say it," grumbled Okihara, when they were out of earshot of their Commander.

So they have found Nakamura's body, thought Takeo in relief, recalling the Company Commander's instruction to "cremate the corpse." He had feared that his comrade's body would still be in the ditch beside the road where they had left it, covered under a thick layer of dust kicked up by the battalion's march past it.

I wonder if I did wrong by taking the hill and advancing without waiting for orders from behind, worriedly thought Corporal Sakamoto to himself, now not so sure of the correctness of his squad's late action.

This worry, however, was very easily dissipated when the squad met their Platoon Commander at the edge of the village. Before Corporal Sakamoto could call his squad to a halt and salute, Lieutenant Kondo, beaming with good-nature and sympathy, said, "Hard work! Hard work! You did well! Put your rucksacks down and rest!"

Corporal Sakamoto hesitated for a moment, but his past discipline got the better of him, and, besides, he was not going to be robbed of his moment of glory. He shouted, "Squad halt!" He presented arms as snappily as ever. The officer who had been squatted comfortably in the shade of a tree (which was one reason why he wanted to waive this ceremony) scrambled to his feet and returned the salute.

"Squad Three now returns from advance patrol mission!" Corporal Sakamoto reported, though he could not attach the usual " . . . without incident," since there had been a casualty.

"Hard work! Hard work!" repeated the Lieutenant. "Take off your rucksacks right away."

Most of the soldiers of the platoon were there, too, resting in the shade, for they had been the first in the village and had had their share already of the excitement of going through the houses.

"Hard work! Hard work!" they all greeted the squad.

There was much prize booty around them, and quite a number of oxen and donkeys were tied to the trees nearby. They sat or lay on expensive-looking rugs and mats spread indiscriminately on the ground, and to their rucksacks were attached many choice items, such as bottles of *chungchiu* and cooking oil, alarm-clocks, bits of leather and cloth, and kitchen utensils, all of which confirmed the advantage the platoon must have had by going through the village before the others. The men of Squad Three looked enviously at these articles of their more fortunate comrades as they lay their unadorned rucksacks on the ground and stacked their rifles.

"The enemy were Communist guerrillas of about a hundred men who had come to plunder food from the farmers' harvests," said Lieutenant Kondo to Corporal Sakamoto, as if he had sensed the envy in the eyes of the returned soldiers and wanted to divert their attention. "Well, sit down and have a smoke before you do anything," continued the Lieutenant.

When the men sat down around him, he continued, "Those who fired on you when you approached the village were a rear-guard squad. They were trying to slow you down while the main body escaped with their pack horses loaded with food. The villagers say they escaped into the hills, and I guess they cannot be caught. The battalion has no time to fool around with them."

This was one thing his men liked about their Platoon Leader. He always confided in them about happenings and did not act as if they were matters beyond their comprehension and interest, as most officers did.

"Where is the corpse of Nakamura?" Corporal Sakamoto asked the question which was in the mind of every man in his squad, after he had laid down his rucksack.

"It is over there," said Lieutenant Kondo in a respectful tone and pointed to a figure covered with a white sheet, lying some distance away from the group. It lay on a clean plank which was raised a little from the ground by logs placed under it and looked as if it had been treated with all respect.

"It was a pity," said Lieutenant Kondo sympathetically. "As soon as you have had your smoke, you had better cremate it. Somebody found a can of kerosene in the village. Use it. It will make it burn faster."

"It is a shame to speak thus of one who has become a Buddha [they all called anyone who died a Buddha], but Nakamura got shot because he had been slow," said Okihara, the butcher.

"No, it was his fate," Lieutenant Kondo protested.

"It was his fate," soldiers grunted in agreement here and there.

Takeo rose to go and look at his late friend.

"You'll find his belongings on his body," said Lieutenant Kondo after him. "The squad must keep them for him until we get into a city. We must send them home together with his ashes to his family."

When Takeo reached the corpse, he lifted the end of the sheet covering the face to take a last look at the kind face of his best comrade. He let the sheet down in disgust, however, for flies had got in under the sheet and were creeping all over the face — into the open mouth, and nostrils, and eyes, and ears. What he saw under the swarm of flies, moreover, did not have the least resemblance to the warm, honest features which he had known as belonging to Nakamura. The lines were there, but the face could have belonged to anybody else.

When the other men came to the corpse, Takeo was hoping they would burn it and get rid of it as soon as possible. They first rummaged curiously through Nakamura's late belongings. There were some pictures of his wife and child, and others of family groups, including his parents, and some letters. There was a shrine charm (a bit of paper on which lucky words to protect one's life were printed) which had been cynically pierced by the fatal bullet. The charm must have been in his breast pocket when the bullet had struck. There were the usual knickknacks — pocket knives, handkerchief, hip towel, purse, nail clipper, and a few others. Corporal Sakamoto ripped a piece of the sheet covering the corpse and wrapped these belongings reverently in it.

"I'll keep them," he said and put the package in his pocket.

With the aid of the soldiers of other squads, the men of Squad Three soon had built a tall pile of dried branches and splintered wood. They poured kerosene liberally over the pile, then lifted the corpse together with the plank onto the pile.

Manju, the drinker, lifted the sheet and began to pour *chung-chiu* from a bottle into the corpse's open mouth. A whole drove of flies flew out of the mouth and began to buzz around the face.

"He liked the stuff, too, you know," gravely observed the Reserve.

"Come, we can't waste time," scolded the Corporal, and he dashed more kerosene on the corpse.

Then more wood was placed on top, and all the kerosene remaining in the can was poured on to it. When Takeo put his lighted match to the pile, the fire spread so swiftly it almost burned his face.

"Say, Nakamura, you don't have to sweat on marches any

more now!" clownishly shouted Manju into the fire. The corpse began to move and writhe most hideously under the strain of the heat from the rising flames, as corpses had a way of doing when burned.

"They all do that, you know," said Hosaka, the farmer, more to console himself than for the benefit of anyone else, since this was not the first time the soldiers were cremating a dead comrade.

Soon the corpse was enveloped and hidden by the flames. The fire finished its work in less than a half-hour, and when the flames died down to smoldering embers, not a visible trace of the body remained. The men of Squad Three surrounded the embers with long improvised chopsticks to pick up the burnt pieces of the charred skeleton. These were fluffy white pieces of bone which crumpled easily under pressure, and the men picked them up gingerly.

"Here's a gold tooth," shouted Manju who had just picked up a shiny object.

But the other soldiers picked up their pieces silently and piled them on a clean strip of cloth spread on the ground. It was customary for the comrades of his own squad to pick up the remains when the body of a dead soldier was cremated, and so, this time too, the soldiers of the other squads merely stood around idly and looked on.

By now, the last vanguard of the battalion had passed into the village. When the Platoon Commander saw that the cremation was over, he ordered his men to prepare for the march. The remains of Nakamura were carefully wrapped in the cloth on which they had been placed, and the ends of the cloth were tied to form a loop. The Corporal took this stringy package and gave it to Takeo.

"Here, you were his best friend. Take it along for him," said the Squad Leader.

Takeo had hoped for it, for now that the remains were white and clean, they seemed more like his friend than the ugly corpse he had seen. He would take good care of it until they reached a city, from which it could be sent home in the customary white wooden box to Nakamura's family, together with his belongings.

When Takeo had put on his equipment and his rucksack, he slung the loop of the improvised package containing his friend's remains around his neck so that the part where the remains were wrapped hung down below his chest.

I will never let it loose from my body, vowed Takeo to himself and he fell in line to pick up his rifle.

CHAPTER 8

WHEN THE PLATOON reached the village square, the company was already lined up and ready to depart. The natives, who had been under investigation by the Company Commander, stood respectfully out of the way, their happy expressions of relief proclaiming more eloquently than words that they had been set free — all, except four, who stood despondently in line with the soldiers beside baskets filled with the rusty weapons which had been collected so diligently in the village. These four had been ordered to carry the baskets on the march until the end of the day when they would be presented together with the "evidences" to the Battalion Commander for final judgment. They were probably the ones with the weakest alibi, and they, along with the weapons, would make excellent material to prove to the Battalion Commander the alertness of the company and its Commander. The natives held long poles to carry on their shoulders with the baskets hanging from them, as they had a way of doing it.

"I was waiting for you," said Captain Hamamoto curtly to Lieutenant Kondo, when the latter arrived in the square with his platoon. "Let us get started. The Battalion Commander has ordered us to burn the village before we leave."

This was the first time the Company Commander had mentioned burning the village to his subordinates, and the hearts of the soldiers beat faster in anticipation of the excitement of setting fire to a village. Some, however, like Takeo felt impatient, since the extra task would only increase the strain of making up for lost time later on, and felt peeved at the superiors for giving them the extra task.

The Company Commander turned to the natives who had been set free and who now stood politely waiting to send off the troops and address them through his interpreter: "We have been ordered to burn your village by our Battalion Commander. That is to punish you for not having informed us about the enemy. Because you did not inform us, one of our comrades was killed. But the Imperial Army does not persecute the innocent citizens. There is some time yet, and if there are any valuables in your home, take them out before they are burned down."

Some of the natives began to whimper protestingly. "What do they say?" Captain Hamamoto asked his interpreter.

"They say they are not at fault. They say that if they had gone out of their village to inform us, they would have been killed by the Communists," answered the interpreter.

"Tell them, I cannot help it," said Captain Hamamoto impatiently. "Tell them it is the order of the Battalion Commander." The Captain turned to his company and was about to assign the platoons their respective duties when one of the natives threw himself at his feet and began to wail loudly and earnestly.

"What does he say?" asked the Captain of his interpreter, somewhat taken aback by this sudden outburst of the native.

"He says that his father and brother were killed by the Communists, because they did not give money when asked for it, and he says the corpses are still in his home. . . . The people hereabout think that the soul will perish if a body is burned," the interpreter explained.

"Then, tell them that four of the natives here should go with him to carry out the corpses before the village is burned, and you go along, too. . . . One squad of the Kondo platoon must go with them and set fire to the house as soon as the corpses are removed," the Company Commander ordered, turning to his men. "The rest of the platoon, set fire to the houses on the other side of the road. Platoon One, burn the houses on this side. Platoon Three and Company Headquarters, come with me to the edge of the village and set fire when the others are finished." Captain Hamamoto was his usual efficient self.

Squad Three was chosen to go to the house from which the corpses were to be borne out. The interpreter selected four natives and ordered the native who was wailing loudly at the Company Commander's feet to rise and lead the way. The soldiers dispersed swiftly to carry out their respective assignments when the company was dismissed, and the group led by the still wailing native had to run to keep ahead of the other soldiers.

The motley group of natives, soldiers, and interpreter went into a narrow lane and arrived at a fairly pretentious house near the village outskirts. The native in the lead showed them into the house and to a wide backyard after passing through several moon-shaped gates, which the soldiers knew were signs of wealth in this country. In the middle of the yard, sure enough, lay two gruesomely disfigured corpses in a puddle of half-dried blood. One was probably shot from the back of the head at close range, and his face was smashed beyond recognition by the outgoing bullet. The other was shot in the stomach, and he must have been shot at close range, too, for his stomach was blown wide open, and the intestines hung out from it.

While the other natives went to look for planks on which to carry the corpses, the one who had led them there began explaining fervently to the interpreter the tragic event which had occurred in that yard that day. He punctuated his sentences liberally with loud wails and turned frequently toward the soldiers, as if he sought their sympathy and hoped to have his home spared.

The interpreter told the native's story on his behalf to the soldiers. He related: "This man's father was the richest land-owner in this district. The Communists came early in the morning and, forcing their way into the house, demanded money from his father. The father lied that the money was in the bank in the city, and one of the Communists went behind him and pointed a pistol to the back of his head and shot him. His brother tried to defend his father, and he was shot in the stomach. While the Communists were ransacking the house, we came. This man was hidden under a bed and was not found."

"If he has his house burned on top of that, he has had the limit of bad luck," said Hosaka sympathetically.

"We can't help it. It's orders," said Corporal Sakamoto with finality.

When the natives saw that there was no hope of having the house saved, they placed the corpses on the planks they had gathered and went out of the house. The lone male survivor of the home (the women must have fled) went hurriedly through the rooms gathering those belongings he wanted to take with him, but he was cut short when the soldiers started setting fire to the house. He carried whatever he had under his arms and ran after the men who had gone out with the dead bodies of his father and brother, wailing louder than ever.

The soldiers had made torches out of bundles of straw and dried kindling wood, and they touched them to various parts of the home. When satisfied that the house was in flames, they dashed out of it and went running down the lane, setting fire with their flaming torches to the thatched straw roofs hanging low over the lane on both sides. When their improvised torches burned down, they hurled them on the roofs or into the houses and built new ones with materials they found in the still untouched houses.

The dried roofs ignited easily and went up in flames very swiftly. The straw and *kaoliang* stalks which reinforced the mud walls caught fire, too, and the walls went crumbling to the ground before the rooms were completely burnt. The fire spread so swiftly in the dry autumn air that the soldiers who were left behind, while their comrades went ahead, had to fight their way through the smoke and sparks to get out into the open again. The crackling of the flames and the crashing of the houses as they tumbled to the ground, mingled with a steady roar, like the sound of a strong wind blowing through a tunnel, soon filled the air and pressed down on the soldiers, who, though used to the sharp sounds of battle, had never experienced such an oppressive concentration of sound before.

The first excitement of setting fire to the houses wore away quickly, and the soldiers were soon beset by an overpowering fear, for they felt as if they were being chased by the flames and the unearthly roar of the fire that they themselves had started. Many, like Takeo, had felt a strong abhorrence to the task from the very outset and ran down the lane, only halfheartedly applying their burning torches to the roofs, but there were enough who went about making a thorough job of it for not a single house along the lane traversed by Squad Three to escape the scourge of the revenging soldiers. Manju danced as he ran down the burning lane with his flaming torch and looked like a real incendiary maniac, singing wildly in the rising flames.

A slight breeze had arisen, as it always does when there is a large conflagration, and it sent the smoke and sparks swirling down into the lanes through which the soldiers ran. The men of Squad Three met with soldiers from other squads at the end of their lane, and they now joined forces to go through the remaining lanes and streets of the village. Animals—hogs, oxen, and donkeys—ran in panic past the soldiers, and even the dogs which had been so irate and pugnacious a moment ago went running helter-skelter down the streets, paying no attention to the soldiers they overtook. Manju had caught a fleeing monkey, and he went dancing along with the comical animal perched tenaciously on his rucksack.

The heat was now oppressive, and soldiers in their haste to get away from the heat, while at the same time performing their duty, were setting fire indiscriminately, and they burned the houses without giving thought to others coming behind them. Those caught in the rear, therefore, were often forced to make a run for it through the burning streets to save themselves, and theirs had become a really dangerous task.

Thus it was that Takeo and some of his comrades of Squad Three found themselves suddenly confronted by a flaming house on each side of a lane when they turned a corner near the end of the village. When they made ready to dash through this dangerous barrier, they became aware of a strange sight. There was an old gray-haired woman kneeling in front of one of the burning houses. The flames were almost upon her as she knelt motionless, as if chained to the ground where she was. This was the first native they had seen since they had started their incendiary destruction of the village, and the sight made them realize for the first time the simple fact they had all but forgotten — that these houses they were burning had been inhabited.

"Hey, old woman! You'll be burned!" Takeo shouted.

They did not know whether the kneeling, gray-haired figure was alive or not, for it had its back turned toward them, but the soldiers now saw it move ever so little when Takeo shouted at it. The front wall of the house before which the old woman crouched was in danger of toppling over any minute, and the soldiers began calling to the forlorn little figure before the flames in earnest. It was a weird sight, and it was a distasteful sight even to these soldiers, hardened by countless ugly, bloody sights of warfare.

"Come back! . . . Old lady, you are in danger! . . . You will burn! . . . " they shouted, and some even made as if to go after her. Hearing the excited commotion behind her, the old woman got shakily to her feet and began groping with her hands before her the way the blind do when searching for something.

"She is blind!" Takeo exclaimed and jumped forward to stop her.

The old woman rushed into the burning house before Takeo

could catch her, as if she were fleeing from something more fearful than the fire before her, and the flames enveloped her in a gush. Hosaka, the farmer, who was a superstitious man, clasped his hands before him and mumbled the Buddhist prayer. Takeo was barely able to jump back to save his face from being scorched.

"Hey, if we don't hurry ourselves, we will get burned too!" somebody shouted, and they all dashed between the two burning houses. They were not too soon, for, as they ran, they could hear the roof of the house which had swallowed the old woman cave in with a resounding crash, and they felt the sparks on the back of their necks as the walls fell across the street.

The soldiers now became aware that all the houses up to the edge of the village were going up in flames. They had probably been forgotten by their more eager comrades in their excitement. They threw away the torches they still had in their hands, for now there was no need for them, and kept running until they were at last out of the madly burning village.

They seemed to have been the last ones out, for the company was already lined up and waiting. Every face of the soldiers in line appeared haggard from the harrowing experience, and there were some with large streaks of soot on them, while other soldiers even showed holes in their uniforms where the sparks had alighted and burnt them. There was no longer among them the enthusiasm with which they had started on their late assignment as they fell in line and counted off. They were facing the burning village, which was now a mountain of flames, and the heat struck their faces and was strong enough almost to push them back. They had certainly done a good job of carrying out their Company Commander's order.

There were no words of praise, however, or instructions for the coming march by the Commander this time, and the company quickly turned about and started up the road after the battalion which was already lost to sight. When Squad Three passed the gully where they had seen the women and children,

Okihara tossed a pebble and shouted an obscene word, but there was no answer, and none of his comrades paid any attention to him, for they were all too tired in spirit to appreciate a joke. Even Manju was silent and almost morose, and the monkey which he still carried on his rucksack seemed the only lively member in the whole column of marching soldiers, for he kept chattering excitedly.

When the column reached the top of a rise in the road, the soldiers turned around to take a last look at the ill-fated village. The fire was now at its height, and out of the flames which licked hungrily into the air, tiers of black, billowy smoke rose high and majestically and spiraled slowly over the village to form a dark veil, as if of mourning, over it. Takeo tried to locate the house which had so mercilessly engulfed the blind old woman near the edge of the village, but everything was in confusion, and he could not distinguish one house from another. He turned away quickly and started down the road on the other side of the rise, relieved that they could no longer see the village.

"They shouldn't let us burn villages," said Hosaka, recovering a little of his talkativeness now that the harassing sight of the burning village was no longer visible.

"They shouldn't let us fight wars," said Aoki, the day laborer, bitterly.

"Really, I have never hated it so much as today," said Hosaka. "It is all right to shoot and be shot at, but I want to be excused from burning a village."

"But it is fun, Honorable Senior Soldier," protested Kan, who always had an idea of his own. "We won't be able to do anything like it when we go home."

"You can do it when you go home. Only they put you in a dark cell if you do it there. The only difference is they give you a medal for it at the front," said Aoki.

"We did right by burning the village," insisted Private First Class Gunji. "If we had not burnt it, they would have thought us weak. From now on, if the enemy should appear around here, the natives will be sure to let us know."

Aoki lighted a cigarette and said, "If it were I, and somebody burned my village, I would hate him surely to the core, and I would revenge myself sometime."

"Well, the Japanese and Chinese are different," said Gunji.

"The people around here are really easygoing," added Kan.

"But they say the Chinese are very vengeful and never forget a wrong," contradicted Hosaka, wiping the sweat from his good-natured face.

"But, on that point, they cannot beat us Japanese," insisted Gunji.

"It is really so. For, in Japan, vengeance has been in existence since long ago," agreed Kan proudly.

Takeo, who had been plodding along silently while listening to the conversation of his comrades without thinking much about it one way or the other, turned now toward Reserve Private Aoki, marching beside him, and asked, "Honorable Senior Soldier, did you see that old woman?" When the Reserve grunted his assent, Takeo added, "She was a pity, wasn't she?"

"That is why I say war is hateful," Aoki almost spat out the words and kept his eyes to the front.

"Do you think that old woman jumped into the fire because she feared us more than the fire?" Takeo asked the question which had been troubling him ever since they had left the burning village. It had seemed that his attempt to save the old woman had been what had scared her into jumping into the flaming house, and his conscience was ill at ease.

"Maybe, that was one reason. But old people are like that — they are easily frightened and do the maddest things. And, besides, she was blind and did not know what she was doing," the older soldier replied in an assuring tone, as if he understood the feelings of his younger comrade.

"There is an old one exactly like her in my home. In such a case, she too would have jumped into the fire," Reserve Private Hosaka now comforted Takeo openly, turning and smiling at him.

Takeo felt a sudden feeling of gratitude for these understanding Reserves and asked Hosaka with genuine concern, "The old woman in your home isn't blind, is she?"

"She is not blind, but she is old and has gray hair," answered Hosaka.

"If the enemy landed in Japan, they would burn our homes, too," Private First Class Gunji said, interrupting the conversation which was beginning to sound very unsoldierlike.

"That would be terrible. Our homes would be wrecked," agreed Private First Class Tanaka. "The enemy are savage and would do more terrible things than we are doing."

"The women of Japan would all be raped," sneered Miki lewdly.

Oka, who had been carrying the machine gun called, "Exchange!" and passed the heavy weapon to Miki, who was marching empty-handed beside him. The two were machine gunners and had no rifles and carried the machine gun in thirty-minute shifts between them on the march.

Oka had been waiting to join the conversation, and he now said in a boastful voice, "We would be in trouble if the enemy came to Japan, and that is why we have come this far to the continent to suffer our hardships and to fight."

"But I don't want to let our parents see something like what we did today," commented Hosaka. He turned toward Miki beside him and said, "If your mother had seen you burning the houses today, she would have wept."

"Honorable Senior Soldier, that would be all right; I have no mother," Miki laughed.

"That fellow Nakamura did the best thing. He can now go home after getting into the 'white box,'" Okihara, the butcher, who had remained silent so far, observed in a cynical voice, and he blew his nose on the road.

This was the first mention anybody had made of their dead comrade since they had cremated his body back in the village.

Takeo quickly felt for the little cloth wrapping hanging from his neck and almost sighed in relief when he still found it hanging in place, for he had almost forgotten about it in the excitement which had happened since the cremation. Nakamura had been so quiet and self-effacing that they had not missed him, and many had even been under the delusion that he was still marching with them.

"That is so. We had completely forgotten about Nakamura," Oka exclaimed, and they all looked at the wrapping hanging from Takeo's neck.

"Nakamura was pitiful," said Hosaka sympathetically.

"His wife and child are more pitiful," observed Aoki. "Sooner or later, if we stay at the front, we are all going to become like that, but those who are left at home are to be pitied."

"On that point, I am at ease. They don't think much about me at home," said Third-Year-Regular Oka, who was still unmarried.

"But, Honorable Senior Soldier, you must have a father and mother," protested Kan in mock sympathy.

"They are living, but they are more at ease if I am not at home," boasted Oka, who took relish in recounting his many wild escapades before joining the Army.

Corporal Sakamoto, who had been marching along in dignified silence and listening to the bits of conversation of his subordinates and forming his own judgments of them all by himself, now joined the conversation for the first time, "I understood Nakamura's parents were alive, too," he said.

"If we look at the picture he had in his breast pocket, he had a very pretty wife," said Hosaka.

Takeo instinctively looked down at the remains of his friend he was carrying hanging from his neck and explained, "Before a year had passed after getting married, he had come to the front. His child was born just a little while before departing, he used to say."

"The baby who was born — was it a girl or a boy?" Hosaka asked, and Takeo answered, "It was a boy."

"That is good. A boy can grow up even if he has no father, but a girl is to be pitied," Hosaka added.

Aoki threw away his cigarette butt and objected, "It should be the opposite. I have three boys, and I think they are to be pitied if I should die."

Hosaka disregarded his friend and continued, "Nakamura is lucky, since there is a father with a reliable business. . . . Wasn't his father a tailor?" Hosaka asked to substantiate his statement, and Takeo answered, "Yes." The Reserve continued, "The father will look after his widow and child."

"Nakamura was a good fellow," said Kan.

"That is so. He was quiet and honest," agreed Private First Class Gunji. Quietness was a virtue among the soldiers, though sometimes they criticized someone for being "too quiet," which meant that he was not aggressive enough, as had been more often the case with Nakamura while he had been living.

"He never got angry," said Takeo.

For once, they all seemed to agree, and no one denied that Nakamura had been a "good fellow." No one mentioned the many faults of their dead comrade, for it was always thus when a soldier died — they never recalled his shortcomings and mentioned only his cardinal points. They did not tell of how the weak soldier had always been a burden to the squad on marches and of how he had not done his duties as aggressively as the other First-Year-Soldiers. Perhaps this habit of forgetting the weaknesses of a dead comrade came from the popular Buddhist conception they were educated in at home that all the dead became Buddhas in Nirvana or from the Shinto conception that a soldier became a guardian-god of the nation. This habit, however, was easily followed in Nakamura's case, for he had been a really "good fellow."

"Honorable Squad Leader, are you going to send Nakamura's parents a letter?" asked Oka of Corporal Sakamoto.

"I guess I have to," said the Corporal in as indifferent a tone as he could master, for indifference was one of the accepted signs of dignity.

"If you are going to write, it is better that you do not write in detail," advised Hosaka, who was older in age and a senior in service of the Squad Leader. "It is enough to say he fought bravely and died. If I should die, I want it done that way."

"I won't write in detail," assured the Squad Leader.

"It is enough to say one 'fell like a cherry blossom,'" added Private First Class Tanaka, mentioning a popular phrase of the time.

Each was thinking to himself, however, that he would want a detailed description of his death sent home if he were to die under the valiant circumstances each hoped to be favored with, like a charge or a special mission, when he died. But the soldiers did not mention it, though they all expected to die, if at all, under nobler circumstances than their late unfortunate friend, Nakamura. A blazing account of the last moment of a soldier always softened the sorrow of those at home, they all knew.

It was the silently accepted duty of the Squad Leader to write a letter of condolence to the home of any of his subordinates who should be killed in action. Sometimes, the Platoon Leader wrote, and even the Company Commander, too. In these letters, as much of the events leading up to one's last moment as could pass the strict censorship was described in the hope of consoling the survivors at home. The official notice of death, of course, was sent by the proper authorities, but even the ordinary comrades of a dead soldier frequently sent letters of condolence. Takeo was thinking of sending one to Nakamura's home, though he was at a loss as to what he would say regarding the way his friend had died.

> *. . . It can be seen, it can be seen,*
> *Through the pine-tree woods,*
> *The sails of Ohara with a circle*
> *round a cross. . . .*

lustily sang Manju the refrain of a famous ballad.

The company had marched swiftly since leaving the village which they had set aflame so thoroughly, and the men could now see still some distance ahead of them the supply wagons which brought up the tail end of the battalion's column of march.

の出

CHAPTER 9

"LEND ME your razor. Mine can't shave," said Aoki in disgust.

"Cheap stuff is no good," chided Hosaka, and he continued to shave meticulously in front of a broken mirror he had standing on his rucksack.

"What do you say! You know you stole it from a native home during the march!" accused Aoki, and he threw his flimsy paper-handled razor, which was the stock-in-trade at the post exchanges those days, into the wastebasket.

"Honorable Senior Soldier, I will shave you," offered Kan, who was shaving Private First Class Gunji's face just then.

"If I let you fellows shave me, you will cut me up terribly," said Aoki, who had a thicker growth of hair on his face than most soldiers. He even had hair on his chest, a phenomenon rare in his race.

The squad room, at that moment, looked more like a beauty parlor than a room of battle-hardened soldiers. Everywhere, soldiers peered into mirrors while they shaved themselves or were shaved by their comrades. Others sat patiently on stools, with very suspicious-looking sheets of white cloth wrapped around their bodies to protect them from the falling hair, while the more adept ones cut their hair to the standard short-crop with the long-handled clippers which were regular equipment in the army.

A few were using short-handled clippers which also must

119

have been "war booty," since the soldiers were too poor to buy them. Others were busy oiling their shoes (polishing was prohibited the soldiers as a sign of effeteness, though the officers were permitted the luxury). There were also soldiers busily patching their uniforms or sewing clean cloth collarbands inside the collars of their coats, as they were compelled to do when going out on leave.

This was leave-day, the first leave-day since the soldiers had arrived in the city on the coast after their long journey from inland and the first leave-day in a city in over half a year, ever since they had started out on the big Suchow campaign. After the little skirmish in the village where Nakamura had been killed, the troops had met no enemy, and they had marched only a week longer when they had been loaded into trains and sent to the city by railway the rest of the way. But the march had been a steady, grinding one, and the trip by train had not been all cozy, for they had been stuffed so closely into the freight cars that they had had little room even to stretch themselves and had to take turns sleeping stretched on the floor. Therefore, the thrill of this first leave in a big city was close to the hearts of all the soldiers of Squad Three as they prepared busily for it.

The room the squad occupied was a classroom of a schoolhouse, converted as closely as possible to look like a regulation squad room of the Japanese Army. One half of the room was raised to the level of a platform, on which straw mats were spread. Against the walls on the platform were piles of neatly folded blankets, which the soldiers spread on the straw mats to sleep on and cover themselves with at night. The mat-covered platform was also where the soldiers ate their meals squatted and where they wrote their letters and lay around in their idle hours during the day. The soldiers removed their shoes to go on this platform. A shelf ran along the whole length of the wall at the head of the platform, on which were stacked the soldiers' rucksacks and belongings in orderly piles. Underneath the shelf were pegs from which hung the bayonet belts, the utilities bags and canteens. The end of the platform farthest away from the entrance was concealed by an improvised wall of tent flaps, which formed a private compartment for the Squad Leader, since a non-commissioned officer was entitled to a private room all to himself.

The other half of the room was conspicuous for its barrenness. There were a long table, benches, some stools, and a rifle rack, and that was all. Simplicity was one of the cardinal points stressed in the army, and a squad room was where the soldiers began practicing it. There were no pictures on the walls, in fact, nothing which could be taken for decoration in the whole room. Simplicity and neatness were the only evident virtues there.

"Hey, has anybody got a pair of scissors?" Corporal Sakamoto's voice called urgently from within the tent flaps.

"Yes, sir," Miki, who was oiling his shoes nearest to the Squad Leader's room, answered promptly, and went and got a pair of scissors from his utilities bag. He proceeded hurriedly in front of the makeshift room and, standing stiffly at attention, reported, "Miki has come with the scissors!"

"Good! Give to me!" the Corporal's gruff voice sounded inside, and a hand was stuck out from between the tent flaps. Miki obligingly placed the scissors in the hand and reported, "Miki will now return!" The voice inside said, "Thank you!"

"Hey, Aoki, come on over and have a drink!" shouted Manju, who was squatted on the platform and had an open bottle of *sake* in front of him. Okihara was squatted beside him, and the two were drinking from large tin cups.

The two were the only ones at ease in the whole room of busy soldiers. Manju never paid much attention to his appearance, and whatever could be done about it was done by the First-Year-Soldiers. Okihara had volunteered to stay behind when each squad had been ordered to leave two soldiers as a precaution against an emergency. Kan, ever alert for a chance to be recognized, had been the other who had volunteered to cancel his leave, but he was busy helping the older soldiers with their various tasks.

"No, thank you," answered Aoki, who was sewing on his collarband. "I won't make a hit with my sweetheart if I don't make myself up."

Manju stroked his month's growth of beard and called, "This is what is going to make a hit with my sweetheart." The soldiers looked up from their work and laughed good-naturedly.

"Kan, what shall I get for you today?" Takeo, who had just finished shaving, went beside his friend, busy polishing the bayonet of Private First Class Tanaka, and asked.

"Sure, get me some cakes and a letter pad," Kan said.

"They are selling letter pads at the exchange," Takeo said.

"I know, but they are no good."

"That is true. I will get you some cakes and a letter pad in the city," Takeo assured his friend.

When Takeo climbed up on the platform to get his bayonet to polish, somebody came running down the hall outside, shouting into the rooms along the way to the squads occupying them. The messenger halted long enough in front of Squad Three's room to call, "Two from each squad, come immediately to Headquarters to get consolation kits!" He was a messenger from Company Headquarters, and he went hurrying down the hall, shouting his message into the rest of the rooms.

The message was greeted by excited cheers from the soldiers, and Private First Class Gunji ordered in a loud voice, "Somebody, go and get them right away!" Of course, he meant First-Year-Soldiers.

"Yes, sir!" answered Kan, but he looked hesitatingly at Private First Class Tanaka, whose bayonet he was polishing.

"Never mind. Leave it. I will do it," the Private First Class said.

Kan dashed to the shelf, where they kept their tent sheets and, taking down his own one, ran out of the room. Takeo, who was already in front of the shelf, took his tent sheet and reached the door about the same time as Kan. The two soldiers returned shortly, carrying each a bulging bundle over his shoulder. They spilled the contents of their bundles in a pile on the platform. Their comrades left whatever they were doing and gathered around, jostling each other like so many happy excited children.

Jumbled in the pile were packages of assorted shapes and sizes. They were all bound by cloth as army regulations required them to be, and the senders' names and addresses were written boldly on them. These were part of the numerous consolation kits contributed by the patriotic citizens at home to the soldiers at the front, and they were gathered from time to time by the patriotic organizations in the nation, especially by the schools and neighborhood associations, and presented to the armed forces.

"Hey, where are the packages from?" called Corporal Sakamoto, who had come out of his private compartment after Miki had gone to call him. He was now standing neglected outside the fringe of the circle formed by his subordinates crowded around the packages.

"They have come from Tokyo," Kan, who had been turning the bundles over in his hands, obligingly answered.

"Let the Honorable Squad Leader come through," Private First Class Gunji, squatted comfortably among the packages, ordered.

The soldiers respectfully made room and the Squad Leader advanced to where the packages were piled. Kan reported proudly, "They said at Headquarters to give one to each soldier, but there are two extras. I stole them for you."

"Nice doing!" Private First Class Tanaka and several others praised immediately.

"Those devils at Company Headquarters always take more than they should, and so, this time, I took a headstart," explained Kan.

"Don't worry. It only means that the packages for the devils at Headquarters are less," assured Aoki.

It was no crime, at least, not much of a crime, to steal in the army, if one could get away with it. "War is a contest to steal each other's life. If you don't watch out, you will get even your own life stolen," the soldiers warned each other. The soldier who lost anything got scolded soundly for being "lax," and his comrades made little effort to find the stolen article for him.

Corporal Sakamoto examined the addresses on some of the packages and exclaimed, "What is this? These are from a girls' school in Toyko."

The soldiers shouted their approval, and Private First Class Gunji said, "Since they are from Toyko, there must be good things in them." Most of the soldiers were from the country, and they had a high respect for the capital.

Hosaka, the oldest in the squad, upon whom always devolved the duty of mediator, was writing the list of numbers which were to be drawn as in a lottery, in order to determine the order by which the soldiers were to select the packages. This lottery procedure was always taken to settle questions too controversial to be left to authority alone. Private First Class Gunji, however, suggested, "Honorable Squad Leader, pick one for yourself," for it was understood that the Squad Leader was exempt from this practice of the common soldiers. Corporal Sakamoto selected the largest package in the pile.

"Come on, call your numbers!" Hosaka announced when his list was done.

"The one in the end . . . the one in the middle . . . the one to the right of that . . ." the soldiers answered, pointing to the numbers which were hidden under a strip of paper. Hosaka diligently wrote their names down where they pointed. The First-Year-Soldiers remained respectfully silent until all the older soldiers were through, and Hosaka himself wrote his name down the last to insure the fairness of the lottery.

When the drawing was ended, Hosaka began to call out the names in the order they had been drawn, and the soldiers happily selected their packages. Hosaka was truly in his element as he urged the soldiers to hurry, for he was an established farmer, and farmers in a village were always having to mediate in petty quarrels among each other.

Okihara, the butcher, got a trim little package bound with a red ribbon. "I could almost swallow it," said Okihara cynically and roughly tore open the package. There was a whole assortment of toilet articles, like perfume, cream, lotion, soap and, even powder. There was also a letter in a pink envelope, and, when he picked it up clumsily in his huge hands, they all began teasing him. "That package must have come from the daughter of a drugstore owner," Aoki chided his friend.

The soldiers, however, did not have much time bantering, for they had their own packages to inspect, and they took their packages and went away to open them, singly or in groups. There was a letter in each package, and the soldiers passed these around, ribbing each other freely the while. All the articles which the imagination of a group of healthy adolescent girls could conjure were in the packages — toilet articles, as in Okihara's package, candies, canned food, dolls, pictures, pressed flowers, books, knitted gloves, and Hosaka even got a massage stick.

"She shows more consideration than my own daughter!" laughed Hosaka, and he held up his unique gift for everyone to see.

The articles in the packages were mostly inexpensive tidbits, for the country was already suffering from the inevitable scarcities of wartime, and the people were being called upon more frequently to contribute packages. Each kit, however, held a letter, and this letter with the name and address of the sender on it was what the soldiers prized the most, for it opened vistas of a pleasant correspondence, enhanced the more by the adventure and mystery of corresponding with a total stranger — and a girl, to boot!

"Say, this is too much for me!" shouted Kan gleefully as he read through his letter.

"Let me see it," said Takeo, who sat in front of him, and made a pass for it.

"No, I can't let you see it," protested Kan and hurriedly shoved his letter into his pocket.

Takeo took his letter out of the envelope and began reading it. "I am a fourth grader in this girls' school," the letter began in a neat, very feminine hand, "so, you see, I will be graduated soon and will have to marry. But when I think of you brave soldiers fighting at the front for our sake, I am afraid I will be cursed if I get married now. That is why I have vowed to wait until all of you have come back before becoming married. . . . " It went on to describe the members of the writer's family and concluded, " . . . Please take good care of yourself. I pray that your fortune of war is long."

Almost more than when he had read a letter from his own folks, Takeo felt an almost overpowering yearning for home. The sweet innocence portrayed in the girl-student's letter had touched a sensitive chord in his heart, which had long gone neglected. Takeo folded the letter neatly and replaced it in the envelope, and before he tucked it away in his coat's breast pocket, surreptitiously sniffed at it and found, as he had expected, that it smelt strongly of sweet perfume. There was also a little silk doll in his package, and he put that, too, in his breast pocket alongside the letter.

"Welcome! Welcome! Sirs! This is the biggest, cheapest sale! These are not articles you find everywhere!" shouted Manju, and he laid out all the articles he had received in his package neatly before him. He was imitating the raucous voice of a stall vendor at home, and his imitation was near perfect. In fact, some said that he had been a stall vendor before joining the army, though he himself remained silent when pressed. Some cheered him on, and a few tried to imitate him, though their performances fell far short of his.

The excitement, however, was over as quickly as it had started, for the soldiers were not forgetting that this was leave-day, and they put their packages away carefully on the shelf together with their belongings which were stacked there. The Squad Leader, too, came out shortly from his compartment, where he had taken his package and the two "extras" Kan had got for him to open and inspect all by himself, and ordered impatiently, "Put away your consolation kits quickly and get ready to take leave."

Soon, all were ready to undergo the usual dress inspection which always preceded a leave in the city. Their uniforms, though torn and patched in places, were freshly washed, and the new unwrinkled collarbands inside the coat collars were conspicuous on all the soldiers. Every button was in place, the shoes oiled, and their puttees rolled according to regulation with the ends showing on the outside of their legs just under the knees. The last speck of rust had been rubbed from their bayonets, and the belts were thoroughly oiled. The bayonet was "the soul of the soldier," and he had to take it along with him on a leave — that is, the bayonet!

Kan helped the Corporal on with his coat, and gave it a last dusting. Then all waited impatiently for their Squad Leader to go to Company Headquarters to get their leave passes. The men wanted their passes before inspection because, sometimes, Headquarters refused to issue them to certain individuals on some minor pretext, and these, if uninformed beforehand, went through the ordeal of inspection for nothing. Corporal Sakamoto, however, returned from Headquarters with passes for all of the men who had asked for leaves that day. The passes were little rectangular wooden pieces with the name of the unit and serial numbers on them.

"I am told to give you salute-training before dress inspection," curtly announced Corporal Sakamoto after he had distributed the passes to his men.

Voices of disappointment and protest greeted the announcement, and Aoki grumbled, "It is ten o'clock already. What is the Company Commander doing?"

"I can't help it," said Corporal Sakamoto dryly. "It is orders. Let us go out and do it, even if just to go through the motions."

The soldiers grudgingly went out to the yard in front of the schoolhouse, where their peevishness was somewhat allayed when they found soldiers from the other squads in the company also filing out for the training. "The quicker we do it, the quicker we will be finished," the Squad Leader prodded his discontented men. After Squad Three was lined up in single file, Privates First Class Gunji and Tanaka were asked to fall out to help the Squad Leader supervise the training.

The Corporal and the two soldiers went up and down the line, stopping before each soldier and commanding, "Attention! . . . Salute! . . . Down! . . . At ease." The soldiers in line went through each motion obediently, but the Reserves, as usual, were sloppy. The Regulars, and especially the First-Year-Soldiers, however, obeyed the commands briskly and in full earnest.

"Your head is a little to the right. . . . Your fingers are apart. . . . Your toes are turned too inward. . . ." The supervisors of the training stopped before each soldier and corrected each with minute care in the usual manner. They did not criticize the Reserves much and did so only in an apologetic voice out of deference to the latters' seniority in service, but they gave the full treatment to the First-Year-Soldiers.

The high, crisp voices of the soldiers, commanding their squads in the monotonous drill, grew in intensity as the drill proceeded, and they seemed to be vying with each other to see who could shout the loudest. There was good reason for this competition, for they all knew that their Company Commander and respective Platoon Commanders would be listening in their rooms not far away. These soldiers shouting their commands tried, as they had been taught, to get their voices from "the bottom of their stomach," where they were told all the strength of a man lay.

Private First Class Tanaka was especially satisfied with the way his voice was coming out this morning. Every time he barked a command, he could feel instantly the muscles of his lower abdomen tightening, and the accompanying sensation was one of boundless strength. Exulting secretly in this feeling of well-being, he stopped before Miki and shouted, "Attention!"

Though a stalwart on the marches, the hulking farmer's lad

was always a clumsy performer in these drills, and his clumsy movement as he pulled himself up to attention highly exasperated Private First Class Tanaka. The sight alone of the large bungling First-Year-Soldier was in complete discord with the brisk, tense feeling he felt this morning. Miki himself was feeling clumsier than usual since his reflexes had been numbed more than he had expected by his anticipation of a free and joyful holiday.

"Your toes, inward! . . . Inward, not outward! . . . Your elbow out! . . . Out! . . . Out! . . . " The Private First Class shouted angrily after he had ordered the posture of salute. The First-Year-Soldier was completely confused by now.

In final exasperation, Private First Class Tanaka went up to the young soldier and kicked his toes inward and shoved his elbow out. He also turned Miki's head a little and pushed his chin in. He corrected his subject's figure like a photographer about to take a picture, and there never was a more pliant, obedient subject for any photographer. Miki now looked like a most unnatural wooden soldier, for he tried to maintain his corrected posture rigidly, and the strain forced him to lose all sense of balance.

Private First Class Tanaka returned to his previous distance to view his corrected subject. He next called, "Chew hard on your molars! . . . Tighten the muscles of your rectum! . . . Put strength in your lower abdomen! . . . Extend the tips of your fingers! . . . Pull your chest in! . . . " Miki tried to follow each instruction the instant it was given, but he felt hopelessly confused. He shared his superior's exasperation at his own self, for every one of the instructions the Private First Class shouted had been given them repeatedly as the essentials for the attainment of the correct posture of "attention," and he seemed to have forgotten them all this morning.

Private First Class Tanaka finally made a helpless gesture as much as to say, "You are hopeless." He ordered the welcome, "At ease!" and, though he would have done plenty to Miki if this had been any other drill but one they were going through merely as a formality before leave-taking, he moved on to the next soldier after caustically instructing, "Practice by yourself!"

Miki took on the drill by himself after the Private First Class had moved on. Seriously and diligently, he went over and over again through the motions of attention. It did not discourage him a bit that no soldier in the Japanese Army was ever called perfect in the execution of the posture of "attention," for the posture of "attention" was called the foundation of the "Spirit of the Soldier," and no one was expected to attain such a far-reaching quality perfectly. Someone was always able to correct a soldier at attention, and even the Reserves were getting it, though mildly, from time to time this morning.

After about half an hour of fretful drilling, the Company Commander at last appeared in the yard and called a halt to the proceeding. The company was assembled in double file, facing each other, and the Company Commander went with his Platoon Commanders and the Warrant Officer between the lines, inspecting each soldier carefully. A few flaws were noted and the guilty ones instructed to correct them before taking leave, but as a whole, the soldiers were up to standard, and the Company Commander seemed highly satisfied with the general appearance of his subordinates.

At the end of the line, the Company Commander ordered, "Show me your handkerchiefs and tissue paper." The soldiers took out these "articles of civilization and sanitation" from their breast pockets where they had been ordered to put them earlier in the morning. Satisfied that everyone had carried out his instructions faithfully, Captain Hamamoto closed the lines and went to the front and center.

"Attention! Eyes center! At ease!" ordered the Captain, as he always did before addressing his troops. "While your comrades are still fighting at the fronts, you have been permitted to take leave in the city," he began gravely. "I ask you not to belittle this favor. You must conduct yourselves with restraint. You know by now what you must do and what you must not

do. Be especially careful of saluting. I need not remind you —
salute every superior you see. . . . Attention! . . . It fills us with
trepidation to note that His Majesty the Emperor has been
pleased to ordain us his 'supports' in the Imperial Rescript. We
must keep this well in mind and conduct ourselves accordingly.
. . . At ease! . . . I have seen you drilling in saluting this morning,
and I think you all did well. . . . "

He saw us from his room! I wonder if he noticed me! thought
Private First Class Tanaka, and his heart beat a little faster.

He said we did well. Maybe I was not as bad as I thought,
Miki told himself, and he felt greatly relieved.

I wish he would end soon and let us out quickly, grumbled
Takeo to himself.

The Company Commander's address continued for a quarter
of an hour, while the soldiers squirmed and fretted invisibly in
line. " . . . Don't forget that feeling when you left home for the
front . . . when you were sent off by your dear ones, waving
their flags and cheering for you. I know if you remember that
feeling, you cannot commit any mistakes."

The Warrant Officer, one of whose main duties was to manage the affairs of personnel, followed the Company Commander
when he was finished and carefully repeated the instructions on
the leave-taking, which had been issued together with the order-
of-the-day during roll-call the previous night. The soldiers were
to return by five-thirty that afternoon, but, to be safe, they
should enter the post gate at four-thirty. The soldiers should
not enter certain restricted areas of the city, which were chiefly
the native sectors, and they would be safe if they spent their
time in the district inhabited by their fellow countrymen. They
must not drink unboiled water, and they should behave themselves before the natives. There was a long list of minute instructions, and the Warrant Officer took another quarter of an
hour reciting them. When he was finally finished, Takeo took a
hasty look at his wrist watch and noticed that the time was
already past eleven o'clock.

The Company Commander finally gave the welcome order, "Dismissed!"

"Salute!" the soldiers cheerfully answered in unison, and they saluted their officers smartly. No longer were their hands down from their salutes than they were off for the gate and precious liberty — for half a day, at least. Some even started running, though the majority pretended nonchalance and restrained themselves from this undignified show of haste.

As Takeo hurried along with the crowd, his heart beating double-time faster than his footsteps, Hosaka came beside him and asked friendlily, "Want me to take you to a good place?"

"Honorable Senior Soldier, what kind of a place is it?" suspiciously asked Takeo in return, for he had decided not to spend any more than for the barest entertainment that day. He was not forgetting the ox he was going to buy for his aged parents with the money he could save from his meager earnings. He had thought of a cup of coffee and maybe a cake in a tea-shop, and, after shopping for Kan's letter pad and cake, he had planned to spend the rest of the day strolling in the park.

"Never mind what kind of a place. You fellows don't know this city, do you?" retorted Hosaka with mock haughtiness.

"Yes, we don't know it. We landed here when we first came to the front, but we were not permitted leave," Takeo admitted.

"We know this place well. We were here once before you came — before the last campaign. A man from my home village is running a good place, and I will take you there," Hosaka assured.

"In that case, it is a good place. Please take me there," Takeo answered eagerly now, for he was sure that a visit to a friend's place would not cost anything, and he felt grateful for the friendship shown him by the elder soldier. The latter had singled Takeo out from all the others, since the First-Year-Soldier was also a farmer like him, and he liked the frugal traits of Takeo.

The men of the Hamamoto Company were soon joined by

soldiers from the other companies of the battalion, and the road leading to the main front gate was crowded with the happy, excited men. They looked awkward in their cleanly washed uniforms and with their neatly shaved faces, for they were thoroughly sunburnt and still had everywhere on their persons marks of the grime and sweat of the marches, and even the blood of combat. The marks were in their sharp, glaring eyes, in their rough gait, and in the way the clean uniforms rested unnaturally on their bodies.

"Why don't they let us out earlier? This is one of our few leaves, and they should let us enjoy it," grumbled Takeo to his Senior Soldier.

"If they let us out too early, we will get too drunk and make mistakes," answered Hosaka obligingly.

"Oh, so that is why! I never thought of it. You can't beat an Honorable Senior Soldier!" exclaimed Takeo, and he felt as if he had gained a valuable insight into the minds of his commanding officers.

"Then, it is so that we will not make mistakes that we are forced every day to go through drills and undertake detail duties even after we have come to the city!" continued Takeo, as if the secret had come to him suddenly in a flash of inspiration.

"That is so," answered Hosaka dryly. Takeo had often wondered why they were not given the rest they deserved after their harsh campaign inland but were compelled to exert themselves and maintain their tension even after coming to the city where the reality of battle seemed far away. The soldiers' life here in the city, Takeo had found, was no different from the strict, disciplined life they had known in the training post at home.

When the soldiers approached the gate, Hosaka suddenly warned, "Be careful about your salute. There is the Officer-of-the-Week standing in front of the sentinel house," and jolted Takeo out of his reverie.

When Takeo looked up, he saw, sure enough, the awe-inspiring figure of the Officer-of-the-Week with his red-and-white sash across his chest standing menacingly in front of the sentinel house and hostilely eyeing the soldiers passing out of the gate before him. The soldiers were saluting smartly as they came in front of him, and the officer returned the salute only occasionally, for he seemed intent on catching every movement of the soldiers passing before him.

They all knew the officer and feared him. He was a young Lieutenant who had only recently come to Battalion Headquarters, but he had made himself quickly known to the soldiers by his severe disciplinary conduct. He especially seemed to relish slapping soldiers who failed to salute him, and the word had gone around quickly among the soldiers, the way it had of doing in a post, to be specially careful of the "new Lieutenant at Battalion Headquarters." They said he was a graduate of the proud Military Academy. He now stood with one hand on the hilt of his long sword and the other hand behind his back, glaring coldly at the saluting soldiers.

Takeo approached the point where everybody was starting his salute and turned his body smartly to the proper angle and was about to raise his hand to his cap when the officer suddenly shouted, "Hey!" His voice exploded like the crack of a gun, and the Lieutenant dashed forward from his proud position in front of the sentinel house, his sword swinging wildly from his hip. Takeo halted frozen in his track when he saw the officer rushing toward him, but felt a great relief when the officer ran past him and halted in front of a soldier marching a little ahead of him.

Without a word, the Lieutenant swung his arm and slapped the soldier soundly on the side of his head. The soldier was an old private and unmistakably a Reserve. The officer's slap sent his cap flying to the ground, and he bent over to pick it up. The officer struck another blow, this time a heavier one, which sent the soldier down on his seat.

"Where is there a fool who will stoop over when there is an

officer in front of him! Get up!" the Lieutenant shouted, and he was fuming with anger.

The private dazedly got to his feet. Bang, bang! He got two more in quick succession on both sides of his face, which was now a flaming red.

"When you were passing by in front of me, you had a cigarette hidden in your left hand, did you not?" shouted the Lieutenant, and he pointed the tip of his boot at a still smoldering cigarette butt lying guiltily on the road beside the soldier.

"Yes, sir," miserably replied the private.

"You, do you think it is proper to salute with a cigarette in your hand?" demanded the officer, who had assumed the haughty position of a moment ago, with one hand on his sword hilt and the other behind his back.

"No, sir," the soldier answered, now stiffly at attention.

"Do you think it is proper for a soldier of the Empire to make such a salute?" continued the officer. His words came out crisply like the crack of a machine gun.

"No, sir," the soldier replied.

"Be careful from now on," the officer said, his voice now low and controlled, as if he had already forgotten his burning anger and the slapping.

"Yes, sir," the soldier replied obediently, and the Lieutenant turned to return to his station in front of the sentinel house. The long column of soldiers approaching the gate had halted completely while the officer raged savagely at the unfortunate Reserve, but now the men made ready to resume their dangerous march out of the gate when they saw the officer was finished, and those soldiers who had been smoking threw their cigarettes away quickly and ground them well under their heels.

Before the Lieutenant reached his post, however, the loud honk of an automobile horn sounded up the road, and the soldiers began making way for a large, brown-colored limousine leisurely making its way toward the gate. The soldiers shouted, "Salute!" as the automobile passed them and saluted respectfully from both sides of the road, for the vehicle was flying the red flag of the Battalion Commander before it.

When the Lieutenant noticed the automobile, he turned himself once again into a concentrated whirlwind of action. "Sentinels, to Guard of Honor!" he shouted to the sentinels in the sentinel house. The men, who had been well trained for occasions like this, dashed out of the house with their rifles and quickly formed in line beside the Lieutenant outside.

The Lieutenant drew his glittering sword from its scabbard and, as the automobile approached, called, "Present arms! Eyes right!" The ringing voice of the young officer drowned the sound of the passing automobile for an instant, and the officer, flourishing his sword dramatically to his side, turned his eyes respectfully to his Commander inside the automobile, while the soldiers raised their rifles in unison in salute and followed the automobile also with their gaze as they were required to do. It was an impressive scene, and the soldiers standing around on their way out of the gate felt a palpitating thrill in the occasion as they, too, saluted with their empty hands.

Takeo, saluting stiffly near the gate, got a fleeting glimpse of his Battalion Commander seated comfortably in the back seat of his automobile. The rotund, well-fed face of the stout officer was expressionless as it stared straight ahead, as if oblivious to all the commotion around him. His hand, however, was weakly raised to the brim of his cap in token of salute.

When the car left the gate and everybody recovered from their salute, Takeo lost all the impression of excitement he had known while saluting and felt an oppressive vacuum in the atmosphere about him. It was as if a hurricane had just passed, leaving everybody in a daze. This feeling prevailed for the minutest infinitesimal instant, and Takeo would not have noticed it except for the fact that he could not sense the atmosphere of excited anticipation that was there among the soldiers only a moment ago, when they started once again moving toward the gate. The past swift succession of events had wrought a sudden change in that mutual interlacing of emotions which followed these men who lived so closely together, wherever they went, to form an atmosphere which they could mutually feel and understand.

The new atmosphere was a depressing and less cheerful one. Takeo heard it in the subdued voices, in the slower shuffling of the shoes; he could see it in the laxer shoulders, in the duller light in the eyes; he could almost smell it in the air — the strong, fresh tang of the healthy perspiring bodies of a moment ago was now more dissipated, and there was an imperceptible something sour in the air. Of course, Takeo did not sense all these changes with his wide-awake outer consciousness as one senses a drama on a stage, but the changes registered on his inner self inexorably and irresistibly and made him feel depressed and reluctant. The sight of the beating and the fleeting glimpse he had caught of his Battalion Commander, sitting so smugly and comfortably in his automobile, had aroused an insistent consciousness of his own insignificant self. He felt futile and forlorn, and the excitement of taking a leave he had felt only until now was no longer there.

As he saluted the Lieutenant, Takeo no longer felt the tension and fear, mingled with respect, which he had felt when he had started to salute the officer a while back, before the latter had interrupted him with his sudden outburst of rage. Takeo did not care any more whether he was saluting properly or not and went through his motions mechanically as he had been taught in repeated drills. It was an audacious feeling, but Takeo felt perfectly at ease, since he was conscious that all the other soldiers were feeling the same as he did, more or less. If the Lieutenant, who kept glaring as menacingly as ever at them had beaten him then, Takeo would have taken the beating with the stoicism he was feeling at that moment.

The Lieutenant was too deeply occupied in a happy reflection, however, to have noticed any little flaws in the many soldiers saluting and passing him, and Takeo and his friends got safely through the gate after showing their passes to the sentinel at guard there.

The Lieutenant was deeply lost in thought. I wonder if the Honorable Battalion Commander saw me put some spirit into that soldier. I hope he did. He is a graduate of the Military Academy, too — he will surely understand . . . he was telling himself.

泰
安

CHAPTER 10

"THIS IS a good place, didn't I tell you?" said Hosaka boastfully and sank down deeper in his plush armchair.

"Honorable Senior Soldier, you certainly know a good place," agreed Takeo in a subdued tone of wonder and respect, and he looked marvelingly about him.

They were in a clean western-style room which was half office and half guest room. All the wooden furniture in it was beautifully lacquered and polished. They were seated in soft armchairs, and they could see expensive-looking scrolls and pictures hanging on the walls. At one corner was a business desk with a stack of books on it.

"This is the master's private office," said Hosaka. "Too bad he isn't here."

They had been told that the master was out and probably would not be back all day, but the mistress of the house had been in. She had immediately invited them into this room and told them that lunch would be served right away.

"But the mistress comes from the same village, too, doesn't she?" asked Takeo, while he tried to make out the pattern of the colored glass in the window before him.

"Sure, she does. We were all friends since childhood days," answered Hosaka. "But if the master were here, we would get much better service."

"This is enough," assured Takeo.

The door opened and the mistress came in carrying a tray loaded with the familiar porcelain *sake*-liquor containers and cups. She was followed by a native boy with a tray full of the usual delicacies which go with *sake* — raw fish, fried shrimp, sweet fried eggs and others which the men had not seen, let alone tasted, for a long time.

"I am sorry I cannot talk leisurely with you," apologized the mistress, who was about Hosaka's age and looked like a very efficient woman, as she put down her tray before the men.

"O-Fumi-san must have a hard time," said Hosaka to the hostess.

"Really, it is a hard time. You saw how it was when you came in. Our house is full of soldiers from morning till night. We are specially crowded today, because it is Sunday, but on other days, too, many customers come, and I have a hard time."

She said this almost in one breath, pausing only to pour the *sake* into the tiny cups she had offered the soldiers. She was dressed in a brilliant-colored kimono and had a loud make-up on her face, which went well with her, for she was of that age in a woman's life when people said, "The fat is on her."

"But you must not know what to do with the money you earn," laughingly joked Hosaka.

"You are joking! If you have fifteen girls, the money which comes in the right hand goes out by the left hand. If you do business with living things as our 'store' is doing, plenty of all kinds of expenses come up, you know, Mr. Hosaka," the woman exclaimed loudly.

Hosaka drank his cup dry and offered it to the mistress as etiquette demanded, and filled it full of the hot wine. The mistress sat down in a seat beside Hosaka and graciously accepted the cup.

"Really, it is pleasant to see you again! It is good that you are well. They say many were killed in the Suchow campaign. Mr. Hosaka, you must be careful. You have a wife and children, you know," she said and returned the cup and poured into it.

"I'm all right. I have a token from the village shrine. Isn't that right, Yamamoto?" asked Hosaka turning toward Takeo, who was listening politely.

"We are all right," answered Takeo modestly.

The unpleasant incident at the sentinel gate of their post a little while back was completely forgotten. In fact, Takeo could almost forget that he was a soldier in the army at the front. Hosaka was doing better in this way, for his face began to turn a cheerful red with each gulp from his tiny cup. He now took off his coat and hung it on the back of his chair.

"Say, Yamamoto, take off yours, too," he said.

"Shall I take it off?" Takeo hesitated, but removed his coat and followed the elder soldier's example and hung it on the back of his chair.

"I once thought of marrying you, O-Fumi-san," said Hosaka.

"Look at you joking! Mr. Hosaka never even gave a look to me," she scolded mockingly as she accepted the cup offered her by Takeo.

"But you were lucky to marry a man like Tetsuo-san. If you had married one like me, you would have had to struggle all your life," said Hosaka.

"This good fortune is possible all because of you soldiers. Because we have you soldiers, we can do business like this and can live in comfort in a foreign land," answered the mistress.

Just then, a girl's high, urgent voice could be heard calling from outside, "Mistress! Mistress!"

The mistress quickly got up and made for the door, saying hurriedly as she did, "Excuse me. A soldier is again mistreating one of my girls. What a nuisance!"

She was about to close the door, but she thrust her head in through the half-closed door and said, "Take it easy, please. If you want anything, just clap your hands. I will get the boy to bring more *sake*," and she was gone.

"She is a busy woman, isn't she? She was like that from the time she was a child," Hosaka said.

"But she has to be like that, or they wouldn't be able to do a business like this," said Takeo.

"That is so. She is, to be sure, the mistress of a prostitution house. . . . But they surely did succeed. Why, they were but poor farmers in the village. But they did well to come with the army to this continent."

"How could one start a business like this?"

"The master of this house was also a soldier at the start of the war. But he was the orderly to the Commander, and he seemed to have caught the old man's favor. He got wounded in the leg and was sent home, but came back soon with a bunch of girls to start this business. It was all the 'pull' of the Commander."

"An orderly is always lucky."

"The master of this house is a hard worker."

Somebody was knocking at the door, and when Hosaka answered, the native boy who had come previously with the food now opened the door quietly and entered with a tray holding more steaming *sake* containers. He set the new containers down and picked up the empty ones and left quietly.

Before he left, Hosaka said, "Bring us more raw fish the next time."

"The girls have some courage to come all the way here to work," said Takeo, pouring steaming *sake* from the containers which had just been placed before them.

"They must make lots of money."

"Surely, they must earn plenty . . . but they have debts to pay. . . . "

"How do they pay their debts? I mean, what kind of contract are they working under?"

"Because her home is poor, the girl's father sells her body. With the money he receives, he pays his debts. The girl works for one year, or two years, or three years, or ten years — I don't know — she works through the period she has promised."

"Then, she must give all the money she earns to her master?"

The door was opened brusquely and the mistress of the house

came bustling in, muttering, "That is really a no-good soldier. He is drunk, and he wants to take my girl out."

"There must be very bad ones among the soldiers," sympathized Hosaka.

"There was one who tried to cut one of my girls with his bayonet not so long ago," said the mistress, picking up the container and pouring into the two soldiers' cups.

Hosaka emptied his cup and handed it to the mistress.

"This soldier here wants to know if your girls get paid?" Hosaka asked.

"Surely! What did you think?" the mistress answered. She drank her cup empty and returned it to Hosaka.

"I thought if you paid the money to buy the body, you did not have to pay until the girl's time was up," said Hosaka.

"There are places like that, but at our place we give them ten per cent, besides feeding and clothing them. When they are sick, we will have to look after them; this is a difficult business."

"Are there girls who take ten customers a day?" asked Takeo, offering his cup to the mistress.

"The most was a girl who took fifty in a night and day," said the mistress returning the cup.

"Fifty?" Hosaka and Takeo repeated in amazement.

"Wait a minute, fifty customers means one hundred twenty-five yen and ten per cent will be twelve-yen-fifty. That's more than I make a month," said Hosaka.

"Really, I hear the soldier's pay is small. How much do you get paid?" asked the mistress.

"We get eight-yen-eighty a month," answered Hosaka.

"Really, that is a pity," said the mistress in mock sympathy, although she had known all along, since most of her customers were soldiers.

"And so if we pay two-yen-fifty for a girl, it is very painful," observed Hosaka with a shrewd light in his eyes.

"Well, are you telling me to make it cheaper? It isn't like you to say such a thing! Don't worry, I will lend my girls free to you any time. And I will tell your wife about it," chided the mistress and added, "How is your wife?"

"She says she is well in her letter. She is probably waiting with the lid on," meaningfully answered Hosaka.

"A wife like yours will never be unfaithful. She is too good for you," said the mistress and, turning to Takeo, said, "This man has a daughter who can almost be your wife. You are not married, are you?"

"No. I am still to be married. That is why I can play a great deal," answered Takeo, and he was surprised at his boldness, though the *sake* was beginning to have its effect on him, and he felt as if he were floating in his chair.

"We told the boy a little while ago to bring us some raw fish, but he hasn't come yet," said Hosaka.

"What a no-good boy!" said the mistress and clapped her hands loudly.

"Yes," a voice answered in the distance, and soon the native boy appeared with more dishes of raw fish.

"You should bring the things more quickly," she scolded in a high voice.

"Yes," the boy answered meekly and quietly went out.

"These natives are slow moving. They surely get you mad," said the woman, who was also showing the effect of the cups which the soldiers were repeatedly offering her.

"But you are lucky the girls work hard for you," said Hosaka. "If a girl takes fifty customers, she must earn a lot for you."

"That is so. On a day like this, they will take thirty or forty each."

"It's a wonder their bodies can stand it!"

"Their bodies are their tools, and so they take good care of themselves. They are also our fortune, so we take good care, too. We give them good things to eat. They are doing heavy labor, you know."

"But some girls must become sick sometimes."

"There isn't a single sick girl in my place, let me tell you!

You can feel safe when you come here. We have them take the best care," the woman boasted.

"Now that I have heard it, I feel safe," said Hosaka.

"Why, this old man, you don't mean to say you want to play here?" the woman ejaculated in mock astonishment.

"No, at least not now," protested Hosaka, "But this fellow — he says he has never once had it out of him since coming to the front. It is pitiful, so see that you do something for him."

"Never mind the other fellow. You want to play yourself, don't you?" the woman leered at Hosaka.

"Really . . . I am all right . . . Right now . . . I want to drink a little more and talk with you about old days," stammered Hosaka guiltily.

"Look at this fellow! He still wants to play afterward. I am going to tell your wife, really."

"I can't help it. I am human."

"Then I will find a good girl for this friend of yours. There are a great many soldiers today, so you won't probably be able to play for long, but you must not mind, for this is war, you know," said the mistress and went out.

She was soon back and beckoned to Takeo. "Come quickly. I found a good one for you," she announced.

Takeo put on his coat and, apologizing in the proper manner, "Excuse me for going first," followed the mistress down the hall.

The hallway was crowded on both sides with long lines of soldiers awaiting their turns in front of doors carrying the names of the girls inside. Some stood almost at attention, but nearly all leaned comfortably against the wall. Some were smoking, others reading, but most remained silent to stare blankly about them. There were a few drunkards roaming the hall and shouting obscenely at the closed doors. A door which Takeo passed as he followed the mistress down the hall opened slightly, and a soldier slipped out of it, hurriedly pulling up and buttoning his trousers. The soldier first in the line patiently waiting before the door went in, but before the door was closed, Takeo caught the smell of cheap perfume and cosmetics coming out of the room.

The mistress took Takeo almost halfway down the hall, and it was a long one, for this house had been a large warehouse once. The woman stopped in front of a door on which was the name *Mariko*. A long line of soldiers was also waiting before it.

She opened the door and said, "Here, get in," and almost shoved Takeo inside.

The soldier at the head of the line grumbled, "Isn't it my turn now?"

Takeo slipped in hurriedly and could hear the mistress answering, "This soldier was waiting from a long time ago."

"Old hag! . . . Let him line up too . . . " Takeo could hear the soldiers in line shouting, and he shut the door behind him in haste.

The room was a little, compact affair with a bed at one end and a desk with a mirror on it. There were two chairs, and ample light filtered in from a large shaded window beyond the the bed. Though a few pictures hung on the wall, the room looked bare, and the coarse unpainted walls and ceiling would have seemed dirty except that the timber was still new. There was a disinfectant container on the wall from which hung a prophylactic tube over a basin, and Takeo felt much assured by the sight of these implements of sanitation.

The girl who sat on the bed, staring curiously at Takeo, had on a single thin pink silk kimono — the kind that was ordinarily worn underneath the thick outer garment. A wide red *obi* was around her waist. Takeo noticed that she was a tall, slender girl and was happy that she had not the usual exaggerated make-up on her face. There was just the slightest trace of rouge and lipstick on her cheeks and lips, and her face was fairer than that of any girl he had known. Although her face was not really what Takeo would have called beautiful, her eyes were intelligent and cheerful. Her ample dark hair was bound tightly at the nape of her neck to accentuate the slender gracefulness of her face.

Takeo felt a strong wave of excitement surge through his body. His heart, which had been beating fast enough already because of the *sake* he had drunk, now began to beat doubly louder and faster.

I want to become friends with her, Takeo thought as he stared back at the girl on the bed, for she looked naïve and sincere, unlike anything he had pictured of girls in her trade and not much different from any of the girls he had known in his village at home. Only this one looked much prettier, and he had never been so close to one so pretty before in his life.

"What are you doing? Come quickly," the girl said coaxingly, and the voice, too, sounded shy and restrained like that of any proper girl of an ordinary home.

Forgotten was the dust and grime of the march. Forgotten, the cold fear and ugly savageries of combat. All the slappings and endless oppressions of military life, the humiliations, sorrows, sufferings, and little jealousies were forgotten in the excitement of this single concentrated moment of meeting with a girl who seemed so amply to represent the softness and beauty of femininity he dreamed of so often. The girl seemed to Takeo to be the very antithesis of all that was hateful and ugly in war, from which he had so fervently hoped to find escape today. Here in this bare room, he had found the ideal opportunity of escape.

"Your name is Mariko, isn't it?" Takeo said as he approached the girl.

"That is so. Are you a relative of the mistress?" the girl asked in return.

"No. A friend who came from the same village as the master and mistress brought me here," Takeo answered and he sat down beside the girl.

"Come, let us sleep," the girl said and raised her legs to stretch out on the bed.

Takeo stopped her and, sitting down beside her, said, "Let us talk a little. We soldiers are lonely."

"Well, look at this soldier! There are so many of your friends lined up and waiting, and what do you want to take your time for?"

"Let them wait a little."

"You may say so, but they won't let you. . . . You can still talk lying down, you know."

"What a nuisance!" Takeo said and began to unroll his puttees.

"Well, look at this soldier! He is unrolling his puttees! You have no time like that!" exclaimed the girl in genuine amazement.

"What! Do we do it with our trousers on?" Now Takeo was the amazed one.

"That is so. If all took their trousers off, there wouldn't be any time to do it."

"You can't help it," grumbled Takeo and began letting his trousers down.

The soldier outside knocked roughly on the door and shouted, "Aren't you over yet?"

"What a nuisance!" said the girl and she turned over on the bed and pulled Takeo beside her.

Takeo lay down beside the girl with his shoes and trousers and everything on. Still, the slender figure which he held in his arms felt warm and soft against his body, and he was careful not to press it too hard.

When it was all over, the girl hung on to Takeo's neck and murmured, "You are just like my sweetheart at home."

"Where are you from?" Takeo asked.

"Kyushu," the girl answered and Takeo did not trouble to ask further, but, instead, he got up and began buttoning his trousers.

"Come again, please," the girl said.

"Yes, I will come again. If not next Sunday, the following one," promised Takeo.

Then he opened the flap of his breast pocket and took out the little cloth doll he had received in his gift package that morning. "Let me give you this in remembrance," he said holding it out to the girl.

The girl took it and said, "Thank you."

"Don't you have a picture?" Takeo asked.

"I have one," the girl answered and pulled a drawer of the desk. She took out a picture of herself dressed in kimono and holding a parasol and handed it to Takeo.

"Thank you," Takeo said and carefully put it into his breast pocket.

"Come again, won't you? Really, you must. I will be waiting for you," the girl said.

"Yes, I will. Be careful of your body."

Takeo gave the girl's hand a last squeeze and opened the door. The soldier standing outside the door almost growled, "You surely took your time," as he brushed past Takeo and entered the room. Though an ordinary private, he looked old enough to be a Senior Soldier, and Takeo quietly slipped past him out of the door.

"Let me take my time, too," Takeo could hear the soldier demanding gruffly inside before the door closed behind him.

He hurried down the hall toward the exit with his head held down, for he wanted to get out as quickly as possible to be by himself with the memory of his pleasant experience. He did not want to lose the feeling of contented elation which filled his body then. He did not care if anybody he knew was among the numerous soldiers lined along both sides of the hall, and he kept his eyes to the floor.

"Hey!" a voice shouted from a line of soldiers beside a door he was passing.

"Yes, sir!" Takeo said and instinctively stopped at attention and looked up at the soldier who had called him. It was a Private First Class who glared at him from the line and demanded in an ominously threatening tone, "You are a First-Year-Soldier, aren't you?"

"Yes, sir!" stammered Takeo, now completely awakened from his trance and returning to his obedient military self again.

"Then why don't you salute?" the Private First Class took a menacing step forward.

"Yes, sir!" Takeo answered and saluted hastily.

The Private First Class returned the salute haughtily and said curtly, "That is all!"

"Yes, sir!" Takeo answered and turned quickly toward the door. He hurried down the hall as fast as he could, but this time was careful to salute every superior he met on the way. Some returned the salute in the proper fashion, but others just kept staring curiously at him as if wondering why anyone should want to salute in a place like this. Takeo felt grateful for the latter, but could not tell them apart from the strict ones and so was careful to salute them all.

Near the end of the hall, when Takeo was just about to gain the exit to the road outside, he heard a familiar voice calling, "Hey, Yamamoto!"

He stopped rigidly and, turning, answered from habit, "Yes, sir!"

It was Private First Class Tanaka calling from inside a spacious waiting room, whose wide doors were open, showing another large group of soldiers sitting on benches against the walls or just standing around and smoking. These were not as glum as the other groups waiting patiently in the hallway, for they chatted freely among each other, and laughed raucously from time to time.

Private First Class Tanaka was standing near the door and, after returning Takeo's salute, said, "Are you already through?"

Takeo lied bravely, "I did not go in," for it would have been a dangerous breach of etiquette to have admitted that he had had his fun ahead of the Honorable Private First Class.

"Then why are you leaving?" the Private First Class asked suspiciously.

"I planned to go in, but they are too crowded, and so I am

going elsewhere," answered Takeo, careful not to reveal the secret of Hosaka's presence in the master's room, for he knew the Reserve hated these authoritative Private First Class Regulars strongly.

"They are crowded elsewhere, too. Wait here and we will make a man of you yet," said Tanaka, and, as he laughed loudly, others joined him, too.

These soldiers, waiting in the room here, were either too proud, or too disinterested, or simply too lazy to line up in the hall with the others. They had little hope of satisfying their urge before time to return to their posts, but still they hung on — some just enjoying the thrill of being in a brothel, others hoping that some unforeseen chance would unfold itself soon, and still others waiting to work up enough courage to get in line in the hall with the rest. Many were drunk and didn't know better.

"I am going back to the post," Takeo said and saluted, desperately trying to find a way to get away.

"That is all!" Tanaka said, regaining his usual dignity, and returned the salute smartly.

Takeo almost sighed with relief as he hurried out of the door and stepped into the refreshing light outside. Some drunks began to sing brashly inside. Takeo picked his way up the road toward the main Japanese district. He was careful to salute every superior he met on the way, but his main purpose was to go somewhere where he could be by himself and enjoy the memory of his late pleasant adventure.

He easily decided on the park on the outskirts of the town, where there were many trees and benches under the trees where one usually could be alone if he wished. There was also a Shinto shrine in the park which soldiers were urged by their officers to go to worship on leave-days, and quite a number went, since worshiping meant no more trouble than merely bowing one's head before the shrine, and the walk through the verdant grounds was pleasant. Sometimes women members of the local Japanese patriotic organization turned out, too, to offer tea at stands specially erected for the soldiers. Most of the elder women, like the mistress of the brothel, moreover, were busy on the soldiers' leave-days, and they were prone to be replaced by their daughters, which was all the more satisfactory to the soldiers.

Takeo, however, was not thinking of the tea stands when he climbed the stone steps leading to the shrine, and he kept looking for a secluded spot among the many trees and shrubs covering the compound.

Stopping before the shrine, which was a plain wooden structure standing among tall trees in the regular fashion of shrines at home, he bowed, more from habit than from any urge to worship. A few soldiers were also bowing beside him, and Takeo was dismayed to see a great many soldiers loitering around the grounds.

There was a tea stand to one side where young girls in school uniforms were serving a large crowd of soldiers, who received their tea and cakes and sat on benches nearby to look at the girls over their cups. The girls were cheerful enough as they busily dispensed their free service, laughing and joking at the soldiers, but the latter were mostly stiff and reserved, for the traditional ideal of manhood, they were taught, was reserve, and the soldiers here seemed to be exerting their best efforts to embody this ideal for the sake of the girls. This was a different matter, indeed, from the way the soldiers looked on the native girls, especially during campaigns, or from the way they enjoyed themselves with the shows put on by the donkeys in occupied villages, or the way they carried on in the brothels not so far away. A few soldiers were forward enough to ask for the girls' names and addresses to write them down in their notebooks, so that they could later correspond with them, but the majority merely vied with each other to see who could appear the most indifferent and reserved.

Takeo was in no mood to test his manhood at the tea stand and so walked around to the rear of the shrine. There he saw a *Kempei* (military police), looking overwhelmingly powerful with his holstered pistol, sword, and awe-inspiring red armband, fiercely upbraiding a soldier, who kept meekly bowing his head in apology. There was a small crowd of curious soldiers standing around them, but Takeo did not join them.

Instead, he continued down the slope on the other side, but everywhere he went he met more soldiers, many of whom were higher in rank and had to be saluted. At last, giving up hope of finding a secluded place in the park, he turned toward the business section of the city.

It was not very far away, and he reached it after a short brisk walk. The stores which lined the streets here were built in the same manner as the general run of stores at home — the front completely open and the goods on sale crowded profusely inside as if they would overflow into the streets before them if people didn't hurry up and buy them. There were the barrels of pickles almost out on the walk for passers-by to look into and smell. There was the officious-looking drugstore with the one long counter, just slightly inside the door, showing the usual medicines, contraceptives, and cosmetics, and lorded over by the usual emaciated-looking clerk who peered down blankly at the passers-by from his raised position behind the counter; and the public baths with the thin makeshift curtains before their entrances — one for the men and one for the women — behind which anybody who wanted to could see the bather's plainly in their naked splendor.

Many of these stores catered directly to the soldiers who crowded into the town on leave-days, and these were doing a busy trade, but still many were mere fronts for questionable operations farther inland under protection of the occupation troops. These had no one to wait on, and whoever was in charge remained in the room in the rear, sipping tea, or discussing deals with prospective clients.

When Takeo approached one of the many drinking restaurants which flourished in this part of the city, the door was roughly opened and a group of loudly declaiming soldiers tumbled out of it. One soldier in the center of the group was desperately attempting to re-enter the restaurant, but his friends held him back and led him away. Somebody inside had probably insulted him, and he had to make a show to defend his honor. Soldiers became very sensitive of their honor when they became drunk and such scenes were common enough on leave-days, so that Takeo did not even stop to look at it.

As Takeo passed the restaurant, he could hear the shrill grating voice of a girl singing a patriotic song with her soldier customers inside. He had never been to one of these places since entering the army, for they were not places for a First-Year-Soldier to patronize. He was liable, too, to be beaten up by the older soldiers who, even among each other, felt a strong jealousy and rivalry to gain the favor of the few girls who waited upon them and sat at their tables, even though the most that a soldier, who had to be back in his post by sundown, could expect from any of these girls was a few kind words and maybe permission to correspond.

He passed many other brothels too, most of which in this part of the city were patterned after those at home, so that one had to remove his shoes to enter them. As in the place he had been to, he could see many soldiers loitering patiently in the waiting rooms in the front. Before one of the brothels an old woman, the usual type to be found in all the brothels at home, was sitting outside the entrance, and she called to Takeo "Come in and become a man." Takeo disgustedly passed her by, and the woman sneered behind him, "Well! He is a snob!"

Passing before an establishment whose door was forbiddingly closed and which had a sign in bold classic characters, Takeo could hear, coming out of the windows above his head, the drunken voices of men singing to the accompaniment of the noisy twang of the stringed Samisen.* This was the superior "Geisha house," which only the officers and certain high non-commissioned officers could afford to patronize, though sometimes some soldiers who were lucky in their loot during an inland campaign succeeded in crashing the forbidding barrier. Takeo could not tell, then, the rank of the jolly singers, though

* A waitress's harp.

he thought it was too early in the day for officers, who could stay out all night, to be carrying on in drunken revelry like the men in that establishment. He looked up enviously at the opened windows but could not see inside.

These houses were abundant in the city, and Takeo felt himself yearning for the privacy of their expensive rooms. Everywhere the army went, these houses flourished and *sake* flowed freely to the accompaniment of the Samisen and the lilting songs of the Geisha girls. They were there to help relieve the officers from the strains of combat and to help replenish the confidence of these overburdened men in their own manhood — a manhood which they had been trained to prize as supreme in the world and to defend as precious legacies of an exaggerated history. Takeo listened to the spirited songs and felt the same gnawing loneliness and vacuum which he had felt when the Battalion Commander's automobile had passed him at the sentinel gate of the post in the morning that day.

Takeo entered the first delicatessen he came to and ordered a box of cakes to take back to Kan, as he had promised. The price was high as were the prices of all articles in this city, since the merchants had long ago relinquished their last pretensions of sacrificing patriotism and were all out now to squeeze as much as they could from the army and its helpless members. There was the post exchange, to be sure, where prices were low, but articles were scarce and the quality poor.

Takeo next entered a bookstore and ordered two letter pads, the other article he had promised to buy for Kan, and bought one for himself. He looked at the clock on the wall and saw that the time was four o'clock. There was still an hour and a half before the deadline of five-thirty, but he remembered that the First-Year-Soldiers especially were expected to be in by four-thirty, on the premise that the quicker they returned to the protecting confines of their company, the less chance they had of committing "mistakes." Furthermore, if all the soldiers returned early, it made the work easier for the Officer-of-the-

Week whose duty it was to see that all the soldiers returned at the end of the day.

As Takeo stood vacantly turning the pages of a popular magazine he had picked up from a stand, he began debating within himself whether to return to the post at once or not. For the truth was that he had begun to feel a strong urge to return to the brothel he had visited earlier in the afternoon to meet, even for a few minutes, the girl named Mariko, who had shown such distinct friendship toward him. Takeo very quickly made up his mind and, paying for the magazine, which he carried under his arm along with his other purchases, he retraced his steps toward the converted warehouse which had given him such heavenly pleasure that day.

He did not go by way of the park, for that was a roundabout way, but made straight for his destination through a narrow back alley. It took him over a quarter of an hour, but it was still some time before four-thirty when he arrived at the low painted house. There were soldiers still loitering in the waiting room, though they were not as numerous as when he had left, and soldiers still patiently waited in the hallway beside the doors which remained unfeelingly closed to them.

Takeo hurried down the hall to the rear of the house, where he knew he could find the mistress, but made sure again to salute all the superior-ranking soldiers he met on the way. He was glad to see only a handful of soldiers in front of Mariko's door when he hurried past it on his way to the rear. When he opened the door to the room at the end of the hall, Takeo found the mistress busily supervising the cooking for supper.

"Where is Honorable Senior Soldier Hosaka?" Takeo asked and he tried to hide his real reason for returning.

"He left long ago to go to town," the mistress answered, and Takeo was surprised to notice in her cool, efficient voice not a single trace of the many cups of *sake* she had exchanged with Takeo and his friend not so long ago.

"Is that so? I am disappointed," said Takeo and tried to look as disappointed as he could.

"That was too bad," sympathized the mistress in a motherly tone. "Anyway, why don't you stay around a little longer. Hosaka may come back before he returns to the post."

"No, I must be going. It is time already . . . " Takeo answered and hesitated before he added in as matter-of-fact a tone as he could master, "Can you let me see that girl I had a while ago — Mariko?"

"Is it Mariko you want? Now, a sergeant is with her, and she won't be free for some time. A non-commissioned officer doesn't have to be back until late, isn't it true?" asked the mistress.

"Yes, he can stay out until roll-call, which is at eight-thirty," Takeo could only mumble, for he felt weak all of a sudden.

He had been quite confident that the mistress would be able to arrange it as she had done earlier in the afternoon, and had even hoped that she would be able to let them meet in the privacy of the office where Hosaka and he had dined. Takeo was truly disappointed, and all of a sudden he felt himself struggling hard to hide the mixed feelings of shame, jealousy, frustration, and loneliness which welled uncontrollably in his heart.

He was not succeeding much in keeping his feelings from showing on his face, for the mistress sympathetically added, "Can I help you with some other girl?"

"No, that is all right. I just wanted to give her this magazine she had asked for. It would be all right if you gave it to her for me," Takeo lied and handed the mistress the magazine he had bought at the bookstore, hoping to enjoy it during the few free hours of the drab days which were sure to follow until the next leave-day.

"Give her my regards," Takeo said and hastily departed down the hall. He did not even look at the door of Mariko's room this time when he passed it but was still careful to salute all the superiors he met.

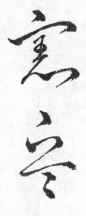

CHAPTER 11

First-Year-Soldier Private Shunzo Miki had fallen in beside Reserve Private Aoki, the former road laborer, when the soldiers had happily walked out of the post on leave that day.

"Honorable Senior Soldier, please take me to a good place," Miki had said, ambling up to Aoki.

"Surely. I will take you to a good place," Aoki had gladly agreed, for he had always liked this blunt country lad.

They made a good pair, these two husky, muscular soldiers — one a farmer's lad and the other a heavy laborer. Miki was taller than the elder soldier, though the latter was broader in the shoulders, and his face was rugged like a chiseled-out piece of rock. But Miki was the one who caught people's eyes, for he was tall for his race of short men.

"Do you drink much?" asked Aoki.

"No, I can hardly drink at all," confessed Miki.

"Good. I do not drink, either. Let's go to a brothel first," suggested Aoki and offered the younger soldier a cigarette.

"I have never been to a brothel yet," said Miki, accepting the cigarette and smiling sheepishly.

"What? You have never been to a brothel! Not even at home!" asked Aoki in astonishment as he stopped to light his cigarette and Miki's.

Miki took a puff and blushed noticeably and confessed, "I was too poor to go to brothels at home."

158

"Why, I started going to brothels from the time I was eighteen," Aoki said.

They were now shuffling along leisurely and were being passed by the main stream of the excited soldiers, most of whom hurried with short quick steps as if they already imagined themselves racing against the limited time allotted them for their leave that day.

"Then, you don't mean to say you don't know a woman at all?" Aoki, now looking genuinely surprised, halted completely and turned toward Miki, as if this thought had struck him all of a sudden.

Miki blushed and hesitated, then mumbled, "I don't know a woman at all."

"Was that it? You are pitiful. I must let you know the taste of a woman quickly," said Aoki laughingly and resumed the walk, now quickening his pace a little.

"I am afraid of sickness," said Miki.

"You can't help sickness. If you contract it, it's your bad luck. It is like being hit by a bullet."

"Can't you tell a sick girl?"

"You can't tell. But if you urinate good and hard afterward, you are safe most of the time."

"I am a little worried somehow."

"Look at you, a big fellow! If you were to be hit by a bullet and die tomorrow, that's all there is to it."

"That is what I think. That is why I think if I don't try it once, I will be reluctant to die."

"That is so. Anyway, I will make a man of you today."

They went first to the brothel where Hosaka and Takeo were receiving their royal treatment unknown to their friends in a special room in the back and, finding it already full of waiting soldiers, went on to the other houses in the main district. They found the others also overcrowded and left them all in disgust to enter a restaurant to eat their lunch.

"Really, I get disgusted," Aoki said over his bowl of rice. "If only for a single day, why can't they let a soldier have fun at leisure?"

"For this crowd, it will be a big task," said Miki, picking up his chopsticks.

"They should build larger and more brothels. There should be any number of girls at home who would be willing to come over. Or they can use Koreans and native girls."

"In the first place, they should not build any brothels. Then we won't want to go at all. We want to go, because they are there," observed Miki.

"That is impossible. If there were no brothels, the native girls would be raped, and there would be plenty of trouble. It is human nature; you can't help it," said Aoki.

"A fellow like me doesn't feel it at all."

"That is so. All the soldiers are not like you."

"Then you mean to say, you can't bear to wait at all!"

"We can wait for a short time but not for long."

"Then how about your wives?" Miki poured some hot tea into the elder soldier's cup from the kettle which stood conveniently on their table.

"Women are different. Women can bear to wait. My wife is like a log. She doesn't think anything of it at all," the Reserve answered nonchalantly.

Aoki sipped his tea and looked dreamily ahead of him, as if his last statement had awakened a deeper contemplation than he had meant for it. They quickly dispatched their meager lunch, which had consisted of a bowl of rice, a piece of fish, and a few slices of pickles. When the waitress came to take the dishes away, Aoki ordered coffee for the two. Coffee was something he had learned to like in the cities, and he always ordered it after a meal wherever it was served.

"What time do you have?" Aoki asked Miki.

The latter looked at his wrist watch and answered, "Twelve-thirty."

Aoki compared it with the clock on the wall and, finding they matched, exclaimed, "Good! It is still early."

The waitress brought the coffee, and they began sipping it.

"Let's go to a native brothel," Aoki suggested suddenly.

"Aren't they forbidden?" asked Miki, surprised.

"They are forbidden, but if you stick around here, you won't get anywhere."

"But if you are caught by the *Kempei*, won't it be bad?"

"Yes, it will be bad — *if you are caught.* . . . If you are scared, you don't have to come."

"No, I am not scared. But is it all right?"

"It is all right. I know all the streets and alleys. I've been to them often. . . . But you must stick close to me."

"It should be safe to be with Honorable Senior Soldier, but don't leave me in the native sector. I will be lost."

"If we are discovered by the *Kempei*, don't lose your head. Keep close to me and run. We can easily run away from him."

"Don't the *Kempei* come to the brothels?"

"If they come, I will have the old woman let us know. There is a back door which the *Kempei* don't know."

"It sounds safe. Let us go."

Miki pushed back his chair. Aoki paid for the meal a price which was exorbitant, and the two left the restaurant and took a narrow back alley which ran between the backyards of their compatriots' stores and into the native sector. Aoki stopped at every corner to look sharply before crossing. He followed the shadows of the narrow winding streets carefully and seemed to be well versed with the layout of this district, as he had boasted to Miki. There were no soldiers here, and the many natives who passed them and whom they passed looked at them curiously. Miki felt an eery sensation that some native might take a shot at him from the back and was glad that they had their bayonets with them at least. They spoke not a word as they went furtively down the crowded streets like two escaping convicts.

They soon came to a large, pretentious arched gate and Aoki pulled Miki in behind him. They found themselves standing in a wide courtyard enclosed on all sides but the entrance by an elaborate two-storied building, with balconies running along the whole front on both floors. Numerous native girls were lounging on the balconies or leaning from the rails when the soldiers entered. At the sight of the strangers, the girls began to shout in glee and to call teasingly. Aoki, plainly no stranger here, made straight for a room directly right of the entrance and next to the floor landing of a stairway leading up to the second floor. Entering it, he hurriedly closed the door after Miki, who was staying close to him as instructed.

To the girl who came inquiringly, Aoki said, "*Muchin, muchin*" (which means "Mother" in the native dialect). He was probably asking for the old lady who made the arrangements, thought Miki. An old kindly looking woman, sure enough, soon came, who seemed to recognize Aoki, and greeted him happily.

"*Shin-san, Shin-san*," she greeted him.

Aoki gave her a five-yen note and asked her, "*Kempei* — are they here?" using the few words of the native dialect that he knew to ask if the dreaded *Kempei* were there. He also pointed at his arm where the *Kempei*'s armband would be to emphasize the meaning of his question.

"*Kempei* — they are not," assured the old woman and shook her head vigorously.

"Girl — one, me — one, my friend — good?" Aoki asked.

"Good, good," the old woman answered, smiling profusely and nodding her head now in assent.

"*Kempei* come — you tell us — we go quickly," Aoki said and made the motion of running.

"Sure, sure," the old woman assured and laughed merrily.

Aoki turned toward Miki, who had been a respectful listener to this seemingly brilliant negotiation of his senior comrade, and said, "Be sure to come with me."

"I will be all right," smilingly answered Miki, who had been highly assured by the extremely friendly attitude of the girls when they had entered the courtyard and especially by the motherly tone of the old woman.

Aoki and Miki now followed the old woman out of the room and began climbing the stairs amid the gleeful shouting and clapping of the many girls, who were all idle at this early hour of the day. Miki smiled back good-naturedly at them and thought, surely, he had never seen such pretty girls before. They seemed much prettier, he thought, than the girls of his own race, and he liked their tight-fitting gowns which accentuated the graceful lines of their bodies so enticingly. He had never seen such fair faces, he thought, and decided that any one of them would be worthy of receiving his virginity.

When they reached the top of the stairs, they turned to proceed down the balcony which extended along the whole length of the building's face. But a slender girl, standing in front of the first room facing the balcony, got hold of Miki's arm and began pulling him persistently.

"Come, come," she said in a voice which Miki thought was the most musical and feminine voice he had ever heard in his life. Miki, who had never been pulled by a woman before in his life, let alone liked overmuch by one, yielded easily and was halfway inside the doorway when Aoki turned around to notice him.

"It's no good," Aoki said nervously. "That room is dangerous."

Miki looked at the almost pleading face of the girl who was pulling him and thought it was just the kind of face he liked. He felt that he must touch its soft fair surface with his hands and caress it and resisted only weakly. "It's all right. They'll let me know if the *Kempei* comes," Miki now said confidently, as if he was the one who knew all about it.

Aoki was getting nervous at the continued shouting and cheering of the other girls, as they watched the little drama on the balcony, and he decided not to expose himself any further. He hastily instructed his friend, "If the *Kempei* comes, come quickly to my room at the end of this lobby. There's a secret door leading out of the building from there. Don't forget . . . at the end of this lobby," Aoki repeated and turned and hurried down the balcony to the room at the end. Miki had surrendered completely to the wiles of his captor and could only smile back helplessly at his elder friend, and when the latter had turned to go, allowed himself to be pulled into the room at the top of the stairs, and the door was shut after him.

The girls, who saw the large figure of Miki finally over-powered by their slender mate, clapped and cheered loudly as if they had seen the end to a drama enacted on a stage. And they kept calling noisily at Aoki until the latter, too, disappeared in the room with the secret exit at the end of the lobby.

Miki found himself in a small, very shabby-looking room. The bedding was soiled, and the furniture was just the conventional shaky wooden bed, bare unpainted stand, and old stool he had seen so often in the peasants' huts farther inland. A brave effort had been made to decorate the walls, which were plastered with newspaper pages carrying colorful advertisements and pictures. This impoverished appearance of the interior contrasted strongly with the lively, cheerful atmosphere exuded by the pretty girl who sat on the bed and pulled Miki down beside her. Though her liveliness and coquettishness had been the things about her which had impressed Miki the most when he entered the room, a close look showed that the dress she was wearing was frayed in spots and that she needed a bath more than anything. A premo-nition of contracting sickness flashed through his mind, but it lasted only for the minutest instant, and he was soon interested solely in the lively, disarming personality of the girl.

She unbuttoned the flap of Miki's breast pocket and pulled out his purse, which she had very accurately guessed to be there from the bulge that it made. Miki took it back good-naturedly, though a little taken aback at the girl's forwardness.

"How much?" he asked in the native tongue, for they were some of the few native words he knew.

The girl raised her hand, stretching the five fingers meaning-fully, and smiled most attractively. Miki took a five-yen note and gave it to her.

The girl pulled at his sleeve and pleaded coaxingly, almost

like a child, "One more, one more," and shook a finger vigorously before Miki's face.

Miki grinned cheerfully and, drawing out another five-yen note from his purse, gave it to the girl, though he knew even five yen was too much according to local practice. What did he care, he thought, he had almost half a year's wages in back pay, covering nearly the entire period they had been campaigning in the inland. . . . He also took out a picture of his family at home and showed it to the girl.

"Father . . . Mother . . . Brothers . . . Sisters . . ." he said pointing them out respectively on the picture.

The girl took the picture in her hands and said "Oh" each time Miki pointed to a member of his family, and the exclamation sent a pleasant feeling down his spine. She said it softly and wistfully and added, when Miki had ended, "I have no father and mother." Her eyes were sensitive and restrained, though they sparkled with an intense light, and the lines of her face looked as if they were made of vapor — so soft and indistinct, yet graceful, they were.

Miki ran his hands caressingly over her shoulders and breast and, knowing nothing else to say, said, "Good, good."

She smiled in his eyes, and the passive, completely submitting and trusting light he saw in them made Miki forget his own oppressed, inferior status in the army. Here was somebody, at last, who not only fully recognized his existence but permitted him to be master of their relationship. She helped him remove his coat and bayonet; then helped him take off his puttees to roll them into neat balls and placed them on the stool. She helped him remove all his clothes and shoes, then took off her own gown. Then she slipped into bed and called softly "Come, come."

It was then they heard the old woman's voice calling urgently and sharply outside the door. "*Kempei* come!" She repeated her warning several times, and, when the girl answered, left in haste down the lobby.

Miki stood dumbfounded for a moment, for the return to

reality was too sudden, and he had already wandered far into the world of unrestrained make-believe. It took time to recollect his senses.

The girl called, "Hurry! Hurry!" and jumped out of bed and went for Miki's clothes which were folded and piled on the table.

The sudden action of the girl shocked Miki into a full awareness of his own danger. Like one awakened from a deep dream, he began moving dazedly, but an intense fear began to rise in his heart, and he hurried to put on the clothes which the girl shoved into his arms.

He was getting into his trousers when somebody began roughly knocking at the door and shouted imperiously in Japanese, "Open up!"

"Wait," the girl whispered to Miki and slipped into her gown. She advanced toward the door and began protesting vehemently in the native language but did not open the door. Miki saw that she was stalling and, quickly buttoning his trousers, looked around him for a place to hide. Finding none, he waited, hoping that whoever was outside would be convinced by the brave tone of the girl and go away.

But the knocking grew louder and the voice angrier. The girl was now pleading. Miki did not understand what she was saying but could tell by the desperate tone of her voice that she was making a last brave effort to drive away the intruder.

"If you don't open, I'll break down this door," the voice threatened outside.

It was a flimsy door at the most, and Miki knew that anybody could break it down if he wished. Pushing aside the girl, he went and loosened the latch holding the door. The door was flung open roughly, and a very angry-looking *Kempei* Corporal with sword, pistol, armband, and all confronted Miki. He was accompanied by a soldier carrying a bayoneted rifle. The pair looked formidable enough to start a little war of their own as they stood glaring savagely at the occupants in the room.

"Who are you?" the Corporal shouted.

"Yes, sir. I am Private Shunzo Miki."

"What are you doing in a place like this?"

"I didn't know it was prohibited," Miki lied as he stood stiffly at attention.

"What did you say?" the Corporal shouted and almost snarled like an angered animal when he said it.

He whipped his arm around and slapped Miki soundly on his cheek. This Corporal looked like a past master at the art of slapping, for Miki did not know until he felt the sting on his cheek that the Corporal had slapped him. The sudden shock of the blow was more painful than the blow itself.

"Yes, sir," Miki said and stiffened his body and waited for more blows.

But before the *Kempei* could slap again, the girl jumped in between Miki and the military police and began haranguing loudly at the intruders. The other girls who had gathered outside the room, too, joined her, and they raised a loud though uncomprehensible clamor. Even those who watched from the balcony across the courtyard lent their voices in berating the unpopular intruders.

"You are a bother!" the *Kempei* shouted and slapped the girl on her cheek and shoved her out of the room.

When she tried to return, the soldier with the rifle drove her off at the point of his bayonet, and her friends, too, held her back and now began consoling and placating her earnestly.

"What year soldier are you?" asked the military police.

"I am a First-Year-Soldier," honestly answered Miki this time.

No sooner had Miki said it than the *Kempei* put a leg behind him and gave him a shove in the well-known *judo* fashion. Miki, who had not expected anything like it and who had been standing rigidly at attention, toppled over easily. The *Kempei* kicked him twice in the jaw and once in his stomach before Miki was able to scramble to his feet.

Miki felt dizzy and wobbly, but he resumed his position of attention. He spat out the blood which flowed freely from a cut in his mouth but remembered the impropriety of spitting before a superior and swallowed the rest. The blood tasted warm and salty and increased the feeling of sickness in his stomach.

The Corporal had knocked Miki over, to get him on the ground where he could kick him, because the latter was almost twice as large as he, and that seemed the only way he could soften him up. It was the usual method of the *Kempei* to beat anyone who came under their custody into a cringing pulp before taking his confession or passing sentence. Whether this came from a definite policy or a common underlying strain of sadism, none of the *Kempei's* innumerable victims had ever dared to determine, and Miki himself was a blank bundle of terror as he patiently awaited whatever further chastisement was in store for him. However confident he was in his own physical strength, he had not the least intention of offering resistance, so inbued he had been with the absolute authority of the *Kempei*.

"Did you come alone?" the *Kempei* demanded, his voice growing higher and more threatening with each question he asked.

"Yes, sir," Miki lied desperately.

"You are lying!" the *Kempei* shouted and cuffed Miki again.

The latter floundered sideways but quickly came to attention and repeated, "I came alone." Nobody could make him betray his comrade Senior Soldier, Miki determined then and there.

"Well! We will search the rooms. If you are lying, I won't pardon you! . . . Put on your clothes!" the police ordered.

"Yes, sir!" Miki answered and was glad that he could move his body again, for he was beginning to ache most terribly. Miki dressed himself with fumbling fingers, struggling intensely within himself between an urge to stall for time, which would be valuable in enabling his comrade to make his getaway, and a strong fear for his savage captor. The *Kempei*, in the meantime, chased away the curious, now silent crowd gathered in front of the room. The girls who had been shouting their invectives

loudly and insistently at these rude intruders to their professional sanctuary had grown suddenly silent when the *Kempei*
had started beating up the soldier, their guest, and the latter had
seemed powerless to resist. The girls had hoped that the soldier,
a member of the victorious Japanese Army, and a large mus-
cular-looking one to boot, would stand up to defend their
professional rights, and their clamor had been partly meant to
cheer him on, but they had been able only to look on with
mixed terror and pity when the latter seemed completely helpless before his captor.

When Miki was dressed, the *Kempei* asked him his name again
and his unit and entered in his notebook the data which Miki
honestly and meekly offered. He asked for the leave permit,
and, finding it in order, ordered the guard with the rifle to take
their "captive" down into the courtyard and to await him there.
The *Kempei* went roughly through all the rooms of the house
and except for a few frightened native customers, did not find
any other soldier in the prohibited native brothel.

Miki almost sighed out aloud when he saw the *Kempei*
coming out of the room where Aoki had said he would be.
There must have been a secret door as the elder soldier had said.
If Miki had only stayed in a room nearby as he had been
urged . . . He felt a sudden upsurge of remorse which left him
weaker.

The unfortunate First-Year-Soldier had to be prodded to get
started when the *Kempei* returned from his search of the rooms,
for Miki's ears rang so from the beating he had received that he
did not hear his captor's peremptory order to march forward.
But when they started, he could hear the shrill voices of the girls
who seemed suddenly to have come to life again and began
shouting angrily and insultingly at the departing *Kempei*. Miki
even thought he could hear the voice of his little friend of a
while ago screaming above all the others, but he did not look up
to the balcony from where it seemed to be coming to find out
for certain.

In cynical contrast to the furtive way in which he and Aoki

had followed the shadows of the back alleys on their way to the forbidden native brothel, the group now walked boldly down the center of the main streets of the native sector. The natives now looked on respectfully, whereas a moment ago they had watched only curiously at the soldiers sneaking so undignifiedly through the streets. The silent group of captors and captive arrived shortly at the *Kempei* headquarters, which looked like a converted bank building. It had been a brisk walk through the native sector back to the Japanese district, but Miki, despite the growing pain of his body, found himself marveling at how deeply his older comrade had taken him into the native sector.

Miki was led through several conventional-looking rooms into a large hall in the rear which was filled with people coming and going, and he was shoved in front of a desk where a Sergeant looked up peevishly from something he was writing hurriedly on a piece of paper.

"What is this?" he asked gruffly as Miki saluted at stiff attention.

"He was in a brothel in a native sector," the Corporal who had found him and who now stood proudly beside him reported respectfully. "We caught him while on patrol."

The Sergeant pulled out a large black book from a stack on his desk and began writing down Miki's name, the unit he belonged to, the time and place of his discovery, and other relevant details, which the Corporal reported from notations in his notebook. The cool, efficient manner in which the latter made his report contrasted sharply with his almost maniacal behavior in the brothel a moment ago. Meanwhile, Miki had opportunity to notice from furtive glances around the room a scene which made his heart grow cold inside of him. At one corner a group of soldiers in their undershirts were forcing water into the open mouth of a kneeling native. The native had his hands bound behind his back, and several soldiers were holding him down in his kneeling position. One *Kempei* had a firm grip of his hair and was holding his head backward with a knee propped against his back, while another kept pouring water into his face. Still more *Kempei* stood around watching grimly while the native kept gasping desperately for breath like a drowning man.

At another corner, a native stripped to his hips was hanging suspended by his fingers from the ceiling, the tips of his toes barely scraping the floor. This one was wailing most wretchedly while a *Kempei*, who probably knew the native tongue, kept screaming in his face. Near him, another native knelt resignedly with hands bound behind his back, while a soldier stood before him with a drawn sword and an interpreter kept questioning him persistently. Miki could see this native merely shaking his head weakly in silent denial and not even troubling to look up. These natives, Miki knew, were suspect agents of the enemy from whom the *Kempei* were trying to draw confessions and intelligence before putting them to the execution sword. There were other natives standing around waiting their turn despondently, but in all the group, Miki could not see any other soldier besides himself who looked like a prisoner of the *Kempei*.

When the Sergeant finished writing in his book, he got up lazily from his desk and came around slowly to stand in front of Miki, mumbling peevishly, "What a nuisance!"

Before he knew it, Miki felt a stinging blow on his cheek. Then about three others who were standing around, including the Corporal, his original captor, jumped upon Miki all at once, and everything went black in the latter's mind. When he became aware of himself, he was sitting weakly on the floor and somebody was pouring water on his head. He felt as if he were a great distance from everything. He could hear a very insistent voice far away shouting, "Get up! Get up!" Somebody kicked him in his leg.

He rose clumsily, and that was when pain shot through his body like a hot flame. He twisted his face but gritted his teeth and came to attention. His ears kept ringing loudly, and his face felt like somebody else's. Tears were in his eyes and kept running down his cheeks, and he could feel the warmth of the tears against the smarting surface of his face. He felt wobbly on his feet, and his head kept swaying — back and forth, back and forth. The figures before him appeared blurred and distorted, and it was not only because of the tears in his eyes. When he had received his indiscriminate beating at the hand of the Corporal back in the brothel, the pain had been great, but there had been something in the center of him, a central force, which had held him together and maintained a conscious resistance; but now, that force was almost gone, and his senses and consciousness seemed to be dispersing hopelessly and uncontrollably all about him, so that he had the greatest difficulty being conscious of even his own self.

A hard object lightly tapped the side of his face, and he heard a familiar rattle, and knew somebody was tapping his face with the scabbard of a sword. Then he heard, as if from a distance, the Sergeant's voice saying, "The next time you go to a native brothel, it's the prison for you!" and he knew it was the Sergeant who was touching his face with the sword scabbard to emphasize his statement.

Miki answered, "Yes, sir," and even as he struggled to get the words out of his aching mouth, his knees gave way under him, and he slumped helplessly to the floor.

He now felt the sword scabbard falling all over his body and head, but though he knew he was being beaten mercilessly, he did not care so much this time, and even wondered why the Sergeant's voice was sounding angry all of a sudden as it shouted from a much greater distance than ever, "You have strength to go to a brothel, but don't you have strength to stand up?" Still in his removed mood, Miki decided to stand up, and he soon found himself standing shakily on his feet once again.

"You bastard!" the Sergeant shouted, and a hard object hit the middle of his stomach, and a sensation, less pain than nausea, shot through his body. Then everything went black again. But even as he blacked out, the thought flashed through Miki's mind, as if from an inspiration, that the Sergeant had poked him in his stomach with the point of his scabbard, and he tried desperately to hang on to this thought, but it was too late.

When Miki regained consciousness, somebody was again pouring water on his head and face, for this time he was sprawled lengthwise on the floor. "Get up! Get up!" he heard them shouting. He made a mighty effort and got to his feet.

"Your nose is bleeding. Don't you have a handkerchief?" the Sergeant's voice reached his ears, and he was relieved to find it sounding a little kindly this time. Miki pulled a handkerchief out from his pocket and pressed it against his nose.

Somebody said, "He must be mad . . . only a First-Year-Soldier!"

"Take him to bed," the Sergeant ordered.

Somebody grabbed Miki's arm and shoved him along. They came to a bed next to the wall and whoever was leading him said haughtily, "Lie down."

Miki stretched his body hesitantly on the bed, expecting any moment to be scolded for taking such liberty, but the bed felt so welcome he did not care and closed his burning eyes. Nobody scolded him. All he heard was the wailing of the tortured natives and the screaming of their tormentors. He felt a closer kindredship with these natives than he had ever felt before, and except for the sympathy he felt for them, there was no other sensation within him as he tried to forget everything in his welcome state of semi-consciousness.

Miki did not know how long he had been lying with his eye closed when a voice, full of dignity and authority, said beside his bed, "What is this?"

Miki opened his eyes and saw several officers standing beside him. He tried to scramble to his feet, but his body ached and his joints were stiff, and it took some time before he could stand up and come to attention. His eyes were so swollen now that they were almost closed, and he could barely discern through the slits which remained that he was confronted by a Major and

174

two Lieutenants. They all wore the red armbands of the *Kempei*, and Miki knew that they were officers of this head-quarters. He tried to speak but his swollen lips would not open, and he could not form the words readily.

The Sergeant at the desk hurried forward to the officers' side and, smiling somewhat apologetically, explained nasally, "He was caught at a native brothel."

"He looks like only a First-Year-Soldier," the Major said in a tone which sounded as if he were more amused than angered.

Miki was able to form the words, "Yes, sir," but his voice sounded weak, and it did not sound like his own.

The Major turned away disinterestedly and began to walk away. A Lieutenant came before Miki and, hissing contemptuously, "Damn fool," shoved his face roughly and Miki slumped down on the bed.

He floundered nervously to regain his feet and come to attention again, but the Lieutenant, too, turned away and followed the Major, and the Sergeant pushed him back and said, "Lie down."

Miki lay back and gratefully closed his eyes. He could hear the Sergeant reporting to the officer who had remained, "We have notified his unit. Somebody should be coming over to get him soon."

It was young Lieutenant Kondo, Miki's Platoon Commander, who came to take him back to the post. After many apologies to the *Kempei* at the desk and to the officers in their private offices, the Lieutenant came to Miki's bedside and said gruffly, "Come, let's go." When Miki got to his feet, the Lieutenant pushed him roughly to get him started.

On their way out, they also met the Corporal, who had caught Miki in the forbidden brothel. Miki halted and, bowing politely, said, "I am sorry."

The Corporal, smiling cordially, as if he had already forgotten everything that had happened, said in a forced brotherly tone, "Next time, don't go to such a place."

"Yes, sir," Miki answered and, after bowing respectfully, followed his Lieutenant outside.

The officer called a taxi, and they got inside. When the vehicle had gone some distance, the Lieutenant turned toward his subordinate and said, "You were beaten up badly." There was genuine concern and sympathy in his tone now.

Miki felt a warm feeling of gratitude surge through him at this first sign of genuine sympathy he had received from anybody since he had fallen into his terrible mishap today. Miki now realized that his Platoon Commander's gruff conduct at the *Kempei* headquarters had been only a show put on to deceive the *Kempei*.

Now fully assured, he leaned back limply against the soft cushion of the automobile seat, and, when he was asked to recount his misadventure, related everything honestly — all except the part which involved mentioning his older comrade's name. However hard he tried, though, to give a full picture to his sympathetic listener, he could only get the sentences out jerkily, and he felt chagrined and as if he was not repaying the officer's kindness fully.

When Miki was finished, the officer said, "Good, I understand now. Don't say anything to anybody. I will fix everything for you. Just go back to your squad and go to sleep." Miki had never felt so grateful in all his life, and he abandoned the intention he had of elaborating some spots in his story which he had thought insufficient. He lay back and closed his eyes and let the smooth motion of the automobile relieve his jangled nerves.

When they reached the post, the sentinel let them in without questioning, though it was way past the hour when a soldier should have been back from his leave. Is it because they already know at Battalion Headquarters and gave special instructions to the sentinel; or is it because I am with an officer? Miki thought, and the possibility that Battalion Headquarters already knew all about him and the conclusion he had to draw from it that he would have to go into stockade made him sick at his stomach.

The crowded interior of his squad room, howbeit with its ever present atmosphere of etiquette and strict discipline, never looked so welcome to Miki as the Lieutenant led him, following shamefully and meekly, through its door. When his comrades showed excited interest in his return and even sympathy for his condition, the beaten-up First-Year-Soldier felt the tension he had had to sustain ever since he was caught in the brothel that afternoon leave him all at once. The Platoon Commander ordered that Miki be put to bed immediately, and Takeo helped his broken comrade off with his clothes, which were still soaked with the water which had been poured on him at *Kempei* Headquarters and with the blood from his bleeding face. The others helped him change completely into clean clothes, though Kan had to lend him his underwear, since Miki's only other pair were soiled, having been changed only that morning in anticipation of the leave.

When Miki was finally warmly and comfortably tucked under the blankets, the Platoon Commander said, "Don't bother him any more. Leave him alone and let him go to sleep." Then he left after asking the Squad Leader to come to his room to discuss the whole matter. The Lieutenant's sympathetic and resigned attitude was quickly communicated to the men of Squad Three, and any thought any of the older soldiers might have had of chastising their younger comrade was abandoned at once.

The company's medical soldier soon came and gave Miki some pills and instructed the men of the squad to cool the sick soldier's forehead with a wet towel to be changed every hour. The men got a washbasin full of water and placed it beside Miki's pillow and, after soaking a towel in the water and rinsing it, spread it across his forehead. Then they left him, as they had been instructed by their Platoon Commander, to gather in little groups to discuss their unfortunate comrade in grave, hushed tones.

Meantime, Aoki went to change the towel on Miki's forehead, though it had been put there only a short while ago and there was some time left yet before the hour specified by the medical soldier was up. There was no one else around, and Aoki, the escaped partner of the day's unfortunate escapade, said consolingly, "You were done in plenty."

Miki recognized the voice and, without opening his eyes, but smiling, said, "I did not tell about you."

"Thank you," the Reserve answered, and Miki went to sleep with the grateful tone of the Reserve's voice ringing assuringly in his ears.

CHAPTER 12

"BRING your rice containers and come to Company Headquarters to get your *sake!*" the orderly went shouting through the lobbies of the converted schoolhouse where the Hamamoto company was billeted.

The squads had been resting after a heavy Sunday dinner, and the First-Year-Soldiers had just finished their regular after-dinner chore of washing the dishes and sweeping the floor when the welcome call was heard. The men leaped into action as if an alarm had been sounded. The noisy clatter of the empty aluminum rice containers and the excited voices of men, who had suddenly had the lids of their forcefully stored energy indiscriminately wrenched open, mingled and reverberated and generated an air of bustling, ebullient excitement seldom seen in the usually depressed and tense squad rooms. The First-Year-Soldiers hurriedly gathered the rice containers from the shelves where they were kept and dashed away with them to the Company Headquarters where the *sake* was waiting in sweet-smelling wooden kegs. The older soldiers cleared the mats for the anticipated bacchanal and began hastily gathering whatever they could find in their rooms which could be used to fortify their stomachs against the wine. Fortunately, every squad had an abundance of canned food which they had received in their comfort kits that morning. They also gathered the pickles left over from earlier meals which were always lying around in the squad rooms, and some soldiers even went to the kitchen to try their luck with the mess sergeants. Once billeted together in a city, as they now were, there was a central kitchen, which cooked the meals for the whole company, and the mess sergeant was a popular man, especially when *sake* was rationed and the squads needed something to go with it.

Many months of frugal campaigning in the inland had passed since the soldiers of the Hamamoto company had had their last ration of *sake*. Of course, there had always been a liberal supply of native liquor wherever they had gone in the interior which had been free for the taking, but *sake* from home was a different matter entirely. "The feeling is different between drinking *chungchiu*, and drinking Japanese *sake*," the soldiers said.

Squad Three, too, was a veritable beehive of excitement after the call was sounded. The men had just put their unfortunate comrade, Miki, to sleep and were feeling more depressed than usual, and the call had come at a most opportune moment. Takeo and Kan had dashed off to Company Headquarters with the squad's rice containers, while Private First Class Tanaka had taken upon himself the duty of gathering the sundry contributions for the feast that evening. Hosaka had brought back some *sushi* (rice cakes) from his friend's place in the city, and he contributed them to the polyglot pile.

When the young soldiers returned with the squad's share of the wine ration, a spontaneous cheer arose from the men who had remained, for Takeo and Kan had five containers full of the fragrant *sake*, or five *sho*, which meant that each soldier of the squad would receive over three *go*, or nearly a pint. This was enough to get one fairly drunk, and, considering the fact that many could not drink so much, the real lovers of the wine were guaranteed a decent inebriation. Takeo and Kan left one container for the older soldiers to start with and hurried with the rest to the kitchen to heat them. *Sake* was ordinarily drunk hot, and the task of heating always went to the First-Year-Soldiers.

The older soldiers were almost through with their one container of cold *sake* when Takeo and Kan came back with the heated, steaming ones. The men were squatted in a wide oblong circle on the mat and were drinking from their large aluminum rice bowls. Some were already showing the first faint signs of inebriation on their flushed faces. The hastily assembled banquet was scattered wildly inside the circle, and the men were stretching their arms and leaning over each other to get at the choice pieces with their chopsticks. There were canned sardines, peanuts, dried cuttlefish, salted plums, pickles, and seaweed paste, among others. Hosaka's rice cakes, which had been the most extravagant among the numerous contributions, had disappeared with the first skirmish of chopsticks.

"Well, this is good!" exclaimed Corporal Sakamoto, when the First-Year-Soldiers returned with their heated *sake*. "You come up, too." The soldiers cheerfully made room for their younger comrades to join their circle, for everybody was in high spirits.

Reserve Private Manju, the habitual drinker, who had already been fairly well steeped during his leave-excursion in the city earlier that day, began to clap his hands and sing in his usual ringing voice, which sounded even louder in the narrow confines of the room. He was naked except for his *fundoshi* or gee-string around his loins, and had a towel tied around his head the way they had of doing when they were feeling cocky. Many were undressed like him, and even those who had their trousers on wore nothing on the upper half of their bodies, and their sunburnt, muscular backs glistened most savagely as they reflected the setting sun's slanting rays which filtered in through the windows.

Everybody began to clap in unison and in time to the song Manju sang, a popular ballad:

> *No more will I fall in love with one from a*
> *foreign land,*
> *For in the end we must part like crying*
> *crows.*

Some joined him in chorus, and when he had sung his stanza, another continued the song into the next stanza:

> *Even if in the end we must part like crying*
> *   crows,*
> *I want to hold you and suffer the pangs of*
> *   love with you.*

The men sang lustily and clapped their hands loudly. They sang the stanzas of the ballad one after the other, and soon the tunes were repeating themselves monotonously, although the men seemed to grow more spirited as the singing continued. There was no one now to frown upon their levity, for it was generally understood that when *sake* was rationed the soldiers had full liberty to have a good time just as long as they stayed within their quarters. Some officers even encouraged their men to let themselves loose on such occasions, for they knew the benefit to be derived from blowing off excess steam once in a while. The soldiers took full advantage of the occasion and quickly worked themselves up into a drunken frenzy.

"Come on, drink! You work hard enough at other times, so drink now!" said Hosaka and held a rice container full of the steaming *sake* and offered to pour into Takeo's bowl.

Takeo had not drunk much, and his bowl was still full of the liquor somebody had poured into it when he had first joined the group. "I do not drink much," Takeo protested weakly, although he had shown a man-sized capacity when he had drunk alone with Hosaka in the brothel's private room while on leave earlier that day. Takeo was not forgetting his status as a First-Year-Soldier and was trying hard to maintain what he thought was a proper modesty for one in his station.

"I know you can drink!" Hosaka said meaningfully. "Come, empty what is in the bowl!"

"You don't have to be bashful now. Drink!" also urged Aoki, and he turned toward their Squad Leader, Corporal Sakamoto, and said "Today, there are no rules, isn't that right, Squad

Leader?" His tongue was a little heavy from the wine, and he did not attach the usual "Honorable" when he addressed his superior, but the soldiers were inclined to drop the honorifics during their drinking bouts, and everybody accepted it in good spirit. Corporal Sakamoto, too, smiled good-naturedly and nodded his head cheerfully in reply to his blunt subordinate, for his mouth was full at that time with a large strip of dried cuttle-fish.

Thus urged by his Senior Soldiers, Takeo raised his bowl to his lips and drank down what was in it, though he tried to do it with as much decorum as he could show under the circumstances. "Thank you," he said modestly as Hosaka now filled his empty bowl, exclaiming the while, "That's the spirit! Work when you have to work; drink heavily when it is time to drink and sing!"

Kan, the other First-Year-Soldier of the squad, was proving himself more formidable. He was stubbornly refusing every offer to empty his bowl and have it refilled. Private First Class Gunji was wildly flourishing a container before the face of the young soldier, but the latter would not budge, though he was taking the greatest care not to hurt the feelings of his Seniors. "Honorable Private First Class, I cannot drink!" he protested loudly. "I was sucking my mother's teats only until a short time ago!" he joked and tried to divert the attention of his older comrades diplomatically.

When everybody laughed at his joke, Kan took advantage of the occasion immediately and, wrenching the container away from the hand of Private First Class Gunji, turned to offer to fill the latter's bowl, exclaiming coaxingly, "Honorable Private First Class, you can drink! Go ahead and drink!"

Everybody knew that Kan could drink and that he had been quite a playboy before joining the army, for he had boasted often of his "escapades" in his civilian life. But no one troubled to accuse him for his insincerity, and many admired his fortitude instead, for a First-Year-Soldier was not expected to drink —

not much, anyway — since he was undergoing a sort of apprenticeship, and an apprenticeship was traditionally, in the country where the soldiers came from, a period of abstention and suffering toil. Even Takeo, who had gulped his *sake* in good spirit; tried hard to keep the effects of the liquor from showing on his face and in his conduct.

The air in the room was now heavy with the sweet-sourish smell of the *sake*, and except for the First-Year-Soldiers, the men of the squad had worked themselves up to a real frenzy. Manju was crazily beating the side of an empty aluminum rice container, while still others drummed on their rice bowls with their chopsticks in time to the songs which continued ceaselessly. Some of the songs became brazenly bawdy. Between songs, the men poured freely into each other's bowls, and they sipped their wine with audible sounds of satisfaction. The racket they raised and their wild deportment, mingled with the oppressing odor in the room, would have made a lunatic feel perfectly at home among them.

At an appropriate break in the singing, Manju began a *dodoitsu*, which was a couplet of well-known pronouncements on anything from love to philosophy to be chanted more than sung in a fixed rhythm and which was usually performed solo. This time, too, Manju performed alone, and his high musical voice seemed to pierce the heavy atmosphere of the room:

> *The strings of a geisha's samisen*
> *are three in number,*
> *But her love is always one.*

Others followed, chanting their verses solo, and the slow rhythm and complicated text of the verses seemed to dampen the exuberance of the soldiers a little, since they were forced to listen to the solo performers silently, and they could not even clap their hands, for the *dodoitsu* was not evenly timed to allow any other accompaniment but the classic twanging of the geisha's samisen. Somebody finally assayed to break the monot-

ony of the slow chanting, and, rudely interrupting a solo performer, began clapping his hands loudly and singing a patriotic
march which was finding wide popularity at home at that time.
Everybody joined in chorus and began clapping their hands and
beating their bowls in unison, for they all knew the song. They
sang:

> We have been called by our Great Emperor;
> How glorious are our lives in the dawn.
> The cheers of our hundred million compa-
>   triots, praising and sending us off, rise to
>   the skies.
> We are off! Warriors! Men of Japan!

The soldiers had now regained their former high spirit, and
they sang several more stanzas of the march. Then someone
began singing the dance-song of the *Yasuki Bushi*. Manju immediately jumped to his feet and began dancing in the middle of
the circle formed by his comrades. He picked his steps with
surprising skill among the many dishes, bowls, and rice containers scattered on the mat where he danced. It was a comical
dance, and Manju rolled his head from side to side in time to
the song's rhythm and assumed numerous weird poses, sticking
his tongue out from time to time and twisting his face into
exaggerated expressions. His comrades applauded raucously,
while others continued the song, clapping their hands and beating their bowls in time to the dance.

The dance, however, soon began to grow monotonous as
Manju went through the same motions over and over again, and
the same refrain too was repeated with seemingly stubborn regu-
larity. Private First Class Tanaka suddenly rose to his feet and,
turning to several Regulars sitting beside him, suggested loudly,
"Let's go to Squad Two to see if they got more *sake* there!"
His comrades welcomed this opportunity to seek a change in the
excitement and followed him drunkenly out of the squad room.

It was dark outside now, and the electric lights were turned on everywhere. A messenger ran down the lobby, shouting, "Tonight's roll-call is by report!" The announcement was greeted by cheers of satisfaction in every squad room, for it meant that the soldiers did not have to go through the onerous ordeal of evening roll-call and they could go on with their carousal until "Lights-out." The Squad Leaders, however, had to report to Company Headquarters, and in Squad Three Corporal Sakamoto felt sudden relief at this opportunity to withdraw, for the increasing license of his subordinates under the influence of the *sake* was dangerously compromising his dignity. Kan ran to get the Squad Leader's coat from his private compartment. Hastily getting into his coat, Corporal Sakamoto, who had taken care not to get too drunk before his subordinates, slipped quietly out of the room.

Manju, meantime, while executing a difficult step in his dance, had kicked over a container still half full of the precious wine, and this had stopped the singing and dancing all of a sudden. Takeo ran for a rag and wiped up the mess. This interlude was welcomed by most of the men, who were not as energetic as Manju, for they had grown a little tired from the concentrated merrymaking which had continued uninterruptedly since the drinking had started. They now began to drink in earnest the little *sake* which remained in the bottoms of the containers.

"Ah, this is good!" exclaimed Hosaka, sipping from his bowl with eyes rapturously closed.

"I would want to drink with my wife seated across from me!" somebody sighed.

"Damn it! When are they going to let us go home?" said Aoki, swallowing his *sake* in a single gulp and refilling his bowl.

"The story of the whole division going home was a fluke again," somebody said.

"When we said we were going home, we were really fooling ourselves. They say they are going to use us soon in a landing operation!" said Aoki.

Just then three soldiers, dressed only in their loincloths and with towels tied cockily around their heads swayed noisily into the room, shouting drunkenly, "Give us some drink!" The soldiers were Reserves from a neighboring squad.

"It is no use! We don't have any more *sake*," Manju protested sadly.

"That is all right. We got two full containers here with us. The men in our squad don't drink. They have now started gambling," assured one of the newcomers, and he set down two containers full of the golden wine before the surprised men of Squad Three.

"Say, this is great! Come on up! Come on up!" Manju cheered, and the others pulled the welcome guests up on the mat beside them.

"Did you say gambling has started?" Okihara, who had drunk little and who had remained glum as usual throughout the frenzied merrymaking, now seemed to come to life all of a sudden.

"There is a big crowd doing it," said one of the newcomers.

"Well, then, shall I go and see?" said Okihara and stood up to leave. Several others, who were also devoted patrons of the elusive art, got up and followed him out of the room. Those, too, were not very drunk, for it was said of them that they did not drink much because they were not sure when gambling would begin.

The soldiers were still singing and making merry in many of the other squads of the company. Voices raised in drunken ribaldry could be heard also from the neighboring buildings where the other companies of the battalion were billeted, and it seemed the whole battalion had been rationed *sake* this night. The lusty songs of the intoxicated soldiers, sung in every scale and tempo known to the human voice, together with the wild racket they raised in accompaniment, mingled and clashed in the still night air and tumbled in irresistible torrents into the room where the men of Squad Three were now drinking their newly replenished stock of wine in relative silence. Drunken soldiers were passing noisily back and forth across the lobby outside, and some banged themselves against the wall or stumbled to the floor.

"Come, this squad has no life!" one of the newcomers said and began singing:

> *Hanako-san, who is prettier than the flowers!*
> *O, Hanako-san! . . .*

Everybody joined the song, and the squad now sang louder than ever, for the short respite had refreshed them, and the added liquor in their stomachs had greatly rejuvenated their morale.

Takeo and Kan, the only First-Year-Soldiers of the squad, were busily cutting more pickles for their drinking superiors on the table at the other end of the room, when a voice was heard shouting persistently from the yard outside, "First-Year-Soldiers, assemble!" Other voices, some unmistakably drunken, soon took up the call, so that everybody in the building heard it above the intoxicated bedlam in the squad rooms.

Takeo turned toward Kan and said lifelessly, "There, it's started." They all knew what it meant when First-Year-Soldiers alone were called to assemble. It meant only one thing — more discipline and having more "spirit-put-into-them." It was nothing new, moreover, to the First-Year-Soldiers to have "spirit put into them" when the elder soldiers were feeling high with liquor, for the latter often took this (to them) absolutely safe means to work off their alcoholic steam, and it had happened even in the post at home.

Kan and Takeo took the pickles they had cut to the Reserves, who kept unconcernedly singing, and Takeo next went to change the wet towel on the swollen forehead of Miki, who was sleeping in the far corner of the room. Miki groaned when the new towel was set on his forehead, but he did not open his eyes, and Takeo looked enviously upon the sleeping face of his comrade who was able thus to remain happily oblivious to all the insane racket around him. Takeo and Kan went before the Reserves and, standing at attention, reported in the proper manner, "We will go and return."

The Reserves stopped their singing and seemed to notice the voices, now pressingly persistent and threatening, outside in the yard for the first time. "Wait! It is the Regulars bragging again," said Aoki, and he leaped down from the platform and ran out to the lobby to shout into the dark yard, "Who is calling the First-Year-Soldiers to assemble?"

"It is I! It is the Warrant Officer!" came back the haughty voice of the company's Warrant Officer.

Aoki turned around silently and, returning into the room, said weakly, "It is the Warrant Officer. It can't be helped."

Takeo and Kan, who had felt a sharp hope when the sympathizing Reserve had gone to make his inquiry into the yard, now meekly repeated, "We will go and return," and left the room.

The Reserves in Squad Three soon heard the young untainted voices of the First-Year-Soldiers counting off crisply in the yard. There were quite a number of them in the Company — over fifty — and their stiff military voices sounded strange and unbelonging amidst the drunken racket which could still be heard from the other buildings and from some of the squad rooms in the Company.

As the Reserves listened attentively and curiously to learn why their younger comrades had been called to assemble by the Warrant Officer at such a time as this, they heard loud footsteps coming down the lobby and approaching their room. They could hear angry voices, and they soon discerned some of them calling, "Miki! Where is Miki?"

The footsteps stopped in front of their room, and a group of Second- and Third-Year Regulars entered, led by Private First Class Yamanaka, a Second-Year Regular in a neighboring squad. Private First Class Tanaka, Squad Three's own Regular, was also in the mob advancing brazenly into the room, but he remained well in the back out of deference to the Reserves in the room who were his direct seniors. Many of the intruding Regulars showed outward signs of advanced intoxication as they swayed from side to side and glared threateningly at the Reserves in the room. The latter looked back peevishly at the Regulars, whom they knew would not be acting so brashly in front of them if they had not been under the uplifting influence of *sake*.

"What do you want?" asked one of the Reserves.

"Where is Miki? First-Year-Soldiers must assemble!" defiantly answered Private First Class Yamanaka, a stocky bull-necked fellow, who they said was a truck driver before being conscripted into the army. When his roving bloodshot eyes caught sight of Miki sleeping in the far corner of the room, he shouted, "Miki, get up!" and made for the sleeping First-Year-Soldier with unsteady, albeit resolute steps.

Aoki jumped from the platform where he was squatted with the other Reserves of the squad and blocked the way of the advancing Regular. He had drunk much, and the sweat shone on his naked muscular body, but he was still steady on his feet — much steadier than the Private First Class whom he blocked. "Miki is sick and cannot go," said Aoki in a low, ominous voice.

"This is my order! This is the order of Private First Class Yamanaka!" the Regular almost screamed and tried to brush aside the interfering Reserve.

Aoki struck with his huge right fist, and he caught the younger soldier squarely on the side of his face. The stocky figure of Private First Class Yamanaka went sprawling helplessly to the floor. The latter seemed dazed for a moment but soon rose to his knees and, snarling, "So, you did it!" sprang fiercely toward his assailant. Aoki, who showed the utmost coolness and seemed well versed in the art of self-defense, now struck with his left fist and sent the Regular sprawling in the opposite direction. The blow sounded loud in the hushed room.

"It is too early for you young ones to try to come at me,"

Aoki jeered in a voice charged with cynicism and spite, and he presented a majestic figure as he looked down scoffingly at his fallen victim with one hand held nonchalantly on his hip.

The Private First Class, sprawled on the floor, seemed really dazed this time and he kept staring blankly at the tip of his shoes, but he got shakily to his feet when he heard the jeering voice of Aoki and started once more for the Reserve. His comrades, however, stopped him and held him back and began to pull him out of the room. None of the other Regulars had tried to go to his aid, for the figure of Aoki alone had seemed too formidable, let alone the presence of the numerous other Reserves in the room and, like the good soldiers they were, they knew when a battle was lost and now decided to make a hasty retreat.

Private First Class Yamanaka, who now seemed completely recovered from the blows which had sent him so ignominiously to the floor, kicked and struggled most desperately. He kept shouting repeatedly, "Let me go! Let me go!" and there was a tragic finality in his voice, as if he felt his prestige was fatally injured and required a final, even life-risking, assault to redeem it.

Aoki remained unmoved and only laughed while the Reserves on the platform called deridingly, "Take him away before he is killed!" The Regulars tried to soothe their madly screaming and struggling comrade and finally succeeded in dragging him out of the room. Before he was dragged out, Private First Class Yamanaka made a last brave effort to break away at the door and went away shouting, "The vengeance for this I will carry out even with the honor of Private First Class Yamanaka!"

Once outside the room, the Private First Class succeeded in shaking off his comrades and now made a dash for his own squad room. He reappeared shortly, wildly brandishing a drawn bayonet and shouting like a maniac, "Aoki, prepare yourself!"

His comrades, who had stopped him previously, again held him back, and this time they made sure to hang on tightly to the arm which gripped the bayonet. Several soldiers held on to the arm while others tried to take the dangerous weapon away from their almost demented comrade. Sweat ran freely down the face of the struggling Private First Class and mingled with the tears which now appeared in his eyes. The thin shirt which he was wearing was soaked with sweat too. Froth formed at the corners of his mouth, and the veins stuck out prominently on his face and neck as he shouted, "I am going to kill Aoki! I am going to kill him and die myself!" He was now weeping openly and beseeching plaintively.

Aoki appeared with several other Reserves in the lobby where the struggle was taking place. Aoki, too, had a bayonet in his hand, but the others were unarmed, and they said tauntingly to the Regulars, "Let him go. He doesn't have the courage to use the bayonet."

Somebody finally succeeded in wrenching the bayonet away from Private First Class Yamanaka, and they all dragged him, shouting threats to the last, down the lobby and into his own squad room. There they found some leftover *sake*, which they poured lavishly for their frustrated comrade. The latter accepted it and, drinking it in wild gulps, kept repeating, "I am disappointed! Why did you stop me?" His comrades also drank with him and consoled him, "We understand your feelings. That bastard Aoki has had his stomach turned upside down for sure."

Private First Class Yamanaka tried several times to rise and go for his bayonet again, but his comrades held him down, and he seemed finally reconciled with his fate and obediently began drinking the *sake* offered him. He made a final speech of defiance, however, and said, "I am not boasting, but the family of Yamanaka is a lineage of warriors. I am going to take vengeance eventually."

His comrades kept consoling him sympathetically. Somebody said, "You have amply regained your honor." They sprinkled their comments amply with insulting remarks about the Reserves, for whom none of the Regulars had much friendly feeling.

CHAPTER 13

IN THE MEANTIME, the Warrant Officer had lined up the First-Year-Soldiers in double file in the yard in front of the building where the company was billeted. It was he who had sent Private First Class Yamanaka and the Regulars to inquire after Miki when the count had shown a soldier missing. When the commotion had started in Squad Three, his sharp intuition had informed him right away what was taking place, and he had decided against going to interfere, since it would have become a messy affair if he went. It was never a wise policy to antagonize the Reserves and the height of folly, he knew, to bother them on a night like this.

He turned his attention sharply to the First-Year-Soldiers assembled before him and called in a voice which sounded like the crack of a whip in the night, "Attention!" He did not seem to notice that the men had already been rigidly at attention for some time since the count-off, and he followed with the usual "Eyes center!" but did not add the ordinary "Rest!"

The yard was lighted dimly by the faint rays filtering out from the rooms of the buildings bordering it, but the Warrant Officer could still notice in the dimness that all eyes were riveted toward him and that not a single figure moved. A weak ray of light from a window in the building behind the First-Year-Soldiers fell squarely on the stern countenance of the Warrant Officer and showed it up unnaturally in the darkness. Its eyelids

192

were puffed and complexion flushed and shiny, and his eyes were bloodshot. They were unmistakable signs of intoxication and seemed exaggeratedly artificial and completely out of place on the athletic-looking face of the Warrant Officer. The First-Year-Soldiers felt dismay growing in their hearts when they noticed the large crowd of Regulars standing fawningly around him. Many of the Regulars were drunk, too, and it was plain that they had been drinking together with the Warrant Officer and had been instrumental in arousing the latter to call an assembly of the First-Year-Soldiers.

"Do you know why the Imperial Army is the Imperial Army?" began the Warrant Officer in his well-trained sonorous voice. He was glaring up and down the line. Then he pointed to a soldier directly in front of him and ordered, "That soldier over there!"

The soldier pointed out was Takeo. He was so surprised by the suddenness of the distinction that, although he was able to mumble, "Yes, sir," he was at a loss to continue, and he felt his throat tightening helplessly. Kan, who was standing beside Takeo, came to his comrade's rescue by raising his hand and shouting, "Yes, sir!" He immediately added in that completely impersonal, singsong voice which they used in answering their superiors, "Because the Imperial Army worships the Emperor as its Commander and, down to the lowliest soldier, makes it its absolute duty to perform patriotism to the Emperor." It was a trite phrase which everybody knew, but Kan recited it with such fervor as to make it sound completely his own expression.

"Good!" the Warrant Officer exclaimed. "That is just so!" Takeo had never felt so grateful to his alert comrade as he did now. The Warrant Officer, who had come smartly to attention when the soldier had mentioned the Emperor, now continued, still unmoving, "It fills us with trepidation that the Emperor has been pleased to note in the Imperial Rescript that we are considered his guardians. We cannot fully repay this honor even by giving up our lives!" There was an impressive pause, and the officer looked up and down the line as if he were peering into the eyes of each soldier.

He was a finished master in the art of lecturing the soldiers. Like all warrant officers, he had come up from the ranks and had gone through the whole gamut of the soldier's life. His knowledge of the phrases and sentiments required to discipline the soldier was monumental. His expertness in the drills, and especially in the bayonet exercises, made him highly respected among the soldiers, and his ability to recite eruditely passages from the Imperial Rescript, or Regulations of Military Conduct, or Regulations of Conduct at the Front, or Infantryman's Manual was nothing short of impressive. The Warrant Officer was a unique being in the Japanese Army, existing in the hazy realm between the commissioned and non-commissioned officer. Unlike the commissioned officers, he commanded no body of troops, but he also had many privileges which the non-commissioned officer did not possess. His duty, moreover, of looking after personnel matters made him about the most respected and feared superior to the lowly soldier, whose main preoccupation was centered on the kind of record which might be sent home to his village or ward offices. They knew that the Warrant Officer was the one who wrote the records and who had about the most say regarding their promotions. The sight of the Warrant Officer, deeply immersed in his stacks of thick, impressive-looking record books with his staff of soldiers and non-commissioned officer, was always awe-inspiring.

After his pause, the Hamamoto company's Warrant Officer continued, this time in a low, ominous voice, "Do you know what one of you did today?"

"Yes, sir!" the First-Year-Soldiers answered in unison, and, although they had guessed all along that their being called together had something to do with Miki's blatant breach of conduct that day, they felt their hearts sink to hear it alluded to thus by their Warrant Officer.

"If you all knew the destiny of the Imperial Army and remembered your folks who are waiting for you at home, you would not be able to commit such a foolish deed." The Warrant Officer's left hand on his sword hilt and his right hand was on his hip, and he presented an awesome sight even in the faint light of the yard. "That even one among you became a straggler is a responsibility of all of you," he continued.

"When we came to the Front, we all came prepared to die. Once we have entered the army, our bodies are no longer ours; we have presented our bodies to the Emperor. We must consider the regulations of the army as regulations from the Emperor to protect our bodies." The Warrant Officer spoke long and eloquently, dramatically changing the tone of his voice to suit the fluctuating moods of his sentences. At one passage, he stopped to ask the soldiers to name the restricted areas in the city. Receiving satisfactory replies from all the soldiers he pointed to, the Warrant Officer concluded, "In the next battle, let each of you do your utmost and wipe out this disgrace!" He then added, "The end!" as it was customary to do at the end of a military speech.

"Salute!" the First-Year-Soldiers shouted and saluted the Warrant Officer, as did the older Regulars standing around him. The officer returned the salute, then turned with a flourish of his sword scabbard and walked pompously back to his room.

The First-Year-Soldiers had not been dismissed and now waited patiently for what they knew was coming. The Warrant Officer never stooped to beating the soldiers himself, and he always left it up to the older Regulars and non-commissioned officers. Tonight, too, he had left without dismissing the First-Year-Soldiers, which was as good as asking the older Regulars to take over from where he left off.

Private First Class Yamanaka, who had been beaten by Aoki in Squad Three, came rushing into the yard with his comrades out of the room where they had been drinking their "consolation *sake*" and shouted drunkenly, "Wait!" He was totally soaked now and swayed wildly on his feet. "Do you know this

Private First Class Yamanaka?" he screamed. Of course, they all knew him, and the First-Year-Soldiers did not answer, but it was only another way of saying, "Listen to me!"

"That a good-for-nothing fool turned up among you is also a responsibility of us Second-Year and Third-Year-Soldiers! We will discipline you with all our might from now on, so bear that in mind!" he blubbered and started to slap the First-Year-Soldiers in the front row, but after the first few blows, he was reeling most hopelessly, and his comrades had to hold him up to keep him from crumpling to the ground. Private First Class Tanaka, who was less intoxicated, now stepped forward and ordered, "Front row, about face!" The First-Year-Soldiers were now facing each other in double file. They knew this "game" well enough and braced themselves for it.

"Slap each other! First, start from the front row!" Private First Class Tanaka ordered, and the other Regulars distributed themselves evenly among the rows to see that the First-Year-Soldiers carried out the order faithfully.

Each First-Year-Soldier began slapping his comrade before him. Takeo, who was standing in a comparatively dark section of the yard, hoped that the darkness would protect him and put as little effort into his motions as possible. Then suddenly somebody struck his head from behind and shoved him roughly in the back so that he went sprawling to the ground, and he heard Private First Class Yamanaka's drunken voice shouting, "Won't you put more strength into it, you fool?" Takeo scrambled quickly to his feet and now began slapping in earnest. His comrade before him stood unflinchingly at attention, but the side of his face where the blows fell turned red, and blood began to trickle from a cut in his lip. Private First Class Yamanaka kept screaming like a maniac behind Takeo, "Slap faster! Slap faster!"

Other First-Year-Soldiers were also being roughly reprimanded for skimping their blows, and the shouts of the older soldiers scolding these hesitating men mingled with the drumlike sound of the slaps to form a bedlam of noise which sounded even

more impressive and sickening as it echoed back and forth between the walls of the buildings bordering the yard. After some
time, the rear row was now ordered to take up the slapping. The
process was alternated back and forth until all the faces of the
First-Year-Soldiers were red and swollen, and the noses of some
began to bleed. This would have gone on until Curfew had not
the Warrant Officer leaned out from his room and called into
the yard, "That is enough. Dismiss them!"

The First-Year-Soldiers returned, dazed and aching, to their
respective squad rooms, but they doused their faces well in the
faucets in the yard before they went back. Takeo and Kan found
that the Reserves had finished their drinking bout, when they
returned to their squad room. The room was in a terrible mess.
Some Reserves, still in their state of immodest undress, were
sleeping on the mat in drunken stupor; another group had started
a card game at the far corner of the room; still others were
smoking and chatting in little groups and letting the ashes from
their cigarettes and their cigarette butts fall all over the mat and
floor; and the relics of the late bacchanal — overturned bowls,
dishes with scraps of food still on them, empty cans, empty rice
containers, spilled *sake* and food, and broken chopsticks — lay
uncared and scattered on the mat.

Takeo and Kan first went to get ash trays for the soldiers who
were smoking. Then they began to clear away the débris, taking
care not to awaken the Reserves who were sleeping in their midst.
They swept the mat as best they could and covered the sleeping
Reserves with blankets. Some of the waking Reserves called sympathetically, "Hard work!" but they did not offer to help.
Takeo and Kan went busily about the task of cleaning up the
room, for they knew "Lights-out" would be called soon, and
they had to get the room ready for the examination of the
Officer-Of-The-Week who was sure to come around after
"Lights-out." The First-Year-Soldiers almost forgot the stinging pain of their faces as they sped feverishly through their
chores.

They paid little attention to the commotion which was taking place at one end of the room, as Private Oka, the Third-Year-Soldier who was still a private, tried desperately to break away from friends who held him back to reach his bayonet which was hanging in its scabbard on the wall. "Let me get my bayonet! I am going to get the Warrant Officer tonight. . . . He keeps me a private all this time. . . . What does he think this Oka is?" The Third-Year-Soldier was weeping in a loud voice and struggling wildly to break away. Private Oka always wept when he got drunk, and his retarded promotion was a favorite peeve, drunk or sober.

Corporal Sakamoto entered the room just then. The Squad Leader, too, seemed quite gone and was wobbly on his feet, but, catching sight of the struggling figure of Oka, he shouted in a commanding voice, "Oka, what are you doing?"

Oka stopped his struggling as if strength had drained from him suddenly, and when he caught sight of his Squad Leader standing in the doorway, dashed toward him as if with a final effort of desperation. Reaching his Squad Leader, he tried to throw his arms around him, but the latter stepped back a little, and he was able only to place his hands on his shoulders. Oka now began weeping in earnest, "Honorable Squad Leader, do anything you want with this Oka! Tell me to go and die in the midst of the enemy! I have no face to show the folks at home with these two stars of mine!"

"All right, all right," Corporal Sakamoto said, his voice expressing only sympathy now. "Come to my room and let us talk," the Corporal said and, circling his arm around the weeping Private, led him to his compartment.

The story of Oka was well known, and his comrades all sympathized with him. He was brave enough in combat and strong on the march, but he was always getting into trouble and breaking some rules in between. For instance, he had beaten up the Company Commander's orderly once in a fight over a chicken during a march, and at another time, he had taken leave without permission and had been caught doing it. His comrades all agreed with Oka and pitied him, since he certainly had little face to show his folks at home after remaining a private for three years as a Regular.

Takeo and Kan had the room cleaned and swept in short order, and the Reserves finally gave them a hand when they began to lay out the blankets which were to be their beds for the night. When everything was in order, the two First-Year-Soldiers sat down to rest before turning in, since there was still a little time left before "Lights-out." The singing and merry-making had practically subsided in all the rooms. In the yard some soldier was ranting loudly and vehemently. In the course of their sweeping, Takeo and Kan had heard some Reserves who had just come in from the outside excitedly recounting how they had hung a Second-Year-Soldier, a Private First Class, by his heels from a tree when the latter had boasted that he was a *judo* expert of the first rank. They thought that he must now have been let down by friends, for he was screaming vengeance. In the Squad Leader's compartment, they could hear Corporal Sakamoto earnestly lecturing Oka on the futility of ranks, and his voice was the only excited voice in the room. Most of the Reserves were now lying on their blankets ready to go to sleep. The Reserves, playing their game of cards in the far corner, were whispering in a low voice, for gambling was prohibited in the army.

The First-Year-Soldiers heard with a deep sense of relief the welcome "Lights-out!" called by the soldiers standing the first watch for the night. Kan hastily threw his cigarette butt into the ash tray which was before him, and he and Takeo went to turn the lights out in the room. Then they gathered all the ash trays in the room and placed them outside in the lobby for the Officer-Of-The-Week to see them, since smoking after curfew was strictly prohibited as a fire precaution. The card players continued their game, now by the light of flashlights, and Oka came out of the Squad Leader's room to go quietly to sleep. Private First Class Tanaka and a few other Regulars were still not back in the squad room, and Takeo thought that they were probably in the Warrant Officer's room, currying his favor.

Takeo and Kan went before the Squad Leader's compartment and said politely, "Honorable Squad Leader, we will be permitted to rest." Then they went to the place on the platform where they were to sleep and removed their coats and trousers, but, before lying down, they said, "Please go to sleep," now for the benefit of the Seniors. As he pulled the blankets over him, Takeo felt the aches and pains he had forgotten for some time come back all at once, and he winced and gritted his teeth to keep from groaning out loud. He heard the Officer-Of-The-Week stamping loudly down the lobby and calling angrily, "Turn the lights off!" Some of the squad rooms had probably not been punctual enough in turning their lights out. The Officer-Of-The-Week stopped noisily in front of Squad Three and beamed his flashlight into the room. Takeo kept his eyes tightly closed in pretended sleep; but he felt his heart pounding wildly, for if the officer found any discrepancy in the room, the First-Year-Soldiers would be the ones to be awakened to remedy it. He had heard the Reserves, who had been engaged in their game of cards, diving under the blankets when the steps of the inspecting officer had approached, but he was not sure whether they had hidden all the evidences of their misbehavior successfully or not, and he was worried about them also, but the officer soon turned off his flashlight and left for the next room.

No sooner had the officer left than the Reserves, who had had their card game interrupted, were at it again, and the scraping of the cards as they were shuffled and the low undertone of the gamblers were the only sounds in the room. The ruckus in the yard, too, had stopped, and it seemed that they had led the vengeance-vowing soldier back to his room and put him to sleep. Silence had descended so suddenly when the Curfew call had sounded that Takeo felt dazed and lost as he lay in his blankets. Miki groaned beside him, and that reminded him that the towel on his comrade's forehead had not been changed for some time now. He pulled himself partly out of his blankets and turned toward his injured comrade. He searched with his hand in the darkness and, finding the towel, rinsed it well in the basin beside him and placed the wet towel back on his comrade's forehead. He touched Miki's face with his hand and found it still hot with fever. He stretched himself back under his blankets and felt a little worried about his friend's condition. He tried to find assurance in the thought that they had asked the night watches to change the towel every thirty minutes. But other thoughts and sensations soon came crowding back to his mind, and he quickly forgot his comrade. The thoughts and sensations whirled crazily in his mind, and he made a mighty effort to brush them aside and go to sleep.

Somebody cut the air noisily at the other end of the room. Soon the room was momentarily filled with the foul odor of it. Somebody made a protesting sound. A soldier just outside their room was vomiting loudly, and he seemed to be putting his whole heart and soul into the act. Takeo tried hard not to have his attention drawn toward the new sound outside the room, and he tried desperately to go to sleep, for tomorrow was going to begin early with Reveille and everything which had happened this day would be forgotten, so that nothing mattered except that he would have to be on his toes again tomorrow if he did not want to get it from his superiors. It was always like this at the end of a day — there was no time to recollect one's thoughts or to formulate plans for the future. Time and the effort required were too precious to be wasted in place of the all-valuable sleep, and they would be a total waste anyway even if they bore fruit, since individuals did not exist in the Imperial Army. Kan began to snore loudly beside Takeo, and Takeo thought, What a shameless fellow! but he did not know what he meant by it and tried once more to go to sleep himself.

CHAPTER 14

It was a large room for a Japanese-style one — a ten *jo* room, or one with ten straw mats, each measuring six feet by two feet. It opened into the hall by way of thin paper sliding doors, while thicker paper doors with simple but graceful designs on them stood between it and the next room. The unpainted woodwork was still new and well polished, emitting an atmosphere of untainted cleanliness unattainable even by the highest quality paint.

The *Tokonoma*, or decorative alcove, which stood conspicuously at the head of the room, was frugally bare except for a suggestive arrangement of flowers on its base and a long paper scroll hanging down its full length from the ceiling. The classic characters, "The Imperial Way Is Truth and Justice," were written with bold brush strokes in black ink on the scroll. They represented a popular saying of the day, and in the bottom corner was the very legible signature of a famous General, of whom it was being rumored that he was going to be the next all-powerful War Minister. He had probably been entertained in this house during his late tour of duty on the continental front and had written the scroll for the host in token of his gratitude. People, these days, as soon as they attained a little renown, seemed to be struck by a mania to leave signed works of their penmanship wherever they went, as if they were not so sure whether posterity would remember them for their deeds and so wanted at least to be remembered by their penmanship.

The scroll and the arrangement of flowers were the only decorations in the room. A long, shiningly lacquered, low table in the middle was the sole piece of furniture. It was loaded with the traditional delicacies-to-go-with-wine, such as slices of raw fish, chopped boiled squid, broiled fish, broiled eel on bamboo spits, and pickled seaweed. The food arranged neatly on artistically shaped dishes and in shiny lacquered bowls harmonized pleasantly with the room's general tone of subdued grace.

The officers who were squatted around the table, however, were conspicuously out of harmony with the room, as if they had forced themselves in where the host had intended to invite some more refined friends, dressed appropriately in formal robed kimono. The men were dressed in their harsh khaki uniforms, which, although clean and pressed, so that one knew they were special ones never worn at the battlefronts, nevertheless belonged only to those places where utility was the primary factor in determining grace and beauty — to the rooms where one sat at desks and tables and to the battlefields. One could believe, on the other hand, that the officers had been invited by the host to lend prestige to a dying grace, as one hires thugs to protect a right or a property, which, in the end, the very existence of the thugs themselves endangered.

But the truth was nothing so complicated. The officers were in neither of the above mentioned categories; they had paid for the room and service they were receiving and were intruding on no one but the atmosphere. And even on the last score, they were not as guilty as at first glance, for on close scrutiny, the room showed discrepancies in many details, attesting to a hurried and careless construction. The sliding paper doors did not fit their grooves evenly; the designs on the partition to the next room were cheap imitations of famous classics; the straw mats were crooked; and even the scroll of the mighty General showed traces of having been written by a hand which preferred the wine cup far more than the art brush.

If the discrepancies were there, however, nobody was to blame for them, for the room belonged to one of the numerous tea houses which had hastily mushroomed wherever the Imperial Japanese Army had settled down on the continent. Reserved almost solely for the entertainment of the officers, these houses were doing a prosperous, booming business everywhere they appeared. Flimsy imitations of their more substantial prototypes at home (which, in their turn, were nothing more than imitations of the aristocrats' homes of the feudal ages), these houses offered almost the only source of relaxation to the overworked officers, burdened by a complex conglomeration of duties, demanding an almost feudalistic spiritual and social conduct, on the one hand, and the knowledge of the most intricate scientific details of modern warfare on the other.

The officers assembled in the food-laden room on this particular evening were from the battalion to which Takeo and his comrades belonged. Like the soldiers who had happily poured out of the post earlier that day, the officers were enjoying their first leave this night since coming to the city after their strenuous campaign inland. There were about ten of them in the room, shiningly washed and shaved and showing not the slightest traces of the grimy, tattered figures they had been at the front. The officers sat around the table, just beaming happily at their clean surrounding, or feasting and drinking eagerly, or listening to the chatter and singing of the geisha girls who sat beside them, or exchanging easy jokes among themselves, or discussing some fine points of philosophy, or religion, or art, and trying, all in all, their hardest to forget the war.

The geisha girls were a great help in this last respect as they sang lustily to the accompaniment of their twanging samisens and unceasingly chattered their harmless line of trade, bordering intentionally on the bawdy and uncouth. They were dressed in brilliantly colored kimonos, and their hair was done high and wide in the classic style and oiled liberally with strongly perfumed pomade. Their faces and necks were hidden under a thick layer of a kind of sickly white liquid cosmetic, which was considered an essential aid to beauty in their trade, though it only made them look unnatural and expressionless. Their lips were painted a uniform crimson red, without imagination or originality.

The effect was one of total artificiality — as if one had painted a new face on a face. The rest of the body was wrapped in layers of colorful silk, which completely hid the original contours of the body, and the whole structure was crowned by an ornate hair-do which was half false hair and which almost dripped the oily black dye covering it. This way the women were unmistakably typed, and the men could feel less weight on their consciences for dallying with them.

"Ha-san, let's have another drink!" the geisha sitting next to Captain Hamamoto pouted coquettishly as she lifted the porcelain bottle containing hot *sake* from the table in front of her. This type of women made it their stock-in-trade to call their customers intimately by the first syllable of their last names.

"If it is *sake* poured by O-kiku-san, I shall rejoice to drink it," said Captain Hamamoto gallantly, and he held forth his wine cup.

"Look at Ha-san! He says that to everybody!" exaggeratedly chided O-kiku-san, and she poured the *sake* into the Captain's cup.

Captain Hamamoto was seated at the head of the table, that is, at that end of the table where one's back was turned to the *Tokonoma* (for that was the place of honor). He was the senior in rank, and also in age, among those present. There were also present, Junior Lieutenant Kondo of Takeo's Second Platoon, who was a graduate of a fashionable college in Tokyo; Junior Lieutenant Miura, younger in age and a graduate of the central Military Academy and commander of Captain Hamamoto's Third Platoon; and Senior Lieutenant Makoto, commander of a neighboring company, who had been an official in a rural government office before being mobilized into the army.

The geisha sitting next to Lieutenant Makoto was twanging away zealously on her samisen and singing a popular ballad in that high nasal tone which was considered the height of elegance in her profession:

> *The sprays fall on my fellow, floating down*
> *the River Tenryu on his log-raft.*
> *Oh, how I wish to give him,*
> *Oh, how I wish to give him —*
> *A fancy umbrella!*

Lieutenant Makoto and a few others near him clapped their hands in time to the song and listened attentively to the geisha, interrupting their clapping only occasionally to sip contentedly from their wine cups. It had been a long time since they had heard a woman's voice so close at hand, and the experience made the shivers run up and down their spines.

Near the foot of the table, the two young Lieutenants, Kondo of the fashionable college and Miura of the classic Military Academy, were engaged in a heated argument. Their young faces were bright and shining with excitement, and they seemed to be the only ones in the room who had not succumbed to the debilitating enchantment of the geishas. The others had already allowed themselves to be taken into the soft world of the geishas, but these two young officers seemed to grow livelier with each cup of *sake* they drank.

"But an order is an order, and if it is from a superior, we must take it as an order from the One Being Supreme," Lieutenant Miura, the proponent of the classic tradition, was insisting loudly.

"That is too much!" laughingly objected Lieutenant Kondo, who seemed to be the more diplomatic of the two. "The Emperor will not just wildly, without reason, order one to commit *harakiri*."

"The question is not whether the Emperor will order it or not. The question is whether we must obey if he does — even if we see not the slightest reason for it. I say that we must," doggedly continued Lieutenant Miura.

"If the One Being Supreme orders it, I will commit *harakiri* without questioning, because the Emperor's order is absolute. But we are talking about a superior, say, a Senior Lieutenant, or even a Colonel," retorted Kondo and gulped down another cup of hot *sake*.

"Then don't you think the Imperial Rescript to the Armed Forces is absolute?" Lieutenant Miura was really excited now and his voice grew so high that everybody turned toward the two young Lieutenants. "What do you think of the Imperial Edict, which says: 'Think that an order from a superior is directly an order from Us'?"

"I still think that I will not carry out such an order immediately but will first take my case to an officer higher up," replied Lieutenant Kondo, but he now sounded a little taken aback by the unexpected vehemence of his companion.

Some of the older officers began offering their good services to mediate in the argument, and even O-Kiku-san chided.

"Say, look at these men. They seem to have come to argue!"

"Hey, let us do this party without arguments," called Captain Hamamoto from his end of the table in a fatherly tone. "You can argue anywhere. But you can't feast and play as you can here, very often."

"Hey, sister! Pour them a drink!" shouted Lieutenant Makoto to the young geisha sitting, completely perplexed, next to the two zealous debaters. "It is because you do not entertain them enough that they start arguing," he scolded good-naturedly.

"Say, Miura! Let's hear you sing a song!" Captain Hamamoto called to Lieutenant Miura, who was sulking openly now, and others took up the suggestion, and some began clapping their hands in anticipation.

Lieutenant Miura picked up his cup and, emptying it in a single gulp, shoved it rudely before the geisha beside him to have it refilled and then gulped that down too. He now took the formal position on his knees and squared his shoulders. His actions were so aggressively dramatic that many felt coerced into silence.

The Lieutenant began singing. It was the "*Shigin*," the martial chant passed down by the warriors from feudal times. It was a repetitious chant, wild and moving like a cry in the wilderness, and was usually sung to accompany an equally wild sword dance, but nobody danced this evening, and Lieutenant Miura had the show all to himself:

> *The Emperor is the Commander-in-chief.*
> *The servicemen of land and sea are his*
> *guardians.*
> *Patriotism and Etiquette compose the will of*
> *loyalty.*
> *Courage and Sincerity form the body of sacri-*
> *fice.*
> *Simplicity should reign, and there will be the*
> *happiness of peace.*
> *These Five Imperial Edicts are the Spirit of*
> *the Armed Forces.*

Everybody listened politely, though the savage enthusiasm of the singer was in complete discord with the jovial atmosphere of the occasion. It is enough to turn the *sake* cold in our stomachs, thought Captain Hamamoto who was not the only one who felt peeved at the young rebel. They were only too glad when the song ended and clapped obligingly, though there was no mistaking that a damp had settled down on the party which would require many more porcelain containers of hot, steaming *sake* to remove.

The late singer, paying little heed to the applause offered him, gulped down his third cup of *sake* in succession and got up shakily to his feet. Swaying dangerously, he glared at the geisha beside him and almost scolded, "Sister! Where is the toilet?"

The geisha immediately came to his rescue and, holding him

up, scolded in that elder-sister tone women in her profession use to such advantage, "Well, this fellow is drunk! Come, I will take you along!"

"If you show me the way, I'll go alone," said Lieutenant Miura angrily and shook the hands of the geisha from his shoulders, at the same time almost shaking himself down to the floor.

He staggered a few steps sideways and then turned toward the door, but stumbled with his next step when he miscalculated the level of the floor and, almost diving forward, now completely out of control, bumped heavily into the paper door, making big holes in the paper with his fingers. Barely holding himself upright with the grip he maintained precariously through the holes in the door, he turned toward his Company Commander and blurted pitifully, "Sir Company Commander, I am drunk! Please forgive me!"

"Come! Don't waste your time here! You'll let it leak!" said the geisha, and, now taking firm hold of him, opened the door and led him out.

"What a helpless fool!" said Lieutenant Makoto, expressing the feeling of nearly all those present, for to hold one's drink was a respected virtue among them.

"Well, don't say it," said Captain Hamamoto, "He is only young. And if he doesn't drink, he is all right."

"I am sorry we caused all this confusion," said young Lieutenant Kondo, sitting stiffly and bowing his head, as if he realized for the first time the discomfort he and his young friend had caused by their ill-timed argument.

"You are not to blame," assured Lieutenant Makoto but added, "Drink when you drink and work when you work. Only don't cause any trouble to others."

Then looking meaningfully at two young Junior Lieutenants sitting before him, who were also, like Lieutenant Miura, graduates of the proud Military Academy, he continued, "Whether we are graduates of the Military Academy, or of the Imperial

University, or of a rural elementary school, our feelings for our country and our courage are the same. The main thing is our sincerity." Lieutenant Makoto was a graduate of a rural middle school.

"Sirs, how about stopping all this chatter, and sir_ing some songs," interposed O-Kiku-san in a tone which sounded like an old teacher scolding her flock of children. "What a drab lot you are!"

"Before we start singing, O-Kiku-san, let someone put Miura to sleep. He seemed to be pretty far gone," said Captain Hama-moto. O-Kiku-san was the eldest geisha, and so she was the proper person to whom to refer such a matter as this.

"That is so. O-Hana-san, the four-and-a-half-mat room under the stairway is free. Take him there and put him to sleep." O-Kiku-san called to the youngest geisha present, who im-mediately got up and went out to do her bidding. There was strict discipline among the geishas, and priority in age as well as service, was observed among them as conscientiously as in the army.

Those remaining now began singing in earnest — solo and in groups. They clapped their hands noisily, and the geishas indus-triously twanged their samisens in accompaniment. They also joined the singing with their high rasping voices. Some began beating the bowls and plates with their chopsticks, and the more adept ones got to their feet to dance.

O-Kiku-san herself stood up to dance the bawdy "Shallow River" dance amid the loud clapping and cheering of the officers. One of her fellow geishas sang the song for the dance, accompanied by the samisen:

> When crossing a shallow river,
> We raise our kimono up to our knees . . .

O-Kiku-san raised her kimono slightly and pretended to cross a river, stumbling over pebbles and pushing against the current. It was not a very graceful dance, but the river became deeper each time in the song, and the dancer had to keep raising the hem of her kimono to keep it from getting wet. Everybody was having a good time.

O-Kiku-san returned to her place beside Captain Hamamoto when her dance was over and her guests had had an ample view of her well-rounded legs. The officers enthusiastically offered her their cups and filled them for her in token of their pleasure, and O-Kiku-san emptied the cups as fast as they were offered her and showed an amazing capacity to take her liquor. She seemed not the least abashed at what she had done and maintained a dignity and poise which only the women in her profession could maintain under such circumstances. A lull seemed to have fallen on the merrymaking after O-Kiku-san's dance, and the geisha now began coaxing the officers to begin their singing again.

"Well, well, wait a while. Let us rest before starting again," protested Captain Hamamoto. "Bring some more raw fish and *sake*." Several geishas got to their feet and hurried out to do the bidding. They had been going in and out of the room, busily replenishing the fast waning stock, ever since the party had started, and seldom needed to be reminded as they now had been. It was their main purpose to run up the food and liquor bills of their guests, and they went at it enthusiastically.

Three young Lieutenants soon got up to excuse themselves. They said that they had promised to join another party. The truth was, however, they had had enough of this drinking and singing with the geishas. They wanted more substantial fun, and they knew they would have no claim on the geishas after the party, since there were more officers than geishas, and the senior officers would have first choice.

"Say, it is only nine o'clock yet," protested Lieutenant Makoto, who knew perfectly well what the young officers wanted, but when they left after apologizing profusely, he added, as if in their defense, "They are still young—those men."

"O-Kiku-san, you have pretty hands." Captain Hamamoto took the geisha's hand and patted it lightly.

"Look! He sounds as if he didn't have a wife!" O-Kiku-san parried, and she withdrew her hand roughly. She had a habit of becoming forthright, it seemed, when the drinks took hold of her. She had drunk almost as much as anyone present, especially since her lively dance. The fact that she did not have to leave the table to carry the service trays back and forth between the room and the kitchen, since she was the head geisha and endowed with special privileges, was a great help.

"A wife is a wife," answered Captain Hamamoto ambiguously to the geisha's playful accusation.

"Look! He tries to fool us by saying such a thing! Your wife is waiting faithfully for you at home, and you should be cursed by the gods for being unfaithful," continued O-Kiku-san in mock seriousness.

"It is only natural that a wife should wait faithfully for us. We are fighting death-defyingly for our country," Lieutenant Makoto came to the aid of his friend. The Lieutenant had a wife and four children.

"You have no right to be unfaithful because you are fighting for your country," O-Kiku-san countered without flinching. Now everybody in the room was listening to this highly entertaining argument, and some took parts and cheered their respective party.

"Come, come. We have not been unfaithful yet," said Captain Hamamoto.

"I am only a good-for-nothing woman, and I have been in this profession since I was very young, and I do not know much about anything. But I know, if I were married and if I knew my husband was being unfaithful even if he were fighting for his country, I would be unfaithful too," said O-Kiku-san, haughtily and all in one breath.

"But that is where you are mistaken. From ancient days, in our country a wife of a warrior has been a model of fidelity.

That is why our fighting men have been so strong. They can leave their homes for the battlefields without worry," said Captain Hamamoto, now quite serious himself.

"That still doesn't give anyone any reason to be unfaithful," stubbornly insisted O-Kiku-san.

"This isn't being unfaithful. This is taking a rest," said Captain Hamamoto. "If we do not rest once in a while, we will not be able to fight."

"My wife has a knife under her *obi* or in her room to defend her chastity," said Lieutenant Makoto.

"That is a true wife of a warrior," quickly followed Captain Hamamoto.

"A woman of Japan will sooner cut her throat than let someone despoil her," said Lieutenant Makoto.

"O-Kiku-san, you are being beaten badly. Get a hold of yourself," several geishas called from around the table. Everybody was now interested in the discussion. It was just one of those moments in a drinking party when interest lags to such a low level that the merest incident focuses the attention of all.

"I just want to show your wives a scene like this," O-Kiku-san swallowed the *sake* from a cup offered her by an officer nearby and retorted. They were offering her more cups of *sake*, and she was accepting them all and dispatching them with indefatigable ease.

"They will think nothing of it," answered Captain Hamamoto. "We are performing our patriotism to our country with a soul that has not the slightest shadow of uncertainty. Our wives are performing their duties to us with the same feeling. If we are willing to lay down our lives for our country, they should be willing to lay down their lives to defend their fidelity toward us."

"That is where we see the glory of Japan," added Lieutenant Makoto, now thoroughly carried away by the eloquence of his superior. "The value of having been born sons of the Japanese race is to be found in that quality."

"In the olden days, a warrior was said to be in enemy territory the moment he stepped out of his home. Then it was the woman's duty to guard the house until her master's return, with her life, if need be. It is the same today, only the home has become the nation, and the national pride, and tradition."

Captain Hamamoto was vehemently preaching to a now completely overcome O-Kiku-san, when the sliding door to the room was suddenly opened, and the stout well-fed figure of a slightly bald man with a tiny mustache on a round sun-tanned face stood peering with blinking eyes in the doorway. He was the Battalion Commander, Major Sagami, though they did not recognize him at once, since he was not in his usual uniform but was dressed in an informal *yukata-kimono*. He was swaying drunkenly on his feet.

"Salute!" Junior Lieutenant Kondo shouted when he recognized who the sudden intruder was and, disentangling himself from the geisha around whose shoulder he had his arm, he tried to scramble to his feet.

The sharp command seemed to have jolted the Battalion Commander, and he stiffened to brace himself and rejoined hastily, "As you were! As you were!"

It took the Major a little time to recover from the shock of the young Lieutenant's sudden salutation, but he soon regained his drunken composure and called cheerfully, "Well, so it is you, Captain Hamamoto. I thought I recognized your voice!"

All the officers were now sitting stiffly in the formal position on their knees, and Captain Hamamoto, grinning sheepishly, answered, "Yes, sir."

"Well, Makoto, too, is here. You are all here!" the Major exclaimed, looking around the room and now beaming most patronizingly.

"Honorable Battalion Commander, will it not please you to drink a cup with us?" Captain Hamamoto invited politely, holding a cup before him.

"That is so. Shall I go a cup?" the Major said and started to enter the room.

A geisha, however, who now appeared behind the Major, suddenly grabbed hold of his sleeve and protested vigorously, "Sa-san, that is not good. You have drunk enough already!"

Major Sagami was not his usual formidable self and was pulled back easily by the protesting geisha. The Major tried hard to maintain his dignity, but the best he could manage was to stroke his mustache and excuse himself weakly, "The truth is, I was drinking farther down the hall. If I had known earlier I would have drunk together with you. I was on my way to sleep when I heard Captain Hamamoto's voice. . . . " The geisha gave an insistent pull. "Take your time and have some fun," the Major was barely able to add, as he was forcibly yanked out of the room and the door closed after him.

"The Battalion Commander is some fellow, all right," Captain Hamamoto commented as they all unbent their knees and resumed the more comfortable squatting position.

"More *sake*! More *sake*!" Lieutenant Makoto began calling to the geisha.

"Look at this man! It is eleven o'clock already. There won't be any *sake*," protested O-Kiku-san. "Think of us a little. We are all tired."

The matron of the house, a plain elderly woman, came in just then. She was an avaricious-looking woman, way past her middle age. "We are sorry. But we are all out of *sake*," she lied brashly and immediately began negotiating with Captain Hamamoto regarding arrangements for the night. Captain Hamamoto, of course, chose to sleep with O-Kiku-san, and nearly all the others were able to get bed partners, too, except Lieutenant Kondo and several other Junior Lieutenants. The house was overcrowded, they were told, and it was now up to the young officers to try their luck elsewhere. Even here, the principle of seniority was the almighty factor.

After a very formal leave-taking by the neglected young officers, those remaining went each to his assigned room with his companion for the night. Captain Hamamoto, however, had the presence of mind to console the young officers at parting. "Please forgive us. Do something about it, though, for yourselves for tonight."

Once in their room, a cozy, neat one, O-Kiku-san helped Captain Hamamoto change into a kimono. As she helped her guest on with his *obi*, she said, "You know, Ha-san, there's a beautiful tortoise-shell brooch in the store on the corner. But it costs too much for us in our station to buy. . . . Won't you please buy it for me?"

"Tomorrow, after we get up, I will buy it for you," Captain Hamamoto promised meekly and lighted a cigarette while he watched O-Kiku-san undress.

CHAPTER 15

IT HAD COME SUDDENLY without prior notice, like all orders in the army — the older Reserves had been ordered home all of a sudden to be discharged, and they had been given only three days to prepare to board their ships. Captain Hamamoto had read the fateful order at the company's roll-call one morning not long after the memorable first leave-day in the city. There had been rumors of demobilization for a long time, but none had been able to forecast the exact time nor the form it would take, and so the order had come as a total surprise. The discipline of the men was such that only a subdued ripple of excitement had greeted the announcement when it was made at roll-call, though tears glistened visibly in the eyes of some of the Reserves affected by the discharge order. There had also been a strong undercurrent of disappointment, for the majority of the men were not to return home, and envy always walks hand in hand with extreme joy.

The night before departure, Reserve Private Aoki, who was one of the lucky ones, had taken his First-Year-Soldier friend, Shunzo Miki, to a secluded spot behind the company kitchen to bid him farewell in private. "I will never forget that you did not tell anybody that I had been the one who had taken you into the restricted area that day," Aoki said.

"No, that was nothing. I was to blame," Miki smiled happily.

"Take good care of your body. If you can return home in

good health, remember, such a thing as promotion and citations is worth nothing," Aoki advised his younger friend. Then he had given Miki his talisman, which, he said, had also seen his father safely through the Russo-Japanese War. It was from a Shinto shrine in his home village, he explained.

After the Reserves had left, those remaining had had little time to mope over their own insufficient fate, for, immediately, a whole batch of fresh Replacements had arrived to take the place of the departed soldiers. The weeks following had been busy ones to help acclimatize the new arrivals to conditions on the continent. They had also been exciting ones for the older soldiers, since the Replacements had brought an almost inexhaustible supply of the latest news regarding conditions and happenings at home.

The price of oxen had gone up considerably since he had first started saving his earnings to buy one, Takeo had learned to his chagrin. They had also heard the term "mobilized economy," for the first time, and they had listened with wonder as they were told about how rice was being rationed to the people by the government and about how no one could now go and buy the staple food whenever he wanted to, even if he had the money to do so. The soldiers from the farms had heard also with a little concern about how rice quotas had been established, so that farmers were now compelled to deliver fixed amounts of their harvest annually to the government.

Less than a month after the Replacements had arrived, the order for the whole division to board ships had been issued. It had come just as suddenly as the previous order of demobilization for the Reserves, but this time there was no rejoicing, for the men were told that the division was to embark on a large-scale landing operation. The new order had not come as a complete surprise, since the men had been undergoing intensive training for some time in landing tactics. Day after day they had gone up and down the trap ladder hanging from the second-story balcony of their building in simulation of going over the side of a ship.

Before boarding their ships, the men were given five days' rations of rice and hard biscuits and more ammunition than they could hold in their cartridge containers, so that they had been forced to put the extra ammunition in their already overcrowded rucksacks. They had not been told the new destination, but one thing was certain — the coming campaign was going to be a long, hard one.

Two weeks at sea, and the men were still ignorant of their coming landing point. The days, however, had grown warmer as the ships had advanced, and it was really hot lately like the hottest days of summer, although it had been chilly and frost had started falling where they had boarded the ships in North China, so that the soldiers had come to realize for certain now that they were heading southward.

"Honorable Senior Soldier, where do you think we are going to land?" Private Seki, a newcomer, asked Miki lying beside him in the squad's berth. The new Replacements addressed the First-Year-Soldiers as "Honorable Senior Soldiers."

"If I knew, I would be God," laughed Miki.

"We are going to land on Fukien Province," said Kan knowingly from the other side. "That place is not occupied yet."

"Kwangsi Province and Kwangtung Province also are not occupied yet," said Takeo.

The soldiers had just finished their lunch, and they were lying closely side by side on mats spread on a racklike structure in the ship's hold near the bow. Except for the new Replacements all the soldiers were in their loincloths only, and even the former had their coats off, but still the sweat kept flowing down their faces and backs, and they kept wiping themselves from time to time with their towels.

The vessel had been a freighter, and the hold where the freight had been previously stored was now crowded with the sweating, naked soldiers. Neat rows of double racks, one above the other, had been built in the hold with rough, unplaned pieces of lumber, and straw mats had been spread on them. The racks were just wide enough to accommodate the full length of a soldier lying down and just high enough to keep one from bumping his head when squatted. Space had been allotted each squad on these racks according to the number of its members, and ropes or rows of rucksacks marked the boundaries between the squads. The space allotted a squad, however, was so limited that there was hardly any room left when the soldiers lay down side by side to sleep at night. Soldiers were packed both on the upper racks and on the lower racks, and those on the upper racks had the disadvantage of having the metal deck over their heads which became uncomfortably heated by the sun during the day and which rang with the sound of soldiers stamping back and forth in their hobnailed shoes all day long; those on the lower racks had to suffer the dust which kept falling constantly upon them through the cracks in the upper racks, and sometimes those on the upper racks spilt soup or tea, and they were a sorry lot then.

Squad Three had received a berth on the upper rack, and they were really feeling the heat waves from the hot deck above them this afternoon. A group of the more energetic members of the squad, including Corporal Sakamoto, joined by a few soldiers from the neighboring squad, were engaged in a card game at one end of the squad's berth, but the majority of the soldiers were lying down and trying to be as motionless as possible, since the slightest motion seemed to enhance the heat markedly.

"It is hot," Miki groaned impetuously. He had recovered fully from the beating he had received at *Kempei* headquarters and was his former outspoken self again.

"It would be cooler if we were nearer the center," said Kan. There was a winch hole in the center of the deck covering the hold, which was the only source of ventilation, since the hold had no portholes, and Squad Three was located in the farthest corner away from the hole.

"It isn't so," said Takeo. "Those near the center are having a hard time with the smell of the horses coming from down below."

The hold was divided into two layers, the upper one of which was the one where the soldiers were packed. The winch hole through the deck also passed through the floor of the upper hold and opened into the bottom hold, which was also the bottom of the vessel. This was where part of the battalion's horses were kept, and the smell of the horses' manure, reinforced by the sour odor of rotting hay, rose constantly through the winch hole and partly infiltrated the hold where the men were and mingled with the already heavy stench of the sweating, crowded soldiers.

"What time can it be?" asked Kan emptily, and he lazily lighted a cigarette he had just placed between his lips.

"It is two o'clock," answered Takeo, looking down at his wrist watch.

"It is the hottest time of the day," observed Kan, and he watched the smoke he had just blown from his mouth stand almost stiff in the thick air.

"When I look in here, I think of the cocoon racks at home," said Miki, but nobody felt strong enough to laugh at his joke.

"Hey! Somebody get me some tea!" Corporal Sakamoto called from where he was playing his game of cards with his friends.

"Yes, sir!" several Replacement soldiers promptly answered, and there was a scramble to get off the berth and into their shoes, but Private Seki was the first to make it, and he took the squad's large teakettle and started for the winch hole where there was a ladder leading up to the deck. There was a constant supply of hot, boiled tea in a tank in the improvised kitchen on deck, and soldiers were going there continuously all day long to replenish their kettles. The heat made the men thirsty, and, since they were forbidden to drink raw water, they had only the tea with which to quench their thirst.

"Hard work," the soldiers called consolingly after Seki. The First-Year-Soldiers, too, had made a motion as if to rise to do the bidding of their Squad Leader, for they were still First-Year-Soldiers after all and were looked down upon by the older soldiers, but the motion had been solely a show, and Kan thought, What a fool Seki is! In this heat!

Some First-Year-Soldiers had started to put on airs when they had heard themselves being called, "Honorable Senior Soldier," by the new Replacements, but this had been stopped immediately. The older soldiers had assembled them in the yard back in the city one night and warned them, "It is still too early for you First-Year-Soldiers to put on the airs of Senior Soldiers!" and they had been slapped soundly on top of it. So the First-Year-Soldiers had continued to do the menial errands, though they were now reinforced by the Replacements, and the latter still called them "Honorable Senior Soldier" as etiquette demanded and, out of deference to their seniority, made the work as light as possible for them.

The Replacements themselves had been given the full treatment soon after their arrival. They were not conscript Regulars and were men who had been dropped for various physical defects when they had gone up for their compulsory military examinations. They were, therefore, much older than the Regulars and had various records of established occupation in civilian life like the Reserves, although, unlike the latter, they had no previous experience in military life. There were clerks, businessmen, and professional men, as well as the common workers and farmers, among the Replacements. They, too, had been assembled by the older soldiers one night and "spirit had been put into them."

"You Replacements still have too much of the civilian's attitude! You may have been important in civilian life, but here in the army, you are only soldiers!" the older Regulars had shouted at them, and the Replacements had received their first beating on the continent, although they had already had their taste of this form of discipline back in their training post at home. Since then, the older soldiers and non-commissioned officers had felt themselves called upon to "put the spirit" into the Replacements individually and in groups from time to time.

When Seki returned from his errand, his comrades greeted him again with their "Hard work!" and Corporal Sakamoto commended him with a liberal "Hard work!" After he had left his kettle of steaming tea and gone back to his friends, Private First Class Tanaka, who was also a member of the card game, turned toward his Squad Leader and observed, "That fellow Seki works hard." They poured the hot tea into their cups and began to sip it noisily. There was one advantage in drinking hot tea in the hot weather — a soldier could not drink very much of it and so was safe from sweating heavily afterward. "Fifty sen is too high. Let us make the stakes ten sen," said Corporal Sakamoto when he had finished with his cup of tea.

Gambling was not officially condoned in the Japanese Army, and orders were issued from time to time, reminding the men of the ban, but it was another one of those restrictions which were given a lax interpretation in deference to inevitable human nature. Like the mischiefs which the men perpetrated in a campaign, and like the adultery which the officers committed in the geisha houses, gambling, too, was dismissed by that convenient phrase in the national vocabulary, "It can't be helped." The lofty professions of the Imperial Army sprang primarily from a belief in the Emperor's divinity and in the divinity of the race also, and they were concerned very little with ideals of moral conduct or with codes of ethics. "If God should misbehave, who was one to question Him?" could have been the attitude underlying much of the extra-combat activities of the Imperial Army, though it never was worded so plainly in the men's consciousness.

When Seki, the industrious Replacement, returned to where his comrades were still lying motionless in their futile attempt to fight off the excessive heat, Miki called out in his usual outspoken manner, "Hard work! If you try hard, you can become a Private First Class." Seki had been a farmer like Miki, though a few years older.

"That is a joke," Seki laughed modestly, and he took off his coat and lay down beside Miki. The soldiers were compelled to put on their coats and trousers when going up on deck.

"It must be cool outside," said Kan.

"Yes, there is a good breeze blowing," answered Seki. They all knew how cool it was outside on deck, but the men preferred the hot interior of the hold to the deck. Here, they could be relaxed and comfortably undressed, whereas on deck they were subject to all the strict rules of discipline, including the obnoxious necessity of saluting all the superiors whom they encountered. There was a certain privacy in their berths inside the hold, and since they were very seldom called out to assemble, except for occasional physical exercises, the men tried to exploit this meager privacy to its maximum extent.

Takeo turned to the Replacement soldier lying down beside him and said, "Hirata, you should move around more like Seki, or you won't become a Private First Class quickly."

Hirata, who looked frailer than the usual run of soldiers, smiled cheerfully and answered, "I don't want to become Private First Class as long as I return home safely." Promotion to Private First Class was considered a high mark of distinction among the youths of Japan, and competition to attain it was keen among the soldiers.

"If you don't become a Private First Class, you lose a lot. A Private First Class has it easy, and, in the first place, his salary is higher than that of a common Private," said Kan. Kan was confident of getting his promotion the first chance.

"They say you were graduated from a university, but why didn't you take the examination to become an officer?" asked Takeo.

"If I became an officer, I would be kept a long time in the army. My temperament just doesn't fit the army," said Hirata.

"If you become an officer, you will have it easy, but you are going to have a hard time," said Takeo.

"Hirata has gone to school, and so he will be pulled quickly to Company Headquarters, or Battalion Headquarters. Duty at headquarters is easy, you know," said Kan.

"Anyway, you must become a Private First Class before you go home. Or else you won't have any face to show your folks at home," Takeo insisted doggedly, like an elder brother giving firm advice. Hirata came from the same village as Takeo — at least, his parents did, although Hirata himself had been born in the capital where his parents had gone many years ago. Therefore Takeo had not known the Replacement soldier back in his village, but the latter was registered in the village ledger and so officially considered a member of it.

"We are distant relatives, you know," said Takeo, who, as a farmer's eldest son, was well versed with village matters. "Your mother is a daughter of a cousin of my grandmother."

"Is that so?" said Hirata politely, who knew almost nothing of the village where he was registered, since he had gone into a law office in the capital soon after his graduation and had been back to the native village of his parents on only a few occasions.

Seki and Miki had been discussing the prospects for the next year's wheat crop at home when Kan had spoken loudly of the advantages accruing to one serving a stretch of duty in Company Headquarters. "There are many soldiers in Company Headquarters," Seki observed.

"That is so. They don't do anything and are just standing around," said Miki.

"We thought that the Company Commander was constantly with his subordinates and that he advanced at the head of his company when fighting started, but, as it is, he seems to be in a separate unit entirely," said Seki.

"It is only in the drills at home that the Company Commander advances at the head. At the front here, the Company Commander stays to the rear with his headquarters and lets the platoons go forward," sneered Miki.

"We can't win the war that way," objected Hirata.

"But we are winning it," said Kan.

"Now, we are winning it but we cannot say we have won it yet," said Hirata.

"You were in Tokyo. You were in the capital of the nation. You ought to know when the war will end," said Takeo.

"People like us don't know. They are telling us by radio and newspapers that the war may last many years. We can't help but leave the whole matter to the great ones. They probably think the war is going to be long. They have put rice under ration, and little by little things we can call our own are being lost," Hirata answered.

"Isn't that communism?" interposed Kan.

"No, that isn't communism. The Communists have been thrown into jail. That is a policy of the army. That is a war policy, although it is very similar to communism," said Hirata.

"Diagnosis patients, assemble!" a soldier climbed down the ladder into the hold and shouted in a loud voice.

"What is 'Iodine' getting excited about?" said Kan, raising his head a little to look at the soldier who was shouting in such a loud voice in the hot, stuffy room. The men called the medical soldiers "Iodine" since that painful article seemed to be their only tool of healing. They used it for wounds and cuts, of course, but they also dabbed it on for toothaches and, sometimes, even for headaches.

"Hey, Miki, has your diarrhea stopped?" Corporal Sakamoto looked up from his card game and called to the big First-Year-Soldier.

"Yes, sir. It has stopped," Miki answered promptly. He had started suffering again from his chronic ailment when they had boarded ship and had been making numerous trips to the improvised toilet on deck for some time, but he had made only one trip today.

"If you are bad, go and get yourself looked over," said Kan.

"It is the same, even if I get myself looked over," said Miki. "Iodine for the wounds, aspirin for headaches, and for diarrhea it is 'stop eating' . . . you don't have to get yourself looked over to know such a thing." It was a fact that the surgeons were brusque and very unsympathetic in the Japanese Army, for they had been schooled to give primary importance to "spiritual strength" and made the soldiers who went to see them for anything else but wounds incurred on the battlefields feel that they lacked in will power. The soldiers themselves went to the surgeons only as a last resort, since they not only disliked the uncomfortable reception in the surgeon's office, but also feared the bad impression a visit to the surgeon would make when reported to the personnel officer, as all such matters inevitably were.

"There are no ailing ones in our squad, are there?" Corporal Sakamoto called out, for it was his duty to see that all his men were in condition for the coming landing and campaign.

"There are none," several soldiers answered promptly, and nobody made a move to get up. Satisfied that none in his squad needed medical attention this day, Corporal Sakamoto went back to his card game.

A small group of weary-looking, wan soldiers were gathered now at the foot of the ladder leading out of the hold. Most of them looked pale and really gone. They were the men who were not as seaworthy as the rest of their comrades and who had not eaten much since boarding ship. The ocean had been fairly rough when they had first started although lately it had calmed down to such an extent that there was hardly any motion except the vibration from the engine's steady beat. Everybody had felt a little sick at the beginning, but most had recovered after a while. The meager food, consisting of rice and a thin soup most of the time, and the confined quarters had kept the weaker ones from recovering, and there were some really sick patients on board after two weeks.

"Aren't there any more who want to be diagnosed?" "Iodine" called impatiently. When nobody answered, he led his bedraggled group up the ladder and toward the medical room in the hold to the stern. Patients seldom had the luxury of having themselves examined while in bed.

All the soldiers on the berths had been eyeing the gathering in the center of the hold curiously, to see who among their friends were down with sickness. When the wan group had left, Miki exclaimed, "Really, I don't blame them for becoming sick."

Takeo now turned toward Seki and asked the Replacement a little self-consciously, "Say, Seki, how much does a two-year ox cost back home now?"

"Lately, the price has gone up plenty. A two-year ox should cost over one hundred and fifty yen. Before I came overseas, we sold a three-month calf, and we were able to sell it for fifty-five yen," Seki answered.

Takeo had already heard the news of the rising cost from other soldiers, but he still persisted in putting the question to those Replacements whom he knew to have been farmers before being mobilized in a hope that someone would mention a price closer to the price he knew when he was farming himself before being inducted into the army. Previously, however, he had taken care to ask the question privately, and this was the first time he was asking it in front of all his friends in his squad.

"Is that so? Then I will have to save plenty more before I can buy an ox," Takeo said when he was given the highly enlightening information by Seki.

"What is this? Do you want to buy an ox?" exclaimed Kan, who knew practically nothing about matters pertaining to farming.

"That is so. My parents are very old, and so I thought if I bought them an ox their work would become much easier. Therefore, I am saving every month," said Takeo earnestly, though he blushed a little. Confinement on a ship always made the men speak intimately of their own private affairs, and they thought nothing of it.

"How much have you saved already?" asked Kan.

"I have saved only fifty-five yen yet," admitted Takeo.

"What? You have saved plenty, all right! It is only nine months since we have come, so you have practically not spent any money from your salary. Or are you having money sent from home?" asked Miki unbelievingly.

"No, my home is not that rich," said Takeo. It was a fact that he had saved assiduously. After that memorable day when he had received such lavish entertainment at the brothel run by Hosaka's friend, Takeo had gone to the city on leave on two other occasions, but both times he had spent most of his day in a moving-picture theater and in the park. Both of which required almost no expenditure at all. To be sure, he had looked in at the brothel where the girl Mariko was supposed to be waiting for his next visit, but each time he had seen a large crowd of waiting soldiers, and he had not felt aggressive enough to push through them to go to his girl's room. Unfortunately, too, his friend Reserve Private Hosaka, who knew the owner of the brothel, had taken his leaves on days other than those chosen by him, and Takeo had not had the courage to go to ask the owner for special treatment when his friend was not with him.

"I have money sent from home, and still I don't have enough," said Kan almost boastfully.

"There are people who are making plenty of money from this war, you know," observed Replacement Private Hirata.

"Yes, I have a friend whose father owns a woodwork shop, and they are making plenty of money. They are making ammunition boxes for the army," said Kan.

"They are making money, too, maybe, but the ones who are really profiting are the big ones, the *zaibatsu*. What the single family of Mitsui makes in one year, they say, can support the whole Japanese Government," said Hirata.

"Ah, is it those families you speak of! Those people would make money whether there is war or no war. Their brains are made different from ours," declared Kan half jokingly, and everybody was silent for a moment.

Then Miki insisted doggedly, "It is the commissariat officers who are making the most money from this war. Don't they say that if he serves once at the front a commissariat officer will become rich?"

Somebody at the other end of the hold shouted in mock

desperation, "Turn on the electric fan!" Of course, there were no electric fans on the ship except in the cabins on deck where the officers were quartered.

Private Oka of Squad Three, who had just left the card game to get a pack of cigarettes from his rucksack, turned around and called back with equal zest, "Bring the ice water!" The joke seemed funny enough this time to cause the hot, suffering men to laugh.

CHAPTER 16

THERE HAD BEEN unusual activity from long before dawn this morning among the soldiers in the transport's crowded hold. The troops were now spending their third week at sea since embarking from the memorable seaport in North China. So monotonous had been the days on board ship that it had seemed to the men that all passage of time had stopped momentarily — until today, when they were once again reminded of the inevitability of time, for this was *Tenchosetsu*, or the Emperor's birthday, and the men had been told to assemble on deck for a sunrise service to worship the Emperor's Palace this morning.

Most of the soldiers were getting into their full uniforms for the first time in weeks. Ample grunts and curses could be heard in the hold as the soldiers fumbled in the dark recesses of their berths for the various accoutrements which went to make the regulation uniform worn for a formal occasion. Coats, trousers, caps, puttees, and shoes were to be worn, of course; but also required were the cartridge belt, bayonet, utilities bag, canteen, helmet, and rifle. Many a soldier felt quite lost wearing so many clothes after spending so many days in a loincloth, and all felt awkward when they started binding the troublesome puttees around their legs, almost as on the first day when they had tried it at the regimental barracks at home.

"I have become used to being naked, and so it feels funny to put clothes on again," exclaimed Private First Class Gunji loudly, jumping off the berth into the aisle with his rifle, the first one dressed among the members of Squad Three. It was the Private First Class's principal boast that he could get dressed faster than anyone in the squad, and no one begrudged him his boast, for he certainly had the knack of getting into clothes fast.

Others soon followed him off the squad's berth, however, for everyone was feeling strongly the excitement of the occasion this morning. Miki and Private Oka carried the squad's machine guns, for they had been selected to carry the heavy weapons for the ceremony. The machine guns shone with unblemished luster even in the dim light of the electric lamps in the hold, for they 'had been taken apart and given a thorough polishing the previous day. The rifles and bayonets, too, of all the soldiers had a special sheen on them this morning, for there had been an "inspection of arms" yesterday, and, as they did whenever such an inspection was announced, the men had spent nearly a whole day polishing and oiling their weapons before lining them up for inspection. The Company Commander, followed by a large staff from Company Headquarters, had gone around examining the weapons, and a few flaws had been found as usual, but they had been negligible at the most, consisting mostly of specks of dust or the tiniest traces of sea rust. Those, however, had been duly noted in the books, and the guilty ones harshly reprimanded and ordered to rectify the flaws at once.

Thus when the troops assembled on deck this morning, each soldier of the Hamamoto company felt a certain pleasure and lightness of conscience in the realization that his weapon was in perfect condition and wholly worthy of the honor to be given it through participation in a ceremony worshiping the Emperor. This, however, did not mean that the soldiers were haphazard in looking after their weapons on ordinary days, for, among the many things the soldiers in the Japanese Armed Forces were compelled to do with fanatic thoroughness, the caring of the weapons ranked the highest. The sacred Chrysanthemum Seal of the Emperor was on nearly all the weapons, and the care of them was almost a religious rite. The soldiers were compelled to polish their weapons daily, although most of the older soldiers left the distasteful task to their younger comrades, and if anyone was scolded and beaten for shirking this duty, he received no sympathy from his comrades. The frugal lives which most of the soldiers had led before joining the army had also been an important factor behind the indefatigable care which the weapons received, for the tools which they used in civilian life had been, to those men, valuable properties of their family fortunes.

As Corporal Sakamoto walked among his men of Squad Three, trimly lined for the ceremony on deck, and peered closely at each in the hazy luminousness of the pre-dawn hour, he felt a happy satisfaction in the neat appearance of his subordinates. He was not the only one, moreover, who felt a certain religious excitement, arising from a sense of purity — a feeling which most knew through observance of the traditional purification rites at home. Many of the soldiers, too, had suffered the trouble the previous day of washing their uniforms in the cramped quarters and with the meager water allotted them on deck for this purpose. It had been a sight to see the many uniforms fluttering in the breeze from hurriedly raised ropes and poles and from the railings all day long yesterday, and, this morning, the wrinkles which remained after the rinsing still showed on the newly washed uniforms and imparted an air of unadorned purity to the wearers as the sacred trees and rocks did to the Shinto shrines.

The officers appeared very soon after the soldiers were lined up on deck. They, too, looked their shiniest best, and it was plain that their orderlies had spent many untiring hours preparing for this occasion. Their well-polished long boots, which came up to their knees and which shone even in the hazy light, were especially conspicuous, as were their freshly shaved, well-fed-looking faces. Many of the soldiers were seeing some of the officers for the first time since boarding ship, for the officers were quartered in the passenger cabins on deck and had found almost no need to go among their men in their foul-smelling holds this trip. The soldiers gazed with mild wonder at the shining, well-nourished appearance of the officers, for they themselves had grown noticeably wan and thinner after three weeks at sea, and they could not help noticing the contrast. The more sensitive ones among them found themselves recalling with a slight tinge of envy how the officers were spending their days like regular passengers in their private cabins and were being fed the fancy fare from the ship's regular kitchen, the same as the captain of the ship.

The Battalion Commander, who appeared last of all as usual, topped this impression of well-being, like the climax to a play on the stage. His round face shone with the fat which seeped through its pores, and his portly figure was ebullient and over-flowing with self-confidence as ever. His long sword swung vigorously as he walked, and its point made a wide arc around him, as if he wanted to make plenty of room through which to pass. The sword became still only when the officer stopped at the head of the assembled troops. The deck was crowded with his men, although only part of the battalion had been able to board this ship and the remainder had been distributed on several other vessels.

Major Sagami was an emotional man, and the sight of his men assembled here on deck to observe the rites of *Tenchosetsu* amidst the mysterious expansiveness of the South China Sea filled his heart with a powerful, unspeakable emotion, charged with a solemnity he had never experienced before. The tears arose in his eyes, and he was glad that the faint light on deck hid them from his subordinates, and he did not bother to wipe them. A consciousness of his own importance formed clearly in his mind as he told himself, These soldiers assembled here are will-ing to lay down their lives to the last man if I should order them. He was also conscious of a deep sense of humility, but the consciousness of power was also strong in him. He felt that he stood closer to the Emperor than these men before him and that in a way he represented the Emperor personally to them.

After the usual counting off, the companies saluted their Battalion Commander, who returned the salute with the ponderous dignity which he maintained on such occasions. The first tinge of gold was showing in the eastern sky, and in the path of light which slowly materialized on the ocean's surface the men could now see the endless motion of the unending rollers. The cool breeze which struck their faces felt invigoratingly refreshing, and the smell of the sea was strong in the air. The only thing which marred this sight of the mighty spectacle of dawn at sea was the row of crude toilets lining the deck's edge in front of the assembled troops. Fortunately, the toilets did not extend the full length of the deck, so that over half of the men had a clear view of the awakening horizon, but the remainder had to be satisfied with the piece of sky they saw over the tops, and all had to share the suggestive smell which came out of the makeshift toilets. These, however, were only highly insignificant defects and were easily overlooked by the soldiers, who felt strongly the poetic importance of the moment as only members of their nature-worshiping race could.

"Fix bayonets!" the Battalion Commander ordered in a low voice, and the soldiers removed the shining bayonets from the sheaths hanging from their hips and attached them to the tips of their rifles. The Major and the other officers and non-commissioned officers drew their long swords from their scabbards and held them against their shoulders. The Major drew his sword with an ease and grace which amply validated the report being circulated among the soldiers that he was of the fifth grade in swordsmanship. He now made an about-face and faced the eastern horizon together with his subordinates. The upper rim of the rising sun was now fully visible, and the gold which shone seemed to be living and vibrant with the excitement of the moment.

"Present arms!" the Battalion Commander called in a voice which sounded tense and suffocating, like the ultimate and total voice of the living. The soldiers raised their bayoneted rifles and guns in precise unison, and the officers lowered their swords with a flourish to their sides. The eastern horizon was now in its full glory, as the sun stood poised and almost unmoving on the horizon's rim for one moment as if in answer to the troops' salute. Then with a last flourish of its mighty, golden rays, which reached out respondingly across the ocean surface to the saluting men, it disengaged itself from the horizon and started on its inevitable journey across the sky. Not a trace of cloud appeared in the sky, and the sun seemed to be smiling happily at this promise of an unhampered journey throughout the rest of the day.

The emotions of the men watching this, one of the greatest spectacles of visible nature, were clear and unclouded also. Their very being seemed to have melted into the powerfully embracing radiance of their surrounding, and there was only awe and humility in their hearts. The only sound coming to the ears of the hushed assembly was the churning ripple of the ship's bow as it cut through the billowing waves. Takeo, like the rest, was carried away by the splendor of the spectacle he was beholding beyond the barrel of his raised rifle. His squad was fortunate to be situated where they had a full view of the horizon. His whole being was concentrated in gazing at the golden brilliance unfolding itself before him. The muscles of his body seemed to have grown rigid and felt as if they would snap at any moment. His eyes became blurred, and there was a moment of total blindness. In that moment, there flashed before his eyes a vision of the unforgettable scene behind his home, upon which he had gazed so often while sipping his tea on the back porch after a hard day's work. There was the green hill covered with the tall, straight fir trees and with the abundant underbrush, and there was the thick patch of bamboos at the base of it, and there was the cool, sparkling stream flowing before it.

When the Battalion Commander called, "Order arms!" the

vision had passed, and Takeo was once again gazing at the brilliant golden ball of fire, now some distance above the horizon, but where there had only been a feeling of awe and reverence one moment ago, there was now a feeling of almost jubilant exultation in his heart. It was an almost irrepressible emotion, and he felt a strong urge to shout his exultation and to let his comrades beside him share with him in his jubilance.

"His Majesty the Emperor is pleased to greet His Fortieth Birthday on this auspicious day," the Battalion Commander began in a high, stentorian tone, after he had sheathed his sword and turned around to face his subordinates. "It fills us with trepidation to learn that His Majesty is in the best of health, and that knowledge is the height of joy to us hundred million subjects of the nation. On this auspicious day, we must renew our gratitude for having an incomparable and infinite Emperor, who is pleased to lead us, and to renew our determination to overcome the hardships of the times, thus putting at ease the August Imperial Will." The Battalion Commander was reciting from a prepared speech, and it was a moving, eloquent recitation.

When the Major had concluded his speech, he added, "Let us shout *Banzai* for the Emperor." Then turning around to face the east again, he drew his sword and raised it high together with his other arm. Then he shouted at the top of his lungs, "*Tenno Heika, Banzai!*" The men followed in unison, raising their rifles and arms, too, and they shouted thrice, "*Banzai! Banzai! Banzai!*" Takeo was surprised to hear those around him shouting just as loudly and lustily as he, for he had put all his strength in his shout, and he had expected his voice to drown out all the others.

The Battalion Commander returned his sword into its scabbard, and turned to face his men. His face was flushed with emotions, and everybody could see now in the clear light of the morning that the Major was deeply moved. "We are going to force a landing, day after tomorrow," Major Sagami began in his everyday conversational voice, and it was plain that he was speaking impromptu now. "We do not know how much resistance the enemy will offer, but all of you must not forget the feeling of this moment and must fully carry out your duty!"

He ended abruptly and said, "The end!" The troops saluted him, and he returned to his room, and the soldiers were dismissed. They went clattering down noisily into the stuffy hold to put away their weapons and their hot uniforms. As usual the Replacement Soldiers and First-Year-Soldiers had to help the elder soldiers off with their puttees and uniforms, and they wound the long puttees into neat rolls and presented them respectfully to their owners. By the time they themselves started removing their own uniforms, the older soldiers were already in their loincloths and smoking their cigarettes and discussing in excited groups the happenings of the morning.

"Hey, somebody, go and get some tea!" Private First Class Gunji called suddenly.

Private Hirata, the college-educated Replacement, who had only removed his utilities bag, canteen, and bayonet belt and was still in his full uniform otherwise, quickly went for the kettle and dashed away with it. Takeo, who saw a newborn resoluteness in his fellow villager, felt happy for his sake, for he knew that was the only way Hirata would be recognized by his superiors. The morning's ceremony must have put a new heart into him, Takeo thought.

"When we presented arms, it was some feeling!" exclaimed Private First Class Tanaka, as he lighted a cigarette and passed the match around.

"At a time like that, you don't care if you die!" Private Oka declared impetuously.

"If the boat had gone down then, no one would have moved," said Tanaka.

"That is why Japan is strong. We are all fighting with that kind of spirit," Corporal Sakamoto observed gravely.

Kan had stripped down to his loincloth by now, and he

joined the group and asked respectfully, "Honorable Squad Leader, why is it that when worshiping the Emperor's Palace, we always face eastward, no matter where we are?"

"That is because the Emperor's first August Ancestor was the Goddess of the Sun, called *Amaterasu Omikami*," the Corporal began eruditely, but he seemed suddenly to feel embarrassed by the academic air he was putting on before his subordinates, some of whom had received more schooling than he, and he hastily added, "Anyway, the Emperor is supposed to be pleased to be in the east." Then he stammered weakly, "I don't know much about these matters."

"That is exactly so. It is exactly as the Honorable Squad Leader says," Private First Class Tanaka came to the rescue of his Squad Leader, and he glared accusingly at Kan.

"Children shouldn't ask too difficult questions," Private Oka made a show of scolding Kan.

His impulsiveness had again put Kan in an embarrassing position, but he was equal to it, and he assumed the appearance of extreme contrition and declared, "I asked because I didn't know."

Hirata, in the meantime, had climbed the ladder to the deck with the squad's kettle. The cool morning air felt fresh and invigorating, and he breathed deeply of it and felt himself one with the newness and sprightliness of the morning all around him. The suddenness of the change when he had entered the army, plus the utter and groveling bestiality of the existence he had led since, had left him dazed and at a complete loss with himself. The college he had attended in the capital was a liberal Christian institution which prided itself with the purity and progressiveness of the training it gave the youths who passed through its gates. This training, however, had not denied the divinity of the Emperor, for, even if the educators denied it in their hearts, they were not free to voice their sentiments under strict compulsion of the higher authorities of the nation. The principle, however, had not been propounded any more than was required, and Hirata and his fellow students had been given ample freedom to form their own conclusions in the light of the basically scientific training they were given in every branch of their highly varied curricula. Hirata had been a zealous student and had constantly maintained a wide open attitude on this question, as well as other questions pertaining to the growing popularity of extreme nationalism among the people. Once in the army, however, he had found himself thrown into a life based openly and inexorably upon the doctrine of the Emperor's divinity. The inflexible discipline and the irrevocable rules of conduct and etiquette had been almost unbearably obnoxious to him, and, as he had frankly explained to Takeo, his dislike for the whole organization had led him to refuse to take the examination to become a commissioned officer.

However, something had snapped in him this morning as he had saluted the rising sun together with his comrades on the vessel's deck. A feeling, not so much a revelation as an inspiration, had gripped him and sent a flash of understanding through his mind, which had assured him strongly and revived his self-confidence. "I will do it!" he had exclaimed within his heart in a moment of sudden exultation. He had meant that he was going to bear his share of the life he now found himself in, fully and audaciously. It was only an animal determination which had arisen in him as he had gazed at the sheer physical beauty of the rising sun, but in a moment of impulsive excitement he had determined to liquidate all the bewilderment and weak-hearted confusion under which he had been laboring. He had decided to live strongly from day to day without questioning the purpose of his actions or the comparative values of the principles involved. In short, he had decided to transform himself into a firm realist and opportunist. What strong propulsion he had received in bringing about the sudden transformation, from a heredity which had been satisfied to remain for centuries in absolute servility and within a strict feudalistic code of conduct and which had come to look upon pure animal courage as the highest asset of life and what complex workings of his mind, exposed since childhood to the widespread conception of national patriotism, were behind the change, he was not able to explain, nor in any mood to try to explain.

As he looked about him on the deck, he saw that the usual lines had already formed in front of the necessarily limited row of toilets. The lines extended along the whole length of the deck up to the central bridge where the cabins and the pilot house were. Most of the soldiers were standing stoically and chatting unconcernedly among each other, but a few were jumping impatiently up and down as if they were having a hard time containing the matter which demanded to be let out before the bodies could start freely on their day's mission. Some were pounding the closed doors roughly and demanding those inside to hurry.

The sight alone of the dirty toilets on deck had been repulsive to the sensitive nature of Hirata, and the ordeal of entering one of the smelly, cramped compartments to do his inevitable errand had been almost unbearable, and, in the three weeks at sea, he had come to suffer a painful constipation. There was only a shallow and narrow tin-plated trough running under the compartments which acted as the receptacle, over which the men crouched to unburden themselves. The sailors washed the trough once a day with their long hose of gushing sea water, but the rest of the time only the urine which the men discharged into a receptacle at the farther end of the row of toilets was depended upon to wash the trough, and sometimes the feces piled so high in the trough that the men who entered the toilets had to be careful not to soil themselves.

This morning, Hirata did not turn his eyes away repulsively, as he had been wont to do when he passed the low, suggestive row of closed compartments, and he looked even with some amusement at the antics of discomfiture of some of the waiting soldiers. When he returned to his squad with his full kettle, he was even able to announce boldly for the benefit of any of his comrades who might be intending to go up, "The toilets are full now."

The other Replacement soldiers soon had breakfast ready, and the soldiers, who were hungrier than usual from the excitement of their early-morning ritual, fell eagerly to disposing of it. Besides the usual rice and soya-bean soup, there was a liberal helping of sweetened boiled beans for everyone this morning. "They said at the kitchen that there will be a special dinner at lunch and that there will be *sake*," Seki, who had heard it from the cook in the kitchen, announced, and his comrades greeted the announcement with loud cheers.

Private Oka, in his enthusiasm, tipped over his cup of tea, and immediately there were loud protestations from the berth underneath. The tea had probably seeped through the joints in the floor and was dripping on the heads of the unlucky soldiers underneath. Oka quickly leaned over the side of his squad's berth and, peeking into the lower berth, apologized profusely, but everyone was in a cheerful mood this morning, and the matter was easily forgotten.

When the breakfast was cleared, and the dishes washed, the older soldiers immediately began their game of cards. The Replacements and the First-Year-Soldiers lay down once again at their end of the berth to rest after the morning's chores.

Miki, who was puffing his cigarette contentedly, said, "That *Banzai* this morning was heard by the Emperor, surely."

"Fool! How can he hear it? He is thousands of *ri* away!" said Kan seriously.

"He may be thousands of *ri* away, but we shouted with all our might, and he must have heard it," stubbornly insisted Miki.

"Really, we shouted with all our might," said Takeo, recalling his almost supernatural exultation of the morning.

"It was perhaps better if the Emperor did not hear it. He is such a quiet man that he would have been frightened to hear such a loud noise," said Hirata jokingly.

"You were in Tokyo, weren't you? Have you ever worshiped the Emperor personally?" asked Kan, turning toward Hirata.

"No, a lowly one like me cannot worship the Emperor personally," laughed Hirata. "But I had a friend who was a soldier in the Imperial Guard, and he told me he saw the Emperor and the Empress several times while standing on sentinel duty within the Palace grounds."

"How was it, did he say?" asked Miki.

"When they passed, they were pleased to say, 'Hard work,' and my friend said everything went cold inside of him," Hirata answered.

"That must be true. If it were I, I would probably have fainted," said Miki in an awed tone.

"The Emperor is pleased to be forty, is he? He is the same age as my father," commented Kan in his usual brash manner.

"Hey, don't say it so loud. If they should hear it, you will get it," cautioned Takeo, and they all glanced a little anxiously toward the older soldiers, some of whom were fanatically particular about even the tone of voice used when speaking of the Emperor.

Kan, however, continued undaunted, "My father looks much older though. He is a heavy drinker, you know."

"I wonder if the Emperor is pleased to drink *sake?*" asked Miki, taking courage from the cool nonchalance of Kan.

"Well, he probably drinks. He is pleased to be alive. Why do you ask such a question?" said Takeo, though in a low cautious voice.

"If he drinks and says, 'Hard work,' and so forth, he is not much different from us," said Miki, and he too was careful to keep his voice low, and he looked about him cautiously to make sure no older soldiers were around.

"Fool! He is pleased to be alive, and so he can't help it. But he is pleased to have his lineal blood from the gods in the divine Era, and so that way he is very different from us," said Takeo.

"I may be scolded for saying such a thing as this, but, really, do you feel that you are fighting for the Emperor?" Hirata, who had been listening silently to the interesting discourse of his Senior Soldiers, now asked politely, for he saw an opportunity to learn the secret behind the will and courage of these soldiers who had gone through the fire of combat.

"That is so. We Japanese are all like that," strongly asserted Takeo, and he looked curiously at his fellow villager.

"Then if the present Emperor should be gone, will you stop fighting?" continued Hirata without flinching. He would not have been so audacious previously, but he was a different man this morning.

"If the present Emperor should be gone, there will be a new one," said Miki.

"So, you are not fighting for the Emperor, but for something with the name 'Emperor,'" said Hirata.

Miki seemed puzzled by this reasoning, which was more than his mind could grasp at the moment, and the others, too, became silent to ruminate upon the implications of Hirata's statement. Takeo seemed the first to grasp its full meaning, and he began in a grave tone, "If you say it that way, I am really fighting for my folks at home." He was recalling with new understanding the strange vision of the hill back of his home which he had seen while saluting the Imperial Palace this morning.

"That is, we are all like that," protested Kan. "Not a single one among us wants the folks at home to feel humiliated before their neighbors. That is why we are doing our best."

"The glory of our family is there, but we are also fighting for the glory of our village," said Miki.

"But we all started out vowing to fight for the Emperor," said Seki in his quiet voice, joining the conversation for the first time.

"That is true," agreed Kan. "Nobody will come this far to fight with his life at stake merely for the honor of his family or his village."

"That is, if it were left to our own free will, no one will come to the front," said Hirata. "They said it was for the sake of the

Emperor and yanked us out, and that is why we are here. But, once sent to the front, as Honorable Senior Soldier Yamamoto has been pleased to say, I believe we are really fighting for the people at home."

"Then how do you explain that feeling on deck this morning, when we saluted the Emperor's Palace?" Kan asked a little peevishly.

"When you worshiped the Emperor's Palace this morning, you were really worshiping your folks at home, and the neighbors and villagers who are guarding your home. And even if you really worshiped the Emperor, it was not an individual, but something bigger — what it is, I cannot say," Hirata said with a fervor which surprised even himself.

Everybody had listened respectfully to this enlightening interpretation of their erudite comrade, and when he had ended, Kan spoke almost apologetically, "If you put it that way, I can understand." Then he hurriedly added, "Hirata's head is different from ours. He has gone to school."

"Anyway, when it comes time to die, all one needs to do is to shout 'Banzai' for the Emperor," said Miki bluntly, to whom the discussion had become hopelessly complicated and incomprehensible.

An orderly came down the ladder into the hold and began calling to the squad leaders to assemble with pencils and paper in the Company Commander's cabin. Corporal Sakamoto gave his hand of cards to Private First Class Tanaka, who was watching the game from behind him, and, with the help of several Replacement soldiers, got into his uniform and left with pencil and paper in hand as he had been instructed.

Another orderly shortly appeared to call to the soldiers from each squad to go to the kitchen to get *sake* to celebrate the Emperor's Birthday. Each squad had its quota of *sake* in the aluminum rice containers in a safe corner of the berth, long before the Squad Leaders returned from their conference with the Company Commander.

Corporal Sakamoto returned to his squad with a grave face and quickly assembled his men. They huddled closely around their Squad Leader, and in the other squads, too, the men were gathering around their squad leaders. Shuffling the pages which seemed to hold the notes he had taken at the conference with Captain Hamamoto, Corporal Sakamoto started by explaining that the conference had been one to discuss the combat plan for the coming landing operation.

He read the points of the plan methodically from his paper: "All the ships carrying our division will assemble tomorrow night, and we are to land at dawn, day after tomorrow, at a point near the southernmost boundary of China. The objective of the campaign will be a place called Canton in Kwangtung Province. The enemy may resist strongly. . . . Whatever happens, we must see that our squad's machine guns get on shore. . . . Once on shore, we will push inland immediately, so see that your equipments are held fast to your bodies. . . . "

Corporal Sakamoto was having difficulty reading from his hurriedly scribbled notes, and, when he paused longer than usual after his last statement, Private First Class Gunji asked impatiently, "Honorable Squad Leader, the whole division is going to land, isn't it?"

"That is so. The whole division is going to land," the Corporal said, looking up from his paper.

"Then our food supply and ammunition will be right behind us, and there will also be field hospitals. If we know that much, that is enough," said Gunji, the squad's second-in-command, emphatically.

"That is so. If we know that much, we leave the rest up to you, Honorable Squad Leader. Isn't that so, everybody? We will go anywhere that the Honorable Squad Leader goes, won't we?" Private First Class Tanaka exclaimed impulsively, not to be outdone by his fellow Private First Class, and he looked around him expectantly at his comrades.

"That is so," everybody assented loudly.

When the Corporal tried to protest and started to dig into his notes again, everybody joined the two Privates First Class in stopping him from attempting further his painful task.

"Today is the happy Birthday of the Emperor, and we have already received our *sake*. Let us drink," said Gunji.

That was how Corporal Sakamoto's squad started drinking long before the other squads did, and, when the others were barely started, Squad Three was already well along in its celebration. The soldiers sang the usual folk songs and clapped their hands as loudly as they had done on land. Soon, dried cuttlefish and fish cakes were distributed as a special ration for the celebration, and the hold resounded all day long with the merrymaking. Some of the officers also came down into the hold to join the soldiers, for they were specially anxious to share the comradeship of their subordinates before a combat. The *sake*, which had been rationed, was not as copious as usual, for the commanders did not want the soldiers to tire their bodies from overdrinking when the landing was only a few hours away.

That evening, after roll-call, in the hour before Curfew, when even the Replacement soldiers could feel free to leave the exacting environment of their squads, Replacement Privates Seki and Hirata went on deck to be by themselves. There was not a single speck of light on deck, for a strict blackout was being maintained, but the stars were out in a clear sky, and an eery light arose from the ocean's surface, so that the men could hazily make out the shapes on the deck. There were quite a number of soldiers out this evening, and it seemed that there were many who wanted to be alone with their thoughts besides Seki and Hirata, now that they all knew the coming battle was close at hand.

The two Replacements found a place behind a pile of canvas near the bow which was comparatively secluded and squatted down closely side by side. The ocean was as calm as it had been that morning, and the gentle rollers striking the ship's sides sounded listless and futile.

"I don't want to die in this coming battle," Hirata said almost forlornly.

"Let us both go through it in good health," said Seki cheer-fully, and he impulsively grasped the arm of his comrade. The coming landing was to be the first combat experience for the Replacements, and they all felt a little anxious, but most of them, like Seki, were imbued so strongly with a sense of duty and obedience that they easily reconciled themselves with the in-evitability of the coming event, and they spoke very little among each other about the coming battle.

Hirata, as if ashamed by his expression of anxiety, now asked his comrade in a more cheerful voice, "How many years have you been married?"

"Four years. How many have you?" Seki asked in return.

"Eight months."

"Then it must have been hard to part."

"It was hard, but it must have been just as hard for you."

"If you are together four years, you do not think so much about it when you part. It seems that we have lost our manners to each other."

"Is your wife in your home?" Hirata now asked.

"That is so. There are two children, and the folks are pretty old, so my wife will have to help on the farm also," Seki replied.

"My wife is in my home also, but my home is in the city, and my father goes to work, while my mother is able to do the housework all by herself, so my wife has it easy. I have a sister, too, and my wife will have almost nothing to do all day, so I hope she gets along all right with everybody. I am a little worried," said Hirata.

"Why don't you send her home for a time?"

"I had thought about it, but I could not make up my mind to let her go."

"She would be with her own mother then, and there would be no trouble."

"That is true, to be sure, but I could not help feeling that she is somehow safer with my mother."

"If you are afraid that she will be fickle, you do not have to worry. If she is an ordinary woman, she can wait. A woman's body is made that way."

"When I think how I can hardly bear it, I am a little afraid. We were so much alike."

"That is all right, I tell you. Woman is different," Hirata repeated.

Somewhere in the hold, the first night watch was calling, "Lights out!" The two soldiers rose to go down into the hold.

CHAPTER 17

WHEN THE SOLDIERS got out of their crowded holds for the last time and lined up on deck in the early morning of the day set for the landing, there was a full moon shining, and it was almost as light as day. The sight which greeted the men as they looked about them was impressive and heartening, for as far as their eyes could discern in the misty light of the full moon, they could see all around them the massive shadows of ships at anchor and waiting like theirs to unload their cargoes of landing soldiers. Land was a low and jagged shadow in the moonlit sky not so far away, and two destroyers were steaming back and forth along its length firing their guns noisily in its direction, but the men on board the transports saw that there was no answering fire.

Takeo felt weak and clumsy with his heavy load on his back and shoulders. His rucksack and utilities bag were filled with provisions and the extra ammunition. The tent roll strapped to the top of the rucksack was bulging with the surplus articles which Takeo had been forced to cram into it, and it kept sagging and hitting the back of his head, so that he had to shove it back from time to time. Miki was a huge shadow of a man among the soldiers massed closely on deck, for added to the great bulk of his body was one whole ammunition box strapped to the top of his rucksack. The box came almost as high as the top of his head, and in the faint light he gave the appearance from behind of a neckless, squareheaded giant.

In spite of the great number of soldiers assembled on deck, there was little confusion there, for the men had gone through this very performance in countless and painstaking drills, both on land and since boarding ship. At a given signal, they began going over the sides with their rifles slung over their shoulders and descended by long rope ladders to the landing boats waiting below. Takeo followed closely after Miki, but the heavy load, including the machine gun, which the big soldier was carrying made him shake the ladder so that Takeo had a hard time finding the rungs with his feet. Fortunately the ocean was calm again this morning, and Takeo found little difficulty, after reaching the end of the ladder, in jumping into the boat at the bottom.

The others came down quickly in an endless stream. Left-right, left-right, they descended the ladder and silently went to their assigned positions on the boat until the whole platoon with its Commander was on board. The pilot started the engine, and the boat left the steamer's side to give room to others waiting in line. In a surprisingly short space of time, all the troops assigned to the first landing had boarded their boats, and these now formed a long line and headed together for shore. The muffled hum of their engines combined to echo loudly in the still air.

The boats were advancing at full speed, and the sprays thrown up by their flat bows flew high all around them, but to Takeo and his comrades they seemed to be moving along at a sluggish pace. The men lost all sense of the passage of time, too, as they crouched huddled closely on the boat's bottom, and they felt as if they had been there for a long time and that they would be there forever, with only the hum of the engine and the splash of water against the boat's hull to offer them solace. Only when they could make out the shapes of things on shore — the white sand beach, trees, and verdant hills — as they peered eagerly over the boat's sides did they become aware of the swiftness with which they were approaching their targets. They kept their eyes glued to the shore line and expected any moment to be greeted with a barrage of enemy fire.

"They probably want to draw us near before opening fire," somebody whispered nervously in the back of the boat.

The boats, however, advanced without drawing any challenging fire from the shore, and the silence hung as unbroken and ominous as ever. The men could now make out the brushes and individual shadows on land. Takeo felt himself oscillating between a feeling of fatalistic abandonment and one of concentrated alertness. At one moment he was telling himself that there was nothing to do but to remain low in his boat until it reached shore. even if the enemy should open fire, and the next, he was desperately scanning the shore to see if he could make out any telltale evidences of enemy positions there and to see where it would be safest to go after landing. His teeth began to chatter and his body to shiver, and be became conscious for the first time of the chill in the early morning air.

When the boat scraped bottom and came to a lurching halt, it was still some distance from land. The trap door forming the boat's bow was immediately lowered, and the men began dashing over it into the cold water below. The water came up to their waists, and they had difficulty wading through it. Each man, as he dashed up onto the rampart and down it into the sea, thought, Now . . . now the enemy will open fire! but the shore remained silent as ever. They were all soon safely off the boat and wading in a wide, open formation, the way they had been taught, toward shore. The feeling that each was a marked target for the enemy, however, followed the soldiers until they made land and took shelter in the crevices and brushes there.

A quick survey showed that there were no enemy along the whole coast, and the troops began immediately to push inland in marching columns over a road which had been thoroughly wrecked by the enemy. By the time all the deployed units had fallen into marching order, the sun was well up in the clear sky and showed a countryside very similar to those the men had been used to seeing at home. There were rice paddies everywhere, and the hills were covered with green shrubs, trees, and tall grass, and the streams were abundant, and clear, and inviting. Only some of the vegetation which they saw from time to time was different from anything they had known at home, for here were the trees and plants of the tropics they had read about with such wonder in their school textbooks and heard so much about — there were bananas, coconuts, pineapple, sugar cane, and many others whose names they did not know.

The tropical heat beat mercilessly on their emaciated bodies, and they all felt grateful that there had been no enemy resistance during their landing. Takeo felt the tightness in his body leaving gradually, but the ground under his feet kept swaying as if he were still on the sea, and his head felt light and unsubstantial, as if what he was passing through was far removed from reality. He was not the only one who kept getting thirsty quickly, and everybody drank eagerly from the cool, sparkling streams they found so abundant here. The soldiers sweated profusely, too, and their uniforms which had been wet when landing had no chance of drying.

The troops encountered no resistance the first day, but the next day, in the morning, the enemy struck back. The advance patrol was crossing a deep river over a pontoon bridge hastily constructed by the engineers when the enemy opened fire from a hill across the river, getting practically everyone on the bridge. The rest of the patrol, which numbered a company, were crossing the river on boats they had found conveniently moored to the river's bank when the boats struck mines and capsized, throwing their occupants into the deep, swirling current. When the main body of the battalion reached the river, there were numerous men floundering and crying in agony in the water. The enemy kept firing at these helpless soldiers, and one by one they stopped struggling and disappeared under the dark surface of the swiftly rushing water.

The battalion's heavy machine guns were immediately brought forward and opened fire against the enemy's positions across the river. The mortars, too, went into action and sent shell after shell into the hill where the enemy seemed to be entrenched. This concentrated barrage cut down markedly the fire from the other side, and some soldiers in the river were able to swim back to shore and ran dripping and shivering up the bank and behind the slope where the battalion was sheltered.

The exchange of fire across the rushing current continued for some time, and the enemy also began to answer with their mortars, so that the battalion was compelled to fall back to a safe distance, but the machine guns and mortars remained to continue their holding fire against the enemy. The Battalion Commander, accompanied by his staff, crept forward to survey the lay of the land, and the order was soon sent back for the Hamamoto company to cross the river and capture the hills on the other side.

The men were ordered to remove their rucksacks, and the company advanced cautiously up the slope where they were still hidden from the enemy and to the edge of the river-bank. They met the Battalion Commander, peering through his binoculars on the top of the rise, and he turned around to call to Captain Hamamoto, "It's up to you!" Fidgeting in line while his comrades jostled to get as close to the river's edge as possible, Takeo wondered why the Battalion Commander did not wait until bigger artillery came up before forcing a crossing of the river, and he felt highly vexed at the Commander for compelling them to undertake a seemingly unnecessary risk. He also felt peeved at his immediate superiors, who, he recalled, acted so almighty at other times but seemed helpless to protest now when there was no doubt about the hopelessness of a crossing. Takeo heard the boom of the heavy artillery far to the right, and the fatalistic side of his nature tried to assure him that the artillery were probably being used in an encircling movement and could not be spared here.

But he was not given much time to continue his rumination. The order was given to advance, and he found himself dashing, together with his comrades, helter-skelter down the riverbank toward the ill-fated bridge across the river. The machine guns and mortars behind them covered them well, and the enemy were able to fire only sporadically, but the bullets whistled close to their ears, and the men ran as they had never run before in their lives. Even as he ran, however, Takeo was conscious of the two opposite natures within himself which had been so out-spoken in the landing barge yesterday morning. One was cool and told him there was no use being scared, because there was nothing he could do until he got to the other side of the river; the other was excited and kept urging him to run the faster and to keep his head low.

When crossing the bridge, too, though his whole soul seemed concentrated solely on getting to the other side, Takeo found time, albeit only for a fleeting moment, to notice the hands of a soldier weakly clutching the side of the bridge, and he noticed the lonesome, reproachful look on the soldier's face as his hands slipped and he was carried away by the onrushing current. Takeo was able to recall that face for a long time afterwards and to feel genuine pity for its owner, whoever he might have been, though at that time he merely gave cognizance to the bare fact that the soldier must have been one of the victims of the previous attempted crossing.

The platoon, led by Lieutenant Kondo, had been ordered to attack the hill to the left of the bridge, and, safely across the bridge, the men followed their Platoon Leader into the protec-tive shelter of a ravine at the foot of the assigned hill. The platoon was able to advance quite a way up the hill within the shelter of the ravine, but soon it grew too shallow to conceal them any longer from the top.

"From here, advance one at a time!" the Platoon Leader ordered, and gave each squad its assignment.

The squad Takeo belonged to was assigned to attack from the very front, and the men began darting forward singly to deploy behind boulders and in shallow hollows formed by the natural contours of the slope, and some had to be satisfied with the flimsy protection offered them by scraggly bushes. The slope was a fairly steep one, and the stones loosened by the men in their desperate dash upward rolled down some distance. The distance to the top was long, and the sparse growth of grass and widely dispersed shrubs offered little protection. The machine guns and mortars to the rear, however, kept up their concentrated barrage, preventing the enemy on the top of the hill from exploiting their advantageous position to its fullest, but there were enough bullets flying around, and ricocheting from the boulders, and striking the ground at their feet for the men to have to take the greatest care in advancing after their first deployment, but they kept darting forward, working their way upward little by little.

Each time Takeo sprinted forward to take shelter, he thought he would be able to go no farther. His heart pounded wildly as if the breast containing it would burst, and his head under the helmet, too, grew heavy with the pressure from inside. Only the realization that the whole battalion was watching from the other side of the river and the sight of his comrades continuing the relentless advance kept him from lying down to rest whenever he made a cover which afforded him perfect concealment from the top. The figure of Kan especially was visible constantly in front of him; it darted expertly from shelter to shelter at the head of the whole platoon, and the sight was a strong challenge to Takeo.

Kan had been the first to dash out of the ravine when the Platoon Leader had given the order to advance individually, and he had kept his lead ever since. His lead, furthermore, gave him the advantage of being able to pick his choice of cover, and this helped him to proceed faster than the rest of his comrades. It was more his instinct to pace the crowd and his innate trait to show off, both of which qualities had been always outstanding in his daily life with his comrades, which drove him doggedly to maintain his lead at the head of the platoon.

More than halfway up the slope, Kan began to notice that the available shelter was growing scarcer and less formidable. This slowed him down a little and gave him time to notice that when the bullets from the battalion's machine guns to the rear sounded as a constant stream over his head, the fire from the top was weak. Only when this sound shifted to his right or left, as the machine gunners swung their guns to new targets, did the fire resume its intensity. So now he began to wait until he heard the steady whistling of his comrades' bullets over his head before advancing, and while he waited, he took pot shots at the top. Sometimes, he thought he saw the figures of the enemy aiming their rifles down at him when he fired, but most of the time he aimed blindly and showed his head from behind his cover for only the tiniest fraction of a second. The others in the platoon, too, began to fire their rifles, and the squad's machine guns also opened fire, so that the sound was very heartening.

The defenders of the hill answered by hurling their hand grenades, some of which exploded very close to Kan. The sound of the grenades exploding near him scared Kan a little, and when he had gained the shelter of a fairly large boulder, he turned around to see if the others were coming up. He noticed that most of his comrades were now creeping flat on their stomachs instead of dashing out in the open, but he also noticed that they were not very far behind. The urge to stay in the lead again took hold of Kan, and he peered out from behind his shelter to survey the lay of the slope in front of him. He noticed a huge overhanging boulder not very far away, which looked like the ideal shelter from which to make his last charge to the top of the hill.

There was a shallow rut, formed probably by the rains, leading from where he was almost to the foot of the boulder ahead, which seemed capable of concealing him completely if he chose to creep through it as his comrades were doing. Then he heard the bullets from his comrades' machine guns whistling over his head, and, in an impulsive moment, ruled out the idea of going through so much trouble to get to his goal and decided to make a dash for it. He sprinted out from behind his cover like a beast springing for his prey and dashed straight for the next boulder.

He had gone no more than four or five steps when something struck his left leg with violent force and knocked him to the ground. Everything went black, but he came to, and he realized that he had been out only for a short instant, for the continuity of sounds was still there — the steady flow of machine gun bullets over his head, the crack-crack of the enemy guns on the top of the hill, the whistle and thud of the bullets as they went past him or struck the ground near him, and the occasional explosion of mortar shells and hand grenades.

When the awareness of life returned to him, Kan was lying on his side on the ground. He instinctively reached for his rifle which lay some distance from him, and he rolled over to get into the excavation through which he had thought of creeping before making his impulsive decision to make a dash for it. His left leg felt weak and helpless, and he was able to roll over only with the greatest effort, but the thought did not enter his mind, even for the shortest moment, that he had been hit by a bullet. Instead, he thought, An unexploded hand grenade hurled from the top hit me, and it puzzled him that the grenade should have struck him with such force.

Only the pain and the weakness of his leg, when he reached the rut and tried to creep forward, made him realize that something more powerful than an unexploded hand grenade had hit his leg. He next thought, A piece of stone chipped off by a flying bullet hit me.

As if reassured by this thought, he tried to make greater use of his injured leg, but a pain pierced his whole consciousness, which left him groaning and sweating. He now had to face the only plausible conclusion — that a bullet fired by an enemy aiming directly at him had struck him. This realization left him cold and weak in the stomach, and only the maddest sense of desperation at the thought of being left alone on the slope, where the enemy could continue to shoot at him, made him drag himself finally into the shelter of the large overhanging boulder for which he had started in the first place.

Kan had suffered a very common delusion of modern man in combat. The savage, when he fought, had a cruel and bloody hatred in him, and he was out through and through to destroy his opponent. Modern man has been softened by a society which frowns upon killing as murder, and when he becomes a soldier in an army, more often than he is aware he is more interested in his rivalry with his fellow soldiers than in his principal mission of killing the enemy. Only when brought face to face with the enemy or struck first by the enemy, as in the case of Kan, is he awakened to a full realization of the grim nature of combat. Then he is dazed by the impact of the sudden awakening, or he reverts to his innate primitive self and acts with all the fury and hatred which went to make his ancestors what they were, or he becomes sick and disgusted with the primitive spitefulness behind it all.

Kan was sick and dazed at the same time, as he lay weak with pain at the foot of the huge boulder, while the sound of battle continued with unabated fury all around him. He began to think for the first time of the enemy on the hill as individuals, and he became conscious of a consuming interest in the one who had shot him. A burning fury seized him, which made his body tremble all over. He swore under his breath and, gritting his teeth against the pain in his leg, removed a hand grenade from his utilities bag and tried to get to his feet to hurl it at the enemy on the hill.

The pain, however, was too much, and he sat down groaning. He looked down at his injured leg for the first time, and he saw that it was bleeding from a wound just above his knee. He took out the towel he always carried in his pocket and tied it around his thigh, near the groin, as he had been taught in the first-aid classes. Then he inserted the handle of his bayonet underneath the towel and began twisting it in order to make a tourniquet out of it.

He was completely engrossed in his task when somebody

jumped into the shallow cavity formed by the overhanging boulder and sat down beside him. Kan looked up and saw that it was Takeo, panting savagely and almost choking for lack of breath.

"Were you hit?" Takeo asked, but that was all he could say, and he did not move. Kan groaned and swore again.

When Takeo recovered his breath sufficiently he turned to look at his comrade's wounded leg. He saw a red blotch where the bullet had struck, and the trouser around the wound was soaked with blood. He looked under the leg and saw that the bullet had gone out.

"It is a clean wound. It isn't much," Takeo assured his comrade. Then he asked, "Where is your first-aid bandage?" Every soldier in the Japanese Army was supposed to carry one in a special pocket inside his coat.

"I am all right. Leave me and go ahead," Kan protested weakly.

It was then that Takeo became aware of the silence which had settled suddenly about them. The enemy fire from the hill-top which had been so insistent until a moment ago had stopped completely, and so had the battalion's machine guns and mortars from across the river to the rear.

Then Takeo heard the high, excited voice of his Platoon Leader to his right, shouting, "Charge!" and he saw the Lieutenant dashing forward with his sword brandished above his head. Somebody sprinted past the hollow where Takeo and Kan were, and Takeo saw the glint of his bayonet as he went by. Soldiers were shouting everywhere at the top of their lungs as they charged up the slope.

Takeo forgot all about his wounded comrade, and, hurriedly fixing his bayonet to his rifle, sprang forward, shouting with the others. Still there was no fire from the top, and long before they reached it, the charging soldiers knew the enemy had fled. Takeo was a fast sprinter, and he was among the first to make the top. There they found a deep trench, but no enemy, as they had surmised. Takeo and a few others jumped across the trench to look down the other side of the hill. They saw a group of the enemy in their reddish-khaki uniforms precipitately fleeing down the slope, and some were already turning a corner of another hill in the front.

Takeo and his comrades eagerly raised their rifles and began firing wildly at the fleeing figures. But they were not long doing it when bullets whistled and cracked, the way they have of doing when they are close, all around them. Some fell flat where they stood, while others, like Takeo, turned and dove into the trench behind them. Carried away by the excitement of shooting at the fleeing enemy, like hunters shooting at game, the soldiers had forgotten that there were enemy to the front who were just as eager to shoot them.

Once inside the trench, however, Takeo was able to speculate upon the closeness of his escape and upon the grimness of the predicament in which he and his comrades were. As in the case of Kan, Takeo's late experience was a grim reminder of what war meant. There were a few enemy corpses lying in the trench, and one was still breathing. Corporal Sakamoto casually thrust his bayonet into it until it stopped breathing.

Takeo reported to his Squad Leader about Kan, and he and Private First Class Tanaka were ordered to go and get their wounded comrade. When the two soldiers started down the slope, they saw that the troops of the battalion were already crossing the river over the improvised pontoon bridge, and they realized that the rest of their company had also succeeded in capturing their objectives, thus removing all the enemy resistance which had been blocking the river.

When the two soldiers of Squad Three reached their injured friend, they found two stretcher bearers from the battalion's transport unit already there. They helped place Kan on the stretcher, and as they did, one of the stretcher bearers told Kan, "The Honorable Battalion Commander was praising you. He was saying that you were brave." Kan smiled happily, and he said to Private First Class Tanaka, "Give my regards to the Honorable Squad Leader," and they carried him down the hill.

Takeo and Tanaka returned up the hill, deeply envying their wounded comrade, who needed no longer now to risk the dangers of combat or to undergo the hardships of the march. They met soldiers from the battalion's heavy machine gun company on the way, lugging two of their heavy guns toward the top where their platoon was now entrenched. When they reached the top, the new arrivals immediately placed their guns on the edge of the trench and began firing at the hill in front. The enemy's answering fire was only scattered and ineffective.

"That is so! Keep firing. We will capture that hill for you!" exclaimed Lieutenant Kondo enthusiastically to the machine gunners.

Corporal Sakamoto, who was standing beside his Platoon Leader, immediately protested, "Honorable Platoon Leader, it is better to wait a little more. There may be enemy on the hill to the left." The Corporal pointed to a low hill some distance to the left, which was almost in line with the hill they were on. If there were any enemy on it, they would have a plain view of the platoon's flank and rear, if it should attempt to charge up the hill to the front.

Lieutenant Kondo, however, had tasted his first feeling of glory, and he was hungry for more. He would still be in full view of his superiors if he should lead his platoon in another charge, this time up the hill in front. "That will be all right. Even if there were enemy on the hill to the left, they won't be able to do much at that distance," he said curtly, and he began assigning the squads their new positions in the coming charge.

The distance between the hills was short, and the incline going down as well as going up the other hill was not as steep as on the side they had just come up, and there were no boulders or shrubs to block the way—only grass which came up to the knees. The land had merely receded a little between the two hills to form a shallow cup, so that the soldiers would be able to charge up their new objective in a single dash from where they were.

Takeo felt himself sympathizing strongly with his Squad Leader, and he thought, Why doesn't the Platoon Leader wait? The battalion's light fieldpieces should be enough to knock the enemy off the hill in front. He could still hear the booming of the heavy artillery far to the right, but this time the sound came from a point much more to the front. . . . They must be making good time with their encircling movement, Takeo thought. There was no need to go ahead here, when they were circling and cutting the enemy in his rear.

The Lieutenant gave the order to charge and cut short Takeo's winding contemplation. They all dashed out of their trench and down the hill through the tall grass. The bullets came surprisingly thicker than in the last attack, and some soldiers were hit and went sprawling in the grass. The squad Takeo belonged to was given the left flank of the attack, and none of its members were hit as it reached the bottom of the hill and started up the slope of the other hill.

Takeo had kept his head low and concentrated solely on his pace while they ran down their side of the hill, but he now raised his head and, grasping his bayoneted rifle with both hands, started giving the usual shout of the charge. His mind was a blank, however, and there was no purpose or initiative behind it. There was only the urge to get to the top of the hill as fast as he could. If he should encounter any enemy on the top, he would thrust and parry as he had been drilled so often, but he felt a little confused and unsure of himself, for he still was not able to make out the enemy in front of him. Like many of his comrades, he too felt no consciousness of the enemy as individuals but knew them only as a vague entity, and he felt no personal hatred for them. His main regard was for the command, which had to be obeyed.

The explosion, therefore, came as a complete surprise to Takeo. There was a loud blast, which, since he was knocked flat and unconscious by the first impact, sounded merely like a short noisy "poof," and the next instant everything went black. He had not been long on his back, Takeo knew, when he opened his eyes and gazed up at the blue sky through the blades of grass hanging over him, for the continuity was still there — the sound of the guns and bullets and the shouting of his comrades charging up the hill.

He ran his hands quickly over his arms and legs and finding them whole, scrambled hastily to his feet. All the while, he was conscious of a weak, whimpering voice to his right. It was the loneliest, most forlorn and hopeless voice Takeo had ever heard.

Takeo paused an instant to puzzle over the voice, but the next instant, he had picked up his rifle and was charging up the hill after his comrades. At the top, Takeo saw some of his comrades using their bayonets while shrieking madly as they had been taught, and he also saw the Platoon Leader striking with his sword, but where his squad had gone, there had been no enemy, and the soldiers immediately jumped into the trench they saw before them and started firing at the terrain ahead with their rifles.

Only after the first excitement had died down did the men in Squad Three become aware that there was only one of the squad's two machine guns among them. The one carried by Private Oka was already firing at the enemy positions in front, but the other one, which Private First Class Tanaka had been carrying, was absent together with the Private First Class. Their Squad Leader, Corporal Sakamoto, was also conspicuously absent. They called to the soldiers in the neighboring squads to ask about their missing comrades, but the replies were not conclusive, since everything was in utter confusion.

It was then Takeo recalled the whimpering voice on the slope after the sudden explosion, and he told his comrades about it. Two Replacements were dispatched to go with Takeo, and he took them to the spot where he had heard the voice. They found Private First Class Tanaka there, lying face upward in the deep grass. He was still whimpering in his forlorn voice. There were two large ugly-looking holes on both sides of his chest, from which blood spurted each time he sighed his melancholy "Hu-gh." His face was deadly pale, and there was no recognition in his unblinking open eyes.

"Honorable Private First Class Tanaka, put strength into you!" Takeo shouted, kneeling down beside him.

Takeo now noticed another prostrate figure, lying face down in the grass not very far away. He went to it and turned it over. The face and the whole front of the body were a mass of broken and bloody flesh. The entrails hung out from the stomach, and there was no way of recognizing the body except for a corporal's insignia which dangled from a coat lapel. This had been Corporal Sakamoto, there was no mistaking it.

While Takeo stood gazing aghast at this grisly sight, he heard the stomach-turning sound of a mortar shell descending upon them, and he fell flat on the ground, calling to the others to follow suit. The shell exploded close enough to send the gravel falling on their prostrate bodies. It was followed closely by another, which also sounded as if it were coming down right on top of them, but it exploded farther down the slope.

When he was sure there was no more following, Takeo grabbed hold of the Corporal's collar and began dragging the body up the slope. He shouted to the others to bring the other body up with them. Bullets, this time, fell close to them, as they labored up the hill with their lifeless burdens. From the direction from which the bullets were coming, Takeo deciphered that they were being fired from the hill to the left. It was the hill about which, ironically enough, his late Squad Leader had so prophetically warned. As the Platoon Leader had pointed out, however, the hill was quite some distance away, and Takeo felt assured that the bullets fired from it had little chance of hitting them.

Takeo recalled the curt manner with which Lieutenant Kondo, their Platoon Leader, had dismissed the warning of their Squad Leader, and felt the old feeling of vexation against his superiors returning. There was no doubt that the mortar shell which had got Corporal Sakamoto and Tanaka, and almost Takeo himself, had been fired from the hill to the left. The shells which had fallen a short while back, too, had come from that direction, and the platoon was now in a precarious position with the enemy to the rear. The pity Takeo felt for nis Squad Leader welled up in his heart as he tugged at his lifeless body, and drowned the feeling of vexation that had been there. In its place, he now began to feel anger for the Platoon Leader.

When Takeo and his comrades reached the trench where their squad was, Private First Class Tanaka was no longer sighing his forlorn "Hu-gh's," and blood was no longer spurting from his chest.

CHAPTER 18

"THE BULLETS very seldom hit you. Even if the enemy is close, they seldom hit you," Miki was saying to a group of newly arrived, wide-eyed First-Year-Soldiers. The soldiers had just come in from drill in the yard and were gathered around the coal stove in their squad room, smoking their cigarettes and getting the cold out of their bodies, for there had been a strong wind outside today.

"How can you tell the bullets that don't hit you?" asked one ruddy-faced young soldier.

"The high ones go 'Pi-ung! Pi-ung!' and the close ones go 'Shi! Shi!' and the really close ones crack 'Pachit! Pachit!' near your ear. It's the ones that don't make any noise that get you," said Miki, and they all laughed loudly at this joke.

"I guess, in that case, when they make the noise, they have already hit you," said a bright-looking, young one, and they all thought it funny and laughed again.

They are a cheerful group of First-Year-Soldiers, Takeo thought, while he looked happily at the laughing faces of the young soldiers. Takeo and Miki were Second-Year-Soldiers now, for they were in the second year of their service. A whole batch of First-Year Regulars had come, too, at the beginning of the year to replace the last remaining Reserves, so that the former First-Year-Soldiers could now feel like real old-timers within their own right.

The campaign in South China had ended as all the campaigns they had participated in so far had ended — the Japanese Army had captured another vital stronghold, but the enemy had merely retreated inland, still intact. After the campaign, the division to which the soldiers in Squad Three belonged had returned to North China, and they were now engaged in garrisoning a village outpost outside the occupied seaport of Tsingtao in Shantung Province. Except for widely scattered guerrilla forays, there was no organized enemy resistance here, and the men had ample time to rest from their late campaign, although they were drilled as relentlessly as ever from day to day. After the tropical heat of the south, too, the intense cold of the North China winter was a great strain on their bodies.

There had been some inevitable changes within Squad Three after their return to North China. Private First Class Gunji had been promoted to Corporal and was the new Squad Leader. Oka, the perennial private, who was a Fourth-Year-Soldier now, had also been promoted, and he was a full-fledged Private First Class and the squad's second-in-command. Kan, too, had returned from the hospital, where he had been sent after being wounded in his leg, and had been promoted to Private First Class. Takeo and Miki had not been promoted, but, as combat-tested Senior Soldiers, they now occupied a respected and authoritative position within the squad.

"Was Honorable Senior Soldier Yamamoto ever hit by a bullet?" asked a First-Year-Soldier.

"No, a virtuous man like me is never hit," Takeo laughed.

Just then, they heard Replacement Private Hirata, who had entered the room from the farther door, making his report regarding his transfer to Battalion Headquarters to the Squad Leader in his private compartment. The building the Hamamoto company was occupying had been a government building, and the room in which Squad Three was quartered had been an office, and tent flaps had again been hung to make a private compartment for the Squad Leader.

Hirata's voice in the Squad Leader's room sounded high and

crisp, as it had to be when making a report. "Army Private Toranoshin Hirata has been ordered, as of February the ninth, to transfer to Battalion Headquarters. I hereby report with all humbleness."

"Over again! You are mistaken!" they heard Corporal Gunji's angry reply.

"Yes, sir," Hirata said nervously, and his comrades heard him repeat his report with the necessary correction in the same sing-song tone he had used previously: "Army Private Toranoshin Hirata has been ordered, as on February the ninth, to transfer from the Third Squad of the Second Platoon of the Hamamoto company to Battalion Headquarters. I hereby report with all humbleness."

"Good! Hard work! Do your best when you go to Battalion Headquarters!" Corporal Gunji's voice was now friendly and patronizing, for it was a distinct honor for a soldier to be assigned to Battalion Headquarters.

"Yes, sir. Honorable Squad Leader, I am much indebted to you," Hirata's voice sounded stiff and formal. His comrades heard him excusing himself in the proper manner, "I will leave," and they pictured him bowing respectfully to the Squad Leader.

The honored soldier soon appeared outside the Squad Leader's room and came to join his comrades around the stove. He was dressed in the regulation uniform of one making a formal report. He was wearing his bayonet and belt and had his puttees on. His uniform was newly washed, and his shoes were cleanly oiled. The order for his transfer had been made at roll-call two nights ago, and he had had ample time to prepare for the necessary formalities. "A report is a sacred thing," they said in the army, and he had gone about preparing for it diligently.

"Hard work!" his comrades greeted Hirata, when he sat down beside them.

"I bet you had to go around plenty," consoled Takeo, proud of the honor falling to this Replacement soldier from his own village, and he offered him a place beside him.

"Thank you," Hirata sat down heavily. "I have had to go

before the Company Commander, Warrant Officer, Sergeant Major, Platoon Leader, and the Squad Leader. Really, I am all tired out."

In the Japanese Army, a report had always to be made when one was transferred, or promoted, or left, or came to a unit in any fashion whatever. For instance, one made a report when one left for sentinel duty or returned from hospitalization. The form was always the same, and only the procedure varied, for sometimes the report had only to be made to one's Squad Leader, while at other times it had to be made to the whole list of one's superiors, as in the case of Hirata.

"When I go to Battalion Headquarters, I will have to make the report all over again. I am really disgusted," said Hirata.

"That is all right. You are going to have it easy from now on," said Takeo.

When Hirata had finished his cigarette, he stood up and, bowing to everyone, said politely, "I am indebted to you." The First-Year-Soldiers got respectfully to their feet, too, and they all answered, "Do your best," and Hirata left for his new assignment.

After the fortunate Replacement soldier had gone, Miki said, "He has gone to school, and so he is good at making a report." He was recalling the smooth, unhesitating manner with which Hirata had recited the report. To Miki, with his sluggish mental habit, the necessity to make reports was one of the greatest banes of his army life.

"If you have a good head, you go to a good post," commented Takeo.

Hirata had not been gone very long when the squad's two Privates First Class, Oka and Kan, came out of the Squad Leader's compartment, where they had been to receive the Replacement soldier's respectful report together with the Squad Leader, and called in an angry voice, "First-Year-Soldiers and Replacements, assemble!"

"Yes, sir!" the young soldiers answered obediently, and they hurried to fall in line before the two Privates First Class. Takeo and Miki, however, remained seated where they were before the stove and looked on stoically at the proceeding, for, as Second-Year-Soldiers, they were no longer subject to being ordered around by the Privates First Class.

"Attention! Count off!" Oka ordered sternly. Then glaring at the assembled soldiers with his head lowered menacingly, he asked, "Is there anyone among you who has washed the Honorable Squad Leader's uniform recently?"

No one answered, for none dared interpret how recent was meant by the word "recently" — although they had been washing the Squad Leader's laundry, as well as those of the Privates First Class and of the Senior Soldiers periodically as usual, and they felt puzzled that they should be taken up on this score.

"Why don't you answer?" Kan almost snarled and went down the line slapping each soldier soundly. There were ten of them in the line, so it took him some time, but he did not miss a single one. It did not bother him that he himself had been on the receiving end until not so long ago and had hated this form of chastisement with consuming passion.

When Kan was through, Oka continued angrily, "Don't you know that the Honorable Squad Leader's uniform is soiled?" He probably soiled his uniform in today's drill, thought Takeo, watching the Fourth-Year-Soldier with little feeling of sympathy. . . . "Lately, you Replacements and First-Year-Soldiers have been lazy. It is too early in your service for you to be lazy. I have already eaten the rice of the army for four years. You have only come in recently," Oka said in a loud voice.

Kan stepped forward and began, "You do not know etiquette. You must not forget your Spirit of the Soldier just because you have come to the front." He was a little hesitant, but he was fast learning the art of lecturing his subordinates, and the sight of him trying to put "spirit" into his subordinates, when they knew how he had been when he had had "spirit" put into him, appeared a little amusing to Takeo and Miki, watching from where they were beside the stove.

"Attention!" Kan continued. "It fills us with trepidation that

His Majesty the Emperor has been pleased to include an article on etiquette in the Imperial Edict to the Armed Forces. . . . Private Seki," he called peremptorily. "Yes, sir," Seki answered. "Recite the Article on Etiquette," Kan ordered.

Seki recited earnestly and without flaw, for he had been a good student:

"A soldier must maintain etiquette. From the Commander-in-Chief down to the lowliest soldier, there are separate ranks of duty among the servicemen, and obedience should be solely according to ranks, but even among those of the same rank, seniority must be respected. A subordinate who receives an order from his superior must think of it instantly as an order from Us. Though not in direct command, a superior, naturally, and anyone senior in service must be saluted. A superior must not have the slightest arrogance or contempt in his conduct toward his subordinates. Aside from such times as when dignity must be maintained for the performance of duty, a subordinate must be treated kindly. One in comradeship and united from top to bottom, serve well the Imperial Mission. If there is one who is a serviceman, who disregards etiquette and does not respect his superiors or show benevolence to his subordinates, thus destroying the unity, he is not only a disgrace to the Armed Forces but also an unpardonable traitor to his nation."

When Seki finished his flawless recitation, even Kan felt called upon to exclaim, "Good!" but he added, "But it is no good only to memorize it. You must put it into action. You must show more respect to the older soldiers from now on." He was not thinking of the part in the edict which enjoined the superiors to treat their subordinates kindly and considerately — no one ever did in the army, for the ones who did the talking were always the superiors.

Carried away by his own eloquence, Kan would have gone on indefinitely, only Oka caught sight just then of a soldier in the rank hiding a cigarette butt in the cup of his right hand. He was a Replacement, and he had pinched out the fire when the call to assemble had been given, but he had thought it wasteful to throw the butt away and had hoped to light it again after they were dismissed.

"The soldier with the cigarette butt still in his hand, come forward!" Oka bellowed. The soldier pointed out stepped timidly forward. Oka was a stout, bull-necked man, and he had great strength in his shoulders. He slapped the Replacement soldier three times, nearly knocking him over, when the soldier's nose began to bleed.

"Hold your nose with a towel," Oka said, and he shoved the unfortunate Replacement back into line.

Takeo watched the proceeding with disgust, but the excitement was catching on to Miki, who was more susceptible to influences coming from his environment, and so when he saw a soldier trying to ease the strain on both legs by putting the weight of his body on one foot, he shouted from his bench, "Who told you to be 'At ease'?"

The guilty soldier snapped back to attention as if hit by lightning. Even Takeo and the Privates First Class were jolted by this sudden show of enthusiasm from the usually stolid Miki, and a momentary silence fell on the room, as if everyone felt embarrassed by the sudden intrusion.

But Kan was not one to be outdone, and he shouted imperiously, "From today, you will do as you did at the home regiment! When you leave, state where you are going. When you return, report where you have come from."

"Do you understand?" Oka, who seemed to have relinquished the main performance of the lecturing to his more voluble comrade, now demanded loudly. "Yes, sir," those in line answered in unison.

"Be careful henceforth!" shouted Kan. "Yes, sir. We will be careful henceforth," the chastised soldiers repeated.

"All right. Dismissed!" Oka ordered.

"Salute!" they called and, saluting the Privates First Class, immediately went about carrying out the instructions just given them. Some dashed for the Squad Leader's room to get the Squad Leader's uniform to be washed. Others asked the Privates First Class if they had any available laundry, and still others even went before Takeo and Miki to ask for their laundry. Those going out began shouting their destinations loudly in the doorway, and those returning also announced from where they had come.

They would say, "Private So-and-So will go to the toilet!" or "Private So-and-So has returned from the toilet!" The squad room reverberated with the loud voices of the soldiers coming and going, and these soldiers kept on the move, since it was embarrassing not to mention one's name as often as the next fellow. Especially when one among them made such an announcement, as, "Private So-and-So will go to wash the laundry of Honorable Private First Class Oka!" it behooved the others also to try to dig up something to do, just as worthwhile in its indication of service industriousness. Those remaining in the room also tried to keep on the move, and they took brooms in hand and began sweeping the floor, or they began wiping the tables, or cleaning the rifles and machine guns. There were sundry tasks to do in a squad room if one looked around, and the Replacements and First-Year-Soldiers found enough to do to keep them on the move constantly.

The older soldiers, including Privates First Class Oka and Kan and the Senior Privates Miki and Takeo, sat comfortably around the warm stove and watched this revived activity of the younger soldiers with critical eyes, though, in the case of Takeo alone, there was more pity than domineering criticism for his oppressively driven subordinates. The transformation in Takeo had been gradual but pronounced. He had started out with a pure, unadulterated desire to perform his patriotism to his Emperor, and, in the performance of it, he had also tried to find a means to accomplish his filial duties to his aged parents. He had also sought to reconcile his patriotism with the deepest meaning of life which his unschooled but intuitive mind could grasp. But the ugly realities of warfare had disproved conclusively the idea that patriotism could be the fountain of life, and the petty rivalry and spiteful discipline of the army had made his original pure patriotic urge look like the empty daydreaming of an adolescent. Even his attempt to unite patriotism with his filial obedience to his parents had turned out to be a sad disappointment, for he knew that his parents could never condone many of the things which he was forced to perform or witness unrestrainedly at the front in the name of patriotism. His uncompromising superiors whom he had started out to trust and obey absolutely, as laid down by the regulations of the army, had come to appear only human, with all the common human foibles that he himself possessed and knew, as time went on and he was enabled to notice the more intimate doings of the life around him. His failure to be promoted in the first promotion of his class of privates at the end of their first year had also been a disappointment, for he could not see how he had lacked any more in sincerity and courage than Kan, who had been promoted. The only sentiment which had remained intact as when he had first formed it was his desire to save enough money to buy an ox for his parents, and he held on to it, now more doggedly than ever, as the last stable pillar of his shifting existence. As for the rest, he had decided to serve out the remainder of his term in the army in a fashion which would place the least burden upon himself and his comrades as possible.

That night at roll-call, Takeo found his name included in the list of night watches. The hour assigned him was the unpopular hour after midnight, and Takeo felt little friendship for his Squad Leader for having assigned him that difficult period when the Officer-Of-The-Week was most likely to come on inspection and when a soldier standing it had his night's sleep interrupted in the very middle. He went to bed harboring this grudge, and his mood was not the least improved when he felt the now familiar shove on his shoulder in the midst of a deep sleep and heard the insistent call, "Change!"

With greater distaste than he had ever felt before, he pulled himself out of his warm blankets, and he vowed to himself for the hundredth time that when he went home he would spend all his spare moments sleeping. He dressed himself hurriedly in the dark, cold room and fixing his bayonet to his rifle as regulation required and still a little dazed from his sleep, he went out of the room into the lobby to go to the assigned post inside the main entrance where he knew the previous watch would be waiting. The cold wind which struck him, when he opened the door and stepped into the lobby, instantly knocked the drowsiness out of him. Knotting his muscles tightly now, he walked briskly to the assigned post.

Miki, who had been the one who had awakened him, was waiting, hunched up and shivering. He had his hands in his pockets and the rifle tucked under his arm, and he was marking time impatiently with his feet. Under the weak light hanging from the ceiling there, his face appeared shriveled up, and his lips were purple.

"What is this? Looking so cold!" Takeo scoffed and made a show as if he didn't mind the cold at all.

"You try and stand a whole hour here, too, and you will freeze up," Miki chattered between his teeth.

"All is well, is it?" Takeo playfully cut his comrade's grudge short.

"All is well, except for the cold," Miki said cynically. "There is no message to pass on tonight. I am going back. Take care of the rest," he mumbled in his mouth and started to turn to leave.

"Wait. Aren't you going to recite the Night-Watch Regulation?" Takeo asked. They were required to recite the Regulation given them at the beginning of the night at the change of a watch, but the older soldiers never bothered to do so, except when there was an officer around, and Takeo was only teasing his comrade.

"You recite it for me," Miki said and disappeared down the lobby.

Takeo looked at his watch under the light and saw that the time was only a little past midnight. He thought Miki had chiseled a few minutes from him, and he felt amused at the idea of his big, clumsy comrade stooping to chisel in order to get out of the cold a little sooner than he was entitled to. He thought, What a fool Miki is! He stands for an hour in such a place as this, and that is why he becomes cold!

Soon after Miki had left, Takeo followed him down the lobby and entered his squad room. It was a dark night, and, since electric lights were allowed to be turned on only in the lobbies after Curfew, it was pitch-black in the room, but Takeo saw a red point of light and knew that it was Miki smoking a cigarette in bed before going to sleep. Smoking in bed was strictly prohibited, but it was another one of the many petty violations of regulation which the conscience of the older soldiers permitted — if there were no officers around.

Takeo went to the head of Miki's bed and sat down silently. It was the height of disobedience for a night watch to sit down while on duty, but the older soldiers knew that there were no enemy around and that there were sufficient sentinels outside to warn them if any enemy should approach. They realized, moreover, that the night watch was more for the prevention of fire and the maintenance of discipline than for protection against the enemy. Just as Miki's smoking in bed had little danger of starting a fire if he should take the ordinary precautions, Takeo's sitting in his squad room did not mean that the whole building was exposed to the danger of being consumed by fire, just as long as he went out into the lobby once in a while to take a look around. Both conducts, however, were prohibited by regulations, and only the older soldiers' confidence in their ability to differentiate the principle from the formality — an ability which they prided themselves in having attained from their long experience in the army — led them to condone their disobedient conducts.

Miki, too, would have gone into his squad room to sit out his watch, but his inability to adapt himself to the varying circumstances arising from such an act had discouraged him from doing it. It was a self-assumed privilege of the older soldiers to try to get away with these petty violations, and their ability to show, at the same time, a faithful compliance to the regulations was called "*Yoryo,*" or "Good judgment." It was a stock phrase among the soldiers, and they were always saying to each other, "Do it with 'good judgment.'" And they would say of a successful soldier that "he has 'good judgment,'" which meant, most of the time, that that soldier had a skillful knack of convincing his superiors of his good conduct, while taking advantage of various violations, at the same time.

Miki and Takeo remained silent in the dark room, understanding each other perfectly. When Miki had finished his cigarette, he gave it to Takeo, saying, "Please," and he covered himself completely with his blankets and went to sleep. Takeo took the butt and went and threw it into the cold stove in the center of the room. He sat down on the bench before it and tried to forget the cold, while he leaned against his rifle. The thoughts which sprang, one after the other, in his mind were many and unfettered.

The First-Year-Soldiers say that the price of oxen has gone down again. I may now be able to buy my ox by saving only half a year longer, Takeo was thinking, when he heard the unmistaking crunch of an officer's boots on the frosted ground outside.

He knew in a flash that that would be the Officer-Of-The-Week making his round of inspection. He got to his feet hurriedly and sneaked out quietly from the squad room. The officer was in the middle of the yard, shining his flashlight up and down the face of the building. In the faint light falling on the officer from the lobby, Takeo saw the distinguishing red-and-white sash of authority across his chest, and he also noticed that, as usual, he was accompanied by his orderly, carrying a rifle with fixed bayonet.

Takeo was halfway down the lobby when the officer's light caught him. He stopped abruptly and, turning toward the officer, presented arms smartly, and called in a low but vigorous voice they were taught to use at night, "Night watch, making his round — all is well!" Then he hurried down the rest of the lobby and down the steps into the yard to where the officer was standing waiting in the yard.

"You were in the room resting!" the officer accused ominously.

Takeo replied without the least hesitation, "No, sir, I was making my round." Takeo knew that the officer would have to take his word for it, since there was no evidence to the contrary, but only his tried and tested knowledge in such ways permitted him to maintain his perfectly calm poise.

"All right. Tell me the Regulation-of-the-Watch," he now demanded gruffly.

Takeo had memorized his Regulation well, and he now recited it in a confident voice without a single mistake:

"The Night Watch should stand in the center of the lobby and make a round of the squad rooms from time to time.

"He should be especially careful about the prevention of fire and theft, and the one mounting watch should receive carefully the messages from the one leaving watch.

"At a change of watch, the one mounting and the one leaving should stand together in the center of the lobby and, after reciting the Regulation to each other, complete the exchange of messages.

"In case anything is amiss, it should be immediately reported to the Non-Commissioned Officer-Of-The-Week. . . . The end!"

"All right. What would you do if there was an enemy attack?" the officer next asked.

"I would shout, 'Enemy attack! Enemy attack!' and fire my rifle," Takeo answered promptly.

"All right. What is your name?" the officer asked and, when

Takeo told him, noted it down in a notebook he drew from his breast pocket.

Takeo recognized the officer as being a Lieutenant from Battalion Headquarters, noted for his strict discipline. But he seemed wholly satisfied with Takeo tonight, and he had written down his name in his notebook. That meant that Takeo would probably be cited for "alertness while on night watch" in the order-of-the-day tomorrow.

As the officer turned to go, Takeo presented arms smartly. The officer returned the salute and left the yard. Takeo went back to his squad room and sat down on the bench in front of the stove to sit out the rest of his hour. He was acting with "good judgment," as they meant it in the army.

泥濘

CHAPTER 19

PRIVATE FIRST CLASS OKA stepped aside suddenly to avoid a rut in the road, and Miki, marching with a machine gun alongside him, also stepped sideways to avoid jostling his stocky superior and himself unwarily set foot in a rut. Abetted by the heavy load on his shoulders and by his innate clumsiness, his foot slipped, and he went crashing resoundingly into the mud on the road. There was a loud thump as his huge body, together with the heavy rucksack on his back and the machine gun on his shoulder, hit the ground; and the empty aluminum rice container strapped to the rucksack clanked loudly against the steel helmet tied over it, while his canteen, bayonet, cartridge containers, and the sundry articles in his utilities bag all rattled and jangled loud enough to cause a miniature commotion in the monotonously marching columns.

The whole platoon heard the fall, and those marching ahead turned around to see what had happened while those marching to the rear had an excellent view of what occurs when both feet of a big soldier are swept completely off the road. There was confusion in the columns following, too, since the soldiers were pushed and crowded by this sudden break in their line of march. A few snickered, but the rest remained silent and continued their march, only glancing curiously at their fallen comrade, for they felt too tired, or too grim, or too respectful to see the humor in the fall. Some noted, however, how Miki had protected the valuable machine gun intentionally with his body when he fell and that he had paid for his effort by having his face almost half-buried in the mud.

"Honorable Senior Soldier, let go of the machine gun," First-Year-Soldier Seki said, and he bent over the unlucky soldier, kicking desperately in the slippery mud in an effort to get to his feet.

Other First-Year-Soldiers also came to Miki's aid, and they took the heavy weapon away from him and helped him to his feet. They asked anxiously, "Honorable Senior Soldier, are you all right?"

"Keep your eyes closed," Takeo said, and he wiped the mud from his comrade's face with his towel. Others tried to get the mud off his uniform.

As soon as Miki was able to open his mouth and talk, he began apologizing to his friends gathered around him, "I am sorry," and to their sympathetic inquiries, he answered, "I am all right. Now, leave me alone." Over half his body was covered with the slimy mud, and they were having a hard time getting it off. Miki drew himself away from his commiserating comrades and protested, "That is all right. Leave it alone," and he took back his machine gun and, shouldering it again, started off strong as ever to overtake his squad, which was marching quite a distance ahead by now, and his friends who had stopped to help him followed him.

As they passed friends in the other squads, some called, "Miki, put strength in you!" Others thought, Miki did it again, for the clumsiness of the big soldier was a well-known fact among them, but these did not say anything, and they gazed wonderingly at his massive figure hurrying past them, without the least sign of a limp or weakening, and they thought, surely, there was no limit to the punishment he could take.

When Miki and his comrades returned to their squad, Miki again began apologizing profusely, this time, to his superiors, who had not bothered to stop when he had fallen. "You should watch your footsteps more carefully," Private First Class Oka scolded.

"I am sorry," Miki apologized, but he felt deeply grateful toward Takeo and the younger soldiers, who continued to show signs of genuine sympathy for him. One offered him a cigarette, and others tried to scrape more mud from his uniform while keeping up the march. Seki suggested, "Honorable Senior Soldier, shall I take the machine gun?" Miki was conscious of a feeling of importance and responsibility he had never before known in his life as a soldier in the army.

The soldiers, however, soon left Miki alone, for they themselves had to keep their eyes carefully on the road to keep from falling in the treacherous mud. Their shoes were constantly slipping, but few went completely off their feet, and none fell with as much gusto as Miki had shown.

It was raining heavily, and the roads which had been fine dust during the dry summer months were well-churned masses of viscous, slippery mud which came up to the ankles of the marching soldiers. It had been raining and snowing alternately for nearly a week now, and the roads were thoroughly soaked. The snow of the previous night had turned into rain early this morning when the men had started, and the rain, after continuing miserably for over half a day, had taken the frozen brittleness completely from the roads' surface. The soldiers said disgustedly of the roads, "One slipped back half a step for every step forward."

The battalion was now on its third day of marching since leaving the town it had been garrisoning outside the seaport city of Tsingtao. With the approach of early spring, reports had started to arrive regarding the appearance of Communist guerrillas in the countryside, and the battalion had been ordered out on another one of those much publicized but little effective "mopping-up operations."

The cold rain beat relentlessly on the bodies of the tired soldiers. It seeped through their raincoats and ran down their necks and over their bodies, until almost nothing they were wearing was dry and untouched. The water found its way into their shoes also, and the soldiers felt so miserable that, as they said, "You couldn't tell whether you were wet from the rain or from your sweat, tears, nose-water, or urine." Miki's muddy appearance, too, was not as conspicuous as it would have been on ordinary marches, for they all had mud on them, more or less, from throwing themselves indiscriminately on the ground during the rest periods.

One soldier, a young First-Year-Soldier in the squad marching in front of Squad Three, had fainted from exhaustion, and his comrades were carrying him laboriously on a stretcher borrowed from Headquarters. They carried the stretcher on their shoulders and took turns carrying it, but the way they slipped and struggled through the mud was a pity to watch. They kept exhorting each other in loud voices, and, even during the rest periods, the stronger ones had to keep up a constant chatter in order to sustain the squad's morale, while the soldiers in the other squads lay down quietly to rest their tired muscles. Those in the neighboring squads, moreover, did not offer to help, for it was an accepted code among them that, when the going became hard, each squad should handle its own trouble.

At one rest toward the middle of the afternoon, Squad Leader Gunji exhorted his men in Squad Three, "If one man should fall exhausted, he will cause trouble to everyone, so try your hardest." Fortunately, except for one or two Replacements who tended to lag from time to time, the men in the squad were bearing up nobly, and the sight of Miki and Private First Class Oka almost monopolizing the killing task of carrying the squad's two machine guns between them was an inspiring incentive, not only to their comrades in their own squad but to the other soldiers of the platoon.

Miki, especially, was a sight to see. He went behind his comrades who showed signs of weakening and pushed them along, or took their hands and pulled them over the more difficult spots. He helped remove the shoulder straps of their rucksacks during rest periods and gave them water from his canteen. "Miki has changed since the First-Year-Soldiers came," they all said of the blunt farmer's lad. Miki had regained his outspokenness early enough since his painful escapade with the *Kempei*, but the spark had seemed to have gone out of his effort. He had shown little initiative, as if he had lost all confidence in himself, and he had lived his days nervously, apologizing at the slightest provocation. He was like a horse which had been given too much of the whip.

Since the arrival of the Replacements and especially the First-Year-Soldiers, however, Miki had come to show less and less of his nervousness and had started once again to exert himself actively in a conscious effort to be of service to his comrades. When the younger soldiers called him, "Honorable Senior Soldier," and treated him with respect, they awakened a long slumbering spark within Miki — a force which we call self-respect and without which no living thing, man or animal, can do much good, and, sometimes, even the plants seem to be aware of it. The joy at being recognized once again had been almost painful to goodhearted Miki, and he had been grateful.

No one had welcomed this reviving interest of the big soldier more than Takeo. Their common background as farmers and over a year of service together through the vicissitudes of the battlefront had awakened a binding friendship between them, and the disappointment they had shared at their failure to be promoted with the first group at the end of the previous year had further deepened their comradeship. So when the troops passed through a village and no natives came out to greet them and Miki fell out of line with the permission of the Squad Leader to go into the houses to gather tea and even sweets for his comrades, Takeo was among the first to share his findings. As he munched hungrily at a mouthful of sweets, Takeo envied his comrade's seemingly boundless energy, though he himself was bearing up well in the march — only it was all he could do to take care of his own self.

Some natives soon appeared in their doorways to offer tea and sweets to the passing troops, for they seemed to have decided that it was better to do so than to have the soldiers rummaging roughly through their homes. They stood smiling politely in their doorways but did not venture out into the rain, and the stronger soldiers ran to them to get the proffered refreshments for themselves and their comrades.

Takeo, now remarkably refreshed by the hot tea and candies Miki had got for him, gazed enviously, and almost longingly, at the natives in their dry homes. His interest in them seemed temporarily to make him forget his misery, though the troops plodded through the drizzling rain past them without easing the pace a bit. When they passed one house near the farther end of the village, Takeo had a glimpse through its open door of a fire burning in a hearth inside, and there was a young woman sitting before it with an infant in her lap. A young man, probably her husband, stood in the open doorway, smiling and bowing respectfully and offering hot tea to the passing troops, and Takeo was sure it was not his bias which made him think there was a happy, contented look on the young man's face.

It had been only a fleeting glimpse, and they had soon passed the house and were out of the village, with only the clouded sky, muddy road, and wide, barren fields to offer them meager solace in the depressing, unceasing rain. The warmth and feeling of coziness which the sight of the room with fire burning in the hearth had imparted had awakened a pleasant reaction in Takeo, but the pleasantness had been just a passing sensation and, the next moment, Takeo was conscious only of a gnawing, hungry loneliness and was feeling painfully the cold and the uncomfortable stickiness of the rain running over his face and underneath his clothes. The room which had met Takeo's chance glance had been a common dirt-floored one, no different from all the other rooms of peasant huts he had seen in this region, but the thought of the young native couple living their days in conjugal contentment in it aroused such a powerful awareness of the misery of his own lot that he felt he could not contain it any longer, and he turned toward Private First Class Oka, who was marching beside him.

"It is better to be a native," Takeo said to his stocky superior.

"That is so. You wouldn't know who won the war," said Oka.

"It is better to be a noncombatant in a conquered nation than to be a soldier in a winning army," Takeo continued.

"That is so," Oka agreed again. "Even if the natives are citizens of a conquered nation, they do not have sentinel duty, or marches, or combats like us, and they do not have to salute, and they can go wherever they please."

Kan, who was listening from the other side of Oka, said, "Rather than have one's country ravaged, it should be better to be a soldier in the winning army."

"Even if one's country is ravaged a little, it is better to have a home, however poor it may be, and to be able to live together with all one's folks," Takeo insisted.

Miki shouted loudly, "I want a bowl of steaming noodles!" The soldiers laughed at this impossible suggestion, and the next instant they had forgotten their argument and were trudging stoically through the mud and rain. At the next short rest, they learned that the exhausted soldier in the next squad who was being carried on a stretcher had died.

"Even that will be recorded in the books as an 'honorable death,' " Oka said, as he sat down in the mud beside the road with the rest of his squad and leaned back heavily against his rucksack.

"His folks at home will also be notified that their son has met an 'honorable death' while engaged in combat," said Kan a little sarcastically.

"Can't we go home unless we become ashes and are placed in a 'little white box'?" exclaimed Takeo somewhat desperately.

"It is the end of you if you become ashes and are placed in a 'little white box.' Let us all go home alive!" said Miki.

After the order to resume march was given, the men did not have very far to go to reach the goal of their three days' march. The town was a fairly large-sized one, situated along a river. "No enemy in the town," the advance patrol reported back when it had passed safely among the first cluster of houses on the outskirt. There was not a single soldier in the whole battalion who did not feel overwhelming relief at this announcement, for they had been warned to expect strong resistance, and they had been looking forward with fearful reluctance to the coming battle at the end of their exhausting march. A few, however, found strength to feel vexed at their superiors for taking them on such a fruitless trek.

When the main body of the battalion entered the town, the men found the streets and houses deserted of their native occupants. At the town's farthest end, where a fairly wide river lay partially frozen, they found the bridge crossing to another town on the other side thoroughly demolished. Before the soldiers had started on their march, they had been told that, according to intelligence from native sources, there was a large concentration of Communist guerrillas in the town, and their objective, they had been instructed, was to "capture" the town. Now safely in the town, without having had to fire a single shot, the men had little time to congratulate each other on their good luck, for it was near sundown, and they had to get busy preparing for the night.

Quarters were assigned each squad in the Hamamoto company after the usual procedure, and Corporal Gunji's Squad Three was given a fairly large house near the town's outskirts on the side opposite to where the river was. The soldiers fell to immediately, laying out their beds and getting ready to cook the evening meal. The livelier soldiers dashed into the side lanes to forage for food.

Takeo, who had volunteered to join the foragers, picked a house up the middle of a lane and kicked open its barred doors. He stood for a moment in the doorway to let his eyes become used to the dim light inside, for all the windows were barred and very little light entered the room. After a while, he began to discern the objects in the room. There were a bed in one corner, a table, stools and a dilapidated bureau, and, except for a few more knickknacks scattered on the hard-packed dirt floor, the room showed nothing more remarkable to satisfy the eager eyes of a foraging soldier.

However impoverished and barren, nevertheless, there was a deep thrill in standing in an unknown room, master of everything and anyone in it, and Takeo, who had not recovered wholly yet from the depressing misery of the late march, drank in this thrill with unrestrained abandon. The lonely yearning which had seized him after his glimpse into the warm interior of a native's home during the march that day found an outlet in a sensuous feeling of satisfaction at finding himself in a room, complete master of it and with power over it beyond the ordinary power even of mere ownership.

He was about to step inside from where he stood in the doorway, when the sight of a figure crouching in the shadow of the bureau stopped him with a jolt. He had not seen it in his first survey of the room, but a close scrutiny showed him that the figure crouching beside the bureau and cringing as if it wanted to bury itself in the very wall or under the floor, if it could, was a young and full-bloomed girl. The thought that the figure might be an enemy, waiting to spring upon him, had almost paralyzed Takeo with fear the first time he had noticed it, for, like most of the soldiers out foraging then, he was unarmed except for his bayonet hanging from his belt at his hip. This sight of the girl, however, had dissipated the fear, but the sense of caution which had taken him the first time remained.

The girl kept staring intensely at Takeo with such stark fear on her face as Takeo had never seen on the face of anyone before, and the silence between the two became almost unbearable, and Takeo said cautiously, "Girl, come, come," using the most appropriate words he knew from his scant knowledge of the local vocabulary.

The girl shrank back, as if struck, at the sound of Takeo's soft voice and began to whimper weakly. The helpless tone in her voice gave Takeo courage and awakened a savage lust in him. The new feeling seized him with such force and suddenness that it left him shivering.

"Good, good," Takeo said in the native vernacular, and he leered at the quaking girl. He had never leered at anyone before, and the new experience, sharing its newness with the raw animal lust coursing wildly through his body, surprised even Takeo himself. With heart pounding wildly so that he felt almost constrained to gasp for breath, Takeo started forward nervously. The girl, seeing the soldier coming toward her, buried her head in her arms, as if the sight was too frightening to look upon, and began to weep pitifully.

Takeo had not expected this total breakdown, and the sudden outcry caused him to halt where he was in the middle of the room. He now began to struggle within himself between an urge to consummate his lust and a newborn pity for the helpless, weeping figure. The slightest sign of resistance on the girl's part might have incited him to a final accomplishment of his intended deed, but the show of total passivity and miserable surrender she had chosen struck a sympathetic chord in his heart — a capacity which had been nurtured by his constant life of oppression in the army.

It was then a strange thing happened to Takeo, while he battled with his two conflicting emotions. He became suddenly aware of the picture he was carrying in his breast pocket of the prostitute, Mariko, which he had received from her after his short moment of pleasure with her in the brothel where Reserve Private Hosaka had so considerately taken him. It was not as if he had suddenly thought, I am carrying Mariko's picture! . . . It was not as cool and objective as that. . . . It was as if the picture itself had suddenly started clamoring, "I am here! Here in your breast pocket! Remember me!"

This sudden awakening to the presence of the girl's picture in his pocket overpowered Takeo. It held him motionless. It left him weak and sweating. It pressed against his body like a heavy, leaden weight and squeezed the last trace of the lust which had seized him a moment ago from it. He stood now, calm and master of himself. Together with the lust, the mysterious awe he had felt at his sudden transformation left him, and he even forgot the strange cause of the transformation as he gazed with an unhampered realistic eye at his surrounding, like one awakened from a bad dream, and only later was he to find occasion to recall his strange transformation.

Removing his eyes from the native girl for the first time since he had become aware of her hiding in the shadow of the bureau, Takeo now coolly studied the room once again. A door in the wall in front of him, and not very far away from the girl, stood open and showed the dark interior of a room in the rear. The other room was in complete darkness, and Takeo found himself puzzling why the girl had not hidden in there in the first place. In order to forage, he realized he had to pass through that room in order to get to the backyard where the natives usually kept their hogs and poultry. The darkness of the room, however, seemed forbidding, and the same feeling of caution which he had felt when he had first noticed the girl now returned to him, and he began to reason that if there was a girl here, there might be others in the house. He warned himself that the others might not be as helpless and surrendering as the girl. He became aware of an unexplainable sense of imminent danger, and he even regretted his folly of having entered a house by himself.

He decided to leave the room to seek his comrades, with whom he could go foraging together through the houses, and he thought the next house he chose to enter would be one with a front room opening directly into the backyard. Without giving another thought to the room he was in and without even a parting glance at the girl who continued to weep against the wall at the foot of the bureau, Takeo turned and left the house. Outside, he met several First-Year-Soldiers from his own squad and, together with them, he went dashing up the lane, filled once again with the excitement of trying to find something, better than anything the others might find, to fill their evening's larder.

They entered the last house on the lane and found a fair-sized pig running about in the backyard. It was easily cornered, and Takeo showed the First-Year-Soldiers how to fell it. He got a knife from the kitchen and, with their help, skinned it and sliced away the choice pieces in the usual manner, for he was adept in the art by now. They put the roughly cut chunks of pork in a basket and ran happily back down the lane to return to their squad.

When they approached the house where Takeo had won his strange victory over his sensuous temptation, they suddenly saw a soldier come reeling drunkenly out of its door with his hands covered over his face. He staggered to the middle of the lane and cried, "I am done for! Somebody come and help me!" Then he fell in a heap on the ground.

The surprised soldiers ran to his side and found blood smeared all over his face, so that they had a hard time recognizing him, but a close look showed them that the soldier lying unconscious on the ground was their own Private First Class Oka. Blood was flowing freely from two deep, ugly-looking gashes running diagonally across his face and formed a dark puddle on the ground. The cuts looked as if they had been made by some not-too-sharp object and appeared to have penetrated the skull. The soldiers lifted their bleeding, unconscious superior between themselves and carried him to the house where their squad was quartered. They set him down in the room which had been cleared for the night's lodging, and a soldier was immediately dispatched to Battalion Headquarters to get the surgeon.

Takeo told his Squad Leader about the girl he had seen in the house from which Private First Class Oka had emerged in his sorry condition and expressed his opinion that the Private First Class had probably been struck by someone hidden in the rear room when he had attempted to make a pass at the girl. Corporal Gunji ordered five of his men to get their rifles and, taking his rifle too, asked Takeo to lead the way back to the fateful house. They found the house easily, for the blood was still plainly visible outside its door, and blood was spattered all over inside the front room.

They started a search of the house at once. They looked into every nook and corner and peered under the beds and tables. They went into the backyard and searched the cowshed and kitchen that were there, and they poked their bayonets into the piles of hay and cow's dung in the cowshed. They found no trace of a girl, or of any other native, in the whole compound, although they found a blunt wood chopper covered with blood in the backyard, which they thought had been the weapon used by the assailant against the unlucky Private First Class. The backyard was surrounded by low mud walls, which anyone in the house could have easily scaled, and the searchers now climbed over them and went into the adjoining houses, but still they found no trace of Oka's attackers and saw not even a single native occupant. The soldiers of Squad Three were shortly reinforced by armed comrades from the other squads of their platoon, from whom they learned that the news of the attack on Oka had already spread throughout the company, and they now went through all the houses along the lane. They searched meticulously and thoroughly, but these houses, too, were empty of all their native occupants. They were debating among each other whether to proceed with the search into the adjoining lanes when an orderly came from Company Headquarters to transmit the Company Commander's order for all to return to their quarters. It was already becoming dark, and there was much to be done in preparation for the next day's departure.

When the soldiers of Squad Three returned with their Squad Leader to their quarters, they found the surgeon there putting the last stitches in the wounds of Private First Class Oka. Oka's face had been washed clean, and his eyes were open and staring painfully at the ceiling, as if he had regained consciousness, but the face was swollen beyond recognition, and the vitality and stern pride which they had been used to seeing on it and respecting were no longer there, and there were only pain and an almost infantile helplessness. The soldiers looked with respectful silence at this pitiful transformation of the Private First Class, and, although there were a few who felt a gloating satisfaction underneath their outward show of hushed respect, the majority were struck by an emotion akin to awe at the sight of this ignoble passing of a force which they had come to think almost as inextinguishable.

The surgeon bandaged the face with deft hands, leaving only the eyes, nostrils, and mouth uncovered. He used such a liberal amount of tape plaster on the bandages that the younger soldiers who were usually begrudged the use even of the tiniest strips for their cuts and bruises, marveled at the extravagance permitted their superior. "There will be no danger to his life," the surgeon said to Corporal Gunji, as he got up from his work. "There is nothing to do but keep him warm until we get back to our garrison."

The surgeon next turned to the soldiers standing around their prostrate comrade and, grinning meaningfully and almost lewdly, said, "This happens when you try to enjoy something all by yourself."

"Yes, sir," the soldiers answered respectfully. When the surgeon turned to leave the room, his long sword dangling uncomfortably from his hip, somebody called, "Salute!" and they all saluted him, but the medical officer, who, they said, had been a children's specialist before being mobilized, did not answer the salute but merely shook his head in acknowledgment and hurried out of the room.

The surgeon had not been gone very long, and the soldiers were placing more blankets on their wounded comrade, when the first explosions were heard. The explosions were loud and sharp, and they seemed to come from the town's center. An unknown explosion was always a matter of vital importance at the front, and some of the men went to the door to look in the direction from which the sudden disruption had come. The rain had now changed to snow, and it was bitingly cold outside, but aside from the soft patter made by the falling snow, an ominous silence seemed to have descended upon the whole town after the explosions.

But the men did not have very long to wonder, for the silence was soon broken by the unmistakable sound of shells falling, followed by more explosions. It was the deliberate and pursuing hiss-hiss of the mortar shells, which seemed mostly to be falling in the center of town, but some began to fall nearby. The roofs of the houses were thin slate affairs which, they all knew, could not stop a mortar shell. Corporal Gunji gave the warning to his men, and they began running around, hurriedly gathering their equipment and weapons.

"It may be an enemy attack!" Corporal Gunji exclaimed in a voice which he tried to keep as calm as possible, but he was feeling as nervous as the next soldier, and he wanted his men out of the house as quickly as possible. From the sound of the shells, no one could tell from what direction they were being fired, and for all they knew, some of the more experienced ones thought, they might be encircled.

When the First-Year-Soldiers began to strap on their rucksacks, the Squad Leader impatiently cut them short and said, "Fools! It may be an enemy attack, and what are you taking your time about it for? If you have your guns and ammunition, that is enough!"

It took the men some time, however, to improvise a stretcher for their wounded comrade from boards they found in the backyard and more valuable time to transfer the wounded Private

First Class on to it. Some of the older soldiers had had their coats off, but they were the first to scramble out of the quarters, ready for combat. The others followed them closely, carrying their heavy, stocky comrade between them but leaving their rucksacks and unnecessary equipment, as well as the materials they had so assiduously gathered for their evening meal, behind them.

Outside, the men found many soldiers already in the street, and these were all running from the direction of the town's center and headed toward the outskirts, away from the river. Corporal Gunji tried to stop one of the soldiers running past them and asked, "Where is the enemy?"

Without stopping, the soldier answered, "Across the river!" and kept on running.

Corporal Gunji led his squad to the town's edge toward which everybody seemed to be converging. There they found many soldiers milling about in disorderly confusion and calling excitedly to each other in a desperate attempt to organize themselves in the half-darkness of the sundown. There were a few horses, stubbornly tugging at their bridles and kicking wildly, adding to the general confusion of the scrambled assembly.

Voices were calling loudly and persistently, "The Hamamoto company assemble here!"

Corporal Gunji and his squad went where the call was being sounded and found quite a number of their company already assembled. The Company Commander and Platoon Leader were there, hastily organizing their men, coming together from every direction. Corporal Gunji immediately announced the arrival of his squad to the Platoon Leader, and Squad Three took its position among the other squads, already lined in the regulation double file before the Platoon Leader. The absent squads shortly arrived in swift succession, and the platoon was fully assembled. The report was transmitted to the Company Commander, and when the whole company was assembled, the platoons went through the usual ceremony of saluting their Company Commander. The other companies of the battalion were organizing themselves in similar fashion, and as fast as they were assembled, they reported the fact to the Battalion Commander.

The troops were gathered on a wide, open field just outside the town, and where there had been near pandemonium until a short while ago, there was order and discipline now. The shells were still falling in the town, but the battalion's mortars had been set into position while the troops were still organizing, and the heavy machine guns had remained at the river's edge, so that these were soon sending a concentrated barrage into the enemy in the town across the river in answer to their fire. Like the soldiers in Squad Three, the men in the other squads had also carried their dead and wounded comrades with them when they had fled out of town, and these were laid out in a group a short distance away from where the troops were organizing themselves. Some had taken more time, it seemed, and long after some semblance of order had been established, these soldiers continued to come out of town with the wounded and the dead, and the gruesome cluster beside the assembled soldiers continued to grow. The shells had fallen where the soldiers had been gathered the thickest in the center of town, and the toll they had taken appeared to have been heavy. The groaning and moaning of the wounded could be heard even above the heavy sound of battle.

The battalion had succeeded in organizing itself in a surprisingly short space of time. It was a credit not only to the training and discipline of the soldiers but to the traditional ability of the race to rally swiftly around a leader in times of emergency. It was born of a habit to look constantly toward leadership for guidance in the daily life of the nation, at the expense, almost totally, of individual freedom and initiative. Some of the soldiers, however, showed noticeably in their appearance the haste and alarm with which they had fled the dreadful area of the falling shells. Some had forgotten their caps, and some did not have their puttees on, and a few had even left their rifles behind them.

The latter were scolded roundly and sent back into town to get their weapons.

The soldiers were standing in the falling snow, waiting tensely for their next order, when, just as suddenly as the shelling had started, the enemy ceased firing abruptly. The battalion's guns continued firing for some time, but when the enemy did not answer, the Battalion Commander ordered a cease-fire. The soldiers were now ordered to return to their quarters in town to get the rest of their equipment and to finish cooking their meals. They were told, however, to bring their meals outside the town to eat, when they were cooked. The commanders felt little fear of the enemy resuming their shelling, for they were well aware by now of the enemy's cunning hit-and-run tactics, but they wanted their men out of town as soon as possible and on the open field where they could be deployed swiftly in case of enemy attack, now that they knew the enemy was near.

Before returning to town, the men of Squad Three built a little roof over Private First Class Oka's face with branches they found on the field and a raincoat. The Private First Class had not been laid out with the group of other wounded soldiers, for he had already been treated, and a First-Year-Soldier was left to watch him, when the squad left to re-enter the town. The squad did not have very far to go, for they had been quartered near the edge away from the river. When they reached their house, they found it untouched by the shells. They had already had a fire started under their pot of rice when they had been forced to make their hasty flight, and they now found the rice thoroughly cooked, though a little scorched. Some began removing the rice containers from the rucksacks and started filling them with two meals — the morrow's breakfast and lunch — as they had been ordered, while others began cooking a stew with the materials the foraging soldiers had gathered. The rice containers were strapped back on to the rucksacks as soon as they were filled, and when the stew was cooked, the soldiers shouldered their rucksacks and, carrying the pots containing the stew and rice for their supper (for they had cooked enough rice for three meals), they left the house and headed for the field outside the town.

They found others in the street also hurrying along with their steaming pots of cooked food, and there was unmistaken relief engraved on their faces, for the feeling that the shelling would start any minute had hung heavily on them, all through the time they had had to spend inside their quarters cooking their meals. To the soldiers, who had been trained mostly in the aggressive offensive tactics, the wide open field presented a more desirable haven than the cramped quarters of the village in the face of the enemy.

When the men of Squad Three neared the edge of the town, a soldier carrying a large bundle of firewood on his shoulders overtook them and hurried past them. Kan called out half jokingly to the soldier, "Are you going to burn a fire and let the enemy know where we are?"

The soldier, who looked like a First-Year-Soldier, merely turned back and answered gravely, "No, this is to get the ashes of a dead comrade."

They all fell silent and hastened to where they had left their wounded comrade, Oka, on the field outside the town. When they reached the spot, they set down the pots containing their cooked meals and, after stacking their rifles and machine guns, began immediately ladling out the stew and rice into bowls which they had found in the house and brought along with them. They ate, squatted on the ground around the pots, and they shoveled the food into their mouths greedily, for the excitement of the past hours had made them enormously hungry. The snow fell dispassionately upon them huddled around their pots, but the hot food warmed them considerably, and they did not mind the cold much. Occasionally a First-Year-Soldier poked a spoon under the shelter over Oka's face and let some soup run into his mouth.

When Squad Three had finished its refreshing meal, most of

the others had barely started theirs, and there were some coming out of the town only then with their pots of hastily cooked meals. Squad Three had been fortunate to be quartered near the edge of town, for many of the others had been quartered near the center, and these had returned to their quarters to find them almost demolished by the enemy shells, and they had been forced to start their cooking all over again. As soon as each squad finished eating, the men kicked over the pots which had held their meals and stamped them to bits under their hard shoes. The temptation offered by the fragile wares was too great for their destructive instinct. The native pots were made of thin cast-iron and broke easily under the slightest pressure.

Huge fires, which sent their flames high up into the darkness that had descended by now, began to appear here and there where the soldiers were burning their dead comrades to get the ashes to send home to their families. Soldiers who had finished their meal and had nothing else to do gathered around these fires to warm themselves. Takeo went to one of these and pushed his way in among the soldiers crowded around it to get near the flames. The smell of burning flesh was strong in the air, but Takeo could not see the corpse, for it was already completely enveloped by the fire.

"Honorable Senior Soldier was standing in the doorway when the first shell exploded right in front of the house," one who looked like a First-Year-Soldier said, and he looked reverently at the fire.

"In all, about ten must have died," another soldier near him was saying.

"Far from it! About twenty have died, I am sure," the soldier next to him argued, and from the number of fires being started on the open field around them, Takeo surmised that the second soldier's estimate had been closer to the truth.

The soldier beside Takeo said, "Some horses were killed, too. They were really to be pitied. There was one running around with the guts hanging from his belly, and another, I saw, kept trying to get to its feet, but its backbone was broken, and it could not stand up."

"They tell that at one squad a shell exploded right in the midst of where everyone was cooking the rice," a soldier with a high excited voice was saying on the other side of the circle gathered around the fire.

"In our squad, the Honorable Squad Leader carried a wounded comrade to safety in the midst of the falling shells," another, who looked like a First-Year-Soldier, recounted boastfully.

The soldier beside Takeo turned to him and asked, "In your squad, wasn't anybody hurt?"

Takeo answered, "No," for he did not want to talk about the case of Honorable Private First Class Oka.

Beyond the fire, Takeo could see the wounded, lying in neat rows on the snow-covered ground, and he estimated that there were nearly thirty of them there. The surgeon, now minus his long dangling sword, was going busily among them, and he kept scolding the soldiers trying to help him in his usual short-tempered way. Other soldiers, probably comrades of the wounded, stood looking worriedly from the fringe, and these were called from time to time to take away those to whom the surgeon's care had been of no avail and who had to be cremated as soon as possible before the next order was given from Battalion Headquarters.

"Really, those who were wounded are to be pitied," said Takeo to the soldier standing next to him.

"We are to be pitied also," the soldier replied. "When I think we will have to carry them back along the road we came, I am disgusted."

"Why? Aren't they going to carry them back on wagons?" Takeo asked, surprised.

"This time, the battalion's transport soldiers did not come, and the fieldpieces also did not come, and so there are no wagons," said the soldier, who obviously belonged to Battalion Headquarters or was closer to it than Takeo to know all these things.

Takeo abruptly left the comfortable circle around the fire and returned to where his squad was. He found his comrades had started a little fire of their own and were gathered about it, warming themselves contentedly. He immediately broke the bad news about the absence of wagons and warned his comrades that they would have to carry Private First Class Oka themselves back over the difficult muddy road.

"Is that true?" Corporal Gunji and several others asked unbelievingly.

Takeo recounted the story he had heard from the soldier a short while back, and he added the painful observation that he could not recall having seen any wagons throughout this march. Others supported him, and they were soon forced to view the situation in the new distasteful light.

"Never mind. The first village, we will find a cart and a donkey, and we will put Oka on it," said Corporal Gunji in an effort to bolster the squad's spirit, but his voice sounded weak. The soldiers, however, determined strongly in their hearts that they would find a cart and donkey in the first village they reached, even if they were forced to turn the whole village inside out to do so.

An orderly began calling loudly from where the wounded were assembled, "Each squad, come and get your wounded!" The soldiers in Squad Three, when they heard this call, were now certain that there would be no wagons to accommodate the helpless ones on the return trip.

"I wonder what they are going to let us do tonight?" Kan turned toward his Squad Leader and asked a question which had been troubling everybody since the first shells had started exploding in the town.

"I wish they would let us sleep right here. I am so tired, I can sleep anywhere," said Miki.

He was not to have his wish, however, for, soon an orderly went running among the huddled groups, shouting, "Prepare to depart!"

The numerous fires which had been started to cremate the corpses were now burning low, and it seemed the ghastly task was completed everywhere. In the faint glow of the dying fires, Takeo could see the Battalion Commander mounting his horse, and he seemed as vigorous as ever. He was the very picture of poise and self-confidence as he gave out swift orders to his staff members on the ground from atop his eagerly prancing horse. Usually, the sight of the Battalion Commander on his sturdy-looking mount had aroused a strong feeling of confidence and assurance in Takeo, but, tonight, it awakened only a shallow sense of envy, for, as he looked forward to returning over the difficult road they had come, he thought how good it would be to have a horse under him.

It took a little more time than usual for the troops to form their columns of march, for it was pitch-dark, and many of the squads had their wounded members to carry. There had not been enough stretchers to go around, and most of the squads, like Squad Three, had to carry their wounded on crudely improvised stretchers. The snow was still falling, and, long before they started, the warmth the men had attained by standing around the fires had left them, and they were only too glad to begin the march when, at last, the order was given, after all the sentinel patrols dispatched to the riverbank had returned. The men found the road less slippery than when they had marched over it during the day, for the snow falling on it had already started to freeze its surface, leaving only a few scattered spots still wet and soft.

The First-Year-Soldiers in Squad Three volunteered to take the first turn in carrying Private First Class Oka, and four of them — one under each corner of the plank bearing the wounded soldier — started the march back with the squad's fate-ordained burden. The soldiers had to be careful, for, this time, they were marching in total darkness and had practically to feel their way over the uneven road. Takeo, marching behind the soldiers carrying their difficult burden, said in a sarcastic tone to Miki beside him, "In spite of this, they will report in the papers at home that we captured a vital enemy stronghold and repulsed the enemy, inflicting heavy losses on them."

Miki answered, "That is so. And they will say that our losses were 'insignificant.' "

The Battalion Commander on his horse was thinking along the same line as the two soldiers of Squad Three, only he was not thinking of what the newspapers would report of this operation but of what he himself would report to his superiors about it. After the shelling duel had shown the enemy unwilling to exploit their first surprise further, he had quickly overruled a plan he had evolved to cross the frozen river and attack the enemy in the town on the other side. It would have cost more lives and would have achieved very little, for the enemy was sure to flee farther inland in their usual manner, once the crossing was achieved, leaving only the satisfaction of occupation to compensate for the added sacrifices. He had decided, instead, to color his report in such a way as to hide the dismal failure of the operation — an operation which he himself had suggested to his Regimental Commander on intelligence gained from native spies he had dispatched. They had, after all, "captured" the town which had been reported as being in enemy hands, and they had "silenced" the enemy's shelling with their own guns, which he could claim had inflicted "losses" many times greater than the enemy guns, which had been "silenced," had inflicted on his own troops. He had ample time to think out the exact wording of his report, as he sat unhampered on his horse, while his orderly on foot held the lower end of the reins to guide the animal over the dark road.

"Change!" Corporal Gunji called, when he thought the thirty minutes they had agreed upon to compose the length of a shift had passed. It was too dark to look at his watch, and, since they were forbidden to strike a match, the Corporal had to go by his instinct.

Takeo went beside Seki, carrying the forward right corner of the improvised stretcher, and said, "Change!" and took over the heavy load. It was then he realized that his left shoulder was much weaker than his right and that he should have gone to the soldier on the other side to relieve him, but it was too late.

CHAPTER 20

"THERE! They have shot the fifteen-centimeter gun!" said Miki.

In the distance there was a sharp reverberating explosion, as if somebody had set off a grenade in an empty steel drum. Then they heard the shell — a lazy *swoosh, swoosh, swoosh* — that went hurtling like an air-borne express over their heads. The men listened intently and, though they knew the shell was way over their heads, felt the strength ebb from their bodies. They ducked their heads instinctively, and some seemed ready to fall flat on their stomachs. After a while there was a loud explosion far to the rear, which shook the ground even where they were, and once again they knew the enemy had aimed its big gun at the Brigade Headquarters and supply dumps behind them.

As they always did after each explosion of the big shells, the soldiers felt overwhelming relief at the conclusion of the shell's suspenseful flight and felt genuinely grateful the enemy was not aiming his big guns at their own front lines. It was the first time they had been faced with such big-calibre artillery since coming to the Chinese Front, and the sound alone was terrifying. Compared to the big shells they were hearing now, the mortar shells and field-artillery shells they were used to hearing sounded abrupt and almost insignificant. The latter were over with in an instant. The big shells exploded with an earth-shaking roar, which rose to a mighty crescendo, then receded in undulating, dignified leisure, invincibly and overpoweringly.

"If that shell ever falls on our trench, we are dead Buddhas," said Kan, and they all looked up worryingly at their makeshift roof of crisscrossed timber, reinforced on top with a heavy mound of dirt.

"We should have taken more time to build our shelter," Takeo said.

A mortar shell exploded outside, but the men paid no attention to it. They knew their roof was strong enough at least for a mortar shell, and after the explosion of the larger shell, it had sounded futile and weak.

"No one thought the battle would turn out like this," Miki said.

"It is seldom that a shell scores a direct hit," answered Corporal Gunji, whose duty it was to keep up the squad's morale at a time like this.

"I wouldn't want to be caught by a direct hit at this stage of my service," said Takeo.

Takeo and his Same-Year-Comrades were now going into their third year of service, and Takeo had been promoted to Private First Class, to the same rank as Kan, although Miki was still an ordinary private. After a dreary year spent in garrisoning villages and chasing elusive Communist guerrillas in North China, their division had been shipped once again to South China, and they had captured the vital base of Nanning in Kwangsi Province after another one of those sleepless marching campaigns. As usual, the enemy had merely withdrawn inland after desultory holding attacks, and the troops had captured their objective with little difficulty.

This time, however, the enemy had struck back with a suddenness and ferocity Takeo and his friends had never before encountered during their long service on the continent. They had been used to dealing with the tricky hit-and-run tactics of the Communist guerrillas, and they had engaged in large-scale campaigns to capture vital enemy bases and important cities, but there had been more marching than fighting in these campaigns, for the enemy had chosen, each time, to retreat and returned only to harass the supply lines and outposts. After Nanning, however, the enemy had returned with a full-scale army to try to recapture their lost city from the North. One brigade dispatched to check the enemy in the pine-wooded hills north of the city had been annihilated, and the brigade Takeo and his comrades belonged to were now undertaking the difficult defense. This was the first time they were fighting a frontal engagement with a powerful enemy and the first time they were fighting a defensive trench war, and the experience was enervating.

"How many days is it since we have come here?" asked Miki, stroking the stubby growth of whiskers which had started to show on his chin.

"This is the second week, Honorable Senior Soldier," said Seki. He was now a Second-Year-Soldier and himself Honorable Senior Soldier to a new batch of First-Year-Soldiers.

"It feels like we have been here about a month already," Takeo said, and he scraped the pine needles under him to make a more comfortable seat. They had spread a thick cushion of dry pine needles on the floor in their trench, and the men were squatted or lying on it while waiting their turn to stand sentinel duty outside in the open trench.

"The squad next door has made a chess board and chess pieces," said Seki. "And they have covered the walls with twigs to keep the dampness away."

"Let us make a chess board, too. At this rate, we do not know till when we will have to stay here," said Miki, looking disgustedly around him in the dark room. The only light filtered in through the gunsight which was a narrow slit in front and through the cracks between the opened gunnysacks hanging over the doorway in the back. Although the darkness was a drawback, the trench was a wide one, and the men had more room in it than they had had on the transports.

"We will have to build another shelter first," said Corporal

Gunji gruffly. "If this many are together, it will be dangerous when we are attacked or get a direct hit."

"The squad next door is using the saw now. If they get through with it, we will cut more timber and build another roof, even tonight," assured·Private First Class Kan, who was second-in-command now. Then he turned to the First-Year-Soldiers, huddled in a group in one corner, and said sternly, "The First-Year-Soldiers will have to move around more. If you had gone quickly, we would have been able to borrow the saw from Company Headquarters before the squad next door." Even at the very front, it was the First-Year-Soldiers' duty to look after the menial tasks.

"Yes, sir!" the First-Year-Soldiers answered respectfully, although it had not been their fault that Squad Three had failed to get the only saw in the company before the "squad next door," since the latter was located closer to Headquarters and had been notified earlier of the saw's availability.

When the First-Year-Soldiers had answered Kan, they had assumed the kneeling position, which was the proper position of "attention" in a room. One of them, however, who had just returned from sentinel duty outside, remained stretched out on the comfortable pine-needle cushion. He was lying in the farthest corner and had hoped the darkness and his comrades would hide him, but Kan's sharp eyes picked him out, and the Private First Class went up to him and, pulling him up by his coat, slapped him soundly in the face. The First-Year-Soldier scrambled hastily to his feet and came to attention.

"Fool!" Kan shouted at him. "Can't you answer, at least?"

"Yes, sir!" the young soldier replied, stiffening as if frozen.

"The tired ones are all of us! Even if we are tired, to maintain discipline is our duty!" Kan said sharply.

"Yes, sir!" the First-Year-Soldier answered meekly.

"Well, sit down!" Kan said, and the young soldier squatted down, but he did not stretch himself this time, for he did not want to be caught again. A mortar shell exploded very close outside, but nobody seemed to notice it, and a heavy silence fell on the group.

"The first time they told us to dig this trench, we did not move," said Takeo to no one in particular, in an attempt to break the uncomfortable silence.

"That is because we had never fought a war like this before," laughed Miki, to whom the atmosphere of enforced silence was also distasteful. "Until now, when we dug trenches, we quickly resumed the offensive — even before the trenches were finished."

"But when the shells started to fall, we surely dug in!" Takeo laughed, too, encouraged by the cheerful support given him by Miki.

When their brigade had been dispatched to the hills north of the city, the Hamamoto company had been ordered to entrench itself on a thickly forested hill next to the main highway. There had been no enemy action the first day, and so the men, who had had practically no experience in defensive warfare, had not taken the order to dig in seriously and had made only a half-hearted show of carrying out the order; but that night, the last remnants of their sister brigade, which had been practically wiped out in the hilly area in front of them, had fallen back, and the next day the enemy, fresh from its recent victory, had come down upon them like an avalanche, and the shells had started falling around them as they had never fallen before. The men had dug then — madly and with everything they had. They had dug with their shovels and picks, with their helmets and rice containers, and with their bare hands. They had dug, lying flat on their stomachs to keep the shrapnel from hitting them; then they had dug, kneeling, when the holes had grown deeper; and, finally, they had connected their holes with deep zig-zagging corridors, until the whole company had entrenched itself on the hill they had been assigned to defend in a long, endless line facing the enemy. Then they had cut the timber at night to build large shelters in which the squads could congregate separately and rest themselves between shifts of sentinel duty, and they had built the roofs also to protect themselves from the falling shells.

They had had to fight, too, while they dug, for the enemy had come in wild, shouting hordes up the slope of their hill, and they had had to lay down their digging tools and pick up their rifles and guns to fight off the charging enemy; but their hill had been a high, steep one, and their advantageous position had helped them repel the attackers. They had fought as they had never fought before, and their morale and combat training had been forced to a test such as they had never faced before. The order had been, "Defend-to-the-Death," and its significance had been impressed upon the soldiers through eloquently worded orders from Headquarters, and they had stood by the order with a fury and tenacity which had surprised even themselves.

Except for a small force held in reserve, the other units of the brigade had been assigned positions on hills along a line facing the enemy, to the right and left of the Hamamoto company. They, too, had had to suffer the same experiences as the Hamamoto company, but, except for minor setbacks, they had also held their positions successfully against the first onslaughts of the enemy. After pounding futilely for over a week at the defense positions on the hills, the enemy had dug in also on the hills facing the defenders, and their attacks had diminished, and their shelling had become more methodical and spaced.

The enemy facing the Hamamoto company had entrenched themselves on a hill not more than a hundred meters away, and the fighting lately had been limited to sporadic sniping exchanges between the two hills, reinforced by occasional shelling attacks from both sides. The brigade was getting the worst of the shelling, since its guns were fewer and of smaller calibre, but the few airplanes which had started to come to help the defenders were a great asset, and their bombing and strafing attacks more than made up for the inferiority in artillery power. The planes had come on the fifth day, and on the sixth day the platoon of Lieutenant Miura, graduate of the orthodox Military

Academy and proponent of the classic life of the warrior, had been dispatched to take over a low unoccupied hill to the right and slightly to the front of the hill defended by the Hamamoto company. The company had thus been compelled to divide its strength over two hills, and its position had become a difficult one, as well as a conspicuous one for the enemy artillery.

The soldiers of Squad Three, too, knew well the precariousness of their company's position, and they were not letting the comparative quiet within their dark shelter lull them into a false sense of security. The air in the crowded shelter was charged with an atmosphere of tenseness and readiness, and even the exaggeratedly cheerful-sounding voices of older soldiers like Takeo and Miki contained a tightness and nervousness which could not be easily hidden.

"They say the enemy outnumber us many score times," Miki said, and he began to roll himself a "cigarette" with a piece of newspaper and dry pine needles, for they had been out of tobacco for some time now.

"No, they are only ten times more than we," scoffed Corporal Gunji. "I heard it at Company Headquarters."

"For certain they have more guns than we. That fifteen-centimeter gun — it is certainly a hateful bother!" said Miki.

He was about to mention more invectives regarding the enemy's big gun when he was cut short by a sudden outburst of explosions somewhere close by. The usual sound of battle — the sporadic explosions of shells and the occasional popping of sniping rifles — had suddenly become a concentrated bedlam, which entered their tight-lidded quarters and reverberated between its hard-packed dirt walls. The soldiers fell silent and listened intently, and it seemed to them that the new commotion was coming from the right. Within their confined dugout shelter, the concentrated explosion of shells sounded like pebbles falling on a tightly stretched drum, and the unending firing of rifles and machine guns sounded like the popping of a whole storehouseful of firecrackers.

"Wait until I go and see what it is," ordered Corporal Gunji, and he got up and, fastening the cartridge belt to his waist, picked up his rifle and went out, without waiting for a report from the sentinel outside.

He was not gone long when his head appeared excitedly between the flaps hanging over the doorway, and he shouted, "Everybody, go to his post!"

The men were out in an instant and took their assigned posts in the open trenches on both sides of the shelter. It was mid-afternoon, and the semi-tropical South China sun was shining in all its glory from a clear sky. It was cool in the shelter, but outside it was scorchingly hot. Inside, the sound of battle had seemed muffled and artificial; but now, it struck the soldiers with its full cacophonous impact and almost deafened them, so close it was.

The sound came from the low hill to the right held by the Miura platoon, where the enemy was concentrating a terrific artillery barrage, and also a barrage of machine-gun and rifle fire. The soldiers of Squad Three had an excellent view of the hill, for they were stationed on the slope of the company's higher hill, facing it, and the hill of the Miura platoon was slightly in front of theirs, and had no trees on it, only grass. They saw their comrades in the besieged platoon firing their rifles and machine guns madly down the slope ahead of them, oblivious to the many shells falling all around them. The men on the higher hill could not see what their comrades were firing at, for that part of the platoon's hill was hidden from their view, but they could easily imagine that the enemy were already charging up the slope and that the defenders were firing at these.

Takeo felt a queer sensation, as if he were witnessing something in a sphere of activities entirely separate from his, and yet he felt a pressing excitement which made his body tremble, as when he had approached the enemy shore on the landing barge. He could hear, above the loud commotion of battle, the voices of the men in the neighboring platoon wildly shouting orders and encouragement to each other. The figure of Lieutenant Miura was especially conspicuous as he ran up and down the trench, brandishing his drawn sword above his head and shouting at the top of his lungs, "Hold on! Hold on!"

No longer able to keep his excitement to himself, Takeo turned to Miki standing beside him and said, "There is very seldom a direct hit." He had meant it as an assurance to his comrades on the heavily shelled hill, and he did not realize that he was repeating a statement which their Squad Leader had made in the shelter a little while ago, but he thought it was doubtful and added, "If the Miura platoon holds on, it will be all right."

Miki himself was concentrating his whole being on the battle taking place on the low hill to the right, and he gripped the machine gun before him until the knuckles were white, as if he already imagined himself blazing away with it in the very midst of his battling comrades. He merely shook his head at Takeo's statement and kept his teeth gritted tightly.

They soon began to hear the explosion of grenades, and they saw some of the soldiers on the hill hurling theirs, so that they knew the enemy must be quite close to the top now. Corporal Gunji went hastily along the trench where Squad Three was lined, correcting the distance between the soldiers and cautioning them, "Don't look only to the right, but look also in front. The enemy may attack this hill at the same time."

They had seen the enemy on several occasions during the first days come dashing around the hill before them and come charging up their hill, and the Squad Leader's warning reminded them of it with a start. They looked anxiously at the hill almost only a stone's throw away from them, but they saw no movement on it directed toward them, although some of the guns in its formidable-looking shelters seemed to be concentrated on the lower hill where the Miura platoon was fighting its desperate defensive battle. Miki sent a sudden volley from his machine gun at one of these guns, which were barely visible through narrow slits in their shelters. The outburst made some of the soldiers jump, and the Squad Leader scolded, "Don't waste your bullets!"

"Yes, sir!" Miki answered. He had felt shamefully helpless, standing there and just watching, while his comrades were under such heavy attack in front of his very eyes. He had known there was practically no chance of his hitting anything by firing at the enemy's well-protected gunsight, for they had tried it before, but he felt better now.

The soldiers could not keep their eyes away from the Miura platoon very long, and when they returned their attention to it, they saw that the shelling had ceased entirely and that their comrades were hurling their grenades in earnest. A Japanese soldier, who was trained to expect offensive tactics only, carried but two hand grenades with him at the most, and the men of the Miura platoon exhausted their meager supply in an instant. They reverted to their rifles and machine guns, but the enemy's hand grenades now began to explode all around them like oil in a hot frying pan.

The men of Squad Three and of other squads in the company entrenched on the slope offering a full view of the besieged hill watched the battle reaching its inevitable climax with bated breath. They could see Lieutenant Miura still brandishing his sword and exhorting his men loudly, and he seemed poised as if to jump out at any moment to charge at the oncoming enemy. The soldiers on the higher hill could not see the enemy yet, but they knew from the explosions of the hand grenades and from the actions of their defending comrades that the enemy must be almost upon them.

Then they saw a strange sight — they saw their comrades of the Miura platoon scramble out of their trench and start falling back down the grassy slope of the hill they had been defending with such seeming valor. The order had been to "defend-to-the-death," and they could not believe what they saw unfolding before their eyes. They, who had been trained so strictly in the absolute obedience of orders, had not had the slightest doubt that the men of the Miura platoon would execute their order faithfully to the last man. It was as if they had given their whole life's energy to expect one thing, and the opposite had happened, and they found themselves at a loss to account for it. They had never been taught that there was a limit to the human will after all and to the power of man to withstand punishment. There had been an order — not an every-day routine order, but a very special one — and they had expected it to be fulfilled. They would have remained silent, every single one of them, and they would have felt the burning passions in their breasts settle, like a pebble dropped in a sparkling pool, if the men of the Miura platoon had stood in their trench and let themselves be wiped out completely.

Miki was the first to recover himself, and he shouted, "Hold on!" Others on the hill took up the cry, and soon they were all shouting, "Hold on! Hold on! It's 'defend-to-the-death'!"

The retreating soldiers did not hear the cry, for the explosive sounds of battle were all around them, and they were running with their whole attention concentrated upon the act of fleeing from the fearful presence upon the top of the hill. But somewhere in the cavernous recesses of the minds of some of the older soldiers, as they ran in panic down the hill, was a reassuring consciousness of their ability to use "good judgment" to explain their shameless conduct to their superiors later. The younger soldiers, however, felt only fear — a consuming, helpless fear. More than the enemy, the sight of the shameless flight of their superiors, to whom they had relinquished all their hopes, their initiative, and their very lives, had scared them. The older soldiers had seemed so self-assured and impregnable in their daily behavior before the younger soldiers, but now it was as if the fountain toward which the latter looked for their source of life had suddenly gone dry.

Even Lieutenant Miura, the Platoon Leader, had taken after his men when they had fled from the top of the hill, although the rest of the company watching the battle from their advantageous position noted that the Lieutenant was the last one to leave the trench. There was no assurance in the heart of the officer, however, as he fled down the hill, for he had at all times made a conscious effort to appear immaculate and correct, according to the highest martial traditions of his country, before his subordinates and fellow officers. He had been proud of his *samurai* ancestry, and he had considered it his heaven-ordained responsibility to uphold the aristocratic and stern traditions of the warrior handed down by his ancestors, especially before such officers as Lieutenant Kondo, who, it appeared to him, were undermining the army with their easygoing, merchant-like ways.

After his first scare, the Lieutenant quickly awakened to the shamefulness of what he was doing. A heart-rending despondency seized him. It sickened him and seemed to tear apart his very insides. He had fled on a sudden impulse when he had seen all his subordinates scramble out of the trench to leave him alone on the hill to face the enemy. Once out on the open slope running downward, however, his conscious self returned and he was overcome by anguish. He wanted to throw himself to the ground and to cry, but he gave vent to his anguish by shouting like a madman, "Come back! Come back! Don't run away! Come with your Platoon Leader! It's to the charge! It's to the charge!" They were now near the foot of the slope, and the Lieutenant had stopped and was brandishing his sword wildly over his head and calling desperately to his men.

They all heard their Platoon Leader, and some stopped from instinct, and these began to take up their commander's cry. Then others began to stop and soon all were turning toward their Platoon Leader. Gone now from the minds of the older soldiers was their cowardly dependence on "good judgment" to see them through and gone was the hopeless fright from the hearts of the young ones — there remained only a will, an instinct, to obey.

"To the charge! Charge in!" Lieutenant Miura shouted when

he saw his men rallying and began dashing back up the hill without turning to see whether his men were following him, his sword still brandished high over his head.

The soldiers followed their Platoon Leader without hesitating, and they held their rifles at the ready and shouted wildly as they charged up the hill. To their comrades watching from the hill to the rear, it was as beautiful and brave a charge as any they had practiced on the drill grounds at home. When the enemy had appeared on the hill after the Miura platoon had fled, some of the soldiers on the company's main hill had started shooting their rifles and machine guns at the new targets, but now they all joined in firing at the hill which their comrades were so valiantly trying to recover. They fired their weapons with such fervor and joyous enthusiasm as they had never felt in combat before.

Even before the Miura platoon reached the top, the enemy fled, for they had not been prepared for a counterattack so soon, and the wild courage of the attackers had shaken them, too. The soldiers immediately jumped into the recaptured trench and went to their former defense posts. But Lieutenant Miura, whether carried away by the fervor of the charge or moved by a wish to redeem himself by an act more courageous than the ordinary, did not stop when he reached the top of the hill but instead jumped across the open trench and started to run down the other slope after the fleeing enemy. A hand grenade, however, exploded in front of him and he was thrown back into the trench.

The men on the hill in the rear saw this plainly, for the Lieutenant had been a conspicuous figure. They now waited expectantly, hoping to see the brave officer rise to his feet again. But instead they soon saw the Platoon's Senior Sergeant, who was second-in-command, rise from where the officer had disappeared in the trench's hidden bottom and, turning around, shout at them, "Honorable Platoon Leader is dead!" In that way the Sergeant was reporting back to Company Headquarters the death of the Lieutenant, and he was doing the proper thing, for it was as if he had said, "I am now taking over the command."

The new Platoon Leader had little time to organize his men, for things began erupting once again. Events happened in the same order as previously. The shells fell first, then the hand grenades, and finally the enemy themselves came charging back up the hill. The platoon, which had already lost nearly half of its men, could not withstand the new attack, and the men scrambled out of their trench again, though this time they fell back down the hill crawling on their stomachs with their faces turned toward the top, and they kept firing their rifles to keep the enemy from becoming too bold. The orderly was carrying the Platoon Leader's body over his shoulder, but halfway down the hill he was shot and went sprawling in the grass together with his load, and nobody else took the trouble to go to recover the officer's dead body.

At the foot of the hill the men of the platoon tried to rally again as they had done previously, but the enemy had brought a machine gun with them this time, and the platoon had little chance in the face of the concentrated barrage. After hesitating a moment, they got to their feet and ran helter-skelter to take cover behind the hill where the rest of the company was entrenched. Once in the protecting shelter of the hill, they were met by an orderly from Company Headquarters who told them that the Company Commander wanted them to report to Headquarters.

Headquarters was on the top of the hill, and the surviving members of the badly cut Miura platoon began climbing it from the rear where they were safe from detection by the enemy. As they passed behind the trench where Squad Three was stationed, Takeo and his comrades called out, "Hard work! Hard work!" The soldiers in the trench looked carefully at the bedraggled group plodding stolidly up the slope to see who among their friends in the Miura platoon had been left on the captured hill and along the way of retreat.

When they reached the summit, the soldiers of the returned platoon lined up in double file behind the large shelter there which was the Company Headquarters. Captain Hamamoto, the Company Commander, came out of the shelter with a stern look on his face, but there was sympathy in his voice as he said, "Hard work! Hard work!"

The Senior Sergeant, who was acting Platoon Leader, presented arms to the Company Commander when he came out and reported in a voice full of passion and anguish, "I have no excuse!"

The Company Commander returned the salute and, looking very tired, said in a fatherly tone, "I understand. I understand." Then he instructed the soldiers to go to the trenches where the Kondo platoon was stationed. That was the platoon to which Corporal Gunji's Squad Three belonged.

Before departing, the Sergeant presented arms smartly and reported, "We shall leave!" Whatever impression the Company Commander had had of the platoon which had fled its defense post, the impression he now got was one of discipline and efficiency. The Sergeant was using "good judgment."

The survivors of the Miura platoon went where the members of the Kondo platoon were still out in their open trenches, awaiting the enemy's next move. They distributed themselves evenly among the different squads of the platoon. One soldier who went to the trench being guarded by Squad Three said excitedly to Takeo, "I don't care what they say. You can't stay in a place like that. You become as if you had lost your mind."

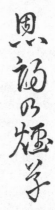

CHAPTER 21

W<small>HEN</small> L<small>IEUTENANT</small> K<small>ONDO</small> was called to Company Headquarters, he did not have the least idea why his Company Commander wanted him. He had been listening, totally absorbed, with his subordinates to the first-hand accounts of the battle of the lost hill related by the surviving members of the Miura platoon when the call had come.

"The Honorable Company Commander is pleased to call the Honorable Platoon Leader," the orderly from Company Headquarters had said, and he had not given the reason.

As the young officer, now Senior Lieutenant, circled the hill and climbed toward the summit from the rear, his heart was still full with the disdain and contempt he had felt toward his rival, Lieutenant Miura, when he had seen the latter scramble out of his trench and flee with the rest of his platoon. Lieutenant Miura, with his outspoken airs of the classic warrior, had always been domineering and almost antagonistic toward his fellow lieutenant. He had been caustically critical at times of the beliefs or habits of Lieutenant Kondo and other young officers with a liberal turn of mind, and the latter had been forced to listen to the reprimands silently, since their fellow officer had the popular trend of the times toward classicism and bigoted nationalism behind him. The presence of the Military Academy graduate had been, to the liberal-minded officers, a nuisance on the one hand and a goad to their conscience on the other, and

Lieutenant Kondo had never felt sufficiently qualified to classify his proud friend in either one of the two categories and had always felt nervously unsettled in his presence. But when he had seen the "exemplary warrior" fleeing from his position this afternoon, when the order had been "defend-to-the-death," all the hesitation he had harbored in judging his friend had disappeared and he had felt free at last to give full vent to the spite and contempt he had nurtured toward him all the time. Not even the sight of the valiant death of the officer could reconcile Lieutenant Kondo to the utter shamefulness of the flight from the defended hill, and it now seemed as if the Lieutenant intentionally accepted the very standard of judgment, stern and uncompromising, which he had so despised in his fellow platoon leader, to judge him in his last moment.

When the young officer entered the dugout shelter of his Company Commander on the top of the hill, he found the stuffy interior dimly lighted by a tall candle on the table in the middle of the room. The Commander, looking extremely haggard and much older than he had ever appeared, was squatted on a folded blanket beside the low table.

"Thank you for coming. Hard work!" the Captain greeted Lieutenant Kondo when the latter reported his arrival in the proper manner. The Captain offered another folded blanket and asked his subordinate to squat down beside him.

"Lieutenant Miura was pitiful," said Kondo since it was the proper thing to say.

"It could not be helped, since the enemy's number was greater. Moreover, the enemy seems to be using National Army troops this time. They are different from guerrilla troops," said Captain Hamamoto.

The Lieutenant remained silent and the Captain, too, did not say anything for some time, but he kept looking intently at his subordinate's face as if trying to ferret out what was going on in his mind. Then he began hesitatingly, almost beseechingly, "I have something to ask of you. . . . I want you to recover that hill."

Lieutenant Kondo felt the pit of his stomach go cold. He had half expected such an order when he had received his summons to Headquarters, but he had quickly overruled it, since its execution had seemed utterly suicidal and impossible to him. Now that he heard it, however, he made a great effort to hide the despair in his heart from showing on his face and he answered obediently, "Yes, sir."

Captain Hamamoto saw the sudden constriction of the muscles on the Lieutenant's face, and he dropped his gaze quickly to a map spread out on the table and, pointing to it, continued, "As you can see, the whole brigade has formed a defense line here. This line extends to the right and to the left of us and is almost a straight line. The hill held by the Miura platoon was located, in relation to this line, in the most forward situation — in other words, it is like the brigade's advance patrol." The Captain pointed to a small mark on the map, and his finger which pointed at the mark was shaking, as well as his voice.

Then he continued in a respectful tone, "When His Excellency the Brigade Commander was pleased to come here on a tour of inspection, he had ordered that hill to be defended by a platoon. As for us, we must defend it to the death for the honor of our company."

When the older officer paused to look intently at the Lieutenant to see the effect of what he had said so far, the latter, who had kept his eyes to the ground to keep them from betraying his innermost feelings, answered softly, "Yes, sir," without raising his eyes. Lieutenant Kondo was struggling fiercely within himself between a hopeless feeling of despair arising from his usual habit of logical deduction and a wild feeling of determination arising from that stern and uncompromising method of judgment with which he had so lately judged his deceased fellow officer.

Captain Hamamoto, receiving no further encouragement from the young Platoon Leader, continued in a hesitating tone, "Take your platoon and carry out a night attack tonight. From experiences hitherto, we know that the enemy is weak before a night attack. I believe you will succeed for sure. I need not say it, but be especially careful about making any sound."

When Lieutenant Kondo heard the word, "night attack," mentioned, he felt the confidence returning to him with a gush, for the night attack was an operation in which he and his men had been trained almost to perfection. The confidence aroused by his logical deduction merged quickly with the classic determination which had been seeking recognition, and the Lieutenant now felt as if all the hesitation and fear which had besieged him a while back had been dispelled from his system. He looked up with eyes glowing with determination and declared almost vehemently, "Honorable Company Commander, I will certainly do it and show you!"

Captain Hamamoto answered immediately in a highly relieved tone, "Is that so? Will you do it for me? I beg of you!" He next continued eagerly, his whole face lighted up as if reflecting the newborn enthusiasm of his young subordinate, "As soon as you capture the hill, carry timber up and build roofs here and there. If you do that, you can take shelter when they shell you. In that case, you can hold the hill for certain."

"Yes, sir! I will do it!" exclaimed Lieutenant Kondo, now complete master of himself. He was conscious of a growing determination to show everybody that one did not have to be a graduate of the Military Academy to be a brave and efficient officer and that one did not have to follow the bothersome code of behavior handed down by tradition in order to be a true warrior and a true patriot of one's country. It had been a constant argument of his and he welcomed the opportunity offered to put it to the test. He never doubted for a moment that he would succeed, and the more he thought about it the more enthusiastic he felt himself becoming.

"For certain, I will do it and show you!" Lieutenant Kondo repeated.

"Is that so? I am grateful!" exclaimed Captain Hamamoto, beaming all over.

He reached behind him and took from a tall white box a bottle of *sake* and, placing two cups on the table, began to fill them. "This was sent to me by His Excellency the Brigade Commander," said the Captain. "Let us make a toast."

The two officers took the cups in their hands and eyed each other for a moment over the cups' rims — the Captain smiling with a fathomless light of relief in his eyes and the Lieutenant almost glaring from the savage determination he felt in his heart.

"I beg of you," the Company Commander toasted.

"I will do it," the Platoon Leader answered and they emptied their cups. Lieutenant Kondo thought he had never tasted any *sake* as delicious and invigorating as this, for it was the first he had tasted in months and really good.

"By this, my face will be saved," the Company Commander said, expressing in an unguarded moment what was foremost in his mind. Lieutenant Kondo did not seem to notice it, and even if he did, he thought nothing of it, for he was not in a critical mood, and it was natural according to the classic tradition of the race for a subordinate to save his superior's face even at the expense of his own life.

Next, the Company Commander, assuming the kneeling position which was the formal position in a room, reached reverently into the same box as the one from which he had removed the *sake* and brought out three flat square boxes which were pure white except for a golden design on their covers. Lieutenant Kondo recognized the design as the Emperor's Chrysanthemum Crest, and he knew at once that the boxes contained the Emperor's personal cigarettes which they had received from time to time at the front. He quickly assumed the kneeling position and bowed reverently.

Stiffly holding the boxes with his arms extended before him, the Captain said in a low, reverent voice, "These Imperial cigarettes were respectfully received from His Excellency the Brigade Commander. Please receive them respectfully and most humbly divide them among the men of your platoon. Let all of you partake of them most gratefully before your night attack tonight."

"Yes, sir," the Lieutenant answered in a voice charged with emotion. He removed a clean sheet of white paper from his breast pocket and, keeping his arms at their full length so that his breath would not fall upon them, received the boxes of Imperial cigarettes on the white paper he held on his hands, without raising his bowed head.

In one brilliant stroke, the shrewd Company Commander had achieved what he could not have achieved in an hour of passionate lecturing. The will to do was now absolute in the heart of the young Lieutenant, and the Commander knew that it would be the same in the hearts of the soldiers of the platoon very shortly. When the orderly had come from Brigade Headquarters, there had been four boxes. The Company Commander had planned to distribute one each to his three platoons and to keep one for Company Headquarters, but now he thought they had been more worthily utilized. He still had one box left which he could use whenever the cigarettes in it could gain as worthy a result as they were now gaining.

Lieutenant Kondo carefully wrapped the boxes of cigarettes in the white sheet of paper on which he had received them and, still holding them reverently at arm's length before him, rose stiffly to his feet and, bowing, said, "Lieutenant Kondo will now start preparing for the night attack."

The Platoon Leader returned to his platoon, still holding his awesome gift at arm's length. Once in his trench, he handed the boxes to his orderly with strict instruction to keep them at arm's length and called an assembly of his men. The sun had already sunk and it was getting dark. The enemy had stopped their shelling completely as if satisfied by their victory that day. The members of the Kondo platoon came out of their shelters where they had just finished their meager supper, consisting of hard biscuits and powdered-soya-bean soup, and gathered around their Platoon Leader.

"I was commanded just now by the Honorable Company Commander to regain the hill previously held by the Miura platoon by a night attack tonight," began Lieutenant Kondo.

The soldiers heard him in silence. Some were too numb already for emotions. Some felt the same coldness in their stomachs which their Platoon Leader had felt earlier in the shelter of the Company Commander when he had first heard of the assignment. Others just felt weak and sick all over, and all felt tired and reluctant.

"When we think of the importance of our mission, we must carry out this order with death-defying determination," the Lieutenant continued. "The fate of our brigade, nay, of the whole division, may be influenced eventually by the outcome of the battle." Nobody moved or made any sound, but they all felt their mutual disappointment. "Be especially careful not to make the least sound tonight," the Lieutenant said, using the stratagem the Company Commander had used on him a while back to break the embarrassing silence. "We will crawl as far as possible up the slope."

The Lieutenant next turned to his orderly and received the white package he was holding with outstretched hands. He removed the boxes and showing them to his men, began in a voice trembling with emotion. "These Imperial cigarettes were respectfully presented us by His Excellency the Brigade Commander. With tonight's night charge ahead of us, let us receive them most gratefully and let us strengthen ourselves through them."

There was a faint rustle among the ranks as the men hastened to attention in the narrow quarters of the trench. It was as if a magic wand had touched them simultaneously. The fatalistic silence which had come upon them when the Platoon Leader had made his first announcement was now charged with a new tenseness. They felt it in the air and in their own bodies. The Lieutenant opened the boxes and passed one cigarette to each soldier, who received his almost sacred gift with his head bowed reverently. The cigarettes were made of the highest quality paper and had pure white paper mouthpieces attached to them. The men took the cigarettes in their dirty hands and gazed silently and worshipfully at the little golden chrysanthemum crests on them, as if they saw the very image of God in them. All their sundry emotions of a moment ago were one now in a sense of submissive, unquestioning reverence.

Lieutenant Kondo lighted his cigarette and, cupping his hands over the lighted tip to hide it from the enemy, began taking deep, respectful puffs on it. Those soldiers who smoked followed his example. If ever the act of smoking had received the ceremonial respect it was now receiving, at any time or at any place in the world, it could still not have included the feeling of worshipful reverence which it was now arousing in the hearts of the men of the Kondo platoon. Many of the men made a strong effort to kill the consciousness of the tobacco's taste and to be aware only of the reverence which they felt as they smoked their cigarettes. But it was a futile attempt, for they had not had a decent smoke now for months, and the smoke they inhaled tasted as delicious and refreshing in their lungs as water did in their mouths after a full day's march in the sun without it — more so, especially, since the paper and tobacco used in the Imperial cigarettes were far superior in quality to the materials used in the cigarettes rationed the soldiers. As the platoon puffed away solemnly thus on their chrysanthemum-crested cigarettes, united in their feeling of reverent gratitude, the men were creating and participating in one of those typical dramatic, sentimental, and grossly simple ceremonies with which their race had inspired itself since time immemorial.

Takeo, who did not smoke, wrapped his cigarette reverently in a piece of paper and put it away carefully in his coat pocket. He was going to store it away in his rucksack when they returned to their shelter, and he decided that he would send it home if he could the next time they reached a city with a post office handling such articles. He did not stop to think for a mo-

ment that he might be killed in the coming attack, for the ceremony of the cigarettes had made him feel immune to death as
well as failure.

When everybody was through smoking, the Platoon Leader
ordered his men to face eastward and commanded, "Worship the
Imperial Palace. The supreme salute." The men bowed silently,
and in the silence of the moment was concentrated the fruits of
years and generations of training in the art of total submission of
the individual will to authority.

The Lieutenant next ordered his men to return to their dugouts and to make preparations and to rest before the order to
depart was given. He asked the Squad Leaders to follow him to
his shelter where he intended to plan the part of each squad in
the night's operation with them, while he ate his supper of hard
biscuits. He requested the members of the Miura platoon who
were sharing their trenches with them to stand guard while his
men rested.

When the platoon at last assembled at the foot of the hill
toward midnight, the night was black as ink. Not even a single
star shone in the sky, for it seemed a thick blanket of clouds had
passed over it since nightfall.

"You wouldn't know it even if somebody pinched your nose,"
the soldiers said of such a night, and they called it "night-attack
weather."

Careful instructions had already been given the men in their
dugouts before starting, and they silently formed a single file and
began to proceed toward the enemy-held hill. Takeo felt himself shaking and his body felt constricted all over. It was a
fairly chilly night, but he knew the trembling and crampness
were not due to the cold air. It was this way every time before
an attack. When he had first come to the front, he had thought
it arose from his cowardice and he had made a conscious effort
to relax, but each time he tried it he had felt himself go limp and
weak all over. Then he had heard from his comrades that they
all felt that way and he had stopped trying to struggle with the

feeling. He had decided that the feeling came because his whole being was concentrating its total energy before an attack, and he found that when the attack started, the feeling of tightness invariably left him.

Tonight, however, as he picked his step carefully behind the bulky figure of his comrade, Miki, walking before him, he felt the tenseness withdraw with each step he took forward and a stable calmness replace it. Strength was in his consciousness, too — a real substantial strength which he felt as if he could almost clutch with his hands in the darkness. He had never felt so strongly the consciousness of just living as he did tonight. It was almost tangible, too, in the co-ordination of his silent steps and the supple swaying of his body, in the keenness of his eyes and ears as they tried to pick out anything suspicious in the almost total blackness of the night, and in the steadiness of his hand which gripped tightly his rifle with fixed bayonet which he was carrying by his side. There were no longer the feelings of vexation and frustration which usually possessed him in moments like this. All the petty feelings he had felt when the order of the attack had been first announced earlier that night had been dispelled in that impressive moment when they had all bowed together toward the Imperial Palace.

The act of obeisance to the Imperial Palace had never satisfied him wholly until his strange experience on the transport when he had seen a vision of his home while bowing toward the Imperial Palace. Since then, the act had come to take on an understandable, inspiring significance, and each time he went through the act, it left him calm and more determined than ever to fulfill his obligations in the service, for the object of worship, he had come to know well, was not anything as intangible and indecipherable as the "Emperor" or the "Imperial Palace" but something more tangible and dear to him — it was his home and his parents — and he had long ago decided that it was amply worth sacrificing his life to fight for them — his home and his parents.

The platoon reached the foot of the enemy's hill undetected and, just as silently as they had come, deployed along the slope and began to climb upward, crouched low over the ground. Their Platoon Leader went ahead of them, and despite the darkness, they could make out faintly the white handkerchief he had tied around his hand as a signal to his men. The officer raised his bandaged hand from time to time and each time the men stopped in their tracks, to proceed cautiously up the slope again only when the hand was lowered.

Halfway up the slope, they saw the Lieutenant swinging his hand widely in a half-arc. They knew it was the signal to lie down, and they went down quietly but swiftly to the ground. Then they saw the signal to advance by crawling and they began to worm themselves forward stealthily through the tall grass. The soldiers went through the movements with perfect co-ordination, for they had been trained countless days and nights in these very tactics even during their spare moments at the front, and they had been told that the bayonet charge in a night attack was the "flower of the infantry."

Takeo felt as if he had been crawling for hours, and his shoulders and leg muscles began to ache. Then suddenly the stillness of the night was pierced by the shrill challenge of an enemy sentinel to the right. The words were unintelligible but the voice was sharp and defiant. The challenge was followed immediately by the loud report of a rifle, and Takeo realized with sudden alarm that they had been discovered.

In a sudden surge of indecision, Takeo felt the old tightness returning, but it was only for an instant, for immediately he heard the inspired voice of his Platoon Leader, shouting, "To the charge! Charge in!"

Takeo sprang to his feet and dashed forward with his rifle at the ready. He could hear his other comrades running, too, all along the slope. He could not tell how far away the enemy were, for the top was not visible, and he had a queer feeling that he would have to keep on running until he fell exhausted. But the enemy began to fire from their trench, and from the flames emitted by their rifles Takeo was surprised to learn that he and his friends were almost upon them. He could hear the alarmed and confused voices of the surprised enemy, and he could hear them dashing about and bumping into each other. He heard voices giving out orders loudly and insistently.

In contrast to all the excited commotion going on in front, their own silence was almost disheartening to Takeo. He wanted to shout — to shout at the top of his lungs as they did in the day charges — not to scare the enemy but to put courage into himself. But they had been strictly forbidden to raise any outcry or even fire their rifles during a night charge, for those who had planned the tactics had thought that the silence would be more terrifying to the enemy, which it generally was. To Takeo, however, it was a powerful temptation to want to shout in that last fearful moment when he was conscious more than ever that he was completely in the open at the mercy of the enemy concealed safely in their trench. But here again his will to obey overcame his baser human nature.

The rest of the platoon, too, was keeping silence faithfully, and it was a silent half-ring of invisible men which closed in on the enemy on the top of the hill all of a sudden out of the darkness of the night. A rifle exploded so close in front of Takeo that he could feel the heat of the blast in his face. In the momentary flash of the explosion, he saw the intent face of the enemy who had fired the rifle and he noticed that he required only a few steps more before reaching the enemy in his trench. With one last spurt he dashed to the edge of the excavation and thrust his bayonet at the blurred figure before him. He felt the bayonet sink into something soft, like a ball of cotton, and when he drew back his rifle, he saw the figure before him slump down and disappear in the darkness of the trench.

Takeo, so far, had merely gone through the motions he had practised in drills. He had done nothing out of his own initiative, and even in the excitement of the moment he felt himself marveling at the ease with which things were developing. When he had thrust at the enemy before him, Takeo had also noticed another figure to his right. He now turned swiftly, with his rifle poised for a thrust again, but he saw the other figure scrambling out of the trench and about to run down the other side of the hill. The distance was too far for his bayonet. Without thinking about it, Takeo removed the safety lock of his rifle and, raising it, fired at the fleeing figure. The enemy fell flat on the ground and was motionless.

"Don't fire your rifle!" Lieutenant Kondo's voice sounded angrily somewhere from the left.

Takeo recalled with a start what he had done and remembered with a sinking feeling the strict instructions they had been given against firing in a night charge. His shot had been the only one fired by the whole platoon so far, and he felt as if the Platoon Leader already knew that he had been the one who had fired it. Even in the very midst of combat, he felt that unpleasant sense of oppression every soldier felt when he was scolded. He looked about him to make sure there were no more enemy, then he pulled back the bolt as quietly as possible to discharge the tell-tale empty shell and shoved it back again just as quietly. Satisfied now that no one would be able to find any evidence of his misconduct on his person, he slid down as inconspicuously as he could into the trench, more to welcome the shelter it offered from his guilt than from any possible counterattack of the enemy.

When they had arrived at the trench, Takeo was almost sure he had seen many enemy tumbling out of it and fleeing, but what with the darkness and the excitement, he had not been sure. Now, however, he heard his comrades moving about easily in the trench to his right and left, and he was sure that most of the enemy had fled without offering any resistance and that the fighting was all over.

The Platoon Leader was calling out in a low voice to his men to make ready for a counterattack. There was unconcealed joy in his voice, and Takeo was glad to hear it, for it meant that the Platoon Leader had forgotten by now the unforgivable offense committed by one of his subordinates during the last moment of the attack.

"Every squad, examine your personnel and let me know," the Lieutenant called after a while when the enemy showed no sign of returning to recover the hill. The Platoon Leader was asking for a report from each squad of its casualties, if any.

Not long after the call was made, Corporal Gunji came behind Takeo and, peering into his face in the dark, said in his usual imperious voice, "You are here, are you?"

"Yes, sir," Takeo answered. As he said it, he recalled for the first time the rifle which had exploded almost in his face when he had reached the trench, and he felt grateful that the bullet obviously intended for him had missed him completely.

Takeo saw the Corporal leave his side and examine another soldier faintly visible to his right. The Corporal asked again, "You are here, are you?"

"That is so. I am no ghost, Honorable Squad Leader," Takeo heard Miki's unmistakable voice laughing softly.

The Squad Leader did not reprimand the undiplomatic soldier for this lightheartedness at a critical moment, as he would have done at other times, but merely said in his same imperious tone, "Do your best!" and moved on down the trench.

It was heartening to hear the cheerful voice of his friend Miki again, and Takeo called to him, "Are you all right, Miki?"

"I am all right. I killed an enemy. Are you all right?" Miki asked in return.

"I am all right. I killed two enemy also," Takeo said boastfully, forgetting completely the guilty feeling he had felt until a short while ago from firing his rifle during the attack.

When the Squad Leaders began making their reports, it felt good to hear them say, one after another, "Personnel and otherwise, there is no change!" It meant that there had not been a single casualty in the whole platoon, wounded or killed, and that the night charge had been a total success.

It had been a beautiful attack — the kind they had read about in their manuals and executed in their drills. It was the kind of thing which increased the men's confidence in the value of their spiritual training, for it had seemed nothing short of a miracle that they should have been able to capture the hill without a single casualty. Like all successes, they attributed this success to "strength," and this "strength" they called "spiritual strength." They all felt, moreover, that the ceremony of worship to the Imperial Palace in which they had participated before undertaking the raid had been principally instrumental in "nurturing" the particular "spiritual strength" which had helped them capture the hill.

"If you charge with a bayonet and the Spirit of the Yamato Race, there will be no enemy who can resist you," they had been taught, and such an experience as this seemed to prove its veracity. It also caused them to place exaggerated worth upon the effectiveness of the bayonet and to participate earnestly and diligently in the numerous and tedious bayonet drills forced upon them.

It was about midnight when all the reports were made and the new assignments given the squads. The rest of the night was spent in concentrated, driving labor. The corpses were dragged out of the trench, and the corpses of the Miura platoon, together with those lying on the slope, were hauled down to the foot of the hill. Timbers were carried up the hill, and new shelters adjacent to the trench were dug, over which the timbers were thrown as protection against falling shells. All the while, sentinels were posted as far down as the middle of the slope in front to keep a sharp lookout for a possible counterattack. The enemy did not come back, and there was only scattered firing from the front. By morning, the work of clearing away the corpses was practically done and the shelters were completed.

With the dawn, the shells began to fall, and the shelling was heavier than on the previous day. This time, however, the men of the Kondo platoon were able to feel comparatively safe within their newly made shelters. They huddled closely together in their reinforced dugouts and listened intently for the warning the few sentinels posted outside in specially constructed foxholes were instructed to give in case of attack. The explosions were so numerous and constant that they drowned out completely the usual hissing sound the soldiers were used to hearing before a shell exploded. The sound consisted of a continuous roar punctuated by the unevenly spaced but unrelenting explosions of the shells. The roofs, the sides of the dugouts, and the very earth beneath the soldiers shook as if in a prolonged earthquake. The men came from a country where earthquakes were not an unusual phenomena, but there had never been anything like this at home.

During a slight lull in the shelling, Miki said, "The enemy are using field artillery guns," and they all knew what he meant, for some shells were louder and seemed to shake the ground more than the mortar shells.

The men had listened nervously to try to locate each shell as it exploded, when the shelling had first started, but they gave it up quickly when the shells began falling like hail, indiscriminately and persistently. They accepted their fate stoically, as they had always been able to do when there seemed to be no other alternative, and they made a conscious effort to shut out the din from their ears, like so many Buddhist monks trying to forget the world's turmoil in meditation in their religious sanctuaries. Some shells must have exploded in the trench, for they sounded very near, and each time, the soldiers felt the blood leave their bodies. But, as a whole, they remained composed and kept staring blankly at each other or at the floor, while the bedlam continued all about them.

After about an hour, the shelling ended just as abruptly as it had started, and simultaneously the men in the dugouts heard their comrades standing sentinel duty outside yelling excitedly, "Enemy attack! Enemy attack!"

Takeo dashed with the others out of the dugout in which his squad had been sheltered and took his assigned place in the open trench beside Miki, who had the machine gun, for Takeo was the assistant machine-gunner and ammunition man. It was a fear-instilling sight which met Takeo's eyes when he peeped over the trench and down the slope in front of him. His whole insides seemed to push upward and choked him, for coming up the slope at the foot of the hill was a seemingly endless horde of wildly shouting men. He felt paralyzed and helpless, and only the sudden burst of Miki's machine gun beside him shocked him into action. He began firing his rifle madly at the onrushing men without taking aim, and he worked the bolt after each shot with such force that soon the very handle of the bolt began to feel hot in his hand. He bent down at intervals to pick up new clips of ammunition for Miki from boxes piled at his feet, but at times he forgot to do it so that Miki had to do it himself.

But even as he fired his rifle like one seized by a demon and looked after his duty as ammunition man, Takeo had time to notice that the enemy rushing up the hill held no weapons but only carried the familiar long-handled grenades in their hands. There were more grenades, Takeo saw, dangling from belts hanging like long collars from their necks. Most of the enemy were barefooted, and some were not in uniform, while not all had helmets on their heads.

The attackers began to hurl their grenades when they were still far down the slope and the missiles exploded a safe distance below the top. But the smoke and dust the explosions kicked up made a fairly effective screen and tended to distract the aim of the defenders. The enemy hurled their grenades together at regular intervals as if in answer to given signals, but they kept up their reckless charge, stopping only to throw their explosives and to take new ones from their belts. More attackers, armed and dressed similarly to those preceeding them, appeared around the corner of the hill in front and came charging up the slope, so that there seemed to be no end to the number of enemy coming to recover the hill. The enemy on the higher hill in front gave effective support to their charging comrades by concentrating a heavy rifle and machine-gun fire upon the defenders, and the bullets flew all around the latter and hit some of them from time to time. Shells fired from a few mortars behind the main hill held by the Hamamoto company exploded among the attackers occasionally, but the explosions did not seem to daunt them.

The exploding grenades kept creeping closer to the top as the enemy continued their daring advance despite heavy casualties. The whole slope was covered with the charging, shouting attackers, and the explosions from their hurled grenades formed one long, unbroken moving line. While he was on the hill in the rear, the enemy's grenade attack had sounded like a frenzied beating of drums to Takeo, but now, in the very midst of it, the sound was one steady, deafening roar, and the flame and dust thrown up by the explosions made it appear as if the very side of the hill was erupting.

There was no longer any consciousness or deliberation in what Takeo did. He was like a man gone mad. The tremendous din, the excitement, and the fear of the moment drove all the reasoning faculties out of the minds of the defending soldiers. They fired their rifles and guns until the barrels were hot. When the grenades started to explode close enough to send pieces of shrapnel whistling over their heads, Miki jumped out of the trench to stand in the open and began firing his machine gun from his hip. Others saw and followed him out of the trench and they began hurling their hand grenades and firing their rifles, standing in the open where they had greater freedom of movement. To these soldiers imbued strongly in the habits of offensive warfare, the thought of being caught by the attacking enemy in the cramped quarters of the trench had seemed nightmarishly unbearable.

Even the Lieutenant was firing a rifle which he had taken

from a fallen subordinate, and he had removed his long sword from its hook on his belt and had laid it down at his feet. He had still some presence of mind left and he did not jump out of the trench with his impulsive subordinates.

More of his men, however, continued to jump out of the trench, and some began to dash down the slope as if they were going to charge into the oncoming enemy. The sight of the soldiers coming at them with their bayonets was frightening to the attackers armed only with their hand grenades, and those in the advance line began to waver and some turned and began to flee down the slope they had come up so recklessly. This marked the turning point in the battle, and soon the whole horde of attackers were pelting down the slope and back into the shelter of the hill from which they had started. A few stubborn ones tried to stop their fleeing comrades, but a shell exploded in their midst, and the panic was complete. Much faster than it had taken them to come up the slope, the attackers fled back to where they had started until shortly the whole terrain in front of the defending Kondo platoon was cleared of the attackers.

Lieutenant Kondo called his men back into their trench and went up and down the line exhorting his men, "Hold on! We must hold on!"

Now that the din of battle was over, the men of the platoon could hear their comrades on the hill to the rear also shouting, "Hold on! Hold on!" They heard, too, loud haranguings from behind the enemy's hill as if the officers were exhorting the grenade-hurling attackers to resume their charge.

"They must be farmers of this region," Miki said to Takeo, and Takeo knew that Miki was talking about the attackers.

"That is so. They are barefooted, and some did not even have uniforms," Takeo said.

"Those farmers — if you hold on, they will flee quickly," Miki said.

Takeo did not answer, but he thought, Since they are defending their own lands, they must be stronger than soldiers.

Then there was a long-drawn-out bugle call, sounding much like the horn of a street vendor at home, and once more the enemy came dashing around the hill in front and came charging up the slope. As Takeo began firing his rifle again, he noticed that this time there were uniformed soldiers armed with rifles among the grenade hurlers. The casualties among the attackers were heavy again, but they continued to advance as resolutely as the first time. Miki jumped out of the trench again to fire away at the approaching enemy, and others started to follow him, but this time they were exposed to the carefully aimed shots of the riflemen among the attackers. As Miki bent over to get fresh clips from Takeo who had stayed back to open a new ammunition box, a bullet struck him and he fell into the trench almost on top of Takeo. The others, too, who had gone forth to meet the enemy on open ground were either hit or driven back into the trench by the unexpected rifle fire.

Takeo placed an arm under Miki, lying limply on the bottom of the trench, and tried to raise him. It was then he noticed that a bullet had pierced his comrade's chest. Although Miki was still breathing, blood was flowing freely from the wound.

"Miki, put strength in you!" Takeo shouted and shook his friend roughly. But before he could stop to notice what effect his shouting had on his wounded comrade, he became aware of the grenades exploding on top of the hill and even in the trench. He took his rifle and was about to stand up to resume the fighting when he noticed Kan scramble out of the rear side of the trench and start falling back.

With a queer sensation in his stomach, as if he had seen a vision in a dream, Takeo straightened up and looked out in front of him. The grenades now seemed to be exploding in front of his eyes, and there were so many of them that he could hardly make out the attackers to the rear. The pressure and the heat from the blasts pressed painfully against his face, so that he could not find strength for some time to raise his rifle and fire at the enemy. The entire area in front of him was crimson with the flames from the bursting hand grenades, and it seemed as if the whole hillside was aflame. In his moment of helplessness, Takeo was able to notice from the corners of his eyes that others were following Kan out of the trench and fleeing down the back of the hill, and he saw that most of them were his own squad's Replacements and First-Year-Soldiers, who were only following one whom they had come to look upon as a beacon for their behavior.

In desperation, Takeo ushered all the strength remaining in him and, raising his rifle, fired blindly in front of him, but even as he did so, he was strangely aware that there were very few comrades anywhere near him. Somewhere he could hear his Platoon Leader calling desperately, "Don't run away! Don't run away!" When he tried to fire a second shot, a grenade exploded almost directly in front of him and threw the dust into his eyes. Sudden panic seized him, and before he knew it, he too had scrambled out of the trench and was running down the hill. He saw so many running on the slope that he knew for certain that the whole platoon was now in flight.

When he had seen all his men flee, even Lieutenant Kondo had jumped out of the trench and taken after them. But it was not until he had reached the foot of the hill that the Lieutenant realized what he had done. He grew weak all of a sudden, almost as if a bullet had struck him, and he threw himself down behind a fairly large rock lying at the bottom of the slope. The enemy were now on the top and they fired their rifles at the fleeing men so that the latter kept running the faster until those who survived were finally safe behind their own hill.

Once behind the rock, Lieutenant Kondo found time to reflect that he still had the rifle he had been using throughout the battle and that he had left his sword behind him in the trench now occupied by the enemy — the sword which was the traditional "Soul of the warrior" and the noble symbol of an officer. The weakness which had seized him previously now overwhelmed him and a mighty anguish filled his heart, for on top of the disgrace of fleeing he was now faced by the greater disgrace of having had his sword taken by the enemy. He felt too weak to want anything more, but at the same time there was the crying passion of a man in deep agony. He felt the agony the more when he remembered his proud determination to outdo his fellow officer, Lieutenant Miura.

Was I no good also? he muttered to himself weakly. A chilly sensation passed through him and calmed his passion and made him almost oblivious to the mad sounds of battle around him. With his confession of his own failure, a humbleness had come to him which dispelled all his sensuous obsessions and developed a dramatic awareness in him of his own insignificance and of the greater, to him unknown, values of life of which he had proven himself unworthy.

He took the formal kneeling position and faced eastward instinctively, for that was the direction in which he thought all goodness lay. Fighting a stronge urge to weep out loudly and unashamedly, he unbuttoned that part of the coat and shirt covering his stomach. Unwinding the band he always wore around his stomach under his shirt to keep it warm, he took from its fold a short black leather case. It was the dagger his father had given him when departing for the front, saying, "This is a family heirloom. Use it, if you must, to preserve the honor of the Kondo family."

He took the black case tenderly in his hands, almost as if he felt communion through it with his father, and his mother, and all the dear ones at home. He thought of them for the warm human beings they were. Then he thought of the Emperor who personified the mystic concentration of all that was good, and noble, and beautiful in life. He tried to think of something more substantial that could represent the goodness and nobility and beauty in life, and his heart yearned for it in his last moment of decision But he could think only of his mother, and he knew she was human like him. He tried desperately, however, to try to link his mother to the supreme goodness, in the consciousness of which he wanted to consummate his last terrible act. But he could not be satisfied, and he returned to the more impersonal contemplation of the Emperor.

He drew the shining blade of the dagger from its case and laying the case beside him, pointed the dagger at his bare stomach. He felt calm and impersonal, and the feeling gave him courage. With a sudden jerk of his hand he thrust the point of the sharp blade into the left side of his abdomen. A pain shot through his body which crushed at once his forced calmness and indifference. He cried in his heart, Mother! Mother! and he drew the blade across the abdomen with all the frantic strength in him. He could hear the blade ripping through the flesh and muscles, and the pain thundered through his body and beat against his brains. There was also the warm feeling of blood flowing down his lower abdomen. He felt, at the same time, as if the whole prop holding up his body had given way, and he doubled up in front of him. The pain now felt as if it were smashing his brains, but he felt too weak to do anything. Not knowing why, he called, "Mother! Mother!" and with the last remaining strength in him he drew the blade from his abdomen and smashed it against his neck. Then everything went black.

The soldiers of the Kondo platoon, who had barely gained the protecting shelter of their own hill and who looked upon this last rite of their Platoon Leader enacted before their very eyes, stood motionless and dumbfounded. What they had just gone through had numbed their senses completely and they could only stare at the dramatic act blankly. Only the Lieutenant's orderly, who had been with the officer for over a year, recovered sufficiently to sense the tragedy of the moment, and he called out loudly, "Honorable Platoon Leader!" even as the latter plunged the blade into his abdomen. But that was all he could say, and he did not move from where he was.

When the act was finished, however, the orderly began to rave like a maniac, "It is vengeance for the Honorable Platoon

Leader! Let us charge! It is the charge!" When the others did not take up his cry, he started to dash out by himself, but they all stopped him. Some were moved now, however, and they began to shout, "Let us charge!"

It was then the airplanes came. They were bombers, four of them, and they came low over the hills and started bombing the enemy positions in front and strafing them with their machine guns. Then, as if the men in the Headquarters of the Hamamoto company had laid out the marker, which they used when the airplanes came, to point out the enemy on the low hill only lately relinquished by the Kondo platoon, one of the bombers began to bomb the hill and to machine-gun it. The bombers continued their aerial attack for nearly an hour and then flew away.

When they were gone, Corporal Gunji said, "Now is a good time. Let us charge!"

The Sergeant, who was second-in-command, gave the command, and they all charged back up the hill from which they had fled so lately. The bombing and machine-gunning from the air seemed to have been too much for the defenders and long before the platoon reached the top, they had fled, leaving behind them their dead and wounded piled high in the trench.

From where he was at the bottom of the trench, Miki, in the depth of his dying consciousness, knew that the enemy had fled. Everything had become silent all of a sudden. When his comrades had fled and the enemy had come before that, he had known it also, for the familiar voices of his comrades had gone and strange voices in a strange tongue had come to replace them. He had also felt it when somebody had poked a bayonet into his stomach, but it had not pained him much. Everything had seemed distant and he felt as if he were alone and aloof from it all. When he heard the familiar voices of his comrades once again, he thought, They have come back, but that was all he thought about it.

Then he heard a very familiar voice which kept shouting insistently beside one of his ears. It required some time and effort before he knew it was Takeo's voice which was shouting repeatedly, "Miki, put strength in you!" It seemed strange, and almost amusing, that his name should be called when he was so distant and remote. The sound of Takeo's voice pleased him as it had always done. He did not know why, but he wanted to tell Takeo, "Such things as the Emperor and promotion in ranks do not matter. What matters is to be happy," but he could not get the voice out of him.

Then he thought he had said it, but the voice in his ear kept calling him insistently, and it sounded almost angry. But everything was like a wave — rising and sinking, rising and sinking. The voice, too, came strong and then faded out. Then there was a large wave and he rose high on it, and Takeo's voice suddenly sounded strong and real. He tried to open his eyes, for he did not know that his eyes were already open and staring unseeingly before him, and the realization came to him all at once that he was dying.

Takeo, his best comrade, was shouting at him to keep him from slipping off. . . . He must hold on! . . . He tried to muster all his strength to take a grip on something before the wave started sinking again. But it seemed no use, for he was at the complete mercy of the wave, and he felt it sinking again. Desperation and fear gripped him, and he made one last, mighty effort. It sounded only a little above a whisper, but Miki thought he was shouting at the top of his voice, "*Tenno Heika, Banzai!*" (Long live the Emperor!) Miki did not know why he had shouted it, but they were the only words he knew which could express his defiance against the dark mystery which seemed to be closing irresistibly about him. But the wave continued to sink, and Miki was now overcome by a boundless loneliness. From the very depth of his forlornness, he cried, "Mother! Mother!" Then the wave sank endlessly and took Miki away with it.

Takeo released the cold wrist of his friend and rose to tell his Squad Leader and others standing around him, "The pulse has stopped."

Though there were tears in them when he said it, Takeo's eyes shone with a vibrant light, for he felt as if he had gained a glimpse into the very core of life. He had been puzzled when Miki had shouted his *"Tenno Heika, Banzai!"* for it had not sounded somehow like Miki's last message to him and it had not sounded like the true honest Miki he had always known. But when he had heard Miki's forlorn cry for his mother, he had felt that the real Miki had reached out across the void which was separating them to clasp his hand warmly and to enter his heart to remain there forever.

故風乃土

CHAPTER 22

THE VAST SILENCE of the Japan Sea was a far cry from the infernal din and turmoil of warfare, but after more months of bloody fighting in the South China hills, Takeo was at last on a steamer and heading for home and discharge. The defensive battle of the trenches had ended when another division had landed and encircled the enemy. The enemy had been routed but, as usual, only routed, though the papers at home made capital news of the "victory." Months had then followed of interminable and wearing combat with guerrillas.

However, as Takeo sat gazing in the twilight at the endlessly heaving expanse of the ocean from the deck of the home-bound transport, the bitter experiences of the war seemed to him like memories of some distant and nearly forgotten past. Takeo was sitting on a pile of canvas behind the bridge, and Kan was beside him. The two had a blanket around them, for it was winter and icy cold, now that they had entered the area of the Japan Sea.

Man has a way of forgetting his unpleasant experiences and remembering his pleasant ones, so that the former are soon lost in a maze of entangled impressions, while the latter remain ever close at hand to cheer him. But just as most values tend to be relative, so it is with memories; what may appear pleasant today may appear unpleasant tomorrow in the light of ensuing circumstances. So with Takeo, those memories of the war which had seemed pleasant when compared with others and which he had cherished to offer him much needed comfort during his three years of service at the front, all seemed now to be little worthy of remembrance in the light of the approaching discharge. As he tried to retrospect from a natural urge to bring order into the crazy pattern of his impressions of the war, he found himself already forgetting many of his experiences and even some of the names of the comrades with whom he had served, and those experiences he remembered already seemed little worthy of possessing any longer.

"Is it three years? . . . It seemed so long and yet was so short," said Takeo wistfully to Kan. There were a few others loitering on the cold deck, for they had just had supper and they were out for the fresh air.

"It seems like only yesterday we crossed this same ocean to go to the front," Kan replied.

"We were so full of spirit when we crossed it the first time," Takeo continued.

"We never thought we would come back alive. We were all prepared to die," said Kan.

"If you say so, I feel a little guilty to return home alive," laughed Takeo weakly, remembering his original determination to die bravely for Emperor and country.

"There's nothing like it," protested Kan seriously. "Only if we are alive can we perform our patriotism. If we die, it is the end."

"Those who died are really to be pitied," said Takeo gravely. He had been confident at the beginning that he understood fully what he was going to die for, but the longer he had stayed at the front the more worthless death had come to appear, and when he had heard Miki calling his mother with his last earthly breath, death had come to take on a totally pitiful aspect. Now he was at a loss to see what it was his comrades had attained by having died for the sole declared purpose of serving the Emperor. To be sure, he was at a loss to see what he himself had gained for having suffered all his hardships in the name of the Emperor, but he was now returning home safely and he could easily forget his hardships. The important thing was to be alive and to be returning home.

The waves dividing at the bow and washing monotonously against the ship's hull sounded forlorn against the expansive broodiness of the ocean. Even the engine, which had sounded so cheerfully purposeful when Takeo had been in the hold below deck, now sounded aimless and futile. Somebody was blowing the *shakuhachi* in the hold and its plaintive notes flowed out on deck and mingled with the lonely sighing of the waves.

Kan took out a cigarette and lighted it. Takeo turned to him and asked, "What are you going to do when you get home?"

"I am going to get married," Kan replied, blowing a thin wisp of smoke into the air.

"Is there anyone fixed already?"

"Yes, I have a fiancée."

"You never told us before!" Takeo said accusingly.

"Once I mentioned it when I was a First-Year-Soldier in the home regiment, and I was scolded by the Squad Leader."

"Why were you scolded?"

"I was told that we should not talk about girls in the army, and so I have never mentioned it since."

"In the army you are scolded for worthless things."

"What do you plan to do when you get home?" Kan asked.

"People like us have nothing else to do but farm," answered Takeo.

"Are you not going to marry?"

"There will be no one to come to my home," Takeo laughed modestly.

Takeo did have his cherished dreams, but he was not confiding them to Kan, for he was sure they would sound too prosaic to his friend from the city. Now, if it were Miki . . . but he and Kan were the only surviving Same-Year-Soldiers of the squad. . . . Takeo's plan, first thing when he got home, was to buy an ox. He had been able to save nearly three hundred yen, and he had been told by the latest newcomers to the front that that amount could get him an ox which could go to work at once. Besides working it on the farm, he planned to use it to do hauling jobs for his neighbors. Takeo also planned to get married as quickly as possible. The idea of having a woman all his own in his home had come to look like a possibility in the near future. The soldiers had been told that they would receive a bonus when they were discharged. They were not told exactly how much it would be, but if it were anything near the wild sums being rumored among them on the ship, why, then, Takeo would already have the money to buy the bedding and to pay the dowry and also the expenses of the wedding ceremony. He was spending more and more hours lately pleasantly ruminating on whom he would select for his wife from among the eligible girls he knew in his village and in neighboring villages, if he could have his own way. But of course there would be relatives and neighbors who would offer themselves as go-betweens and they would do the selecting for him. For a returned-soldier like him, Takeo was sure there would be many offers. His parents, moreover, were not too old and whoever became his wife would not have much work to do. Besides, he did not have any brothers or sisters to make matters complicated for a newcomer into the family. These factors, he knew, would be great assets in his favor when it came time for any parent to consider giving his daughter in marriage to him.

"How much bonus do you think they will pay us?" Takeo asked Kan somewhat timidly, for he was afraid his friend might divine the reason behind his concern.

"It will not be much," Kan replied curtly.

Now this was what Takeo did not like about his comrade, for the latter was always belittling the things which meant so much to him. But Takeo hid his disappointment and said, "If we think of the things we did at the front, there is nothing we cannot do."

"That is really so. If we work day and night until we fall exhausted as we did on the marches, we shall be rich in a short time," said Kan.

"I am prepared to do anything when I go home," said Takeo. He was thinking of earning an extra income by hauling night-soil from the city for his neighbors when he got home.

"Let us work hard!" said Kan.

"It is cold," Takeo stammered and pulled the blanket tighter around his body.

"It must have snowed already at home."

"In South China, they must still be sweating and going at it."

"Dodging the bullets, you mean? When I think of it, the hairs all over my body feel like they are standing up. It is much better to stay home, even if it is cold," Kan exclaimed.

"Will our remobilization order come soon?" asked Takeo worriedly. It was a question worrying all the Regulars going home this time, for after being discharged, a Regular was placed on the Reserve List and he was liable to be called back into service at any time.

"Did not the Company Commander say that it will come soon? He said that since the war was not over yet, we were being sent home only for a temporary rest."

"He must have said it only to keep us from relaxing our spirit. There are any number of young ones," Takeo said but his voice did not sound very sure.

"When I go home, I am going to Manchuria. I heard the Manchurian Railway was looking for lathe mechanics. When my wedding is over, I am going to take my wife and go at once," said Kan.

"Is it true that the mobilization order does not come if you are in Manchuria?" said Takeo a little enviously.

"That is so. That is why I am going. And I am a second-son, too."

"How good it is for you. A fellow like me cannot go any-where. If the remobilization order comes, I must go again, and

I hate even to think of it. But next time I go, I won't do any-thing."

However, in a more submissive moment Takeo had confided to Miki once that his one wish to get home was to buy an ox for his aged parents, so that they would not have to work so hard even if he was not with them. "If they would only let me do this one thing, I will truly give my all and work for the country — even if I should come to the front again," he had said then. But that had been while they were still new at the front and were still laboring under the semi-mystical conception of their destiny. Three years at the front, however, while giving him greater confidence and poise, had taught Takeo just exactly what he could do and withstand and had engendered a strong dislike against any part of the system which tried to impose upon him duties under the presupposition that his capacity was boundless. On the very threshold of returning home, the idea of going back again to the front had appeared unbearably repugnant to Takeo and Kan, and these soldiers had felt little compunction in utter-ing their genuine feelings — something which they would have thought sacrilegious even to think about during their first year of service.

"Really, war is hateful! This kind of war is especially hateful. Even if they are our enemy, they are not a bit different from us. The old men and women we saw in the villages are exactly like the ones we see in our own country villages. Maybe, if we fight the white man, it will be different," said Kan.

"Whomever we fight, it is the same. A war is a war," replied Takeo.

"I guess you are right," said Kan and continued, "The army might be a better place if they did not beat you up and scold you so much."

"Even so, I would hate it."

"Since entering the army and until now, we were beaten at least a hundred times," said Kan.

"You were quite a man yourself when it came to beating the young soldiers," Takeo said accusingly.

"That was handing down to them what we had received ourselves," said Kan in righteous protest.

It was getting quite dark now and their blanket was no longer capable of keeping the chill out. The two stood up and, folding their blanket, went down into the hold where they were quartered. It was warm inside, for there was practically no ventilation and as usual hundreds had been crowded into the windowless chamber. The heat from the occupants' bodies had fused with the smell to form such a thick atmosphere that the prevailing warmth was well preserved despite the chilliness outside. The smell this time, however, was not as acrid as usual, for there were no horses in the bottom hold. The atmosphere, too, was not tense and expectant as it was before a landing operation. Nearly all were lying in their blankets, and they talked in a low, subdued tone. Some were singing, but their songs were quiet and melancholy. These men going home had all seen three or more years of service at the front. Many had been wounded, and none felt now the necessity of showing the forced tension which they had been compelled to maintain throughout their years of service. There was not even a card game going on as Takeo and Kan went to their assigned berth and lay down among their comrades.

Takeo closed his eyes and tried to forget the thick odor of tobacco in the air. He had never tried to smoke and so had never become used to the unnatural odor. The soldiers lying beside him were talking earnestly to each other, and Takeo soon found himself listening intently to their words.

" 'Prolonged war,' it is called, but it must end sometime," one with a voice very much like Miki's was saying almost angrily.

"The more the war is prolonged, the more Japan stands to gain," his friend said.

"Why is it so?"

"Did not the Company Commander say so? The customs from Hankow alone, which the army is taking, is enough to pay all the pensions for the army."

"But the war must cost much," the one with the voice like Miki's persisted.

"That is what I told you. What is spent comes back, and, on top of that, we are making a profit."

"Who is making a profit?"

"If you ask me that, I do not know."

"I am certainly not making any profit," said the voice like Miki's.

"Do you want me to tell you how to end the war quickly?" his friend asked.

"Yes. Tell me."

"Like Germany, if they will mechanize the units and capture all the enemy's bases with one stroke, the war will end."

"Don't they say that we are going to fight America and Britain next? It is said they have already formed mechanized units at home, and since they are going to send them out when the war with America and Britain starts, they are keeping it a secret, so I have heard. I have also heard that many new weapons have been made."

"You know a lot," the other laughed and added jokingly, "They may really start a war with Britain and America. If it starts, let us meet once again at the battlefront."

"I want to excuse myself," the one with Miki's voice said seriously. "I am going to make it so that I will serve in the rear or at home."

"I am going to get into a munitions factory. They say if you get into a munitions factory, you will not be pulled out," the other said.

Kan had turned on his stomach and had lighted a cigarette. He was talking to a soldier on the other side. "Are you going to let your folks know as soon as you reach port?" Kan asked.

"If they will let us send a telegram, I will let them know. But if they will not let us, I will have to wait until I am discharged. I will wire before I get on a train, so my folks will know before I reach home," the soldier beside Kan answered.

"I live in the city and my home is near the port, so I plan to let my folks know by telephone somehow as soon as we land," Kan said.

Somebody had opened the door leading to the deck and left it open. A cold draft was coming in, and Takeo pulled the blankets on his body completely over his head.

"If we fight with Britain and America, it will mostly be a war for the navy. This time, we should let the fellows in the navy do the fighting," Takeo heard the voice which sounded like Miki's continuing.

"The next time we go to war, our lives will not be spared," his friend said.

Takeo repeated to himself with his eyes still closed, "I am going home alive . . . that is enough."

"Our homes come first. They say it is for the Emperor and for the country, but in the end it is for the home," Kan was saying.

"That is so. If we did not have homes, we would not have exerted ourselves like fools as we did," the other soldier said.

Again Takeo saw the hill behind his home with the sparkling stream running under it. He did not know why, but ever since going to the front, every time he had thought of home he had pictured the hill. He remembered with a queer sensation that morning on the transport when they had bowed in worship toward the Imperial Palace and the picture of the hill behind his home had flashed before his eyes. Takeo felt now as if the hill had been his guardian throughout his service at the front. He tried to picture how the trees and shrubs on the hill would be at this time of the year.

The sound of the engine came strongly through the partition

at the end of the hold. There was a new cheerfulness and purposefulness in the sound, and it seemed to harmonize with the exultant beat of Takeo's heart as he thought of home. Each beat of the engine was taking him closer to home . . . and the engine was hurrying. . . . When Takeo fell asleep, it was with the happy sound of the engine still in his ears.

Nothing had appeared as beautiful and welcome to the men crowded on deck as the lights on land did on that early morning when their transport finally anchored outside their home port. They went through a hurried, though thorough, inspection and fumigation on an island in the harbor which took them one whole precious day. Some of the returning soldiers were carrying articles for which they could not show receipts attesting to their legitimate purchase, and these were taken away from them. A strict censorship which only the coldly efficient Military Police knew how to maintain prevented the people at home from learning of the widespread plundering engaged in by the Emperor's Army on the continent. When the barges took them in, there were no crowds on the wharves to welcome them, for their return was being conducted with the greatest secrecy possible. The men had not been permitted to inform their families of their return beforehand and even now were strictly forbidden to get in contact with anybody until they reached their regimental post. Only the stevedores stopped in their work long enough to call out, "Hard work! Many thanks for your labor!" as the soldiers made their way eagerly through the tall stacks of ammunition crates and other supplies intended for the front which crowded the wharves from end to end.

They passed a group of young, fresh-looking soldiers, probably waiting for their boats to take them to the front, and the latter called cheerfully, "Many thanks for your labor!" The returning soldiers replied, "Do your best. We depend upon you!" Some of them recognized friends among the outgoing group, and there were hurried exchanges of greetings. Many among the returned soldiers felt a cynical superiority toward the departing replacements and some even whispered, "They do not know what is waiting for them." A few, like Takeo, felt an almost brotherly commiseration for the youngsters and looked pityingly at their bright, hopeful faces. The sight made them tired all at once and killed temporarily the excitement of returning home at long last.

Even these recovered their excitement and joy swiftly, and there was not a single soldier among them who was not supremely conscious of every step he took when he first felt the soil of his homeland under his feet once again. They had been told, when they had left the country for the front, in songs, in speeches, and in every form of literature, that they were departing to die for a greater glory than ever life at home could bring them. Though bewildered by the vagueness of what they were told, they had naïvely accepted their instructions, and none had expected to return home alive. Such had been the deep-rooted influence of their mystical training that they had all hoped to discover the meaning of the "greater glory" for which they were to die, after they arrived at the front, and to gain heroic courage from it. Home again, however, without having given up their lives or having made the supreme discovery, they were unanimous in their elation — an elation just as naïve and childlike as their original determination to die for their country.

The returned soldiers were led into a wide, walled-in enclosure not very far from the wharves. There they saw a long tent pavilion under which women in the immaculate white aprons of the National Defense Women's Association were serving hot, steaming tea from large aluminum kettles. They were volunteers from the local branch of the Association who had been called out by the army authorities to serve the soldiers passing through the port that day. They had not been told who the soldiers would be, or where they had come from, or where they were going, and they went about their task in their usual unquestioning, kindly way. They were the first ordinary and respectable women of their race they had seen in years, and how good, honest, and understanding they looked to Takeo and his friends! When the soldiers were finally dismissed, they dashed toward the pavilion, and while they were having their cups filled, gazed long and hungrily at these images of their own mothers or wives waiting patiently for them in their homes. Whatever else in their faith had been shaken by their carnal experiences at the front, they knew for certain that their faith in their own womanhood had not been in vain.

After they had had their first cups of tea, Kan told Takeo, "There may be a woman I know. Let us go around and look."

The two of them went along the whole length of the pavilion, and although they met some women who tried to stop them to offer them more tea, they did not see anyone whom Kan knew. Kan went to the last woman in the row and said, "Lady, I live in the city. Will you not telephone to my home for me?" The woman gladly accepted, and Kan gave her a strip of paper on which he had written his father's name and the telephone number of his home, for his was a fairly well-to-do home and one of the few which boasted a telephone. "Tell my father that his son has returned," Kan said.

When the men were assembled after a short rest and marched out the enclosure, there was quite a crowd gathered outside the gate, since the news had already spread in the neighborhood that soldiers of the home regiment had returned. Those eager to see if any kin or friends had returned jostled each other roughly and called names at random in the hope that they might receive from the marching columns the answers they had waited for so long. Others cheered and waved their little flags with the Rising Sun emblem on them.

This spontaneous show of welcome was more than the soldiers had expected. They had had the return described to them by their superiors only in terms of the absolute secrecy which had to be maintained and in terms of the temporary nature of the coming discharge, and they had felt like truants sneaking home before their time. That is. they had felt like truants until they had encountered this sudden outburst of genuine welcome. It was nearly an hour's march to the regimental barracks, they knew, for they had marched over this same road when they had embarked for the front. But an hour's march had never seemed so sweet and their feet had never felt so light, despite the numerous knickknacks — gifts which they had bought with their meager wages before leaving the continent — which filled their rucksacks and utilities bags. Their hobnailed shoes sounded loud and cheerful on the asphalt road.

The news of their return spread swiftly before them, and people leaned out of the buildings along the road to cheer and wave at them, while many came running out of the side alleys until there were large crowds to greet them all along the way. At one place, an entire school had let out its children, who stood in line on the sidewalk and waved tiny red-and-white paper flags. Led by their teachers, the children shouted, *"Banzai!"* in unison over and over again until the whole length of the column had passed them. Their shrill voices sounded weak and innocent against the rough beat of the soldiers' shoes, but Takeo thought he had never heard anything so inspiring and the tears rose in his eyes. The eyes of many another soldier glistened, too, as they passed the cheering children.

A trolley line ran over the road they were passing, and all the streetcars they met stopped, while their occupants bowed and cheered from the windows. On the slope of a short incline, a streetcar coming toward the marching soldiers again halted, but this time a girl in a colorful kimono got off it and came running excitedly toward them. By now, all the soldiers marching in the outside column were aware of this strange figure. The girl came running almost directly toward Takeo, and as she approached, Takeo nearly had his breath taken away, for she was a beautiful girl!

She stopped abruptly in front of Kan, who was marching,

also on the outside, ahead of Takeo. Impulsively, yet with modest restraint, placing her hands on Kan's arm, she cried, "Kansan, well have you come back!" All her actions, since getting off the streetcar, had been precipitate and emotional but there had not been anything vulgar and forward in them — qualities which were most detested in the womanhood of her race. Her refined natural grace and her beauty made what might have appeared immodest and shameless, if attempted by others, appear spontaneous and even charming.

"Yes, I have come back!" Kan said a little gruffly and turned his body only slightly in the direction of the girl, for restraint and reserve were necessary qualities also of the respected manhood of their race. But there was no hiding the happy light which appeared suddenly in his eyes.

Surely, I have never seen such a beautiful girl! Takeo thought and he took in hungrily every graceful line of the girl's features and her hair like black shining silk. This must be the fiancée, Kan mentioned, he thought and he felt a deep envy toward his friend.

The girl started walking beside Kan with short, hurried steps, for her tight kimono did not permit her to take the wide, easy strides necessary to keep up with the marching soldiers. She hung on with one hand to Kan's sleeve, but that was all the show of elation she felt free to indulge in, although tears glistened immodestly in her eyes. As she walked thus proudly beside her lover, she said, almost out of breath from her effort to keep up and from her excitement, "Your Father and Mother . . . are waiting for you . . . in front of the regiment . . . I could not wait . . . so I came first. . . . "

Kan merely nodded his head and he was blushing perceptibly, for his comrades had started teasing him loudly, "Hey Kan! That is unfair!" and "Show us more of your face!" Kan was already beginning to regret the impulsiveness of his fiancée, which had turned their meeting almost into a public demonstration.

But he did not have very long to undergo his ordeal, for soon a Lieutenant who was bringing up the rear of the column came up to where they were and said in a stern voice, "Don't walk together! Go away!" Then he shoved the girl unceremoniously toward the sidewalk. When the girl left meekly to join the crowd of spectators lining the road, the officer turned toward the soldiers and shouted angrily, "Don't forget that we are not a victorious returning army! You must preserve the discipline of the Imperial Army to the last!" The officer, however, did not stop to reprimand Kan individually, for that would have been too vulgar a demonstration in front of the numerous people watching from both sides of the road.

Takeo was not the only one among the soldiers who felt a sudden sympathy for Kan, but he was relieved to notice from the corner of his eyes that Kan's fiancée had not been hurt much by the unfeeling treatment she had received at the hands of the gruff Lieutenant, for she was keeping up bravely with the marching soldiers from her side of the road, half running at times to keep abreast of her lover, Kan. She seemed oblivious of the scolding she had just received or of the many people on the walk who gave way obligingly to her hurrying figure. Her eyes were kept almost constantly on Kan, and it was a wonder she did not bump into more people than she did and she did not trip over their feet.

The strict surveillance of the superiors, however, did not prevent the crowds gathered along the street from cheering at the returned soldiers. Some of the spectators recognized friends and kin in the marching columns, and these, too, tried to join the marchers, but this time they were waved back by the soldiers themselves. These lucky ones, however, kept abreast like Kan's fiancée on the sidewalks and they shouted greetings and the latest home news from where they were. By the time the soldiers reached the regiment, there were quite a number of these garrulous welcomers walking with them at a safe distance on both sides of the road.

Outside the wide parade ground which stood in front of the high wall enclosing the regimental barracks, there was a still greater crowd awaiting the arrival of the returned soldiers. A cordon of angrily frowning Military Police held back the motley group from the parade ground. There were men and women, aged and young, and children among the crowd. Some were dressed formally, and these, like Kan's folks, had been surreptitiously informed of some dear ones' return; others were dressed in their ordinary work clothes, and these were mostly out in the vain hope that the cherished ones of their dreams had returned. When the soldiers reached the fringe, a path was made for them through the crowd by the Military Police, and they were hustled on to the parade ground without being permitted to pause or to glance, except fleetingly, at the waiting people. Names were called, and some cheered while others just blabbered unintelligibly; and such a rumble of voices arose from the crowd that the soldiers were hardly able to know it even if their own names had been called. Those who had accompanied the marchers along the road were also stopped outside the parade ground, and there were several thousand there, pushing and craning to get a view of the passing columns.

The soldiers were led to the edge of the parade ground where stood the National Guardian Shinto Shrine which they all knew so well. Halted before the shrine, they were ordered to Present-Arms. Thus they reported in proper military fashion their safe arrival home to the Patriotic God enshrined there. But the soldiers were so overcome already with the excitement caused by the noisy welcome they had received all along the way from the port that they went through the motion mechanically and almost without feeling, and were only too glad when the short ceremony was over and they were led away to halt, next, in front of a simple platform erected in the center of the wide, barren parade ground. The platform was unoccupied yet, but it was a high one and looked very imposing with a microphone standing in front of it. There were also large horn-shaped speakers protruding from all around it.

When the soldiers were halted, an officer told them, "Correct your uniforms. There will be addresses by His Excellency the Division Commander and the Prefectural Governor."

As the soldiers smoothed the wrinkles which had formed on their uniforms under their shoulder straps and bayonet belts and dusted themselves with their caps, they became conscious for the first time of the irritating pain in their shoulders where the straps of their heavy rucksacks had bitten into them and of their hunger, for it was near noon and they had eaten a very early breakfast that morning.

But to Takeo, the pain and the hunger seemed insignificant in the light of the great excitement which still filled him. He turned toward Kan and asked, "Did you see your parents?"

"There were so many, I was not able to see them," Kan answered.

An icy wind was blowing across the open ground, and the soldiers who had been hot from marching and from the excitement now began to feel the cold. They were told to remove their gloves as they were always compelled to do when about to go into the presence of some high dignitary, and in no time their hands became numb, so that they had to rub them briskly against the sides of their trousers or shake them vigorously to keep them warm. Takeo now began to feel in earnest the strain of his rucksack against his shoulders and he bent over from time to time to relieve the pain. Others were doing it, too, for it was a favorite trick among them.

For a long time after they had corrected their uniforms as they had been ordered, the expected dignitaries did not appear. Now the men began to gaze expectantly and impatiently at the gate to the barracks ground and at the entrance to the parade ground, through either one of which they hoped to see the dignitaries arrive. They could see the crowd still waiting patiently and submissively outside the line formed by the Military Police at the edge of the parade ground, and the soldiers felt more than ever the mutual bond uniting them with the crowd.

Nearly half an hour passed, and yet no dignitaries appeared. Kan turned toward Takeo and almost spat out, "That gate to the barracks — this will be the last time we go in. The next time I come out, I will never go in again." Takeo knew his friend was alluding to his plan to go to Manchuria where the remobilization order could not get him, and, now that he had seen Kan's fiancée, he understood well his friend's desperate determination not to re-enter the army after his discharge.

"That gate has certainly made many a man weep," said Takeo and he bent over again to relieve the strain on his shoulders.

Somebody behind Takeo was grumbling, "Why don't they come quickly? It is enough that they have already made us wait three years!"

Soldiers were asking the officers permission from time to time to go to urinate, and when the permission was given, they went a short distance away from where their comrades were assembled to relieve themselves. Takeo, too, asked permission once and, giving his rifle to Kan, went and urinated facing the hateful gate. It was a bold act of defiance, for which he could have been scolded roundly if the officers had been careful enough to notice him, but they, too, were fretting from the long wait, and had little thought left for anything else but their own discomfort.

After nearly an hour, they finally came — a group of officers on well-groomed horses prancing gracefully out of the barracks gate. As they approached, Takeo could see that the one in the lead was the Division Commander, for he wore the all-gold insignia of a general on his collars. He was followed by a retinue of officers with the shiny golden braids attesting to their membership in his staff flung across their chests. Takeo had never seen so many important-looking officers all at once before, and he momentarily forgot his fatigue and fretfulness and felt the muscles tightening all over his body, just as he had felt them tighten at the front when about to start on a combat operation. The group on horseback was followed by a large shiny automobile, and Takeo knew that it held the Prefectural Governor.

The officer in charge of the returned soldiers ordered them to attention and, in a ringing voice, shouted, "Salute to His Excellency the Division Commander, present arms!" Buglers had come out of the sentinel house inside the gate, where they were usually stationed in the home regiment, and they began to blow the fancy "Salute Call."

The Division Commander answered the salute ponderously and dignifiedly, as they had a way of doing it, and looked down gravely from his high perch on horseback at the soldiers saluting him. After the salute, which lasted until the bugle call was ended, the Division Commander alighted from his horse and, giving the reins to his horse-orderly, climbed up on the platform. His staff officers got off their horses, too, and they likewise followed their Commander on to the platform. At the same time, several men in formal morning coats and striped trousers and wearing tall silk hats alighted from the automobile. These removed their hats and bowed profusely to the officers and also went on the platform, hats still in their hands and keeping respectfully in the back.

The Division Commander stepped briskly to the microphone and, turning to his Adjutant standing beside him, said, "Let them be at ease." All the soldiers heard him, for the voice came out strongly through the speakers, but they did not move. The Adjutant relayed the order to the officer in charge on the ground below, and only when the soldiers heard that officer give the order did they feel free to move.

The Division Commander was next handed a white roll of paper, which he received in his white-gloved hands from his

Adjutant. Unrolling it expertly with his right hand, he began to read the words written across it:

"You have well defended the honor of our historic division and fulfilled your duties as soldiers of the Imperial Army, and you have now returned safely after more than several years of campaigning on the battlefields on the endless plains of the continent. . . . "

It was a powerful and impressive voice which came ringing sonorously out of the speakers on the platform. The wording, moreover, was in the classic language, and the General was reading his speech in the grave manner used in a formal ceremony, which was solemn and impressive. Takeo and his friends had now completely forgotten their discomforts of a moment ago and they were deeply impressed. Takeo tried to listen intently, but he was not used to hearing the difficult words which were of necessity abundant in a formal style and he began to encounter difficulty in following the speech. His attention began to wander from time to time and returned only when he heard some familiar words mentioned.

"Wherever the Imperial Army goes, there are no enemy. Even now, the enemy realizes the irresistible power of our Imperial Army and, abandoning hope of victory, are proclaiming a prolonged warfare. . . . "

Takeo lost track of the speech again and thought instead, It is strange how such a large voice comes from such a small body, for the General was a small, dark man, the handle of whose sword seemed almost to come up under his armpit. Then he found himself next asking, I wonder if he has ever served at the front. He knew the General had never commanded their division at the front, and he was only commander of the home division now.

When next Takeo's attention reverted to the speech, the Commander was saying, "Now the world situation is growing tense. . . . "

Takeo lost track of what followed, for the straps of his rucksack were biting painfully into his shoulders again, but he had
the presence to realize that he would not be able to bend over
now to relieve the strain. He gave the rucksack on his back a
light, imperceptible shake, which lightened the pain surprisingly. He next thought, I should have gone to urinate one more
time.

Then everybody snapped to attention around him and he did,
too, though he was a little late. But that brought his attention
back to the speech, and he heard the Commander saying in a
voice charged with emotion, " . . . we vow to put ᷄ Imperial
Anxiety at rest. Under the Illustrious Virtue of His Majesty the
Emperor, we must further raise our morale and advance toward
the consummation of the holy war. . . ."

The General ordered "At ease" directly now when the passage regarding the Throne was finished. My Mother will be
surprised. Will I be able to send a telegram home today? I wish
this would end quickly, Takeo thought.

The speaker was reading, "You have returned today, but
never think that your duty has ended. Leaving the corpses of
many of your comrades on the battlefields and returning after
parting from many other comrades, who are even now fighting
our enemy, you must quickly adjust your family affairs and wish
that you will be called once again to rally under the regimental
colors at the front. . . ." The General had unwound his rolled
script some distance now, and the unwound end was dangling
uselessly by his side.

Takeo understood the words he had just heard well, and for
the first time his mind was concentrated fully upon the speech.
A vague sense of anger began to build up deep within him. All
the venom he had felt on the transport at the thought of being
remobilized after his well-earned discharge to serve again at the
front awoke in him. He searched for a reason for the anger he
was beginning to harbor toward the speaker and toward all the
dignitaries on the platform. He found it in the General's mention

of the "corpses of the many comrades left on the battlefields."
. . . It is sacrilegious for these men in their prim uniforms and
suits to speak of our dead comrades thus, Takeo told himself and
felt the anger growing in him. Then he thought of the many
good people who were even now left standing in the cold outside the parade ground, patiently waiting for it all to end. Takeo
tried to convince himself that many among them probably had
sons and fathers and husbands who had become "corpses on the
battlefields." And in his pity for them, he tried to find a mutual
bond, and he tried to luxuriate in his own self-pity.

He did not have long to develop his new mood, for everybody snapped to attention again and Takeo was forced to follow
suit. " . . . Long is the Imperial Way. We subjects who live to
follow the Imperial Way must die to become guardian gods of
the nation and must live to offer humbly our whole lives to the
Imperial Throne. I repeat, *Long is the Imperial Way*. Begun
when we were born to our proud nation and continuing through
eternal death, this glorious Way is our destiny and our incomparable good fortune. . . ."

Takeo understood these words, too. Long is the Imperial
Way, he repeated to himself, and the music of the phrase lulled
his thorny nerves momentarily. It had been the only short line
in the speech of long sentences and it sounded almost soothing
to his tired senses. "Long . . . Long . . . " Takeo repeated to himself, then the meaning of the passage suddenly began to dawn in
him. "Long . . . " Takeo said again, and an almost unbearable
weariness swept through him. His head began to feel heavy and
a new cold, which now came from the inside, seized his body
and he leaned desperately against his rifle to keep himself from
slipping to the ground where he stood. A few soldiers had
fainted in the ranks in the course of the speech, and they had
been taken to lie on the ground outside the fringe of the gathering. Takeo had wondered why they had fainted so easily —
those men who had withstood the punishments of warfare so
capably for so long — but now he understood. He made a

mighty effort and recalled all the anger toward the speaker which had been brewing in him. The anger returned easily and the new mood revived him immensely, and he felt even more vigorous than he had ever felt before.

"How could the Division Commander be so impersonal in speaking of Life?" Takeo heard the new strength shouting inside of him. It was then he felt such a yearning as he had never felt before for something warm and personal to guide him through his daily contacts with his fellow men and to protect him in his goodness. It was a clear and concrete yearning. Though it was not in precise language, since he did not know the words to describe it, he felt its presence and its meaning was clear. He recalled Miki's last call for his mother before he died, and he thought that there was somehow a connection between that and his present yearning.

He now felt himself completely alienated from the speaker on the platform. He told himself that the General was merely speaking to show off his voice. The figure before the microphone came to take on the appearance of a boastful, strutting old man, and Takeo was able to look at it and to listen to his voice with a completely detached, objective feeling. The glitter which had surrounded him as he had ponderously returned the soldiers' salute from his horse and the impressiveness of his voice when he had first started reading his speech were no longer there, and only the impression of an insincere old man was there.

I am hungry, Takeo thought, and he shook the rucksack lightly on his back and leaned ever so imperceptibly against his rifle to ease the strain on his legs.

". . . However long the war may last from now, we vow to follow the eternal Imperial Way with an unchanging heart. We determine firmly with you who have just returned from the still bloody battlefields to perpetuate unto infinity the glorious destiny of our nation which has come down to us through two thousand years and more. I have ended." The General concluded and handed the long strip of written paper he had now unrolled completely to its end to the Adjutant beside him. The latter did not take the trouble to rewind the manuscript but, folding it neatly, placed it respectfully into his pocket.

The ceasing of the tense, monotonously droning voice from the platform seemed to ease the tension it had created among the soldiers all at once. They began to shake the rucksacks noisily on their backs, and a sudden wave of fidgeting swept through the ranks. And as always happens when a prolonged tension is broken in an audience, there were loud coughs and audible sighs, and some soldiers even had the audacity to cut the air noisily. No one spoke, however, for the soldiers were not at liberty to speak while in line.

The dignitaries on the platform seemed completely unperturbed by these signs of uneasiness among the soldiers. They had remained stoically expressionless throughout the long reading of the Division Commander's speech and they had maintained a rigid posture of attention. The speech had taken nearly all of half an hour, and even now that it had ended, it seemed to have no effect upon them. Only the Division Commander, who stepped back from the microphone, and the Adjutant, who was folding the long manuscript, seemed to be moving on the platform.

Then one of the men in morning coats stepped before the microphone. He was a thin man, though taller than the General, and wore thick, horn-rimmed glasses, and also had a mustache. He did not read from a prepared script and be began, "I am your Governor." His voice was the exact antithesis of the Division Commander's voice which had preceded him. It was soft and uncertain, and the sentences he used were in the polite conversational form.

"Many thanks for your labor of many years. I congratulate you from the bottom of my heart upon your safe return. . . . " His voice, though weak, sounded sincere and homey. Takeo was not the only one who felt high relief at this change after listening to the proud, domineering voice of the General. Takeo felt, too, that he could understand every word of the speaker now, though the pain in his shoulders was greater than ever and the base of his head was beginning to feel numb again.

"We all prayed for your safe return, and we at home worked as hard as we could. Henceforth I wish that you will become one with us here at the home front and lead us by utilizing the valuable experiences you have learned at the front. . . ." The Governor's voice was soothing and his speech perfectly understandable.

Takeo followed the simple words of the new speaker with friendly, though dogged, attention, and he tried to forget the growing fatigue and hunger of his body. He began to think of his village and the good people in it, and he tried to glean phrases from the speech which he might be able to use when he would be called upon to deliver an address at home, as inevitably happened to a returned soldier.

Then Takeo's attention concentrated upon the speech with a start. The Governor was saying: "The world situation is growing tense. We do not know when we will be dragged into the World War being waged on the European continent. . . ." Why, they are almost the same things the General mentioned! Takeo thought.

The Governor continued in his soft, almost paternal voice, "Take good care of your bodies and always keep your personal affairs in good order, so that if you should be remobilized, you can leave without any worries about home. . . ."

Why, the wretch! Takeo thought. He has never been a soldier a single time himself! Takeo began to feel weak again and he even felt a little sick this time. He was conscious of the rucksack straps around his shoulders more than ever before.

"His Excellency, the Division Commander, has been pleased to say that the Imperial Way is long. We who do not wear

uniforms are one with you in defending the Imperial Way. . . . "
the Governor continued.

Now Takeo was no longer listening to the speech. He was
feeling really sick and felt almost like vomiting. He remembered
his former trick and now tried to arouse a mighty anger against
the new speaker too.

THE END

79537